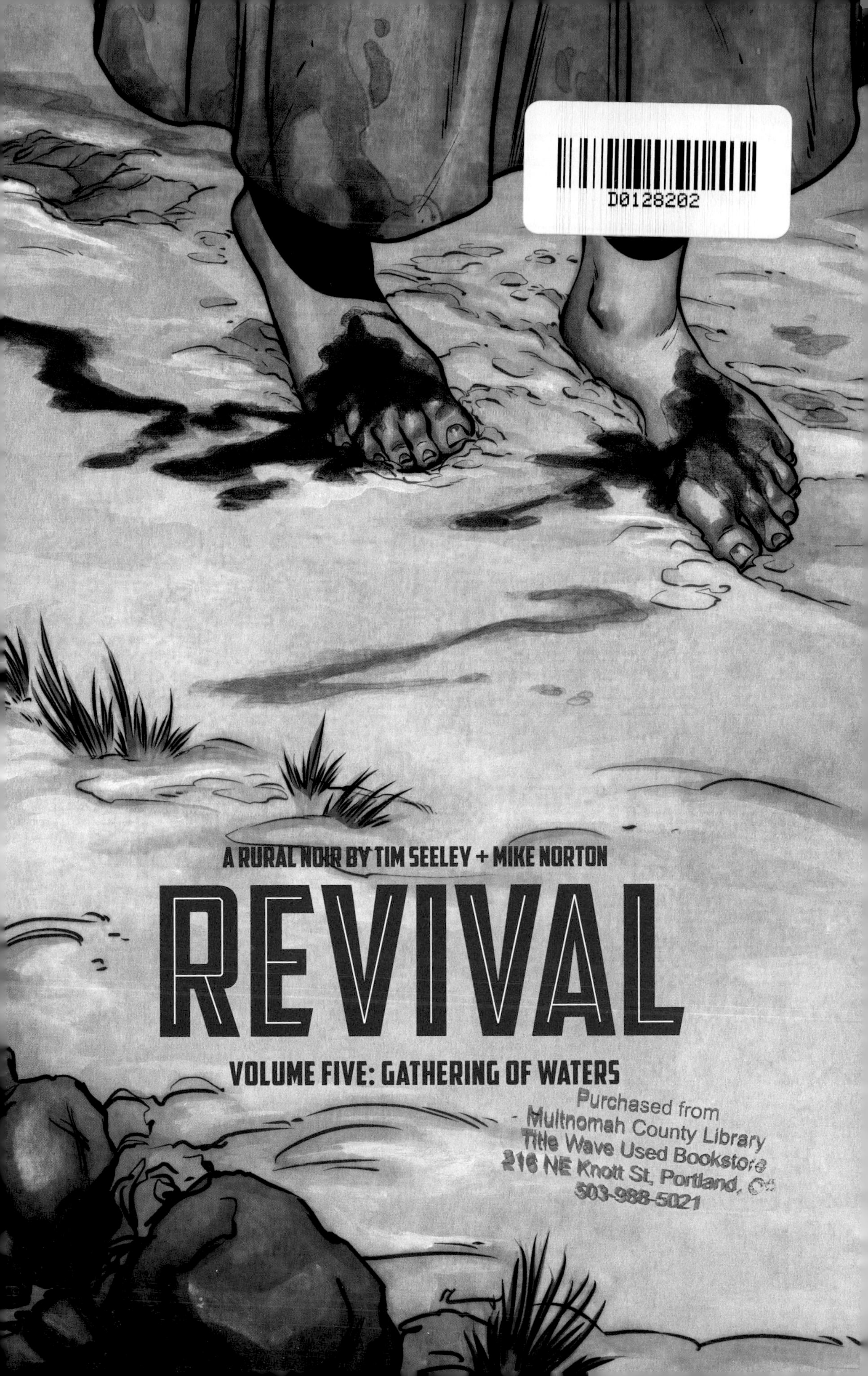
A RURAL NOIR BY TIM SEELEY + MIKE NORTON
REVIVAL
VOLUME FIVE: GATHERING OF WATERS

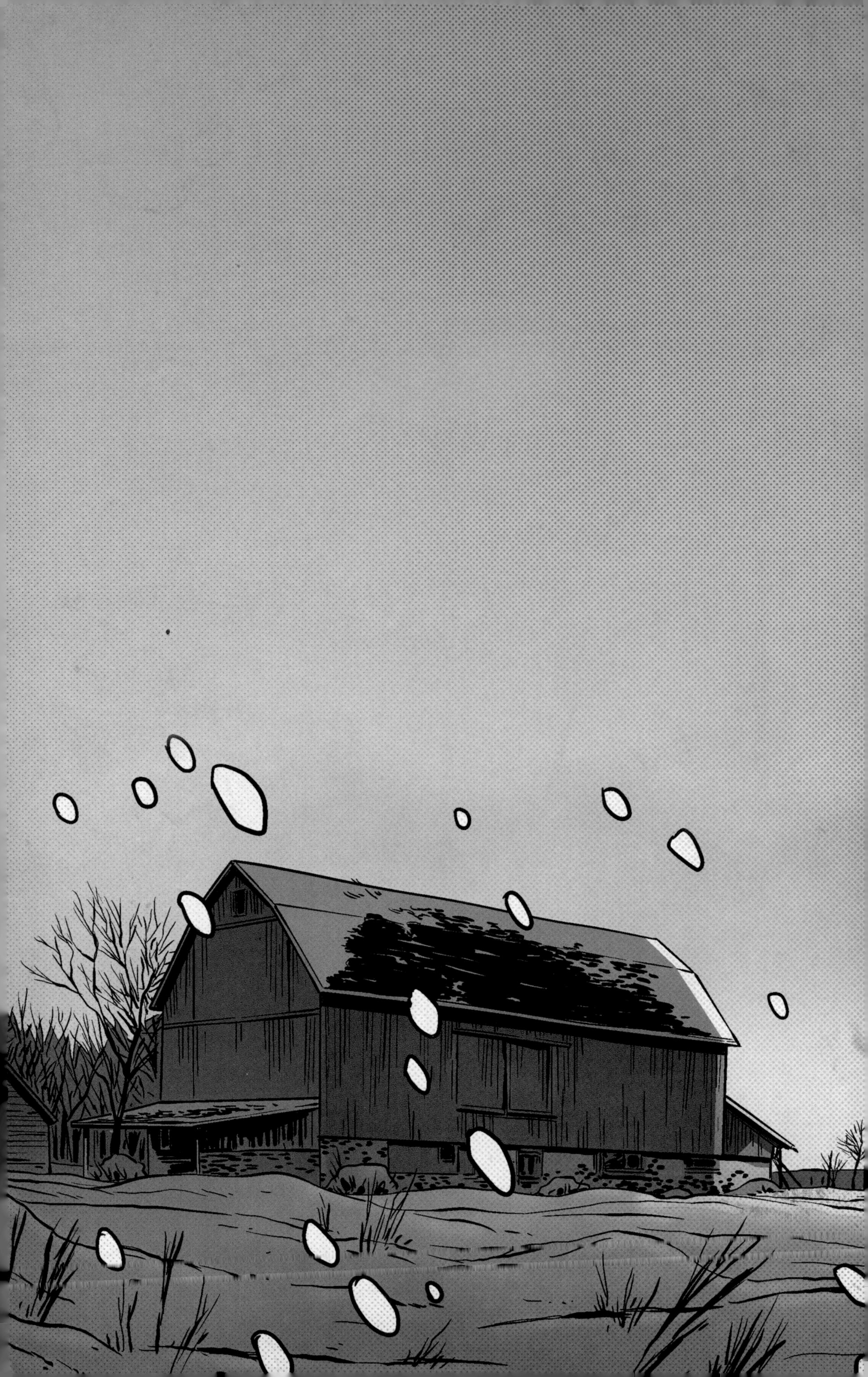

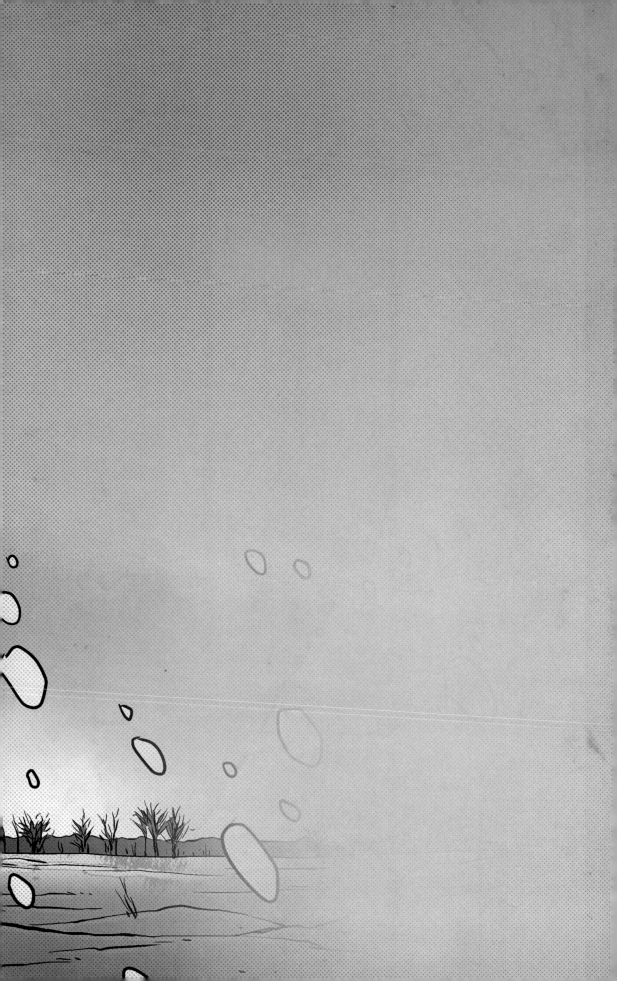

STORY BY
TIM SEELEY

ART BY
MIKE NORTON

COLORS BY
MARK ENGLERT

LETTERS BY
CRANK!

CHAPTER ART BY
JENNY FRISON

EDITED BY
4 STAR STUDIOS

DESIGN BY
SEAN DOVE

FOR MORE INFO CHECK OUT
WWW.REVIVALCOMIC.COM

ALSO CHECK OUT THE SOUNDTRACK BY
SONO MORTI AT **SONOMORTI.BANDCAMP.COM**

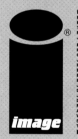

IMAGE COMICS, INC.
Robert Kirkman – Chief Operating Officer
Erik Larsen – Chief Financial Officer
Todd McFarlane – President
Marc Silvestri – Chief Executive Officer
Jim Valentino – Vice-President

Eric Stephenson – Publisher
Kat Salazar – Director of PR & Marketing
Corey Murphy – Director of Retail Sales
Jeremy Sullivan – Director of Digital Sales
Randy Okamura – Marketing Production Designer
Emilio Bautista – Sales Assistant
Branwyn Bigglestone – Senior Accounts Manager
Emily Miller – Accounts Manager
Jessica Ambriz – Administrative Assistant
David Brothers – Content Manager
Jonathan Chan – Production Manager
Drew Gill – Art Director
Meredith Wallace – Print Manager
Addison Duke – Production Artist
Vincent Kukua – Production Artist
Sasha Head – Production Artist
Tricia Ramos – Production Assistant
IMAGECOMICS.COM

REVIVAL Vol. 5: GATHERING OF WATERS. First Printing. May 2015. Published by Image Comics, Inc. Office of publication: 2001 Center Street, 6th Floor, Berkeley, CA 94704.

PRINTED IN USA. For information regarding the UPSIA on this printed material call: 203-595-3636 and provide reference # RICH – 613698.
ISBN: 978-1-63215-379-1.
International Rights / Foreign Licensing – foreignlicensing@imagecomics.com.

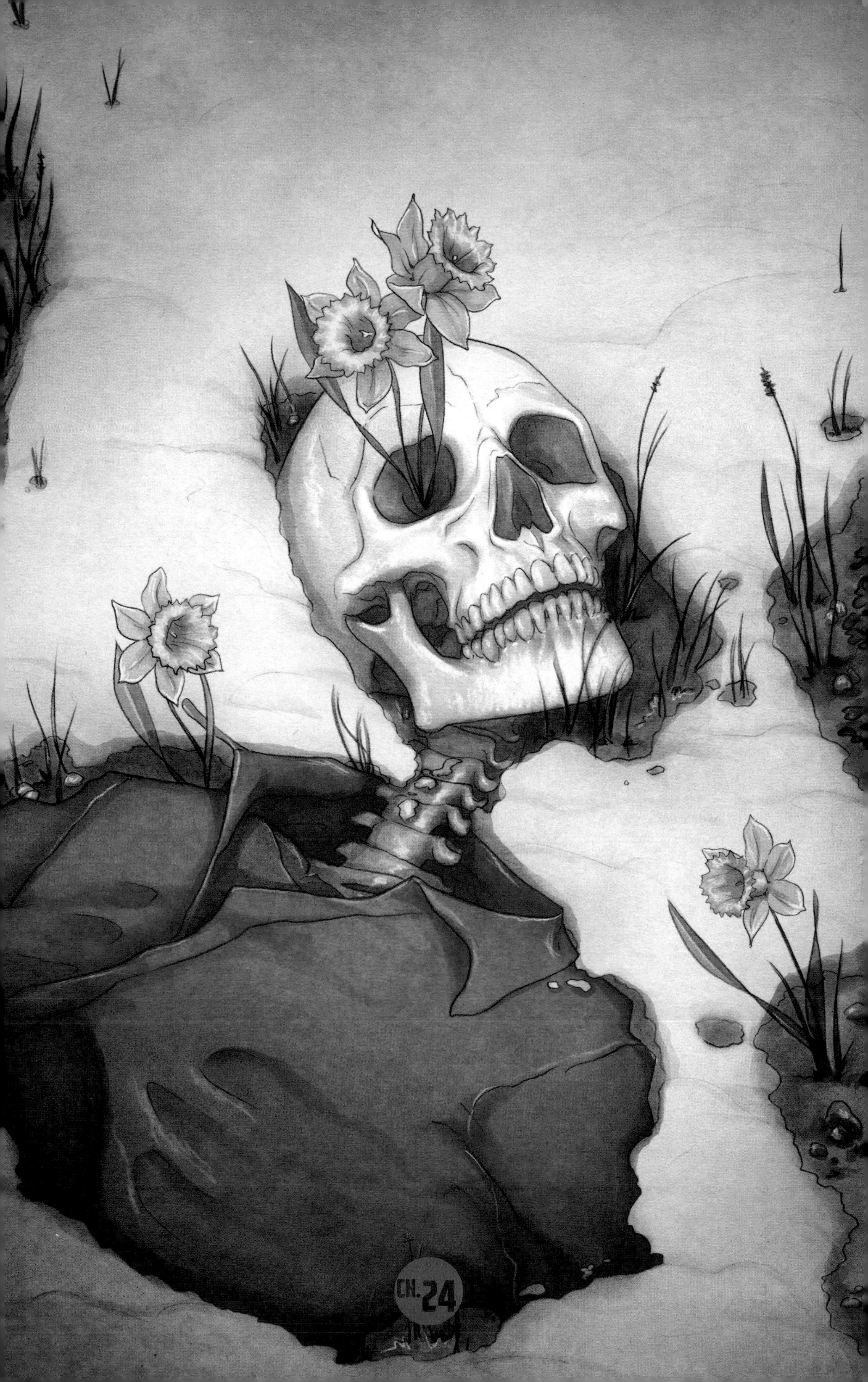
CH. 24

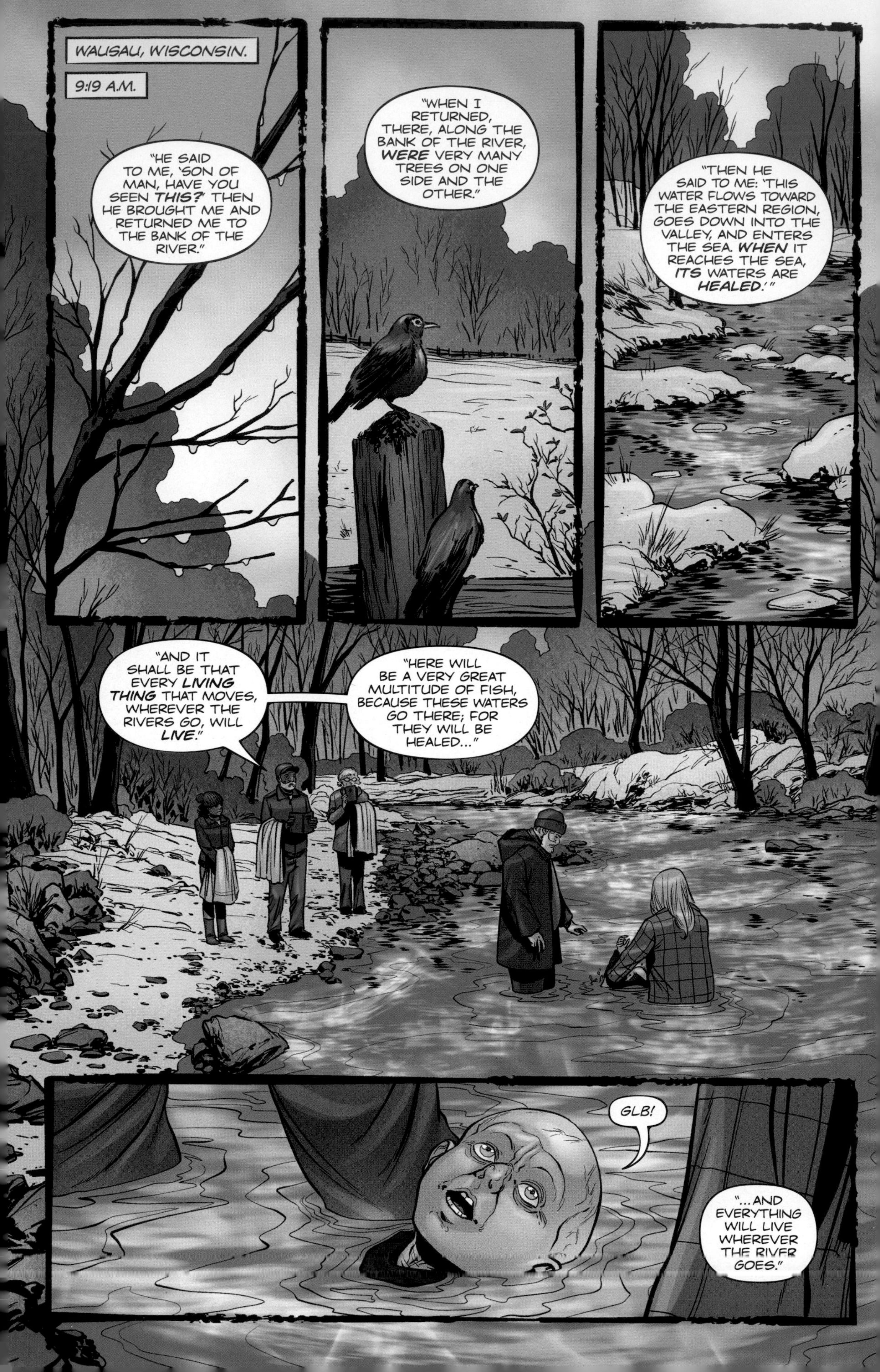

WAUSAU, WISCONSIN.
9:19 A.M.
"HE SAID TO ME, 'SON OF MAN, HAVE YOU SEEN THIS?' THEN HE BROUGHT ME AND RETURNED ME TO THE BANK OF THE RIVER."
"WHEN I RETURNED, THERE, ALONG THE BANK OF THE RIVER, WERE VERY MANY TREES ON ONE SIDE AND THE OTHER."
"THEN HE SAID TO ME: 'THIS WATER FLOWS TOWARD THE EASTERN REGION, GOES DOWN INTO THE VALLEY, AND ENTERS THE SEA. WHEN IT REACHES THE SEA, ITS WATERS ARE HEALED.'"
"AND IT SHALL BE THAT EVERY LIVING THING THAT MOVES, WHEREVER THE RIVERS GO, WILL LIVE."
"HERE WILL BE A VERY GREAT MULTITUDE OF FISH, BECAUSE THESE WATERS GO THERE; FOR THEY WILL BE HEALED..."
GLB!
"...AND EVERYTHING WILL LIVE WHEREVER THE RIVER GOES."

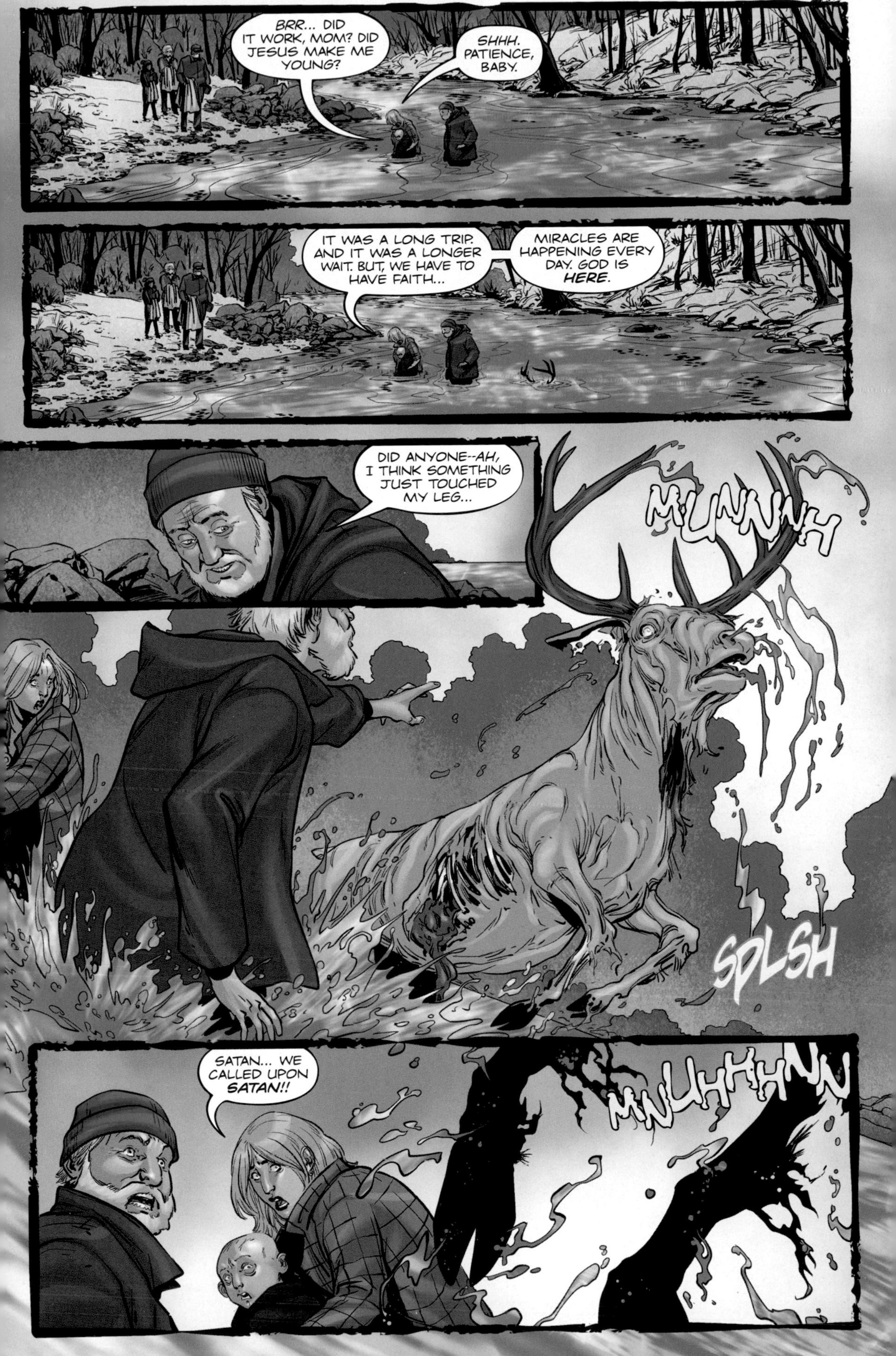
BRR... DID IT WORK, MOM? DID JESUS MAKE ME YOUNG?
SHHH. PATIENCE, BABY.
IT WAS A LONG TRIP. AND IT WAS A LONGER WAIT. BUT, WE HAVE TO HAVE FAITH...
MIRACLES ARE HAPPENING EVERY DAY. GOD IS HERE.
DID ANYONE--AH, I THINK SOMETHING JUST TOUCHED MY LEG...
MUNNNH
SPLSH
SATAN... WE CALLED UPON SATAN!!
MNUHHHNN

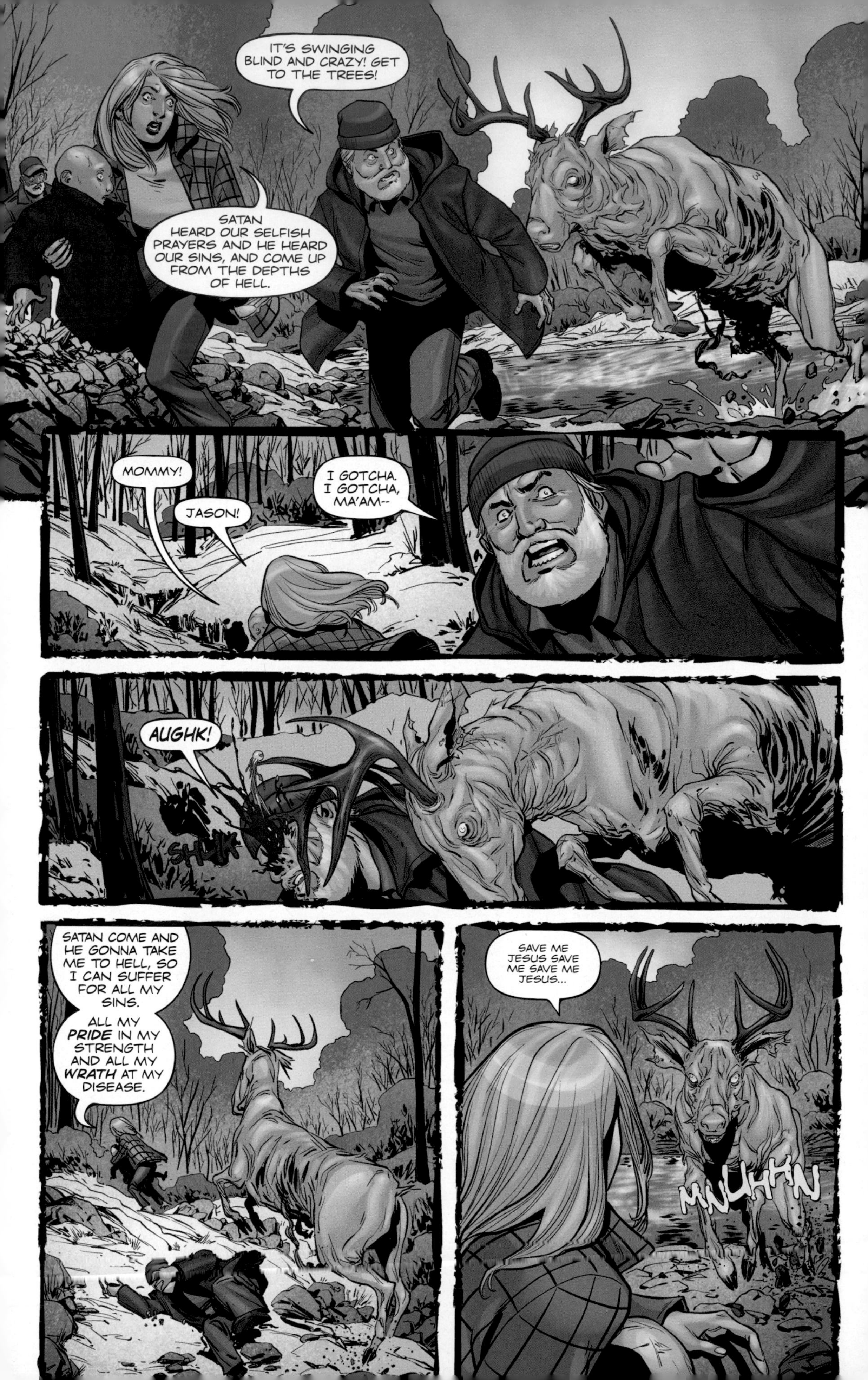
IT'S SWINGING BLIND AND CRAZY! GET TO THE TREES!
SATAN HEARD OUR SELFISH PRAYERS AND HE HEARD OUR SINS, AND COME UP FROM THE DEPTHS OF HELL.
MOMMY!
JASON!
I GOTCHA. I GOTCHA, MA'AM--
AUGHK!
SHUK
SATAN COME AND HE GONNA TAKE ME TO HELL, SO I CAN SUFFER FOR ALL MY SINS.
ALL MY PRIDE IN MY STRENGTH AND ALL MY WRATH AT MY DISEASE.
SAVE ME JESUS SAVE ME SAVE ME JESUS...
MNUHH'N

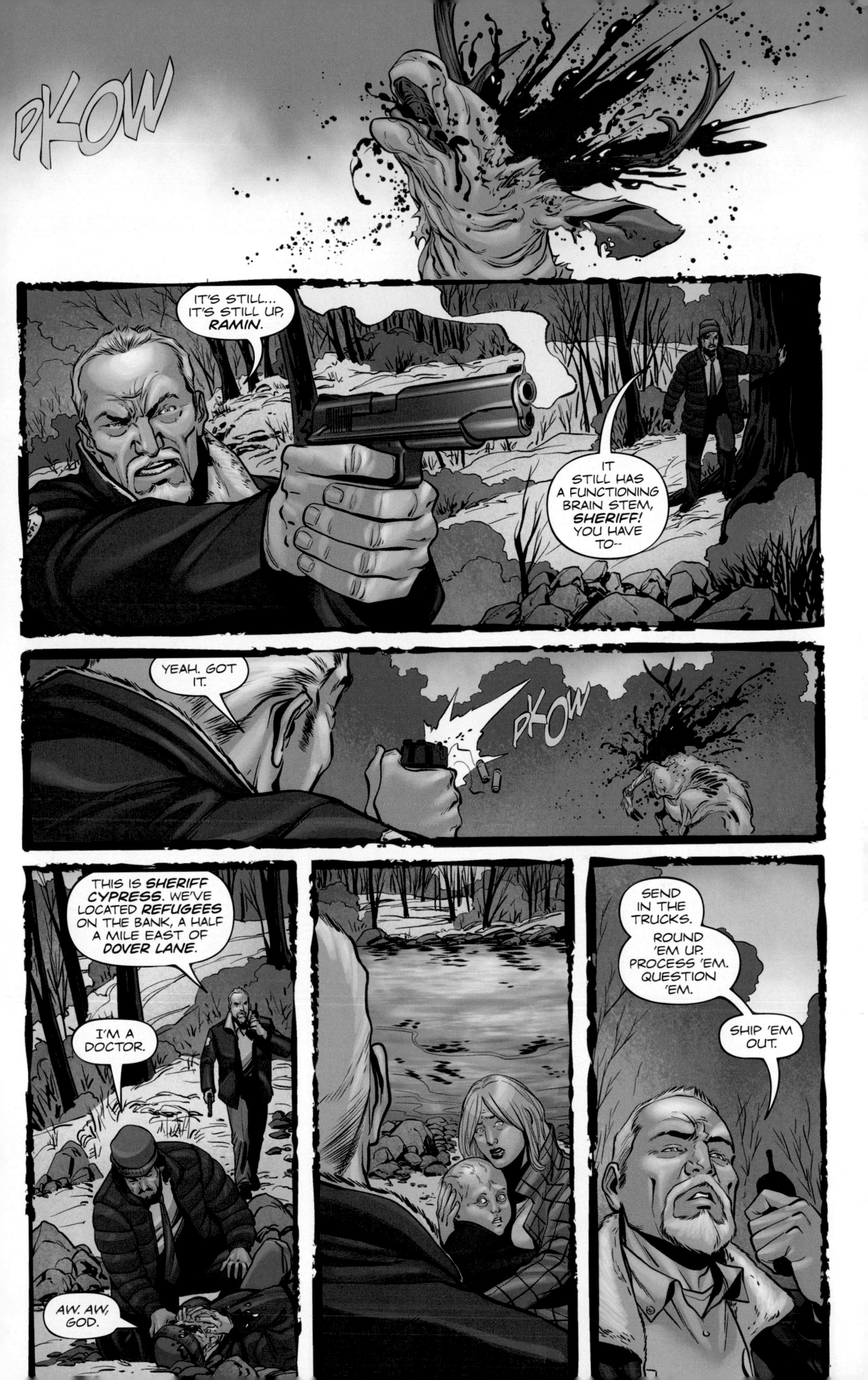
PKOW
IT'S STILL... IT'S STILL UP, RAMIN.
IT STILL HAS A FUNCTIONING BRAIN STEM, SHERIFF! YOU HAVE TO--
YEAH. GOT IT.
PKOW
THIS IS SHERIFF CYPRESS. WE'VE LOCATED REFUGEES ON THE BANK, A HALF A MILE EAST OF DOVER LANE.
I'M A DOCTOR.
AW. AW, GOD.
SEND IN THE TRUCKS.
ROUND 'EM UP. PROCESS 'EM. QUESTION 'EM.
SHIP 'EM OUT.

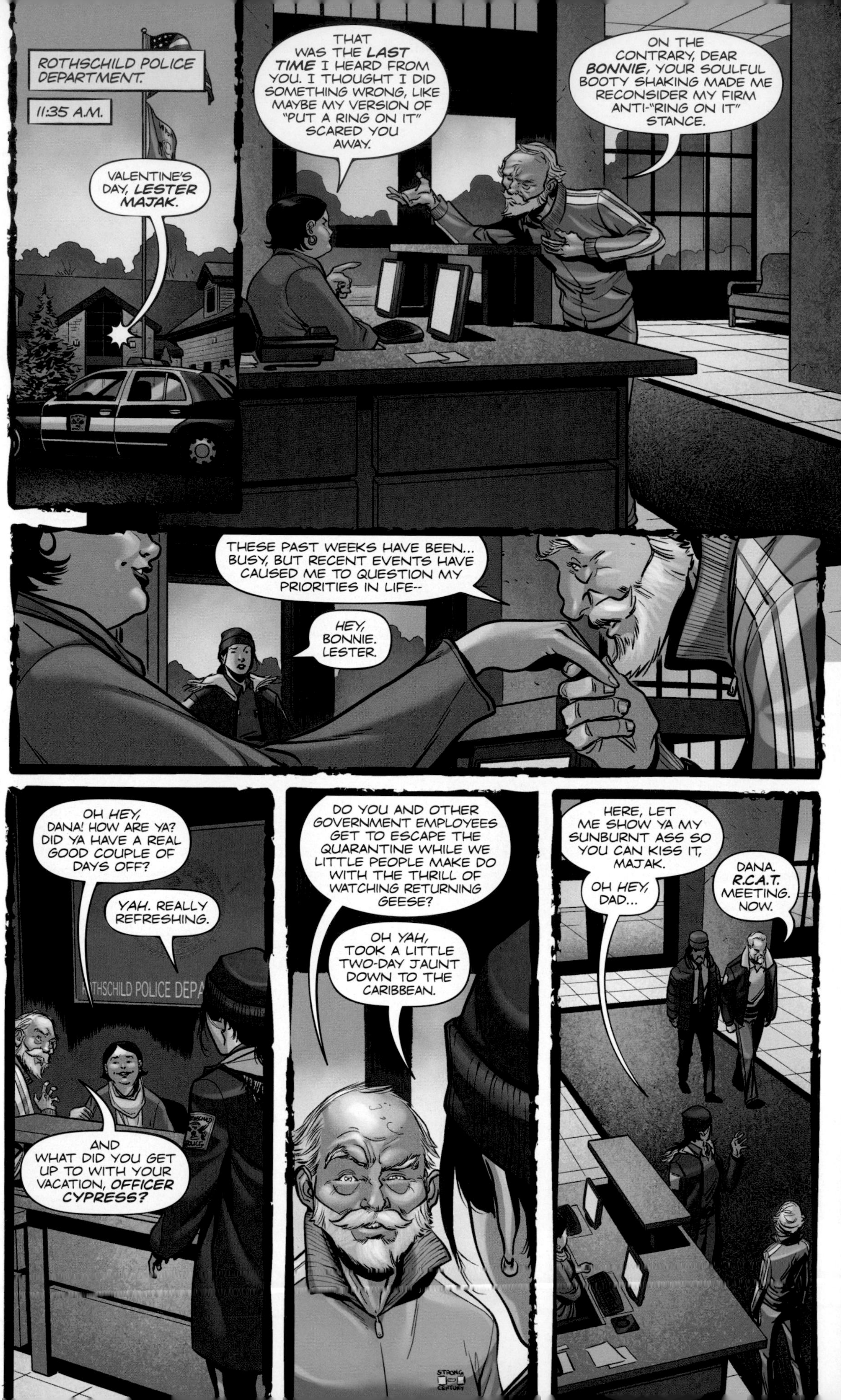
ROTHSCHILD POLICE DEPARTMENT.
11:35 A.M.
VALENTINE'S DAY, LESTER MAJAK.
THAT WAS THE LAST TIME I HEARD FROM YOU. I THOUGHT I DID SOMETHING WRONG, LIKE MAYBE MY VERSION OF "PUT A RING ON IT" SCARED YOU AWAY.
ON THE CONTRARY, DEAR BONNIE, YOUR SOULFUL BOOTY SHAKING MADE ME RECONSIDER MY FIRM ANTI-"RING ON IT" STANCE.
THESE PAST WEEKS HAVE BEEN... BUSY, BUT RECENT EVENTS HAVE CAUSED ME TO QUESTION MY PRIORITIES IN LIFE--
HEY, BONNIE. LESTER.
OH HEY, DANA! HOW ARE YA? DID YA HAVE A REAL GOOD COUPLE OF DAYS OFF?
YAH. REALLY REFRESHING.
AND WHAT DID YOU GET UP TO WITH YOUR VACATION, OFFICER CYPRESS?
DO YOU AND OTHER GOVERNMENT EMPLOYEES GET TO ESCAPE THE QUARANTINE WHILE WE LITTLE PEOPLE MAKE DO WITH THE THRILL OF WATCHING RETURNING GEESE?
OH YAH, TOOK A LITTLE TWO-DAY JAUNT DOWN TO THE CARIBBEAN.
HERE, LET ME SHOW YA MY SUNBURNT ASS SO YOU CAN KISS IT, MAJAK.
OH HEY, DAD...
DANA. R.C.A.T. MEETING. NOW.
STRONG CENTURY

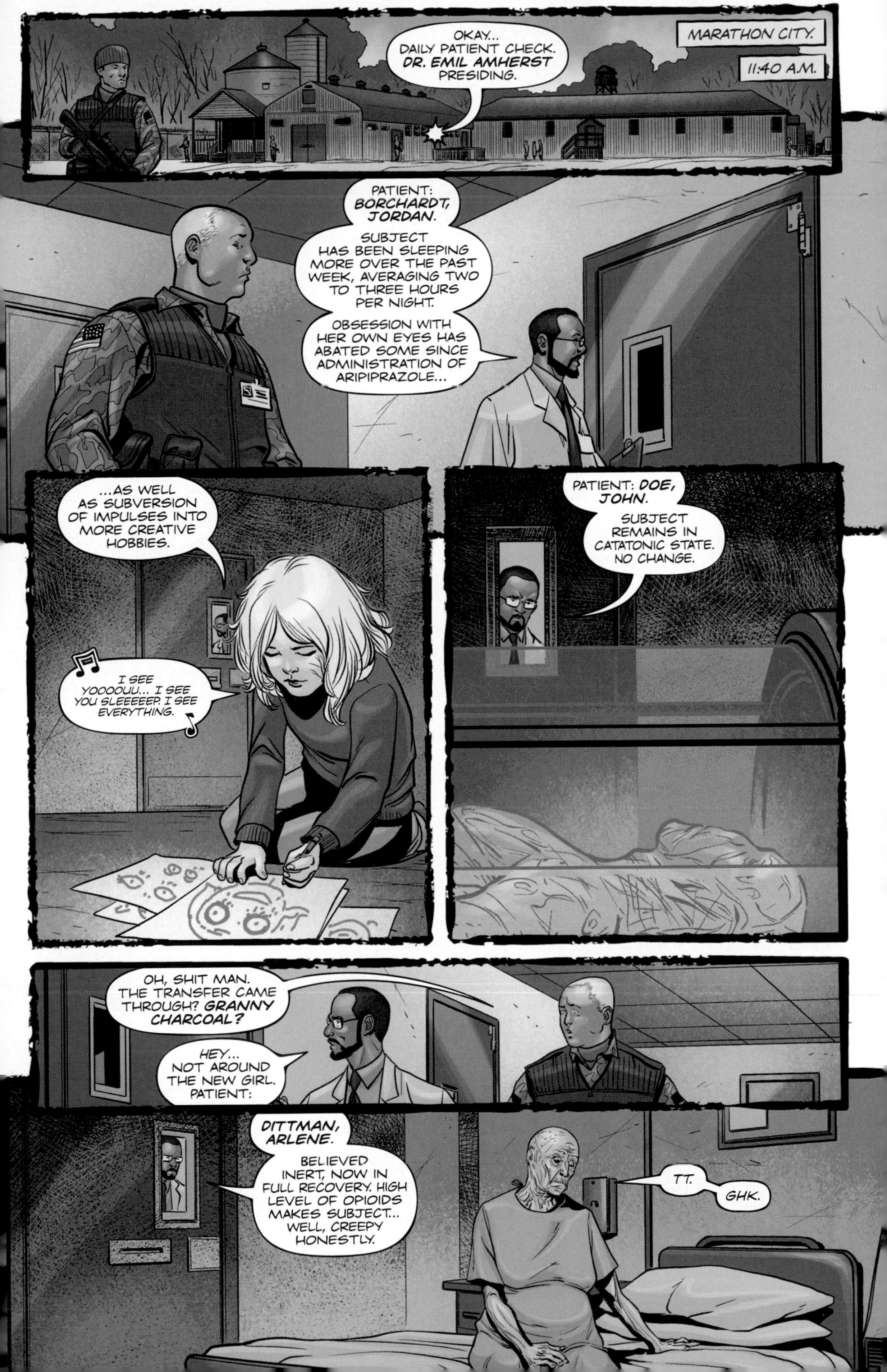
MARATHON CITY.
11:40 A.M.
OKAY... DAILY PATIENT CHECK. DR. EMIL AMHERST PRESIDING.
PATIENT: BORCHARDT, JORDAN.
SUBJECT HAS BEEN SLEEPING MORE OVER THE PAST WEEK, AVERAGING TWO TO THREE HOURS PER NIGHT.
OBSESSION WITH HER OWN EYES HAS ABATED SOME SINCE ADMINISTRATION OF ARIPIPRAZOLE...
...AS WELL AS SUBVERSION OF IMPULSES INTO MORE CREATIVE HOBBIES.
I SEE YOOOOUU... I SEE YOU SLEEEEEP. I SEE EVERYTHING.
PATIENT: DOE, JOHN.
SUBJECT REMAINS IN CATATONIC STATE. NO CHANGE.
OH, SHIT MAN. THE TRANSFER CAME THROUGH? GRANNY CHARCOAL?
HEY... NOT AROUND THE NEW GIRL. PATIENT:
DITTMAN, ARLENE.
BELIEVED INERT, NOW IN FULL RECOVERY. HIGH LEVEL OF OPIOIDS MAKES SUBJECT... WELL, CREEPY HONESTLY.
TT.
GHK.

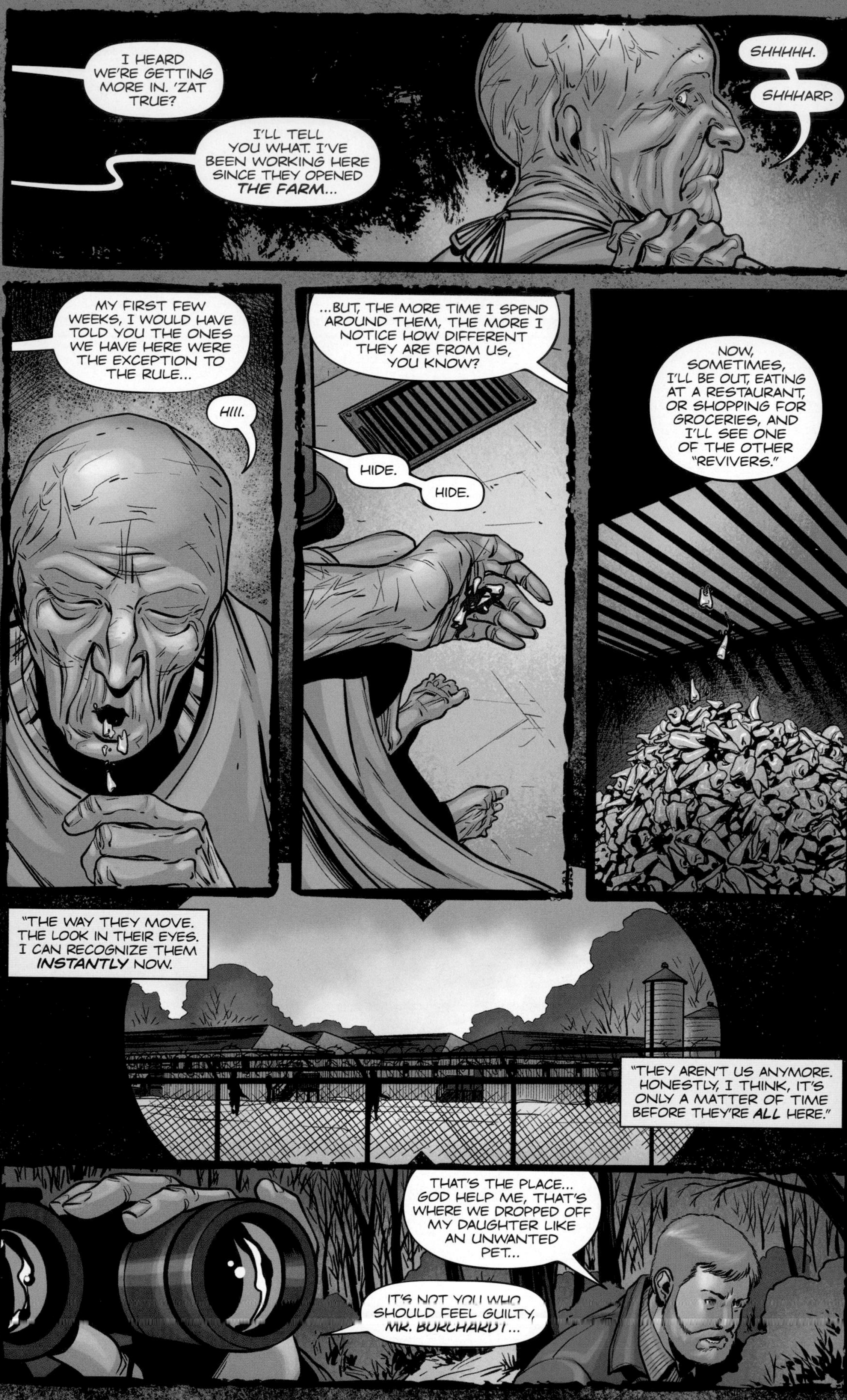
I HEARD WE'RE GETTING MORE IN. 'ZAT TRUE?
I'LL TELL YOU WHAT. I'VE BEEN WORKING HERE SINCE THEY OPENED **THE FARM**...
SHHHHH.
SHHHARP.
MY FIRST FEW WEEKS, I WOULD HAVE TOLD YOU THE ONES WE HAVE HERE WERE THE EXCEPTION TO THE RULE...
HIII.
...BUT, THE MORE TIME I SPEND AROUND THEM, THE MORE I NOTICE HOW DIFFERENT THEY ARE FROM US, YOU KNOW?
HIDE.
HIDE.
NOW, SOMETIMES, I'LL BE OUT, EATING AT A RESTAURANT, OR SHOPPING FOR GROCERIES, AND I'LL SEE ONE OF THE OTHER "REVIVERS."
"THE WAY THEY MOVE. THE LOOK IN THEIR EYES. I CAN RECOGNIZE THEM **INSTANTLY** NOW.
"THEY AREN'T US ANYMORE. HONESTLY, I THINK, IT'S ONLY A MATTER OF TIME BEFORE THEY'RE **ALL** HERE."
THAT'S THE PLACE... GOD HELP ME, THAT'S WHERE WE DROPPED OFF MY DAUGHTER LIKE AN UNWANTED PET...
IT'S NOT YOU WHO SHOULD FEEL GUILTY, **MR. BURCHARDT**...

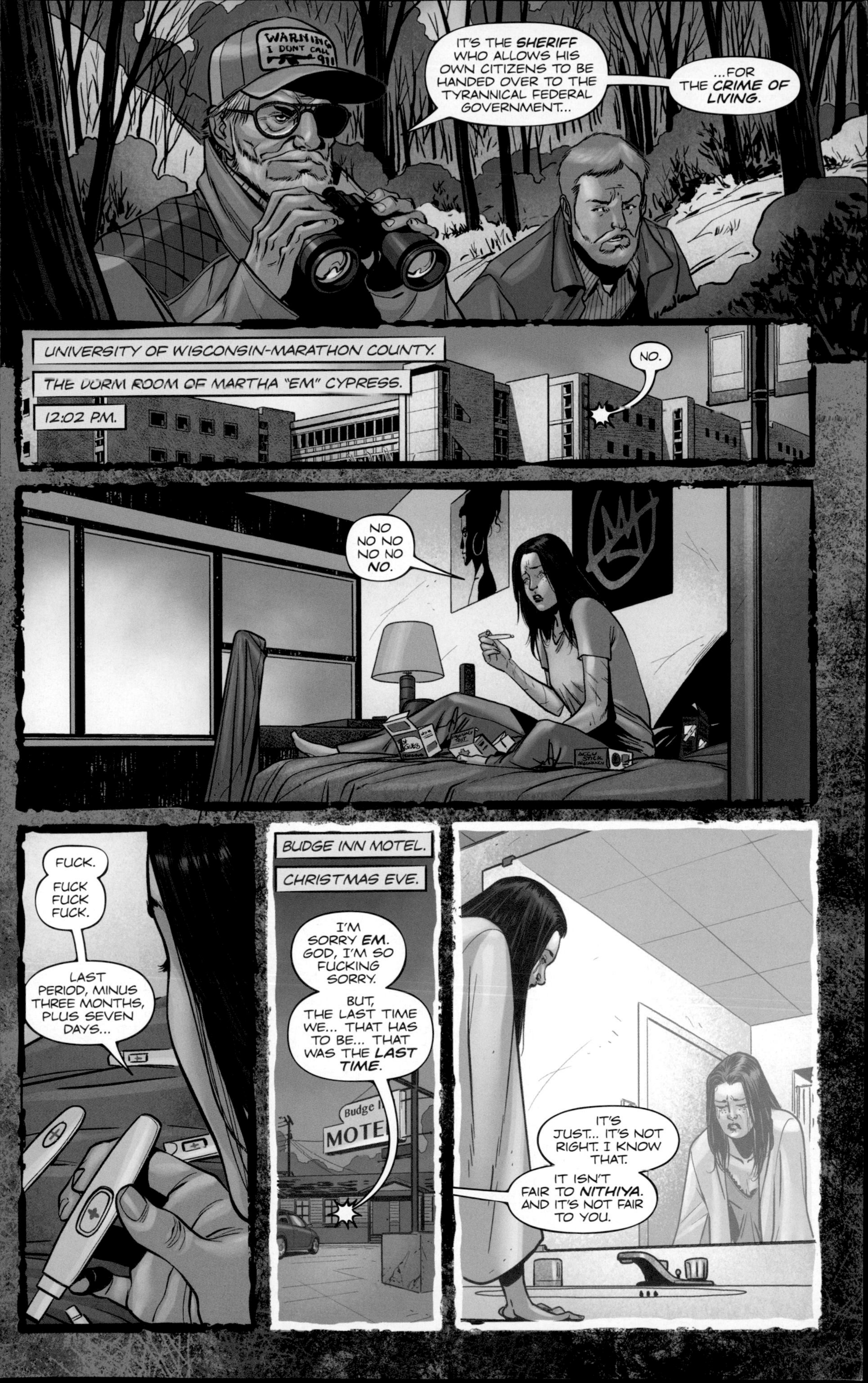
WARNING I DONT CALL 911
IT'S THE SHERIFF WHO ALLOWS HIS OWN CITIZENS TO BE HANDED OVER TO THE TYRANNICAL FEDERAL GOVERNMENT...
...FOR THE CRIME OF LIVING.
UNIVERSITY OF WISCONSIN-MARATHON COUNTY.
THE DORM ROOM OF MARTHA "EM" CYPRESS.
12:02 P.M.
NO.
NO NO NO NO NO NO.
FUCK.
FUCK FUCK FUCK.
LAST PERIOD, MINUS THREE MONTHS, PLUS SEVEN DAYS...
BUDGE INN MOTEL.
CHRISTMAS EVE.
I'M SORRY EM. GOD, I'M SO FUCKING SORRY.
BUT, THE LAST TIME WE... THAT HAS TO BE... THAT WAS THE LAST TIME.
IT'S JUST... IT'S NOT RIGHT. I KNOW THAT.
IT ISN'T FAIR TO NITHIYA. AND IT'S NOT FAIR TO YOU.

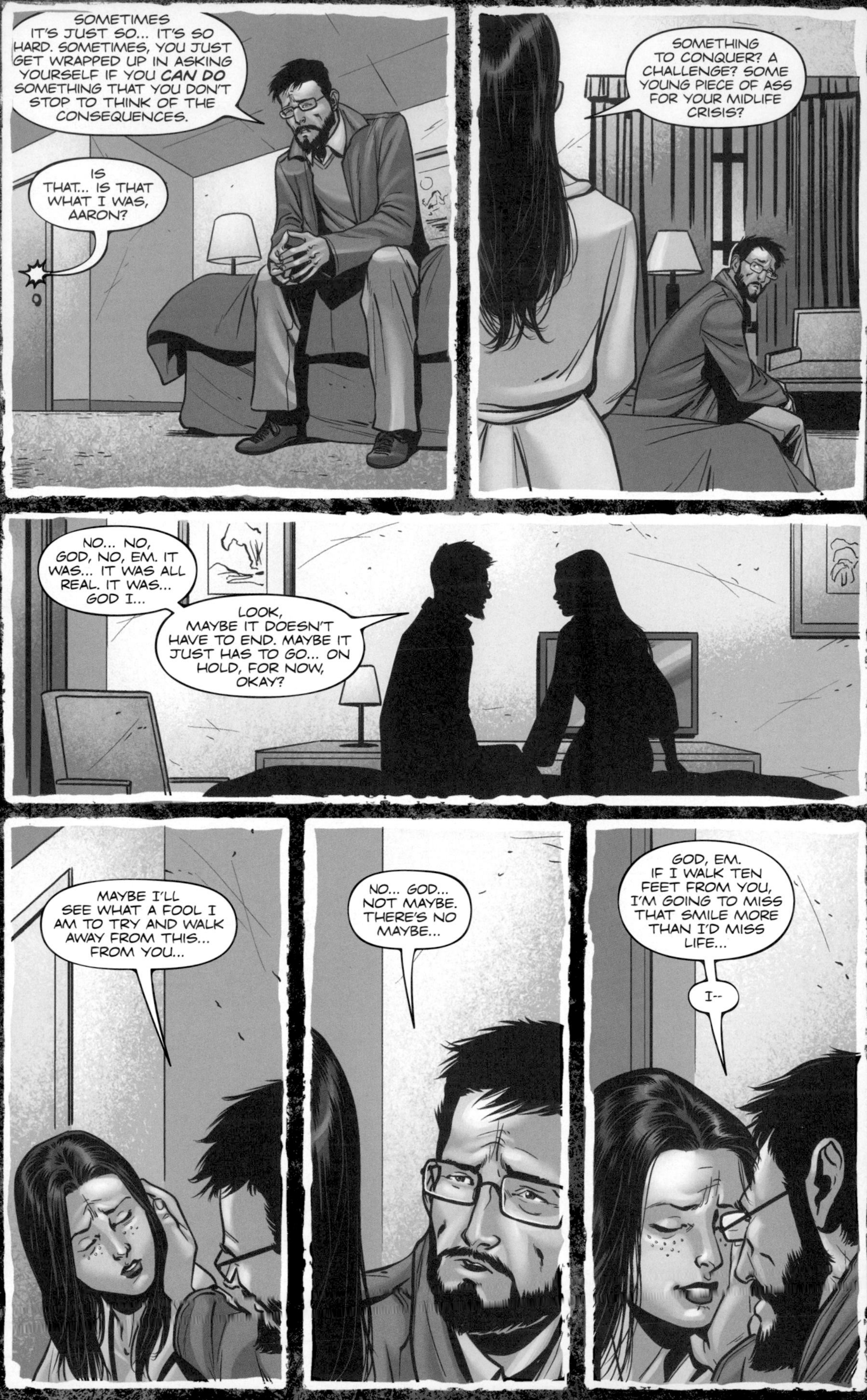
SOMETIMES IT'S JUST SO... IT'S SO HARD. SOMETIMES, YOU JUST GET WRAPPED UP IN ASKING YOURSELF IF YOU **CAN DO** SOMETHING THAT YOU DON'T STOP TO THINK OF THE CONSEQUENCES.
IS THAT... IS THAT WHAT I WAS, AARON?
SOMETHING TO CONQUER? A CHALLENGE? SOME YOUNG PIECE OF ASS FOR YOUR MIDLIFE CRISIS?
NO... NO, GOD, NO, EM. IT WAS... IT WAS ALL REAL. IT WAS... GOD I...
LOOK, MAYBE IT DOESN'T HAVE TO END. MAYBE IT JUST HAS TO GO... ON HOLD, FOR NOW, OKAY?
MAYBE I'LL SEE WHAT A FOOL I AM TO TRY AND WALK AWAY FROM THIS... FROM YOU...
NO... GOD... NOT MAYBE. THERE'S NO MAYBE...
GOD, EM. IF I WALK TEN FEET FROM YOU, I'M GOING TO MISS THAT SMILE MORE THAN I'D MISS LIFE...
I--

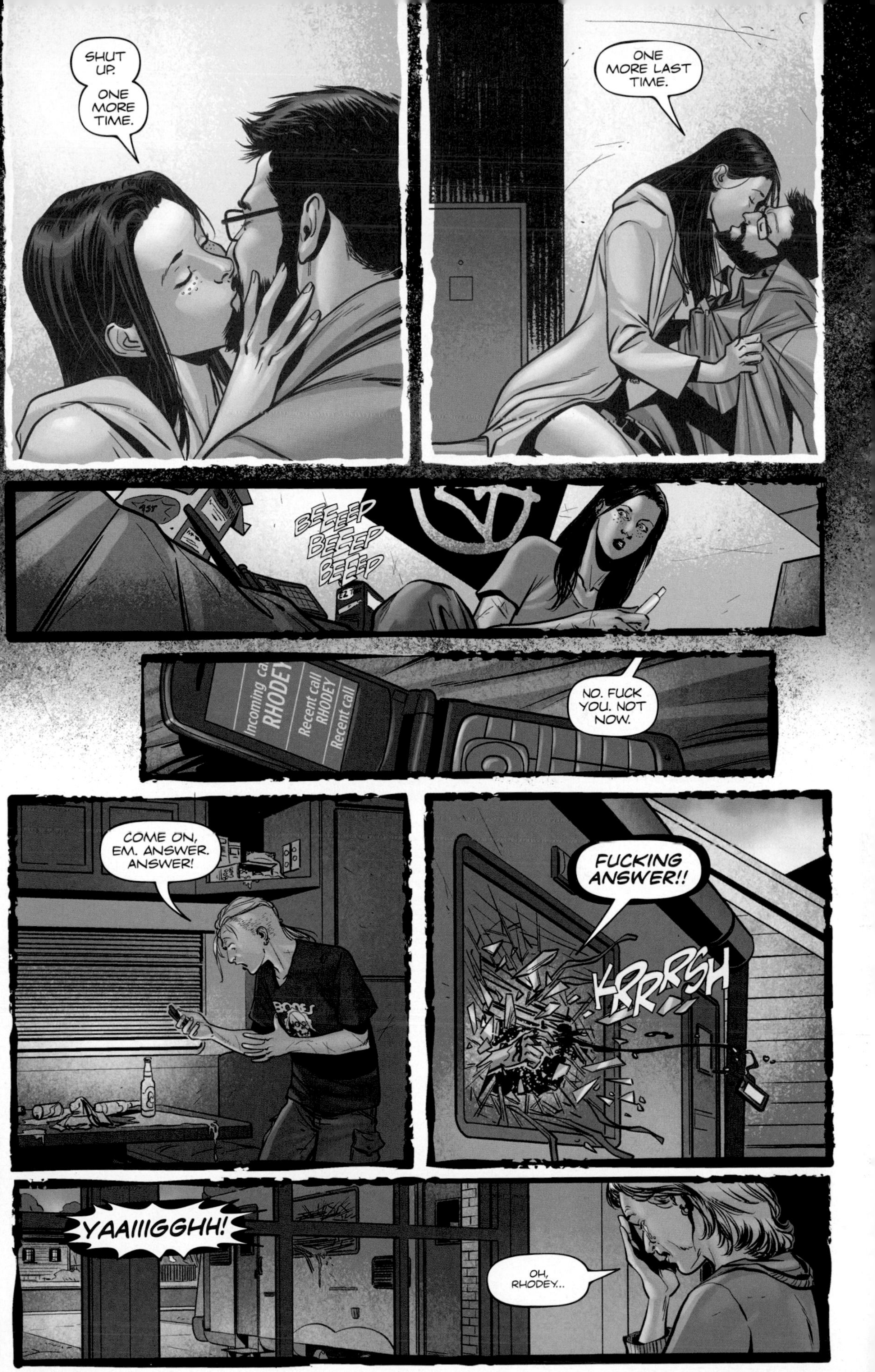
SHUT UP. ONE MORE TIME.
ONE MORE LAST TIME.
BEEEEP BEEEP BEEEP
Incoming call RHODEY
Recent call RHODEY
Recent call
NO. FUCK YOU. NOT NOW.
COME ON, EM. ANSWER. ANSWER!
FUCKING ANSWER!!
KRRRRSH
YAAIIIGGHH!
OH, RHODEY...

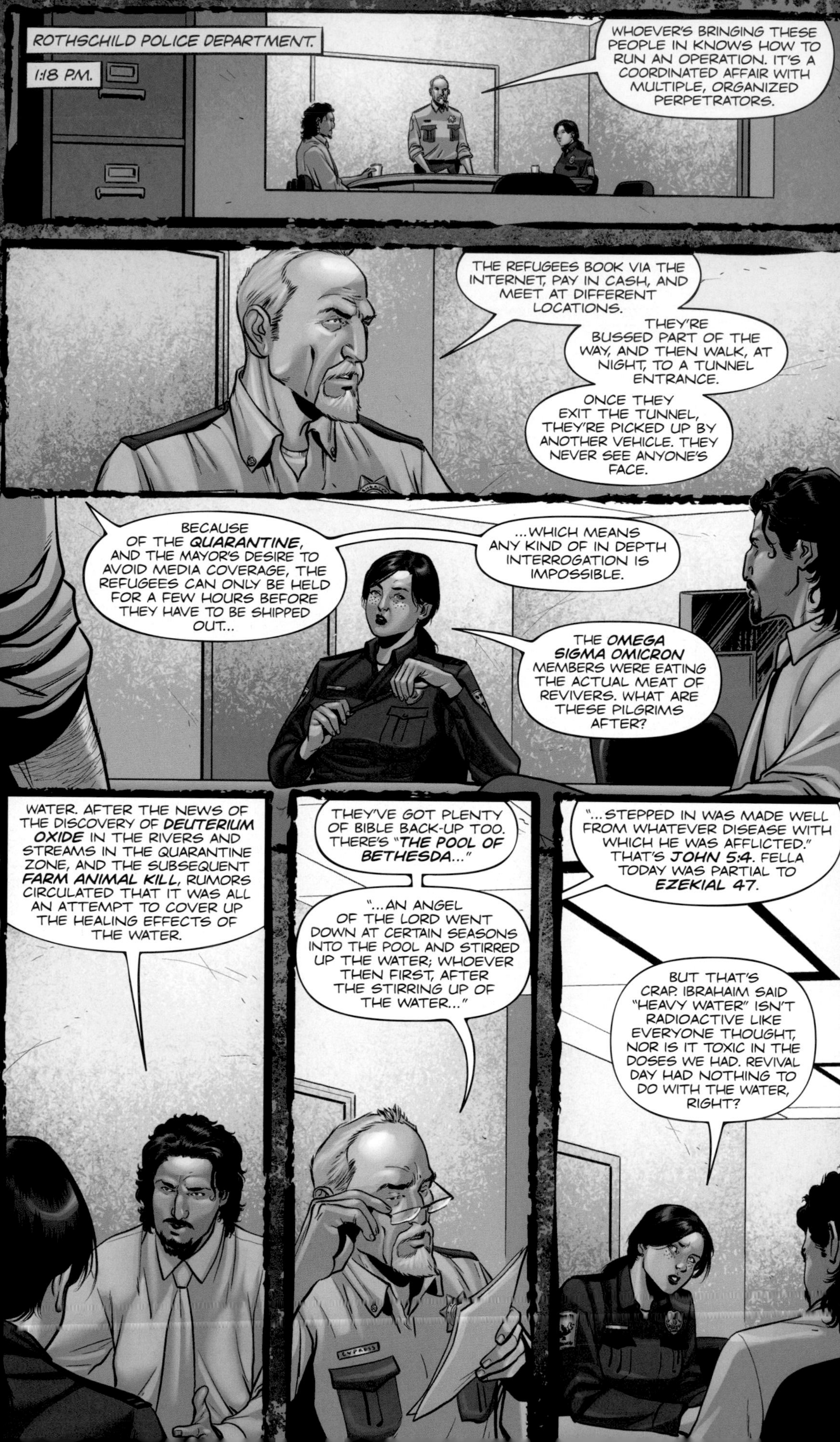
ROTHSCHILD POLICE DEPARTMENT.
1:18 P.M.
WHOEVER'S BRINGING THESE PEOPLE IN KNOWS HOW TO RUN AN OPERATION. IT'S A COORDINATED AFFAIR WITH MULTIPLE, ORGANIZED PERPETRATORS.
THE REFUGEES BOOK VIA THE INTERNET, PAY IN CASH, AND MEET AT DIFFERENT LOCATIONS.
THEY'RE BUSSED PART OF THE WAY, AND THEN WALK, AT NIGHT, TO A TUNNEL ENTRANCE.
ONCE THEY EXIT THE TUNNEL, THEY'RE PICKED UP BY ANOTHER VEHICLE. THEY NEVER SEE ANYONE'S FACE.
BECAUSE OF THE ***QUARANTINE***, AND THE MAYOR'S DESIRE TO AVOID MEDIA COVERAGE, THE REFUGEES CAN ONLY BE HELD FOR A FEW HOURS BEFORE THEY HAVE TO BE SHIPPED OUT...
...WHICH MEANS ANY KIND OF IN DEPTH INTERROGATION IS IMPOSSIBLE.
THE ***OMEGA SIGMA OMICRON*** MEMBERS WERE EATING THE ACTUAL MEAT OF REVIVERS. WHAT ARE THESE PILGRIMS AFTER?
WATER. AFTER THE NEWS OF THE DISCOVERY OF ***DEUTERIUM OXIDE*** IN THE RIVERS AND STREAMS IN THE QUARANTINE ZONE, AND THE SUBSEQUENT ***FARM ANIMAL KILL***, RUMORS CIRCULATED THAT IT WAS ALL AN ATTEMPT TO COVER UP THE HEALING EFFECTS OF THE WATER.
THEY'VE GOT PLENTY OF BIBLE BACK-UP TOO. THERE'S "***THE POOL OF BETHESDA***..."
"...AN ANGEL OF THE LORD WENT DOWN AT CERTAIN SEASONS INTO THE POOL AND STIRRED UP THE WATER; WHOEVER THEN FIRST, AFTER THE STIRRING UP OF THE WATER..."
"...STEPPED IN WAS MADE WELL FROM WHATEVER DISEASE WITH WHICH HE WAS AFFLICTED." THAT'S ***JOHN 5:4***. FELLA TODAY WAS PARTIAL TO ***EZEKIAL 47***.
BUT THAT'S CRAP. IBRAHAIM SAID "HEAVY WATER" ISN'T RADIOACTIVE LIKE EVERYONE THOUGHT, NOR IS IT TOXIC IN THE DOSES WE HAD. REVIVAL DAY HAD NOTHING TO DO WITH THE WATER, RIGHT?

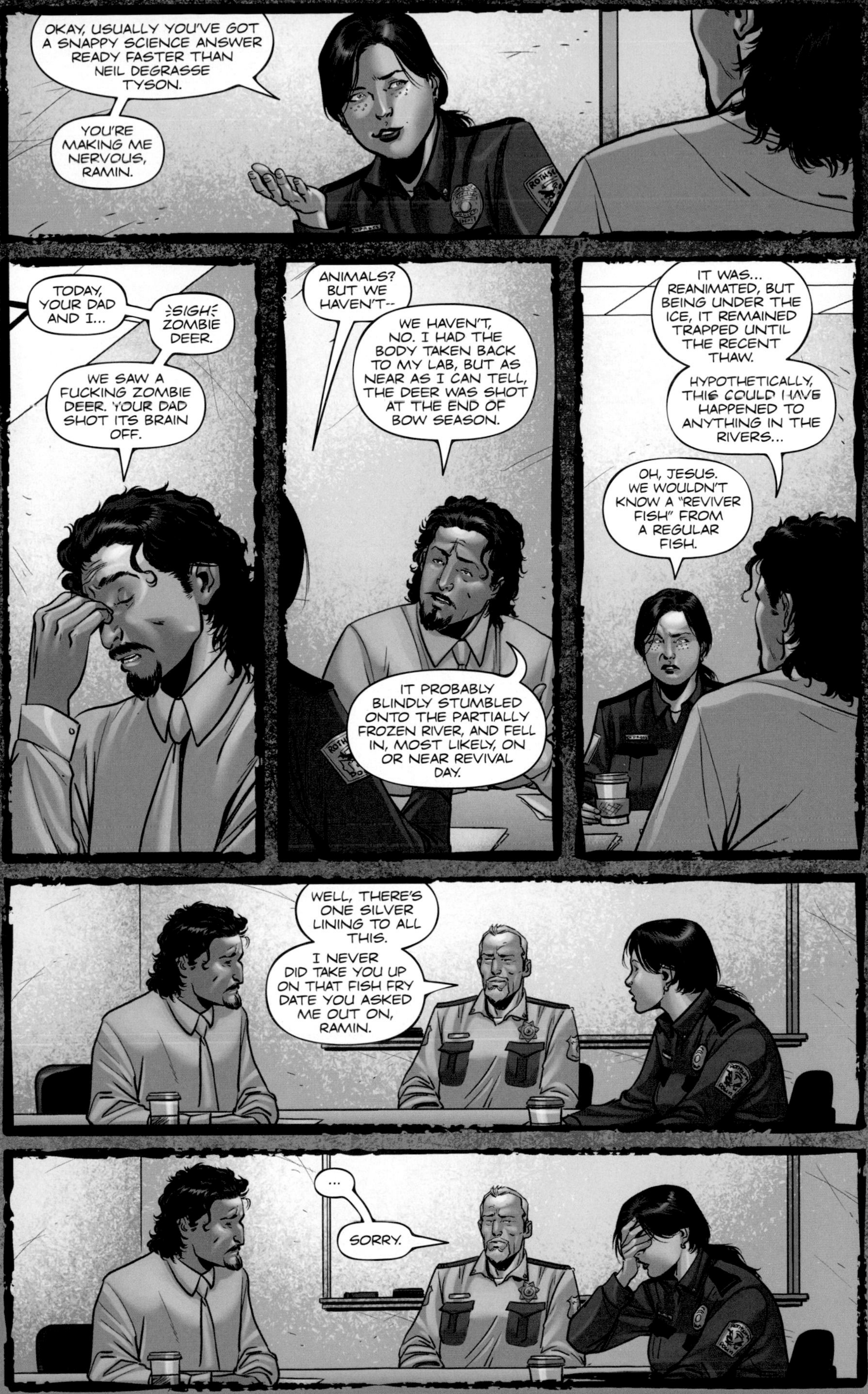
OKAY, USUALLY YOU'VE GOT A SNAPPY SCIENCE ANSWER READY FASTER THAN NEIL DEGRASSE TYSON.
YOU'RE MAKING ME NERVOUS, RAMIN.
TODAY, YOUR DAD AND I...
SIGH ZOMBIE DEER.
WE SAW A FUCKING ZOMBIE DEER. YOUR DAD SHOT ITS BRAIN OFF.
ANIMALS? BUT WE HAVEN'T--
WE HAVEN'T, NO. I HAD THE BODY TAKEN BACK TO MY LAB, BUT AS NEAR AS I CAN TELL, THE DEER WAS SHOT AT THE END OF BOW SEASON.
IT PROBABLY BLINDLY STUMBLED ONTO THE PARTIALLY FROZEN RIVER, AND FELL IN, MOST LIKELY, ON OR NEAR REVIVAL DAY.
IT WAS... REANIMATED, BUT BEING UNDER THE ICE, IT REMAINED TRAPPED UNTIL THE RECENT THAW.
HYPOTHETICALLY, THIS COULD HAVE HAPPENED TO ANYTHING IN THE RIVERS...
OH, JESUS. WE WOULDN'T KNOW A "REVIVER FISH" FROM A REGULAR FISH.
WELL, THERE'S ONE SILVER LINING TO ALL THIS.
I NEVER DID TAKE YOU UP ON THAT FISH FRY DATE YOU ASKED ME OUT ON, RAMIN.
...
SORRY.

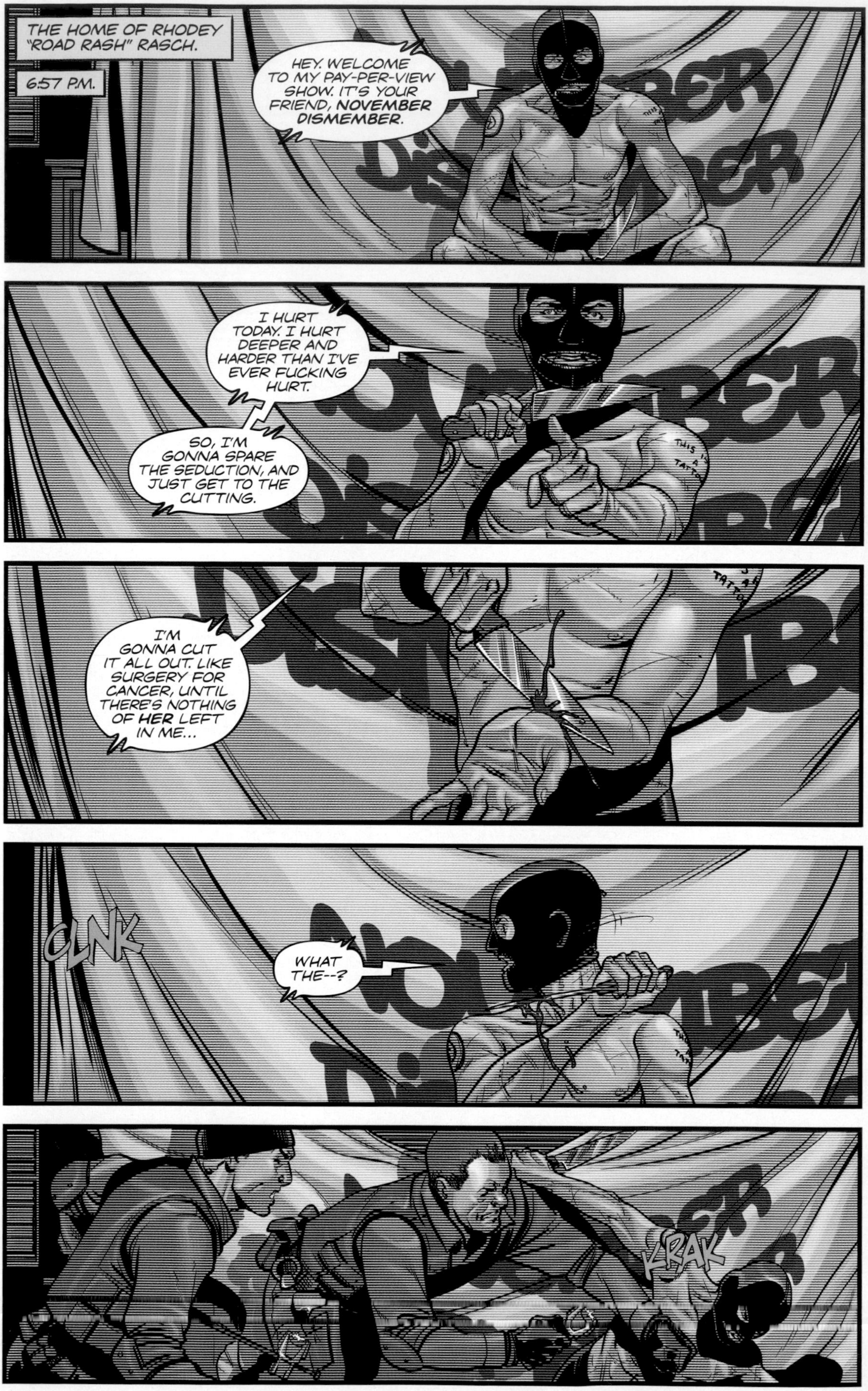
THE HOME OF RHODEY "ROAD RASH" RASCH.
6:57 P.M.
HEY. WELCOME TO MY PAY-PER-VIEW SHOW. IT'S YOUR FRIEND, NOVEMBER DISMEMBER.
I HURT TODAY. I HURT DEEPER AND HARDER THAN I'VE EVER FUCKING HURT.
SO, I'M GONNA SPARE THE SEDUCTION, AND JUST GET TO THE CUTTING.
I'M GONNA CUT IT ALL OUT. LIKE SURGERY FOR CANCER, UNTIL THERE'S NOTHING OF HER LEFT IN ME...
CLNK
WHAT THE--?
KRAK

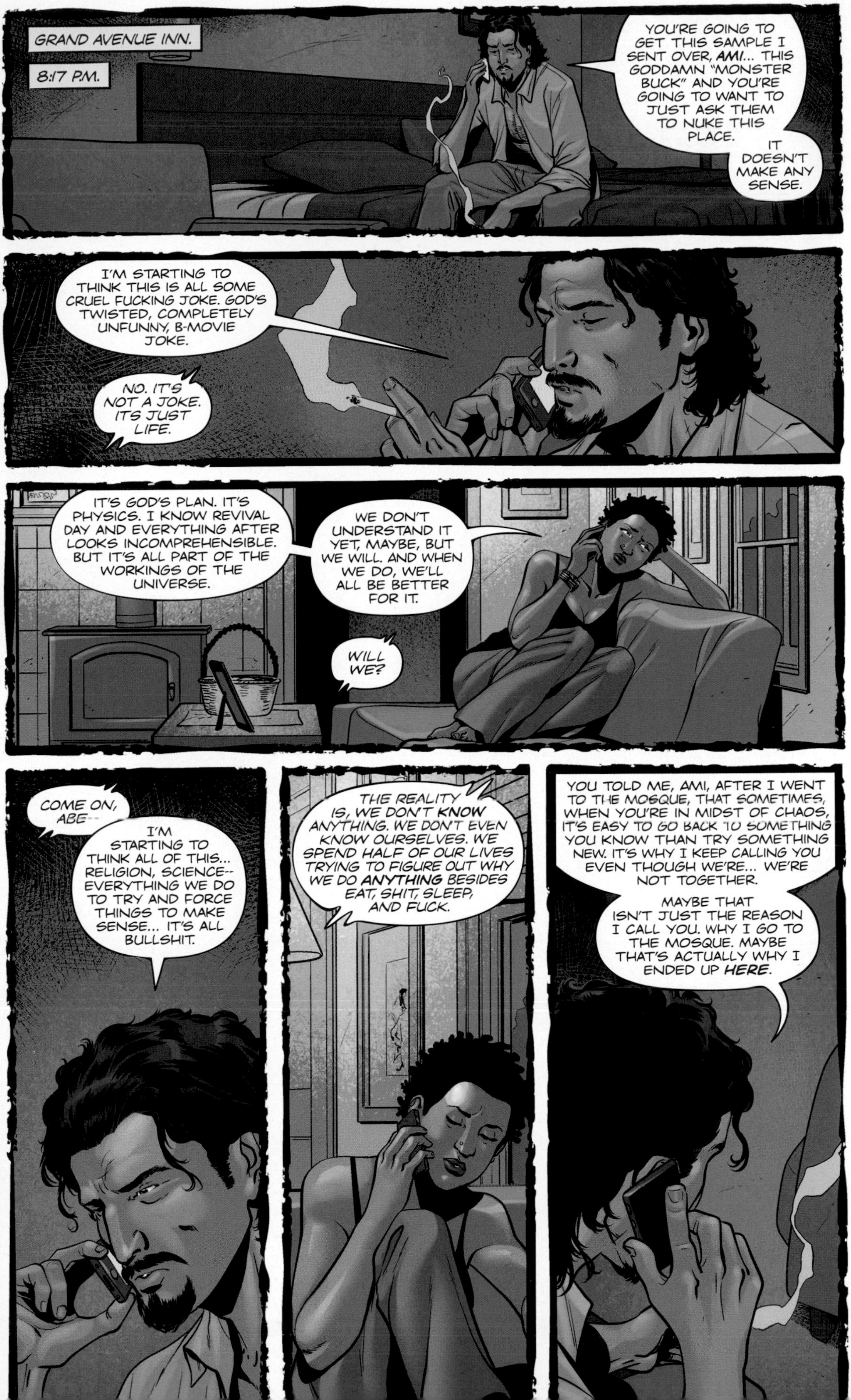
GRAND AVENUE INN.
8:17 P.M.
YOU'RE GOING TO GET THIS SAMPLE I SENT OVER, AMI... THIS GODDAMN "MONSTER BUCK" AND YOU'RE GOING TO WANT TO JUST ASK THEM TO NUKE THIS PLACE.
IT DOESN'T MAKE ANY SENSE.
I'M STARTING TO THINK THIS IS ALL SOME CRUEL FUCKING JOKE. GOD'S TWISTED, COMPLETELY UNFUNNY, B-MOVIE JOKE.
NO. IT'S NOT A JOKE. IT'S JUST LIFE.
IT'S GOD'S PLAN. IT'S PHYSICS. I KNOW REVIVAL DAY AND EVERYTHING AFTER LOOKS INCOMPREHENSIBLE. BUT IT'S ALL PART OF THE WORKINGS OF THE UNIVERSE.
WE DON'T UNDERSTAND IT YET, MAYBE, BUT WE WILL. AND WHEN WE DO, WE'LL ALL BE BETTER FOR IT.
WILL WE?
COME ON, ABE--
I'M STARTING TO THINK ALL OF THIS... RELIGION, SCIENCE--EVERYTHING WE DO TO TRY AND FORCE THINGS TO MAKE SENSE... IT'S ALL BULLSHIT.
THE REALITY IS, WE DON'T KNOW ANYTHING. WE DON'T EVEN KNOW OURSELVES. WE SPEND HALF OF OUR LIVES TRYING TO FIGURE OUT WHY WE DO ANYTHING BESIDES EAT, SHIT, SLEEP, AND FUCK.
YOU TOLD ME, AMI, AFTER I WENT TO THE MOSQUE, THAT SOMETIMES, WHEN YOU'RE IN MIDST OF CHAOS, IT'S EASY TO GO BACK TO SOMETHING YOU KNOW THAN TRY SOMETHING NEW. IT'S WHY I KEEP CALLING YOU EVEN THOUGH WE'RE... WE'RE NOT TOGETHER.
MAYBE THAT ISN'T JUST THE REASON I CALL YOU. WHY I GO TO THE MOSQUE. MAYBE THAT'S ACTUALLY WHY I ENDED UP HERE.

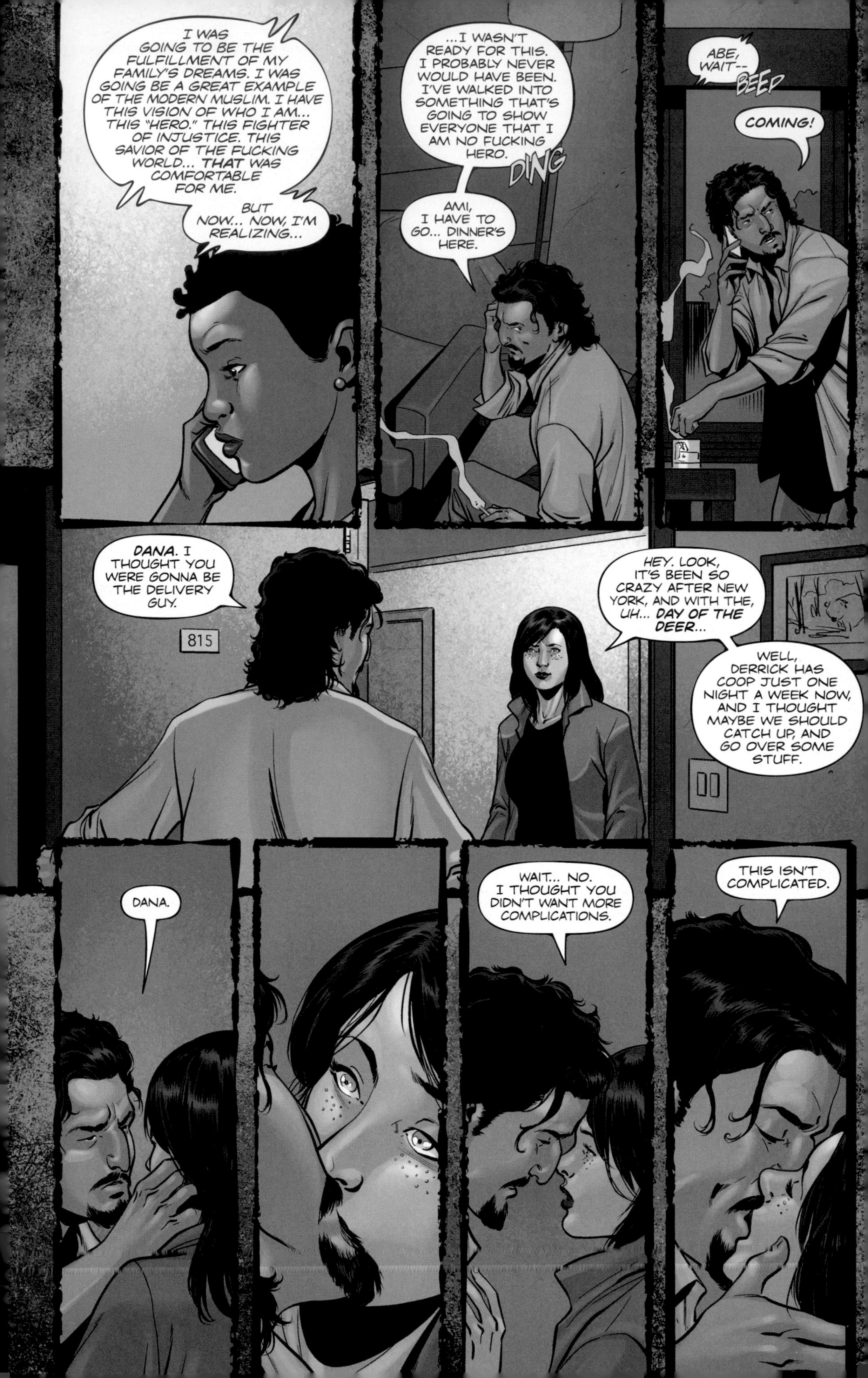

I WAS GOING TO BE THE FULFILLMENT OF MY FAMILY'S DREAMS. I WAS GOING BE A GREAT EXAMPLE OF THE MODERN MUSLIM. I HAVE THIS VISION OF WHO I AM... THIS "HERO." THIS FIGHTER OF INJUSTICE. THIS SAVIOR OF THE FUCKING WORLD... THAT WAS COMFORTABLE FOR ME.
BUT NOW... NOW, I'M REALIZING...
...I WASN'T READY FOR THIS. I PROBABLY NEVER WOULD HAVE BEEN. I'VE WALKED INTO SOMETHING THAT'S GOING TO SHOW EVERYONE THAT I AM NO FUCKING HERO.
DING
AMI, I HAVE TO GO... DINNER'S HERE.
ABE, WAIT--
BEEP
COMING!
DANA. I THOUGHT YOU WERE GONNA BE THE DELIVERY GUY.
815
HEY. LOOK, IT'S BEEN SO CRAZY AFTER NEW YORK, AND WITH THE, UH... DAY OF THE DEER...
WELL, DERRICK HAS COOP JUST ONE NIGHT A WEEK NOW, AND I THOUGHT MAYBE WE SHOULD CATCH UP, AND GO OVER SOME STUFF.
DANA.
WAIT... NO. I THOUGHT YOU DIDN'T WANT MORE COMPLICATIONS.
THIS ISN'T COMPLICATED.

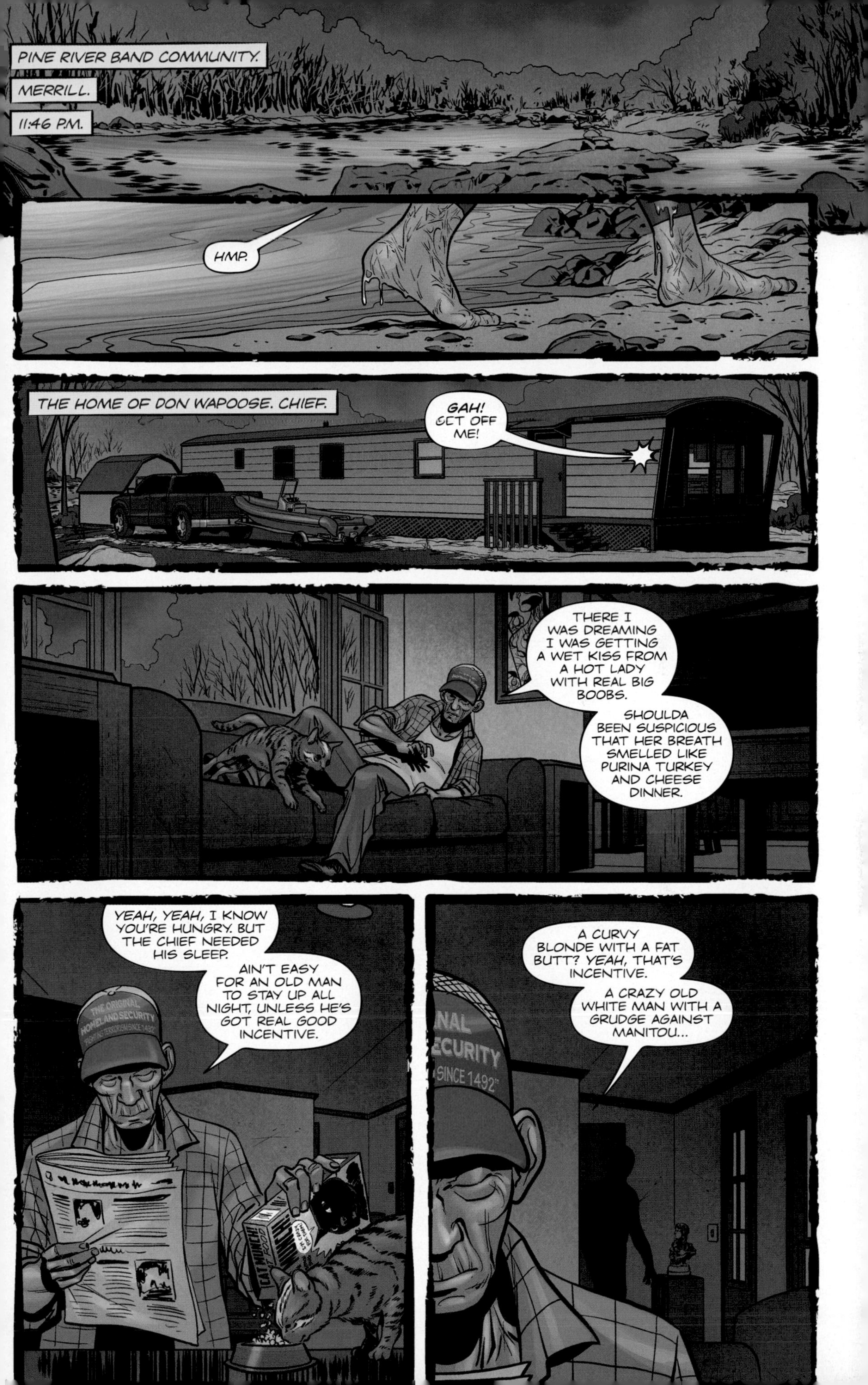
PINE RIVER BAND COMMUNITY.
MERRILL.
11:46 P.M.
HMP.
THE HOME OF DON WAPOOSE. CHIEF.
GAH! GET OFF ME!
THERE I WAS DREAMING I WAS GETTING A WET KISS FROM A HOT LADY WITH REAL BIG BOOBS.
SHOULDA BEEN SUSPICIOUS THAT HER BREATH SMELLED LIKE PURINA TURKEY AND CHEESE DINNER.
YEAH, YEAH, I KNOW YOU'RE HUNGRY. BUT THE CHIEF NEEDED HIS SLEEP.
AIN'T EASY FOR AN OLD MAN TO STAY UP ALL NIGHT, UNLESS HE'S GOT REAL GOOD INCENTIVE.
THE ORIGINAL HOMELAND SECURITY
A CURVY BLONDE WITH A FAT BUTT? YEAH, THAT'S INCENTIVE.
A CRAZY OLD WHITE MAN WITH A GRUDGE AGAINST MANITOU...

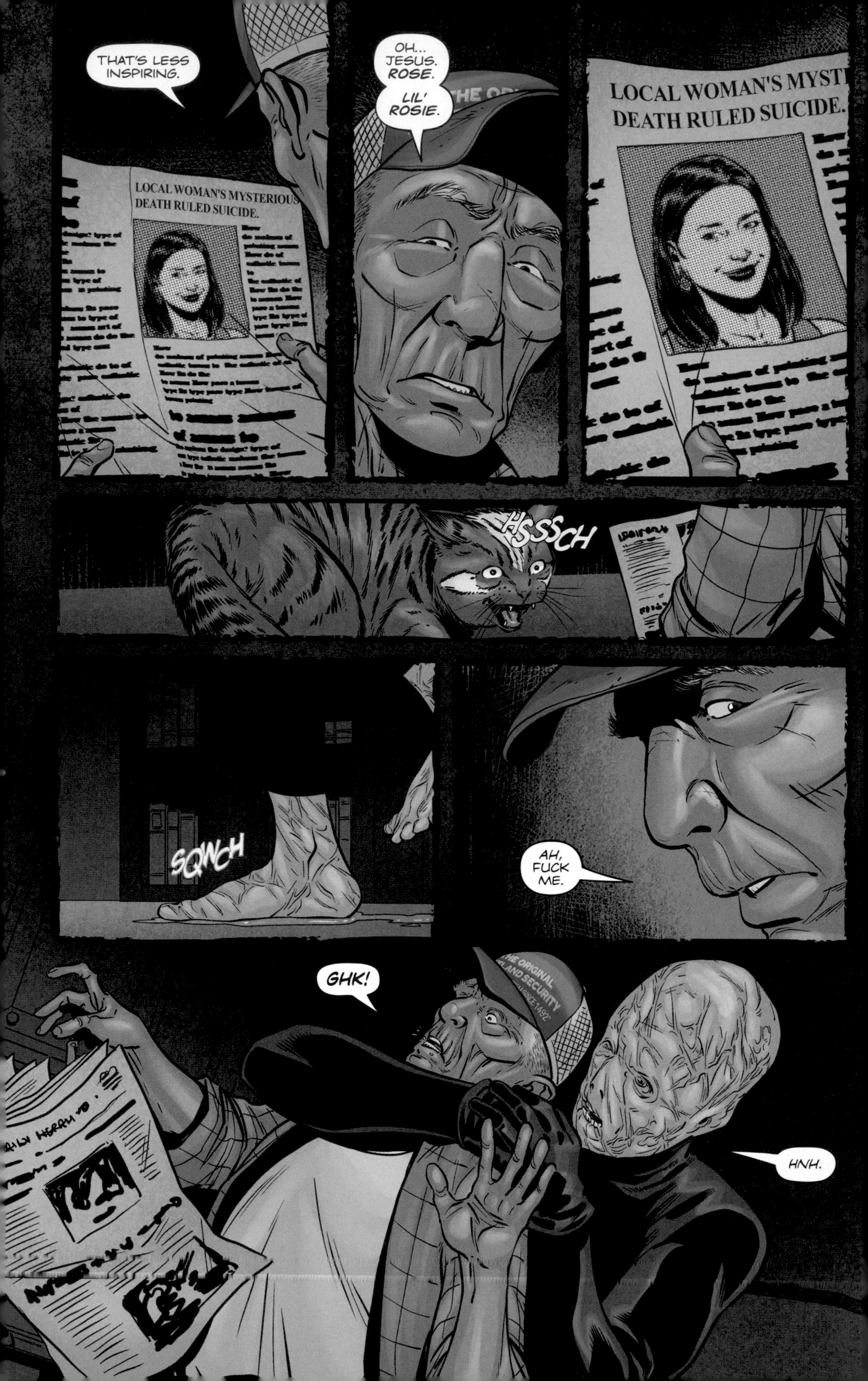
THAT'S LESS INSPIRING.
LOCAL WOMAN'S MYSTERIOUS DEATH RULED SUICIDE.
OH... JESUS. ROSE.
LIL' ROSIE.
HSSSCH
SQWCH
AH, FUCK ME.
GHK!
HNH.

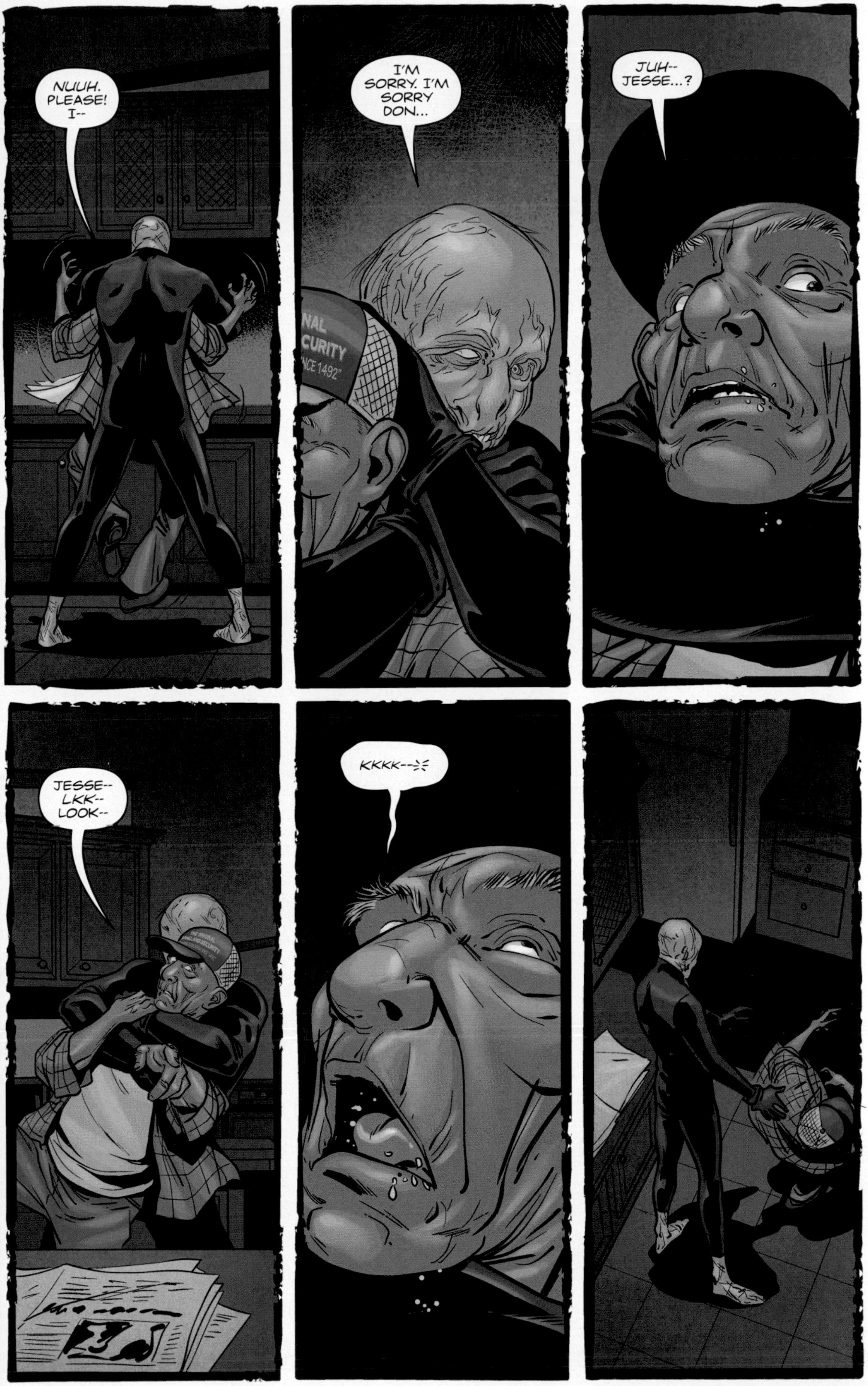
NUUH. PLEASE! I--
I'M SORRY. I'M SORRY DON...
JUH-- JESSE...?
JESSE-- LKK-- LOOK--
KKKK--

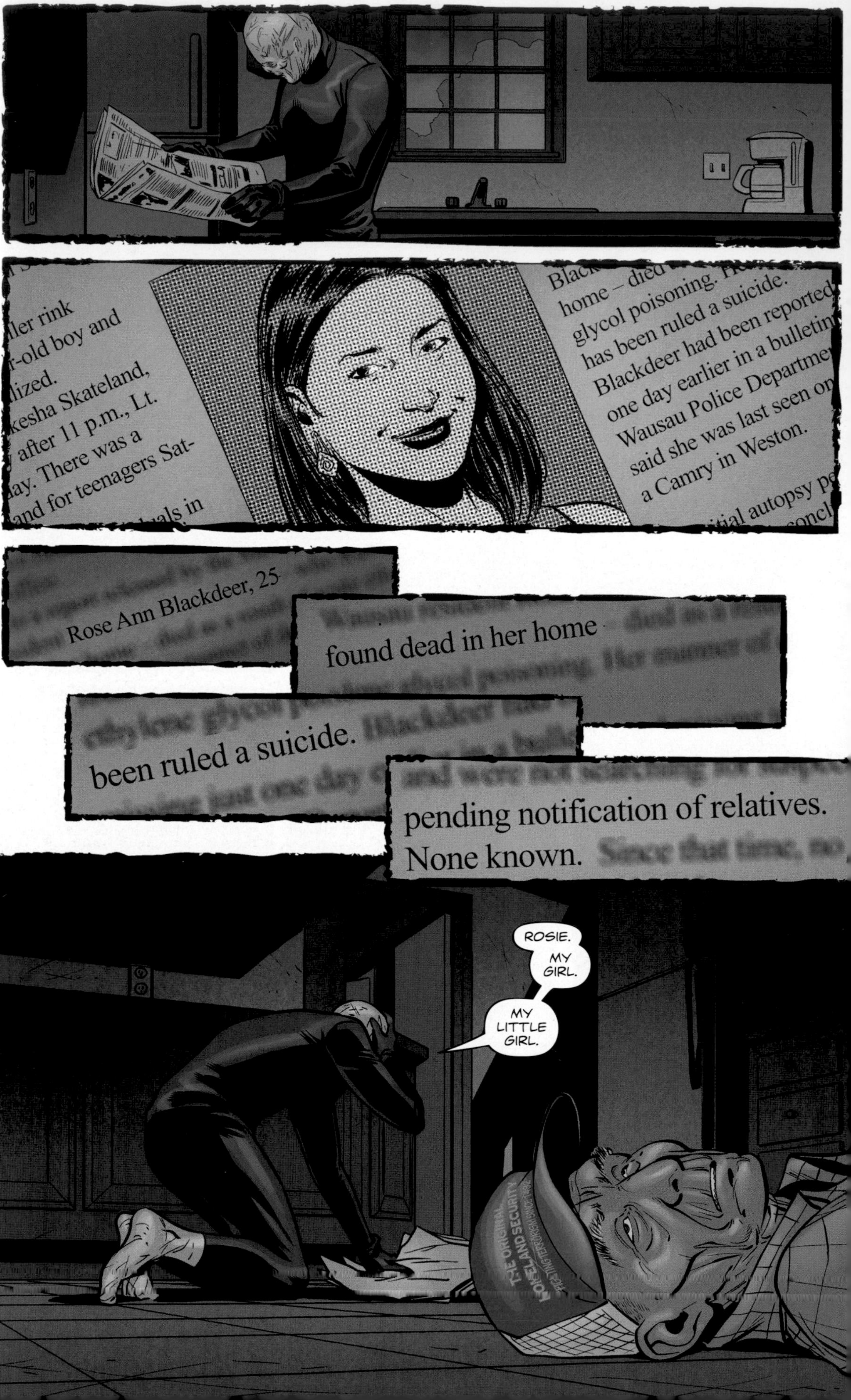

ller rink
-old boy and
lized.
kesha Skateland,
after 11 p.m., Lt.
ay. There was a
and for teenagers Sat-
home – died
glycol poisoning.
has been ruled a suicide.
Blackdeer had been reported
one day earlier in a bulletin
Wausau Police Departme
said she was last seen on
a Camry in Weston.
Rose Ann Blackdeer, 25
found dead in her home
been ruled a suicide.
pending notification of relatives.
None known.
ROSIE.
MY GIRL.
MY LITTLE GIRL.

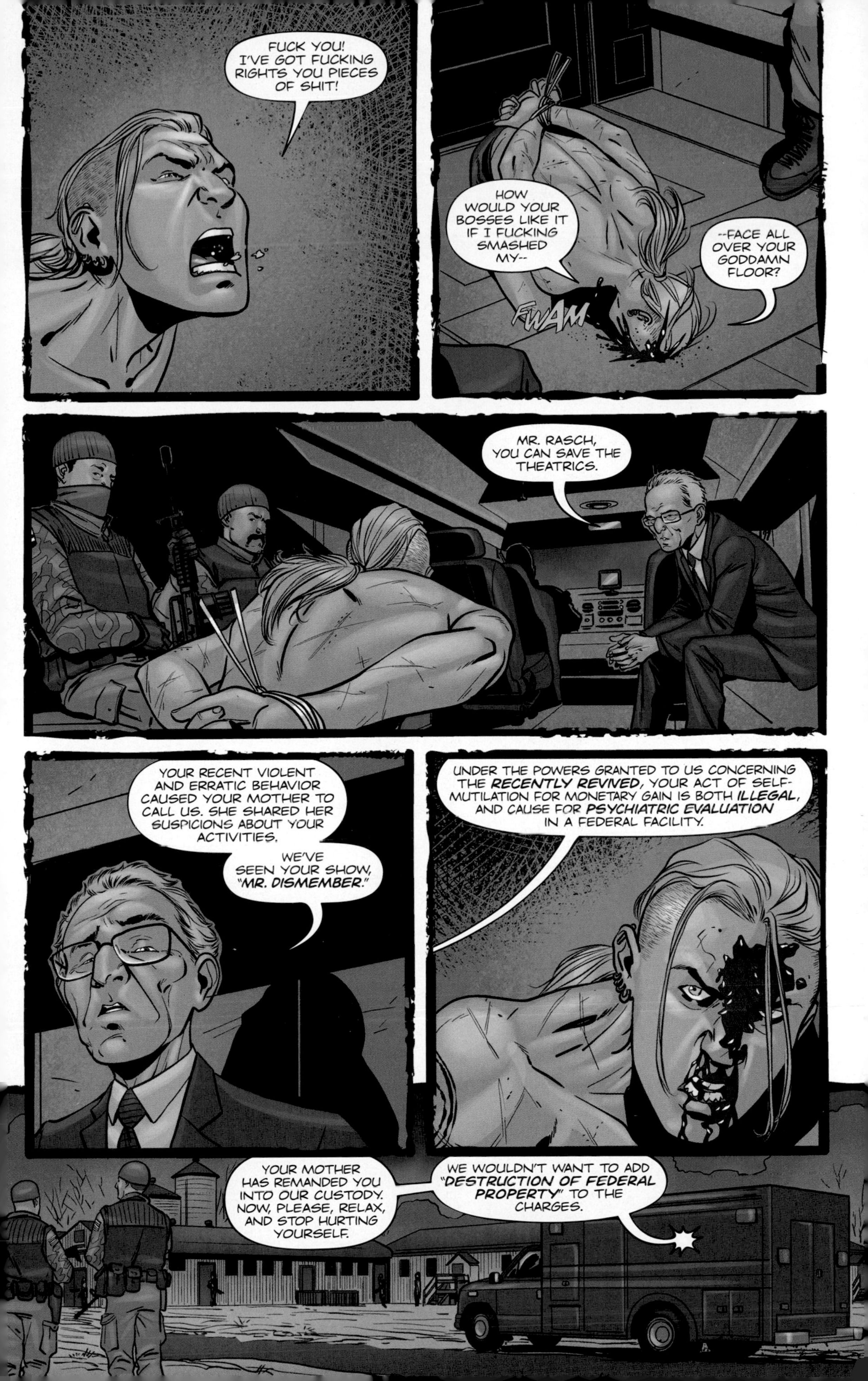
FUCK YOU! I'VE GOT FUCKING RIGHTS YOU PIECES OF SHIT!
HOW WOULD YOUR BOSSES LIKE IT IF I FUCKING SMASHED MY--
FWAM
--FACE ALL OVER YOUR GODDAMN FLOOR?
MR. RASCH, YOU CAN SAVE THE THEATRICS.
YOUR RECENT VIOLENT AND ERRATIC BEHAVIOR CAUSED YOUR MOTHER TO CALL US. SHE SHARED HER SUSPICIONS ABOUT YOUR ACTIVITIES.
WE'VE SEEN YOUR SHOW, "MR. DISMEMBER."
UNDER THE POWERS GRANTED TO US CONCERNING THE RECENTLY REVIVED, YOUR ACT OF SELF-MUTILATION FOR MONETARY GAIN IS BOTH ILLEGAL, AND CAUSE FOR PSYCHIATRIC EVALUATION IN A FEDERAL FACILITY.
YOUR MOTHER HAS REMANDED YOU INTO OUR CUSTODY. NOW, PLEASE, RELAX, AND STOP HURTING YOURSELF.
WE WOULDN'T WANT TO ADD "DESTRUCTION OF FEDERAL PROPERTY" TO THE CHARGES.

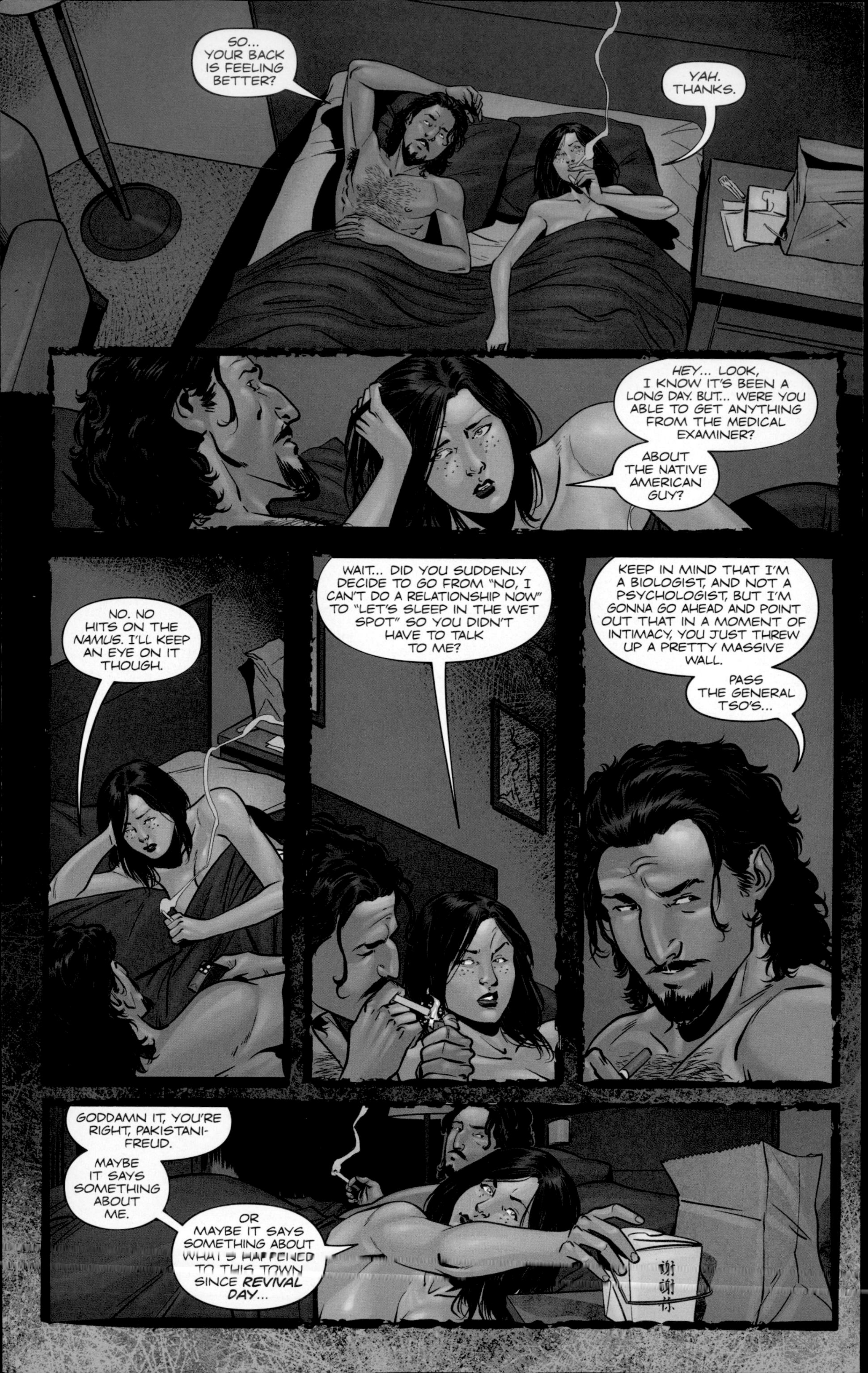
SO... YOUR BACK IS FEELING BETTER?
YAH. THANKS.
HEY... LOOK, I KNOW IT'S BEEN A LONG DAY. BUT... WERE YOU ABLE TO GET ANYTHING FROM THE MEDICAL EXAMINER?
ABOUT THE NATIVE AMERICAN GUY?
NO. NO HITS ON THE NAMUS. I'LL KEEP AN EYE ON IT THOUGH.
WAIT... DID YOU SUDDENLY DECIDE TO GO FROM "NO, I CAN'T DO A RELATIONSHIP NOW" TO "LET'S SLEEP IN THE WET SPOT" SO YOU DIDN'T HAVE TO TALK TO ME?
KEEP IN MIND THAT I'M A BIOLOGIST, AND NOT A PSYCHOLOGIST, BUT I'M GONNA GO AHEAD AND POINT OUT THAT IN A MOMENT OF INTIMACY, YOU JUST THREW UP A PRETTY MASSIVE WALL.
PASS THE GENERAL TSO'S...
GODDAMN IT, YOU'RE RIGHT, PAKISTANI-FREUD.
MAYBE IT SAYS SOMETHING ABOUT ME.
OR MAYBE IT SAYS SOMETHING ABOUT WHAT'S HAPPENED TO THIS TOWN SINCE REVIVAL DAY...

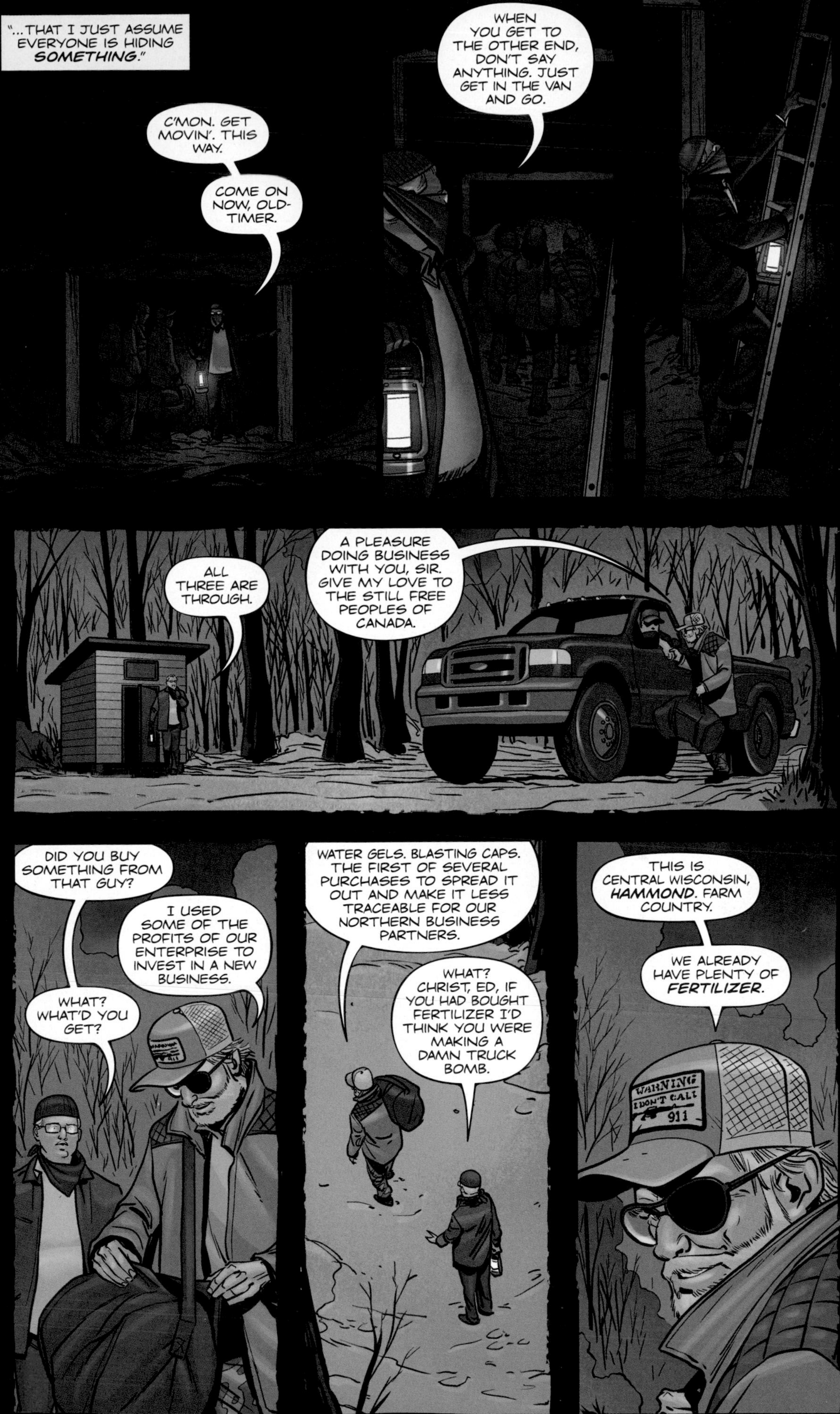
"...THAT I JUST ASSUME EVERYONE IS HIDING *SOMETHING*."
C'MON. GET MOVIN'. THIS WAY.
COME ON NOW, OLD-TIMER.
WHEN YOU GET TO THE OTHER END, DON'T SAY ANYTHING. JUST GET IN THE VAN AND GO.
ALL THREE ARE THROUGH.
A PLEASURE DOING BUSINESS WITH YOU, SIR. GIVE MY LOVE TO THE STILL FREE PEOPLES OF CANADA.
DID YOU BUY SOMETHING FROM THAT GUY?
I USED SOME OF THE PROFITS OF OUR ENTERPRISE TO INVEST IN A NEW BUSINESS.
WHAT? WHAT'D YOU GET?
WATER GELS. BLASTING CAPS. THE FIRST OF SEVERAL PURCHASES TO SPREAD IT OUT AND MAKE IT LESS TRACEABLE FOR OUR NORTHERN BUSINESS PARTNERS.
WHAT? CHRIST, ED, IF YOU HAD BOUGHT FERTILIZER I'D THINK YOU WERE MAKING A DAMN TRUCK BOMB.
THIS IS CENTRAL WISCONSIN, *HAMMOND*. FARM COUNTRY.
WE ALREADY HAVE PLENTY OF *FERTILIZER*.
WARNING
I DON'T CALL
911

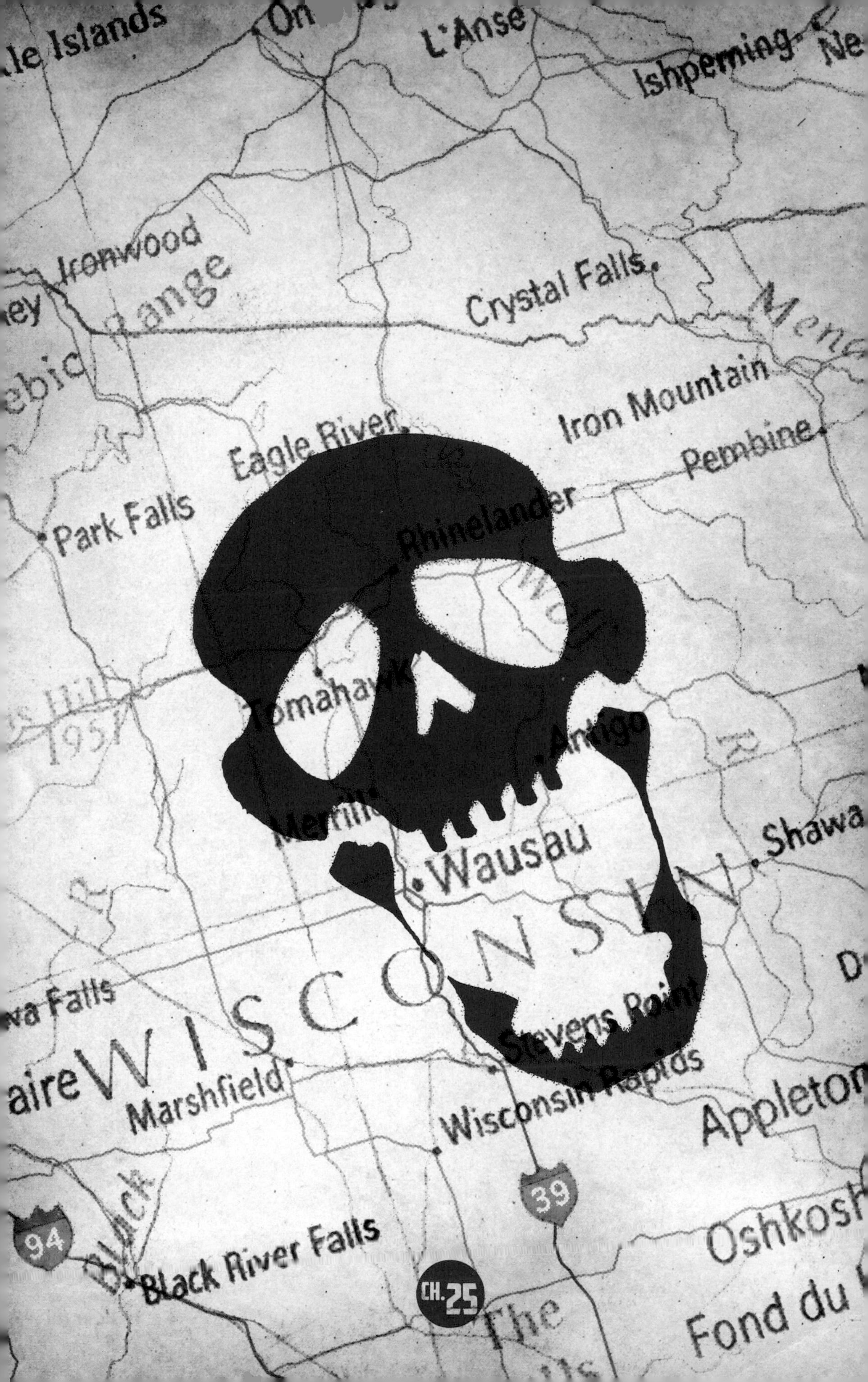

Islands
L'Anse
Ishpeming
Ironwood
Range
Crystal Falls
Iron Mountain
Eagle River
Pembine
Park Falls
Rhinelander
Tomahawk
1957
Antigo
Merrill
Wausau
Shawa
WISCONSIN
Falls
Stevens Point
aire
Marshfield
Wisconsin Rapids
Appleton
Black
94
39
Black River Falls
Oshkosh
Fond du
The
CH. 25

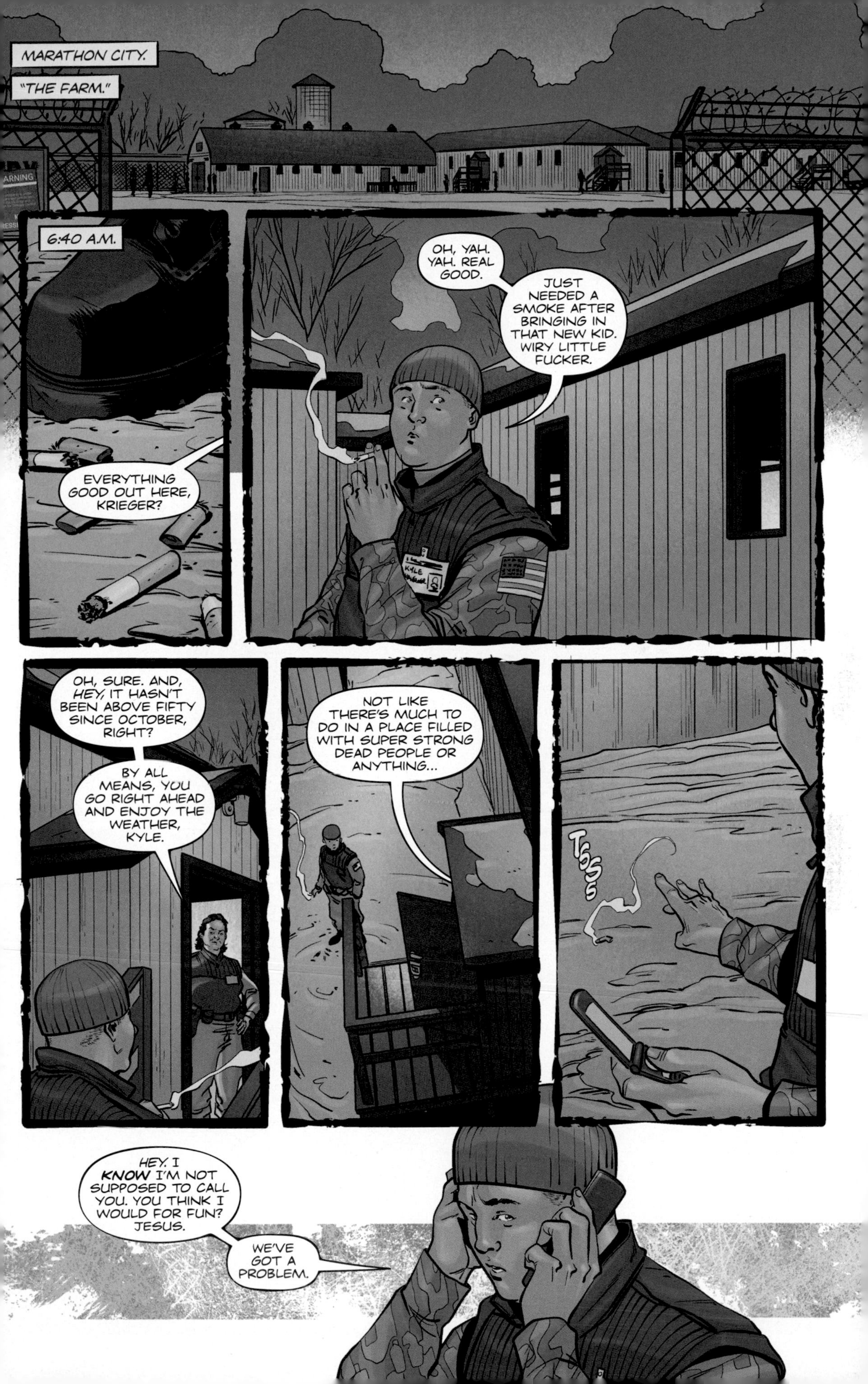
MARATHON CITY.
"THE FARM."
WARNING
6:40 A.M.
EVERYTHING GOOD OUT HERE, KRIEGER?
OH, YAH. YAH. REAL GOOD.
JUST NEEDED A SMOKE AFTER BRINGING IN THAT NEW KID. WIRY LITTLE FUCKER.
KYLE
OH, SURE. AND, HEY, IT HASN'T BEEN ABOVE FIFTY SINCE OCTOBER, RIGHT?
BY ALL MEANS, YOU GO RIGHT AHEAD AND ENJOY THE WEATHER, KYLE.
NOT LIKE THERE'S MUCH TO DO IN A PLACE FILLED WITH SUPER STRONG DEAD PEOPLE OR ANYTHING...
TOSS
HEY. I KNOW I'M NOT SUPPOSED TO CALL YOU. YOU THINK I WOULD FOR FUN? JESUS.
WE'VE GOT A PROBLEM.

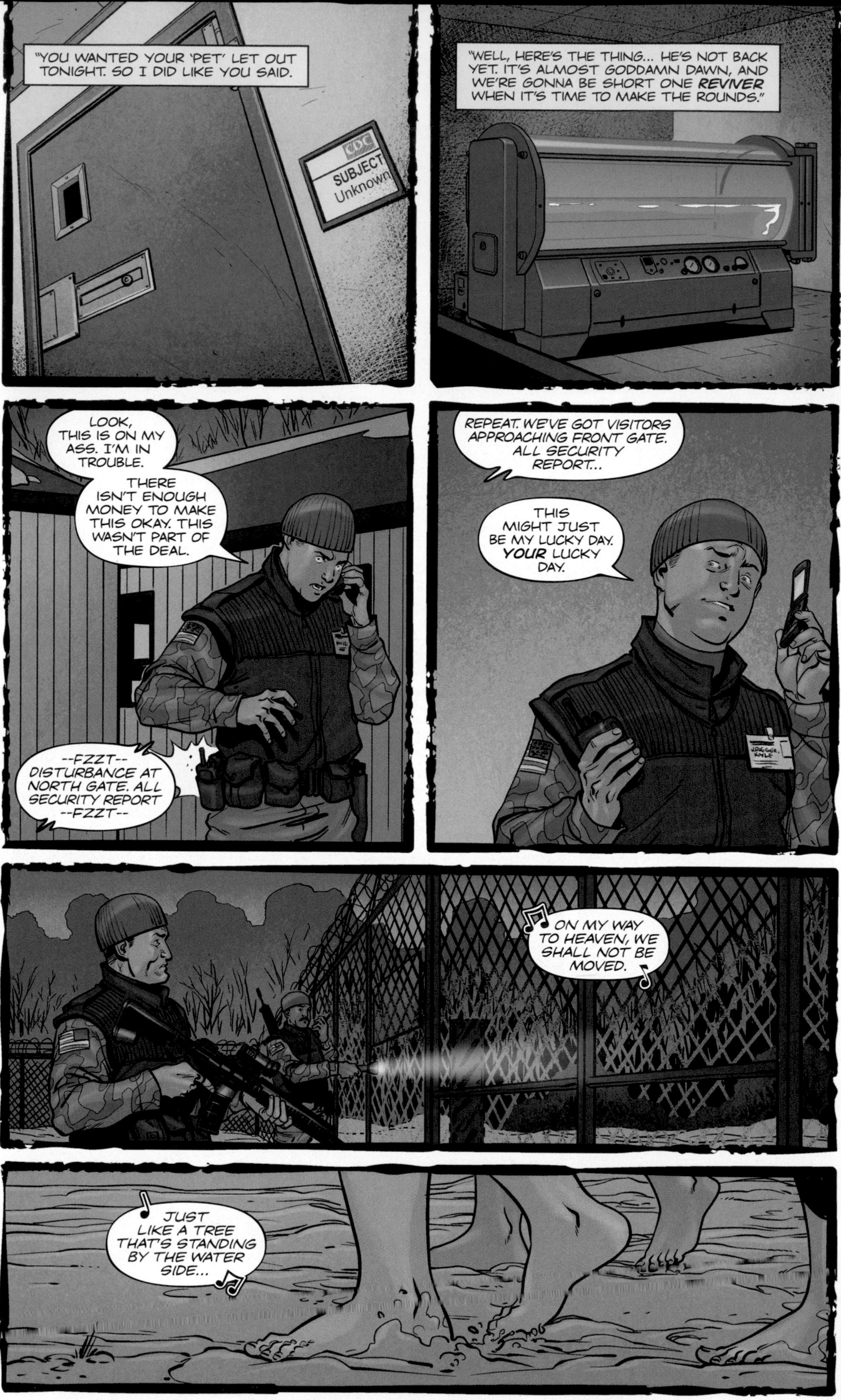
"YOU WANTED YOUR 'PET' LET OUT TONIGHT. SO I DID LIKE YOU SAID.
SUBJECT Unknown
"WELL, HERE'S THE THING... HE'S NOT BACK YET. IT'S ALMOST GODDAMN DAWN, AND WE'RE GONNA BE SHORT ONE REVIVER WHEN IT'S TIME TO MAKE THE ROUNDS."
LOOK, THIS IS ON MY ASS. I'M IN TROUBLE.
THERE ISN'T ENOUGH MONEY TO MAKE THIS OKAY. THIS WASN'T PART OF THE DEAL.
--FZZT-- DISTURBANCE AT NORTH GATE. ALL SECURITY REPORT --FZZT--
REPEAT. WE'VE GOT VISITORS APPROACHING FRONT GATE. ALL SECURITY REPORT...
THIS MIGHT JUST BE MY LUCKY DAY. YOUR LUCKY DAY.
ON MY WAY TO HEAVEN, WE SHALL NOT BE MOVED.
JUST LIKE A TREE THAT'S STANDING BY THE WATER SIDE...

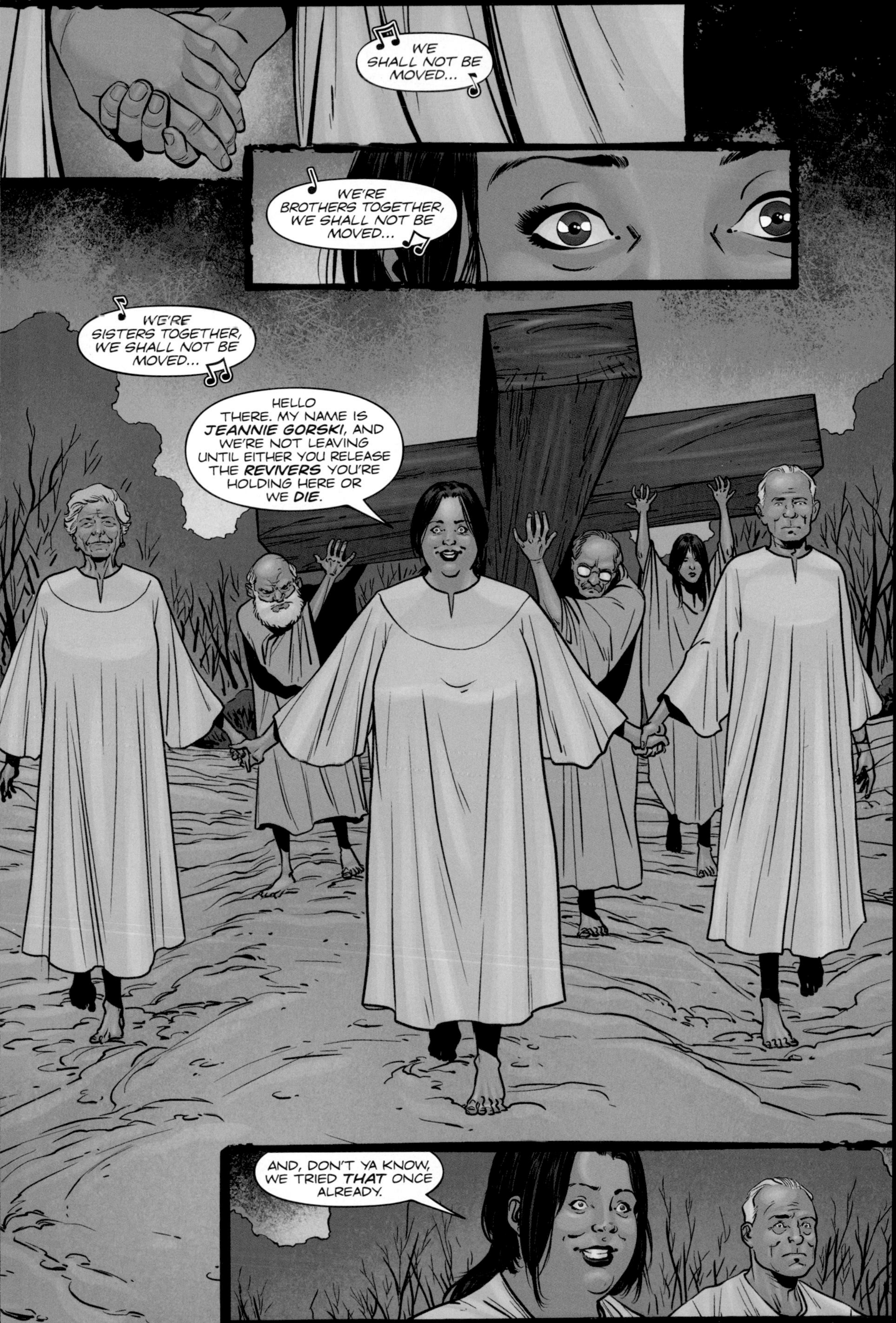
WE SHALL NOT BE MOVED...
WE'RE BROTHERS TOGETHER, WE SHALL NOT BE MOVED...
WE'RE SISTERS TOGETHER, WE SHALL NOT BE MOVED...
HELLO THERE. MY NAME IS JEANNIE GORSKI, AND WE'RE NOT LEAVING UNTIL EITHER YOU RELEASE THE REVIVERS YOU'RE HOLDING HERE OR WE DIE.
AND, DON'T YA KNOW, WE TRIED THAT ONCE ALREADY.

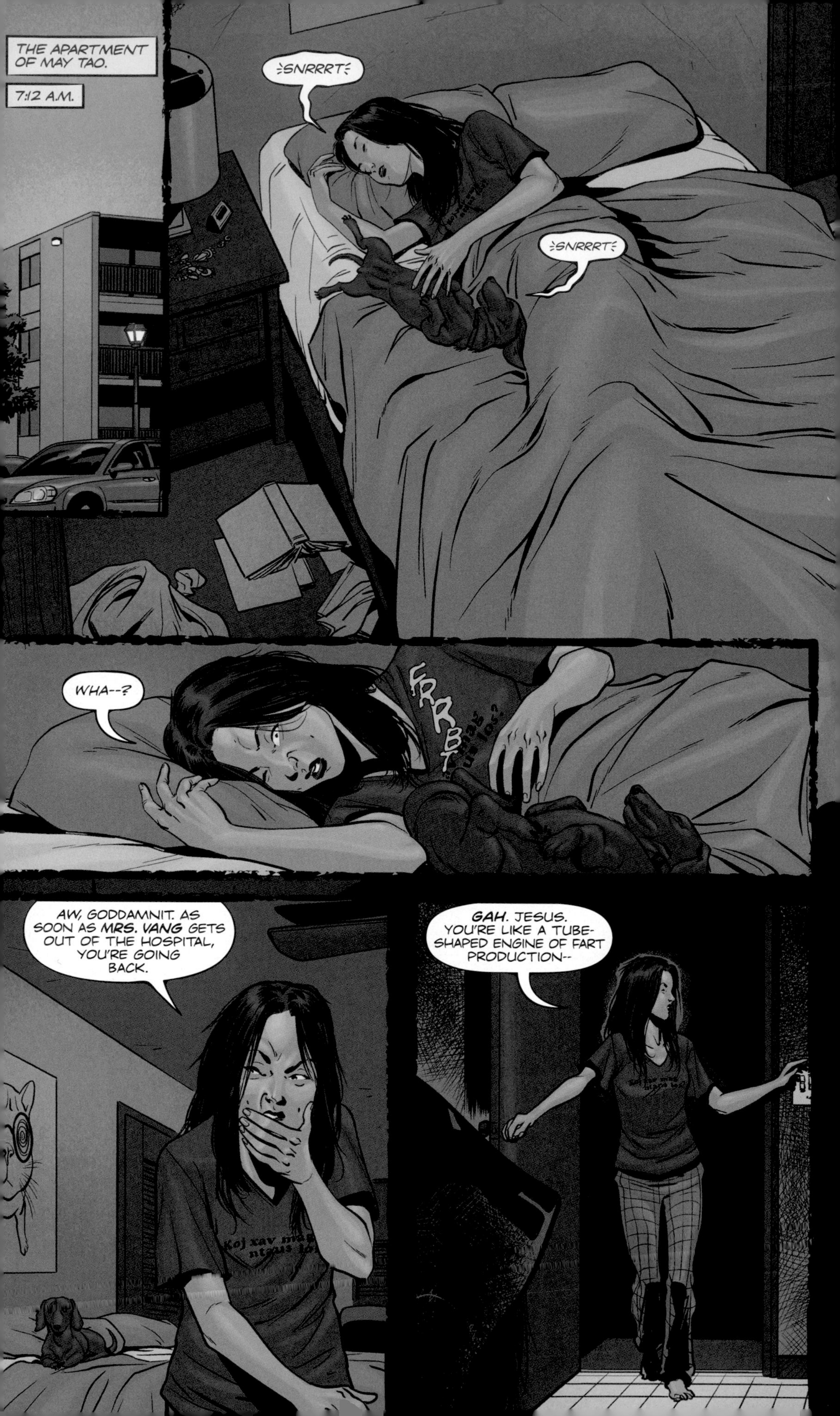
THE APARTMENT OF MAY TAO.
7:12 A.M.
SNRRRT
SNRRRT
WHA--?
FRRRBT
AW, GODDAMNIT. AS SOON AS MRS. VANG GETS OUT OF THE HOSPITAL, YOU'RE GOING BACK.
GAH. JESUS. YOU'RE LIKE A TUBE-SHAPED ENGINE OF FART PRODUCTION--
Koj xav mag ntaus los?

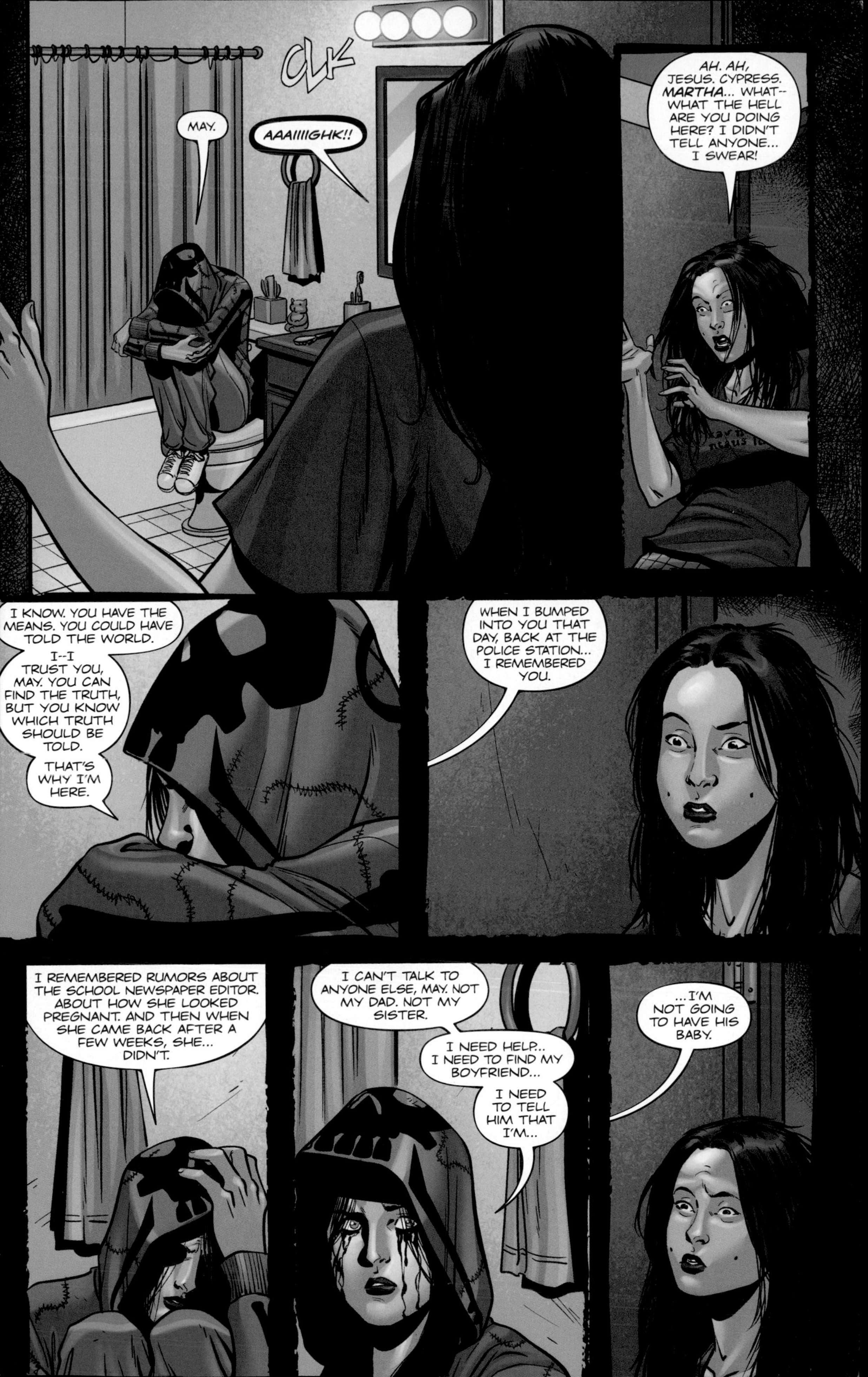

CLK
MAY.
AAAIIIIGHK!!
AH. AH, JESUS. CYPRESS. MARTHA... WHAT-- WHAT THE HELL ARE YOU DOING HERE? I DIDN'T TELL ANYONE... I SWEAR!
I KNOW. YOU HAVE THE MEANS. YOU COULD HAVE TOLD THE WORLD.
I--I TRUST YOU, MAY. YOU CAN FIND THE TRUTH, BUT YOU KNOW WHICH TRUTH SHOULD BE TOLD.
THAT'S WHY I'M HERE.
WHEN I BUMPED INTO YOU THAT DAY, BACK AT THE POLICE STATION... I REMEMBERED YOU.
I REMEMBERED RUMORS ABOUT THE SCHOOL NEWSPAPER EDITOR. ABOUT HOW SHE LOOKED PREGNANT. AND THEN WHEN SHE CAME BACK AFTER A FEW WEEKS, SHE... DIDN'T.
I CAN'T TALK TO ANYONE ELSE, MAY. NOT MY DAD. NOT MY SISTER.
I NEED HELP... I NEED TO FIND MY BOYFRIEND...
I NEED TO TELL HIM THAT I'M...
...I'M NOT GOING TO HAVE HIS BABY.

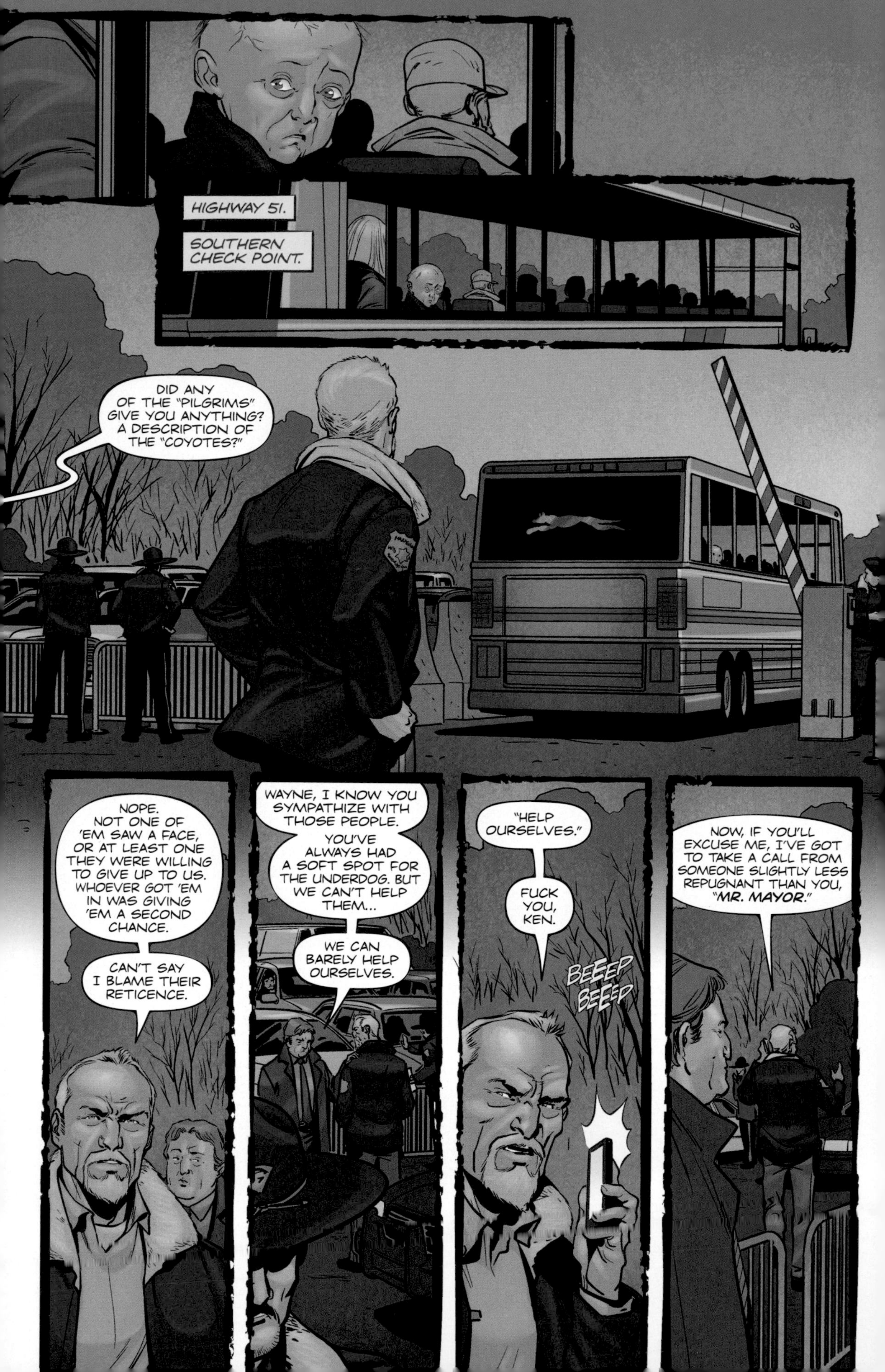
HIGHWAY 51.
SOUTHERN CHECK POINT.
DID ANY OF THE "PILGRIMS" GIVE YOU ANYTHING? A DESCRIPTION OF THE "COYOTES?"
NOPE. NOT ONE OF 'EM SAW A FACE, OR AT LEAST ONE THEY WERE WILLING TO GIVE UP TO US. WHOEVER GOT 'EM IN WAS GIVING 'EM A SECOND CHANCE.
CAN'T SAY I BLAME THEIR RETICENCE.
WAYNE, I KNOW YOU SYMPATHIZE WITH THOSE PEOPLE.
YOU'VE ALWAYS HAD A SOFT SPOT FOR THE UNDERDOG. BUT WE CAN'T HELP THEM...
WE CAN BARELY HELP OURSELVES.
"HELP OURSELVES."
FUCK YOU, KEN.
BEEEP BEEEP
NOW, IF YOU'LL EXCUSE ME, I'VE GOT TO TAKE A CALL FROM SOMEONE SLIGHTLY LESS REPUGNANT THAN YOU, "MR. MAYOR."

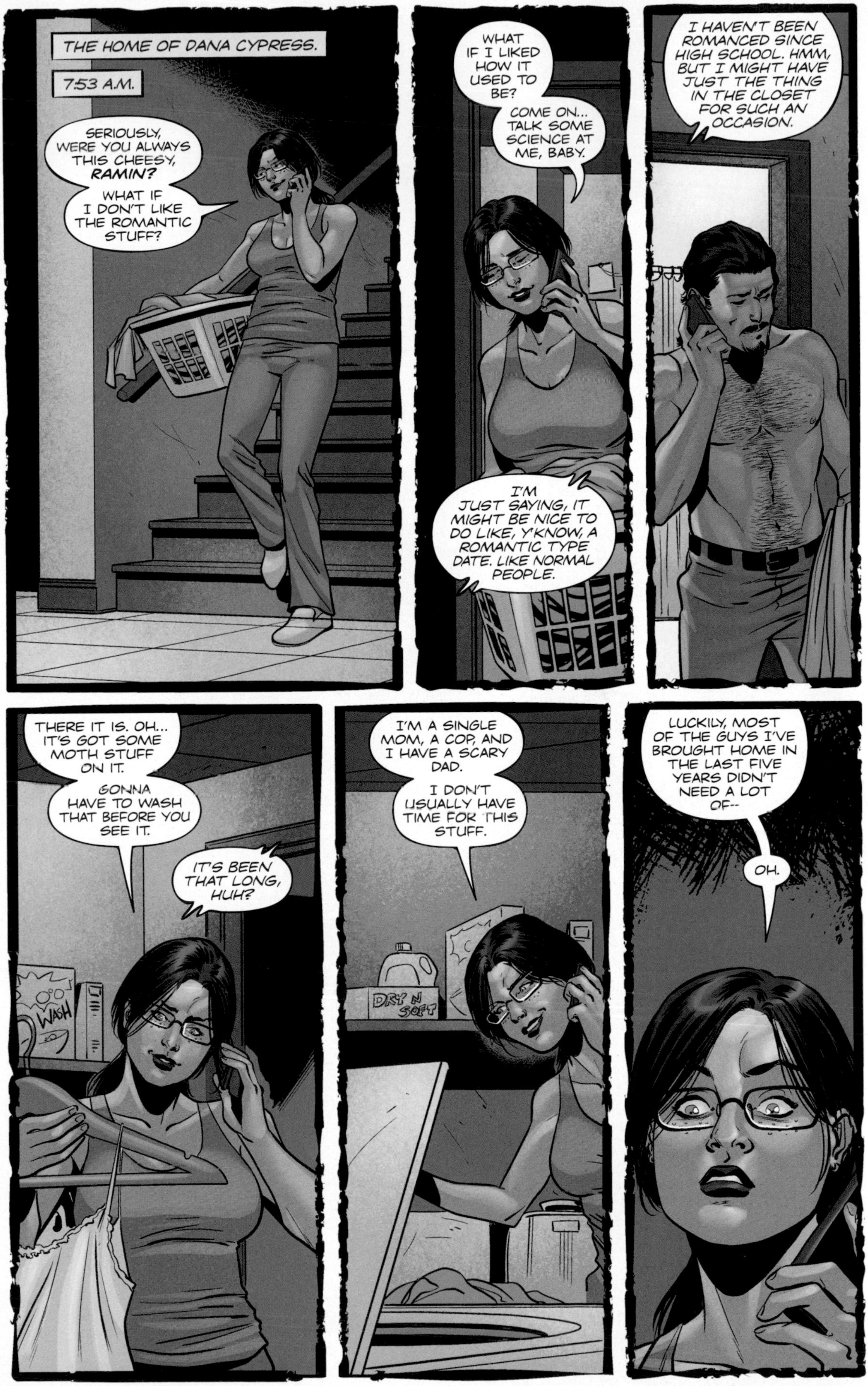

THE HOME OF DANA CYPRESS.
7:53 A.M.
SERIOUSLY, WERE YOU ALWAYS THIS CHEESY, RAMIN?
WHAT IF I DON'T LIKE THE ROMANTIC STUFF?
WHAT IF I LIKED HOW IT USED TO BE?
COME ON... TALK SOME SCIENCE AT ME, BABY.
I'M JUST SAYING, IT MIGHT BE NICE TO DO LIKE, Y'KNOW, A ROMANTIC TYPE DATE. LIKE NORMAL PEOPLE.
I HAVEN'T BEEN ROMANCED SINCE HIGH SCHOOL. HMM, BUT I MIGHT HAVE JUST THE THING IN THE CLOSET FOR SUCH AN OCCASION.
THERE IT IS. OH... IT'S GOT SOME MOTH STUFF ON IT.
GONNA HAVE TO WASH THAT BEFORE YOU SEE IT.
IT'S BEEN THAT LONG, HUH?
WASH
I'M A SINGLE MOM, A COP, AND I HAVE A SCARY DAD.
I DON'T USUALLY HAVE TIME FOR THIS STUFF.
DRY N SOFT
LUCKILY, MOST OF THE GUYS I'VE BROUGHT HOME IN THE LAST FIVE YEARS DIDN'T NEED A LOT OF--
OH.

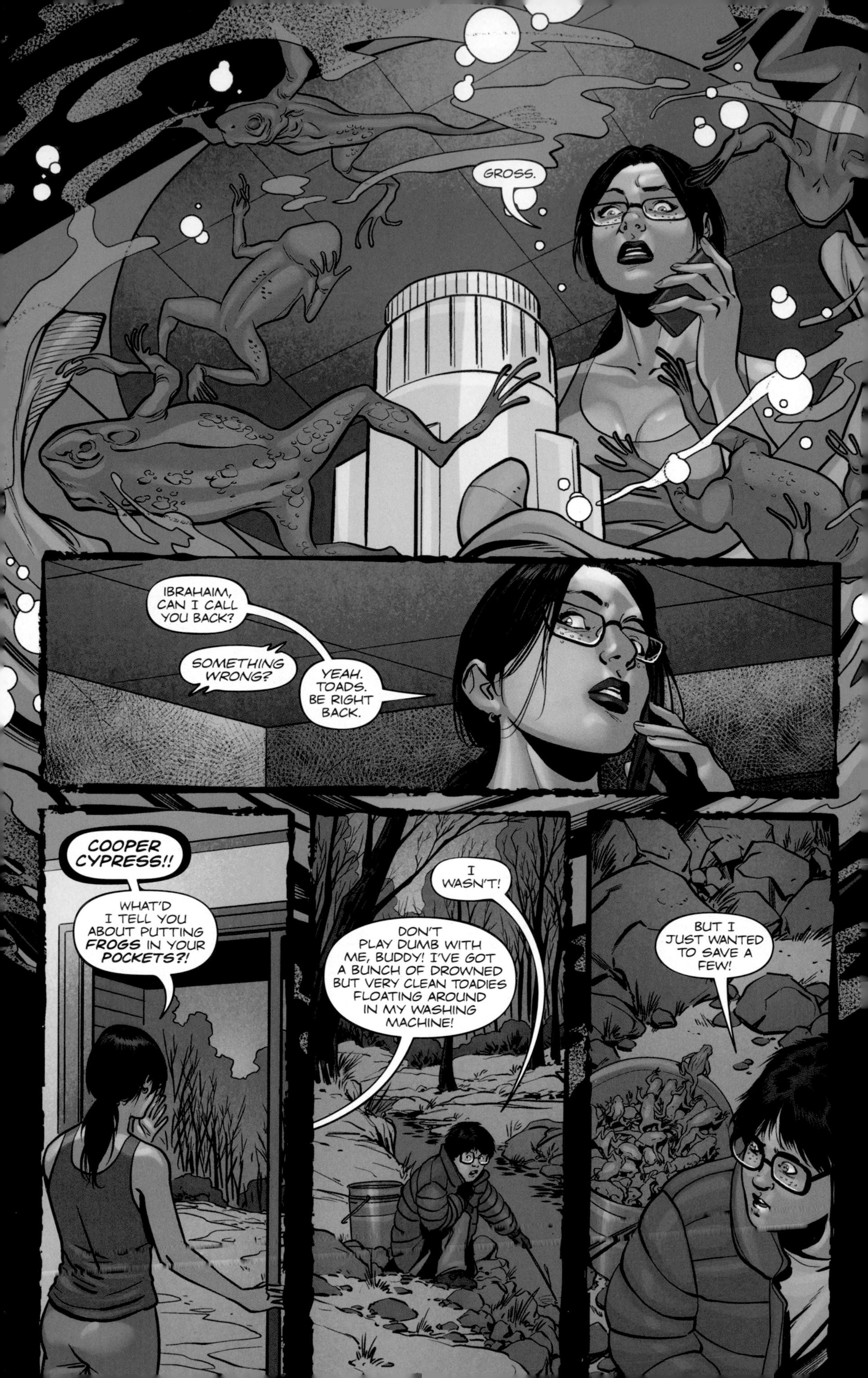
GROSS.
IBRAHAIM, CAN I CALL YOU BACK?
SOMETHING WRONG?
YEAH. TOADS. BE RIGHT BACK.
COOPER CYPRESS!!
WHAT'D I TELL YOU ABOUT PUTTING FROGS IN YOUR POCKETS?!
I WASN'T!
DON'T PLAY DUMB WITH ME, BUDDY! I'VE GOT A BUNCH OF DROWNED BUT VERY CLEAN TOADIES FLOATING AROUND IN MY WASHING MACHINE!
BUT I JUST WANTED TO SAVE A FEW!

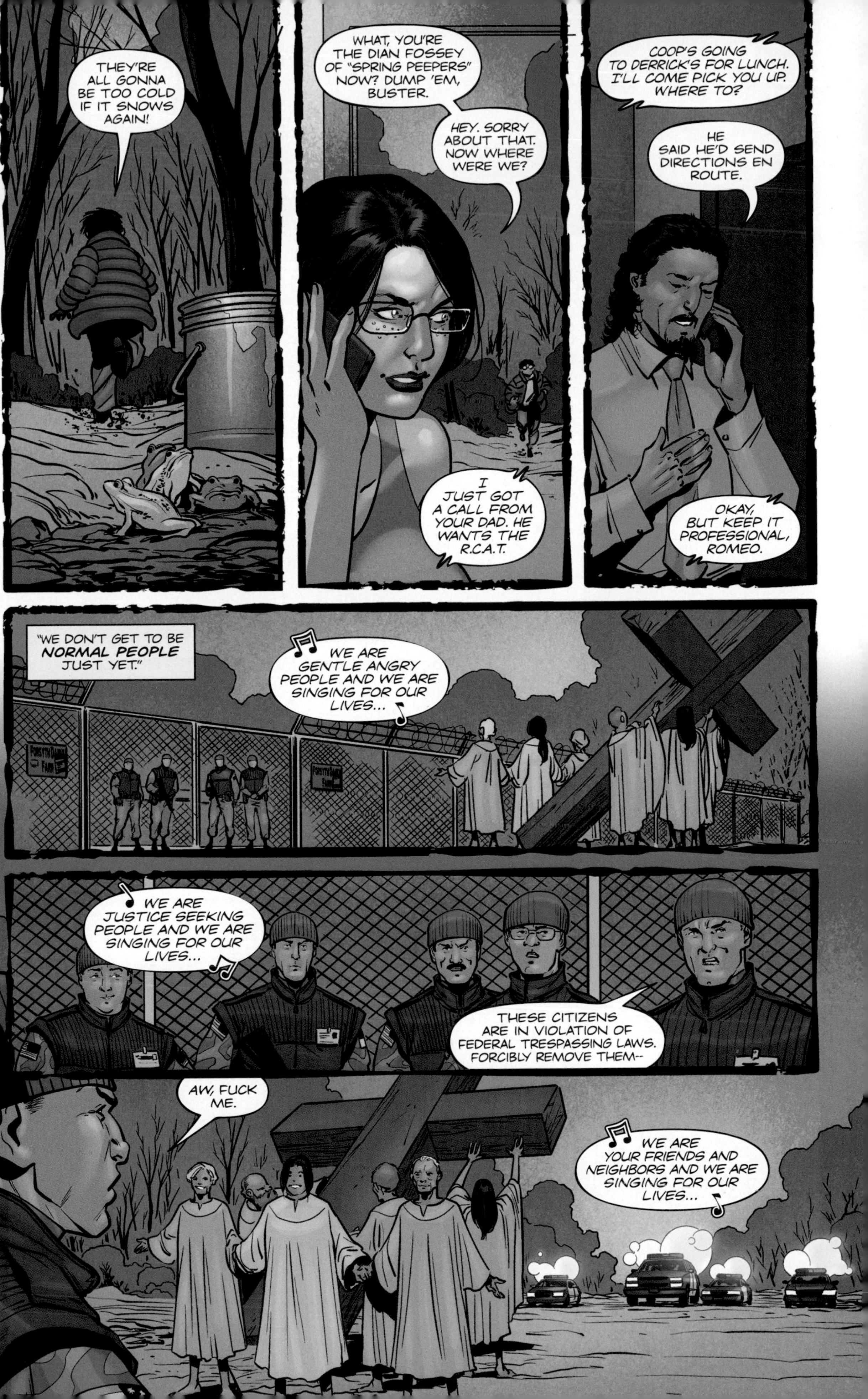

THEY'RE ALL GONNA BE TOO COLD IF IT SNOWS AGAIN!
WHAT, YOU'RE THE DIAN FOSSEY OF "SPRING PEEPERS" NOW? DUMP 'EM, BUSTER.
HEY. SORRY ABOUT THAT. NOW WHERE WERE WE?
I JUST GOT A CALL FROM YOUR DAD. HE WANTS THE R.C.A.T.
COOP'S GOING TO DERRICK'S FOR LUNCH. I'LL COME PICK YOU UP. WHERE TO?
HE SAID HE'D SEND DIRECTIONS EN ROUTE.
OKAY, BUT KEEP IT PROFESSIONAL, ROMEO.
"WE DON'T GET TO BE NORMAL PEOPLE JUST YET."
WE ARE GENTLE ANGRY PEOPLE AND WE ARE SINGING FOR OUR LIVES...
WE ARE JUSTICE SEEKING PEOPLE AND WE ARE SINGING FOR OUR LIVES...
THESE CITIZENS ARE IN VIOLATION OF FEDERAL TRESPASSING LAWS. FORCIBLY REMOVE THEM--
AW, FUCK ME.
WE ARE YOUR FRIENDS AND NEIGHBORS AND WE ARE SINGING FOR OUR LIVES...

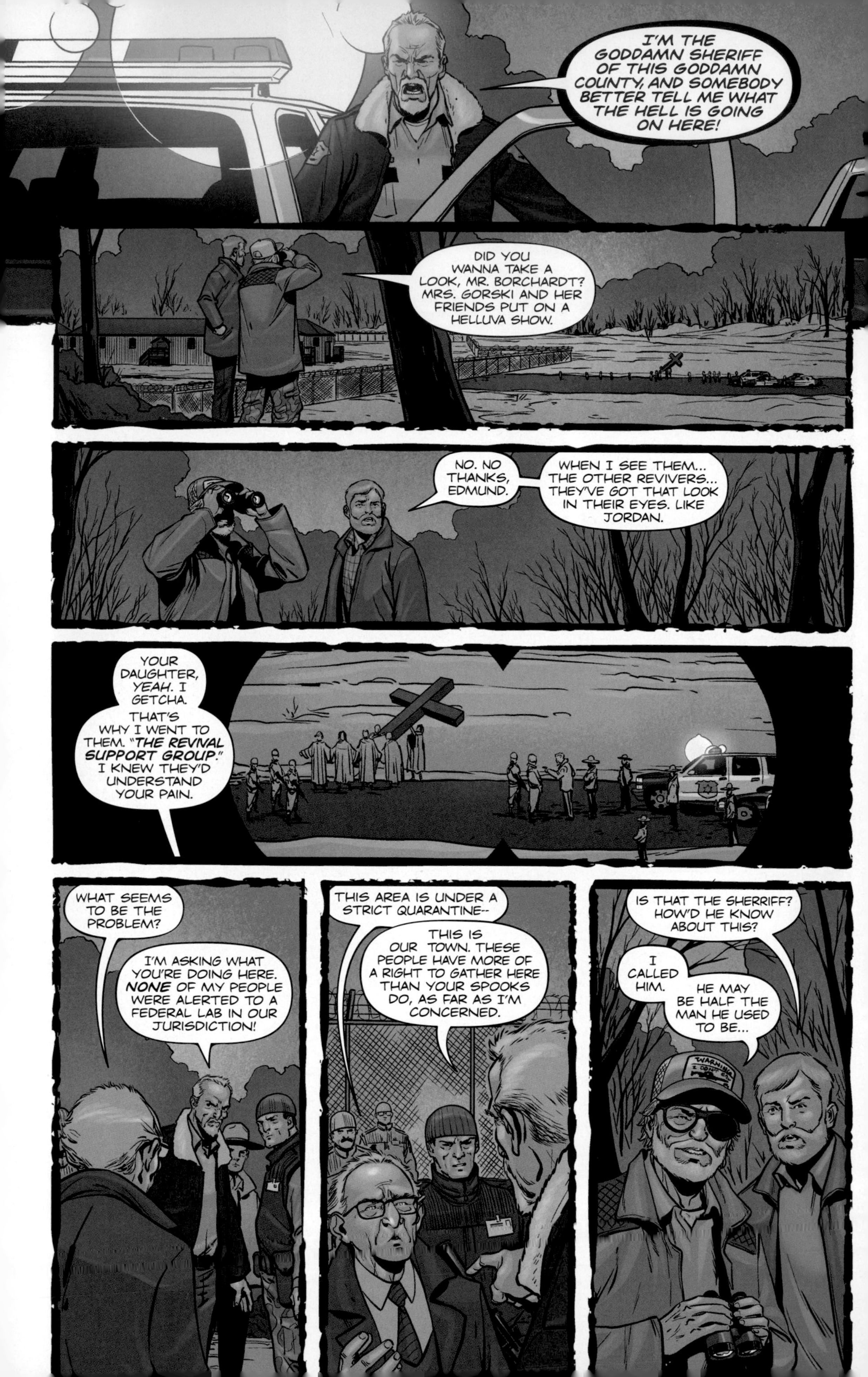
I'M THE GODDAMN SHERIFF OF THIS GODDAMN COUNTY, AND SOMEBODY BETTER TELL ME WHAT THE HELL IS GOING ON HERE!
DID YOU WANNA TAKE A LOOK, MR. BORCHARDT? MRS. GORSKI AND HER FRIENDS PUT ON A HELLUVA SHOW.
NO. NO THANKS, EDMUND.
WHEN I SEE THEM... THE OTHER REVIVERS... THEY'VE GOT THAT LOOK IN THEIR EYES. LIKE JORDAN.
YOUR DAUGHTER, YEAH. I GETCHA.
THAT'S WHY I WENT TO THEM. "THE REVIVAL SUPPORT GROUP." I KNEW THEY'D UNDERSTAND YOUR PAIN.
WHAT SEEMS TO BE THE PROBLEM?
I'M ASKING WHAT YOU'RE DOING HERE. NONE OF MY PEOPLE WERE ALERTED TO A FEDERAL LAB IN OUR JURISDICTION!
THIS AREA IS UNDER A STRICT QUARANTINE--
THIS IS OUR TOWN. THESE PEOPLE HAVE MORE OF A RIGHT TO GATHER HERE THAN YOUR SPOOKS DO, AS FAR AS I'M CONCERNED.
IS THAT THE SHERRIFF? HOW'D HE KNOW ABOUT THIS?
I CALLED HIM.
HE MAY BE HALF THE MAN HE USED TO BE...

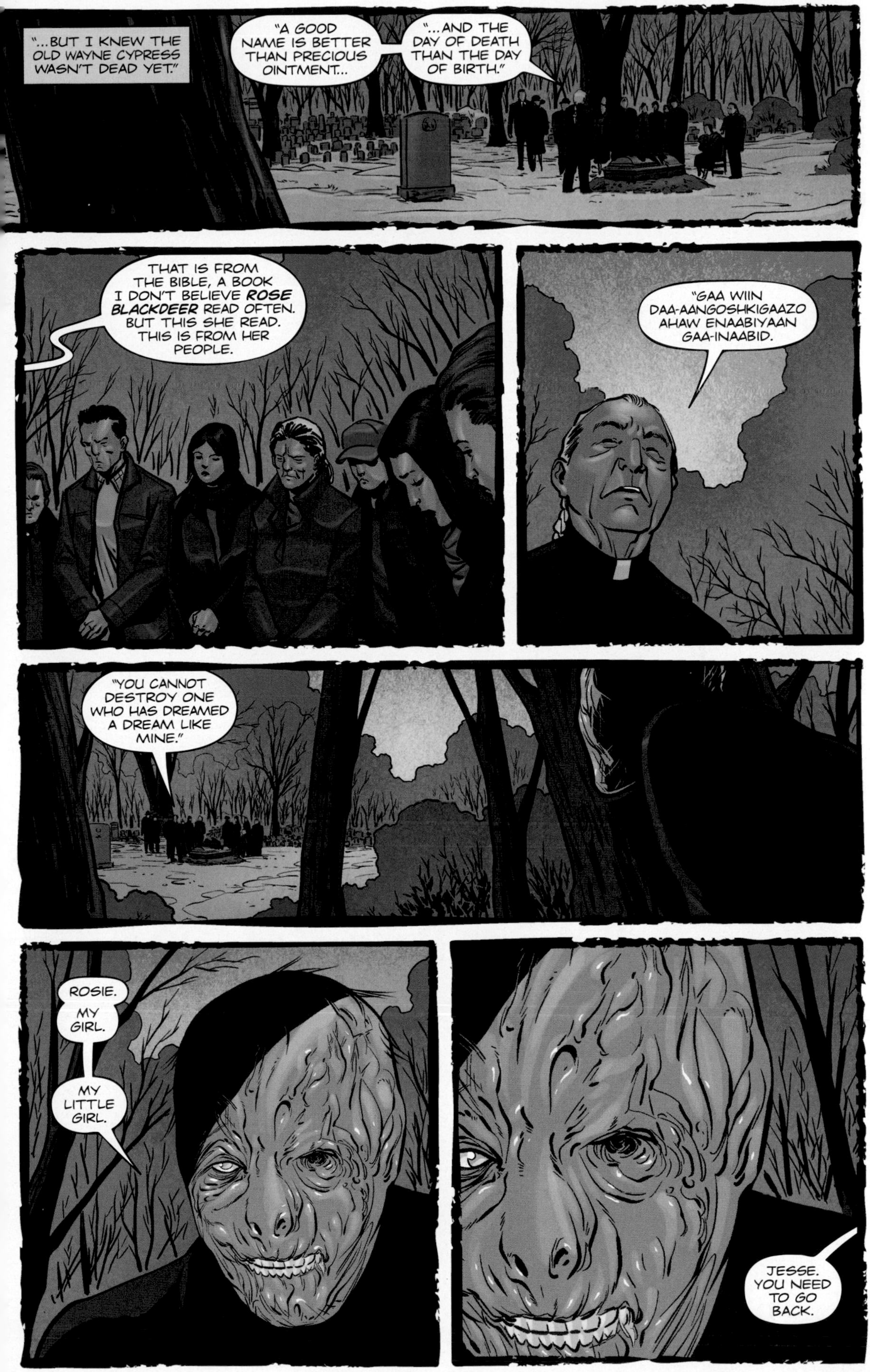

"...BUT I KNEW THE OLD WAYNE CYPRESS WASN'T DEAD YET."
"A GOOD NAME IS BETTER THAN PRECIOUS OINTMENT...
"...AND THE DAY OF DEATH THAN THE DAY OF BIRTH."
THAT IS FROM THE BIBLE, A BOOK I DON'T BELIEVE ROSE BLACKDEER READ OFTEN. BUT THIS SHE READ. THIS IS FROM HER PEOPLE.
"GAA WIIN DAA-AANGOSHKIGAAZO AHAW ENAABIYAAN GAA-INAABID.
"YOU CANNOT DESTROY ONE WHO HAS DREAMED A DREAM LIKE MINE."
ROSIE.
MY GIRL.
MY LITTLE GIRL.
JESSE. YOU NEED TO GO BACK.

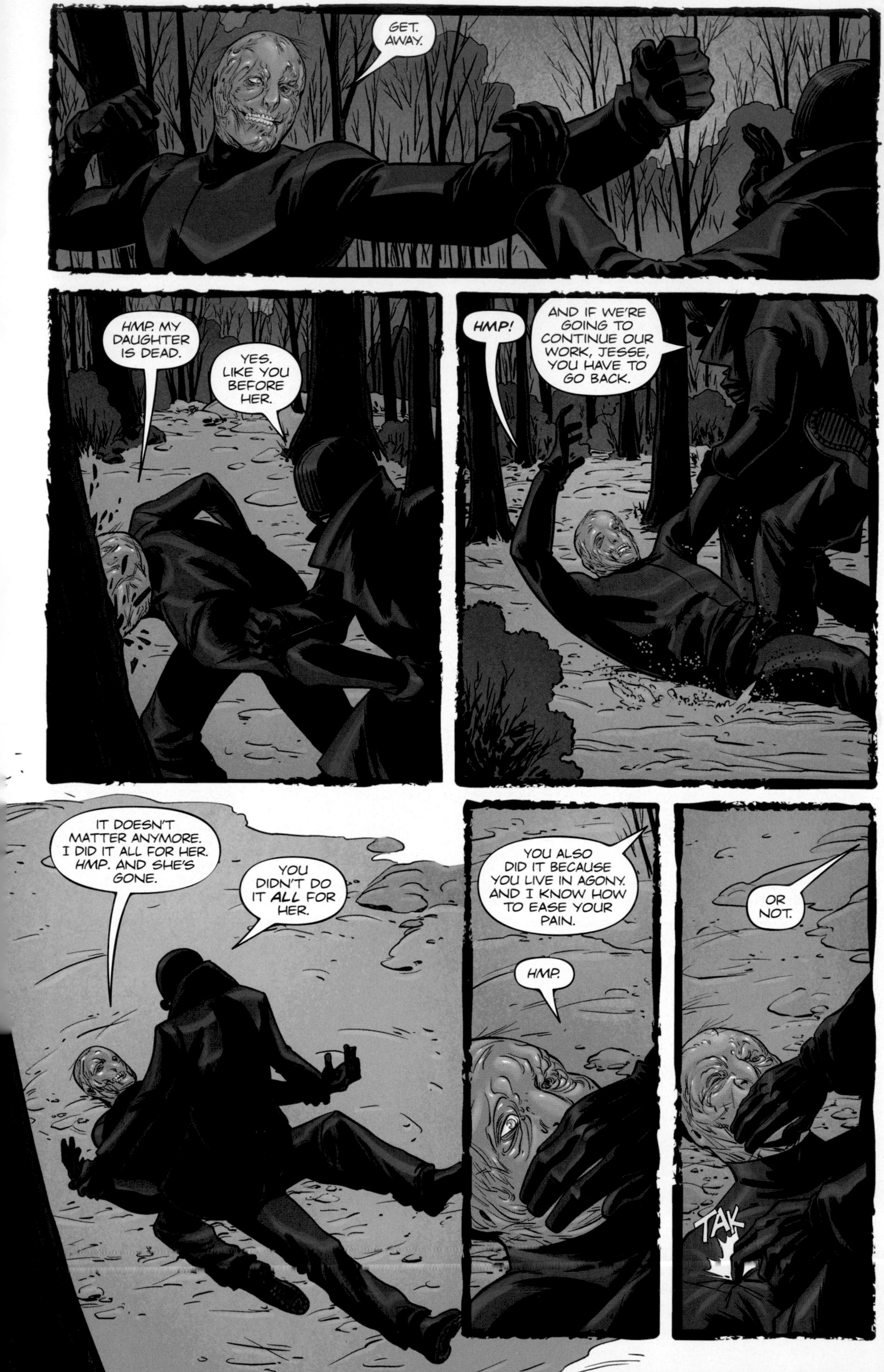
GET. AWAY.
HMP. MY DAUGHTER IS DEAD.
YES. LIKE YOU BEFORE HER.
HMP!
AND IF WE'RE GOING TO CONTINUE OUR WORK, JESSE, YOU HAVE TO GO BACK.
IT DOESN'T MATTER ANYMORE. I DID IT ALL FOR HER. HMP. AND SHE'S GONE.
YOU DIDN'T DO IT ALL FOR HER.
YOU ALSO DID IT BECAUSE YOU LIVE IN AGONY. AND I KNOW HOW TO EASE YOUR PAIN.
HMP.
OR NOT.
TAK

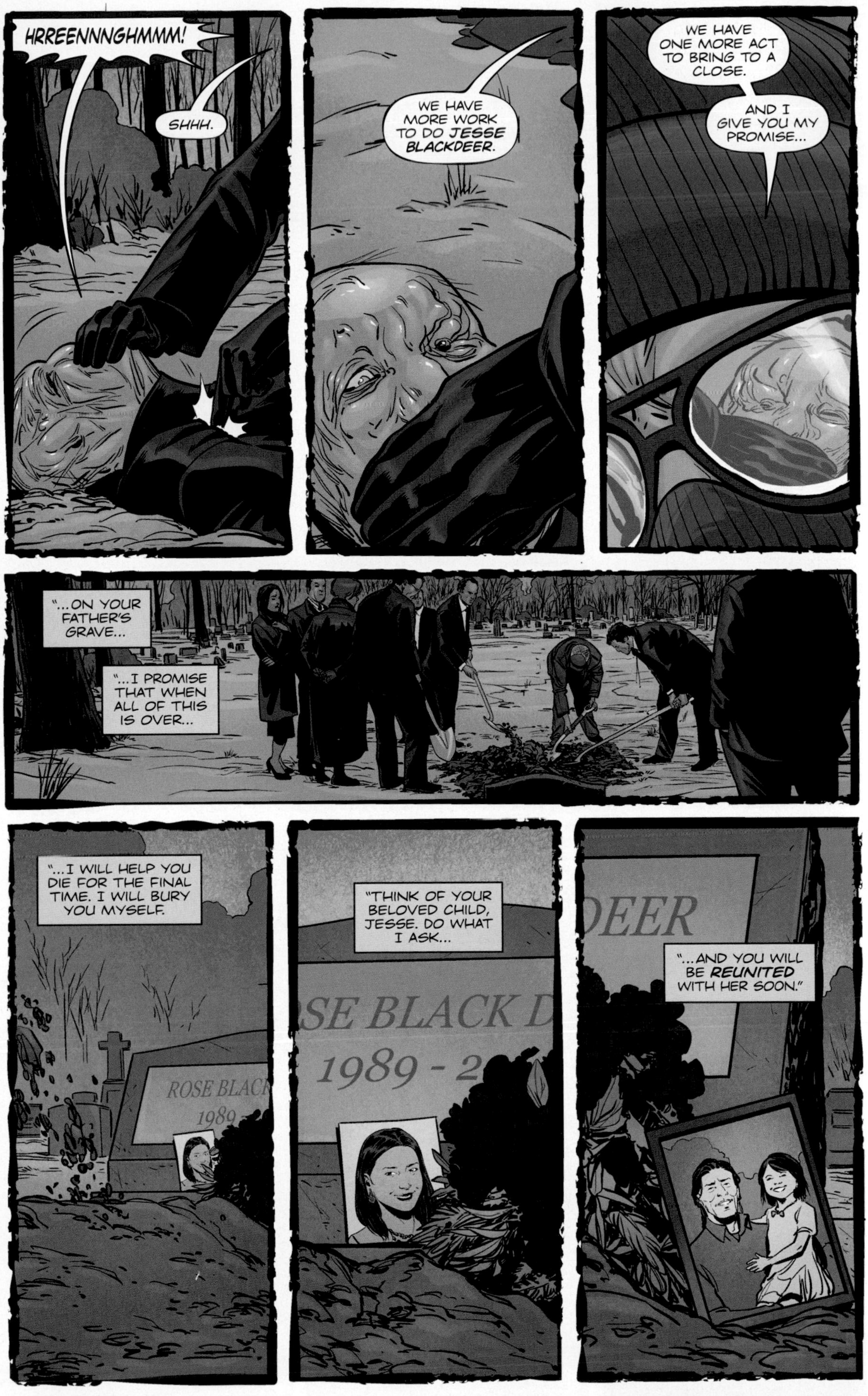
HRREENNNGHMMM!
SHHH.
WE HAVE MORE WORK TO DO JESSE BLACKDEER.
WE HAVE ONE MORE ACT TO BRING TO A CLOSE.
AND I GIVE YOU MY PROMISE...
"...ON YOUR FATHER'S GRAVE...
"...I PROMISE THAT WHEN ALL OF THIS IS OVER...
"...I WILL HELP YOU DIE FOR THE FINAL TIME. I WILL BURY YOU MYSELF.
ROSE BLACK
1989
"THINK OF YOUR BELOVED CHILD, JESSE. DO WHAT I ASK...
SE BLACK D
1989 - 2
DEER
"...AND YOU WILL BE REUNITED WITH HER SOON."

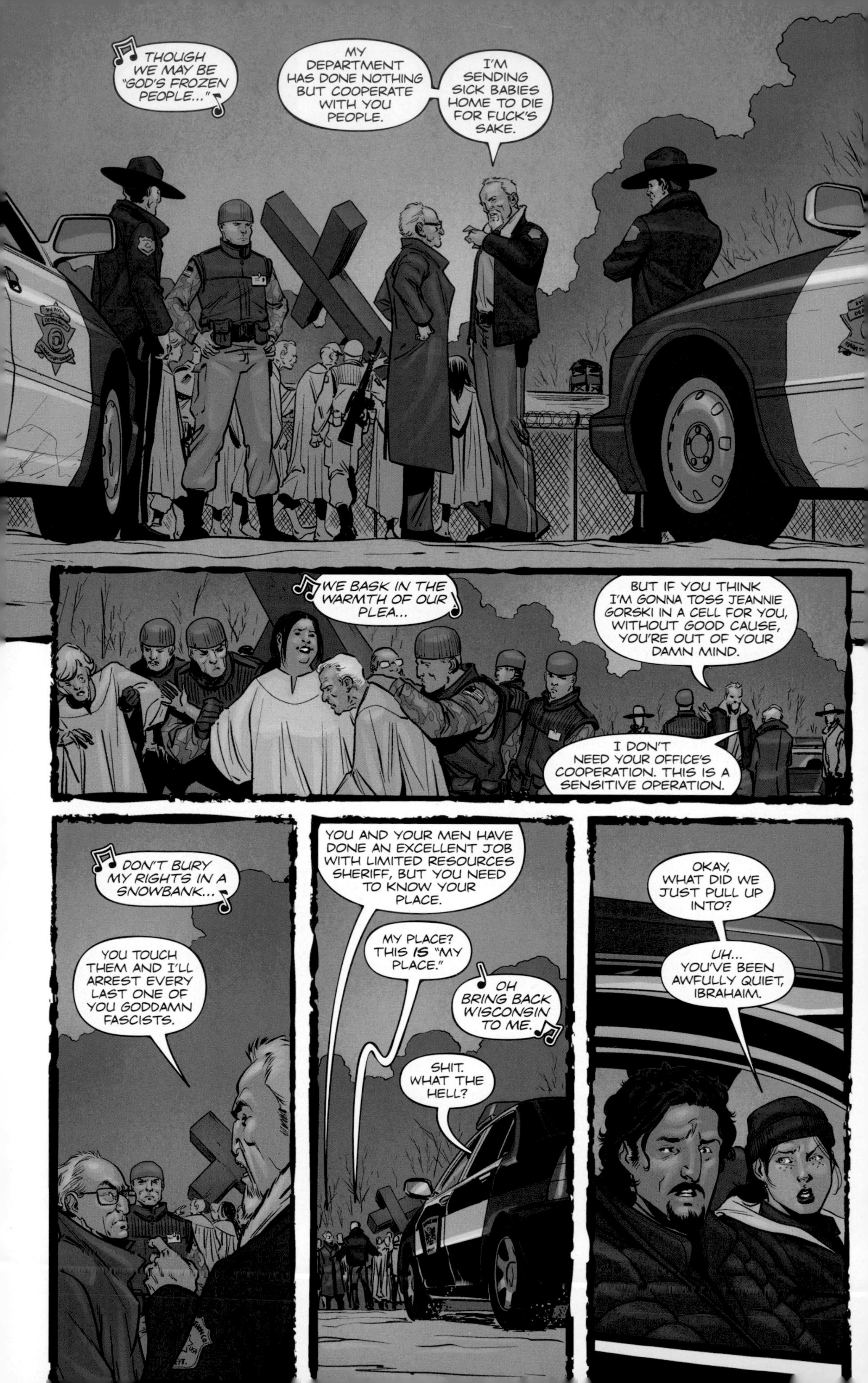
THOUGH WE MAY BE "GOD'S FROZEN PEOPLE..."
MY DEPARTMENT HAS DONE NOTHING BUT COOPERATE WITH YOU PEOPLE.
I'M SENDING SICK BABIES HOME TO DIE FOR FUCK'S SAKE.
WE BASK IN THE WARMTH OF OUR PLEA...
BUT IF YOU THINK I'M GONNA TOSS JEANNIE GORSKI IN A CELL FOR YOU, WITHOUT GOOD CAUSE, YOU'RE OUT OF YOUR DAMN MIND.
I DON'T NEED YOUR OFFICE'S COOPERATION. THIS IS A SENSITIVE OPERATION.
DON'T BURY MY RIGHTS IN A SNOWBANK...
YOU TOUCH THEM AND I'LL ARREST EVERY LAST ONE OF YOU GODDAMN FASCISTS.
YOU AND YOUR MEN HAVE DONE AN EXCELLENT JOB WITH LIMITED RESOURCES SHERIFF, BUT YOU NEED TO KNOW YOUR PLACE.
MY PLACE? THIS IS "MY PLACE."
OH BRING BACK WISCONSIN TO ME.
SHIT. WHAT THE HELL?
OKAY, WHAT DID WE JUST PULL UP INTO?
UH... YOU'VE BEEN AWFULLY QUIET, IBRAHAIM.

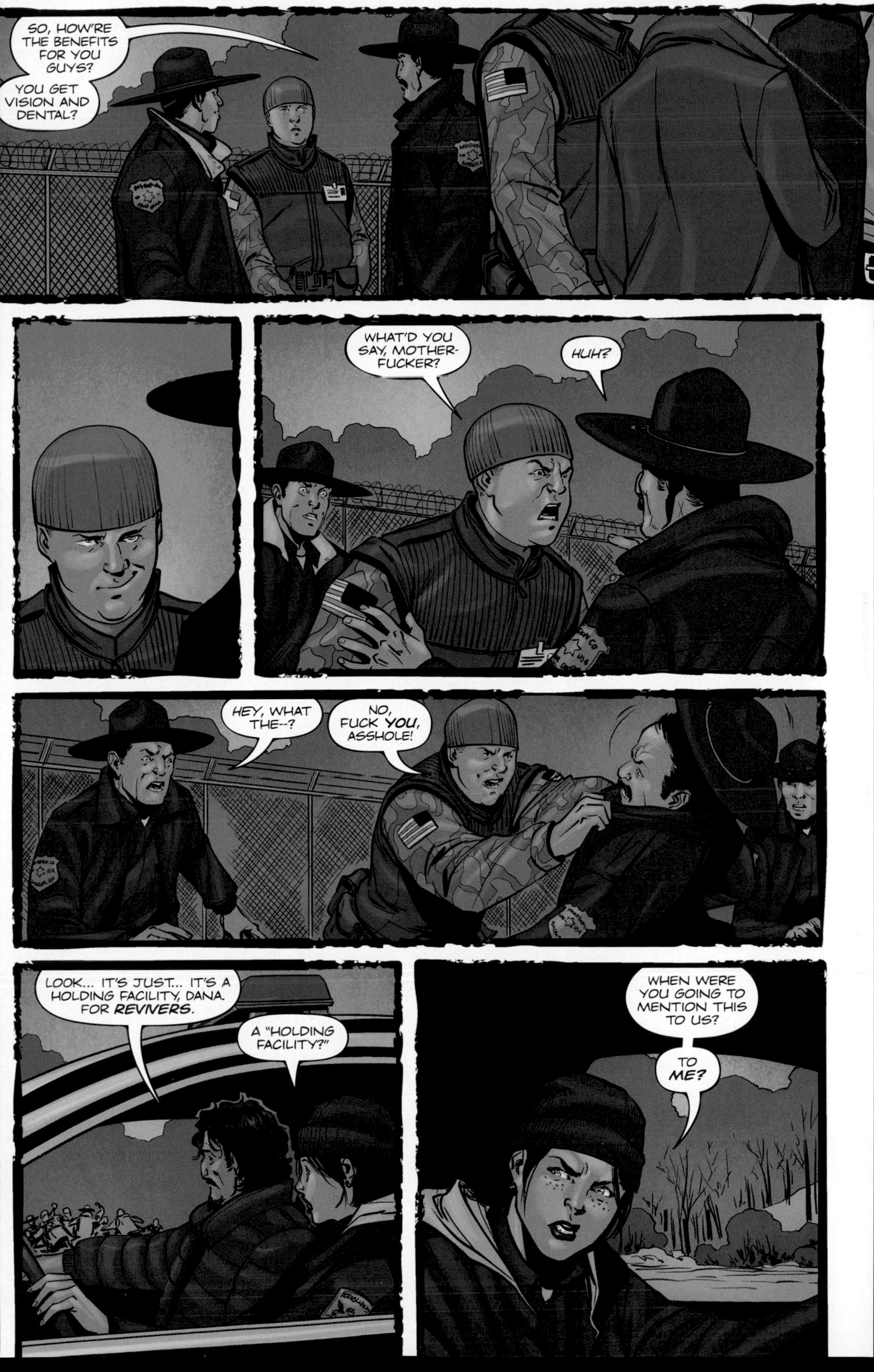

SO, HOW'RE THE BENEFITS FOR YOU GUYS?
YOU GET VISION AND DENTAL?
WHAT'D YOU SAY, MOTHER-FUCKER?
HUH?
HEY, WHAT THE--?
NO, FUCK *YOU*, ASSHOLE!
LOOK... IT'S JUST... IT'S A HOLDING FACILITY, DANA. FOR *REVIVERS*.
A "HOLDING FACILITY?"
WHEN WERE YOU GOING TO MENTION THIS TO US?
TO *ME?*

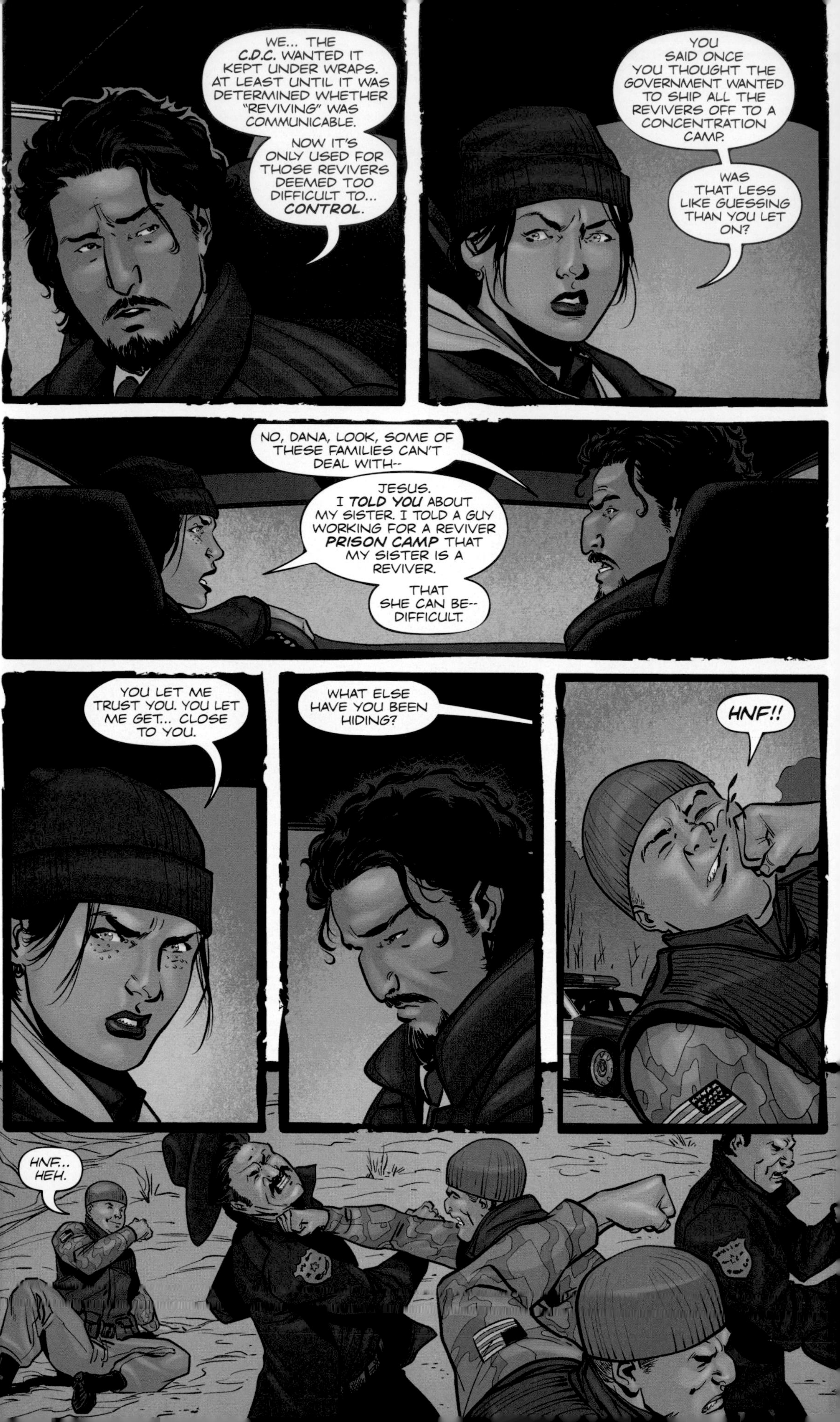

WE... THE C.D.C. WANTED IT KEPT UNDER WRAPS. AT LEAST UNTIL IT WAS DETERMINED WHETHER "REVIVING" WAS COMMUNICABLE.
NOW IT'S ONLY USED FOR THOSE REVIVERS DEEMED TOO DIFFICULT TO... CONTROL.
YOU SAID ONCE YOU THOUGHT THE GOVERNMENT WANTED TO SHIP ALL THE REVIVERS OFF TO A CONCENTRATION CAMP.
WAS THAT LESS LIKE GUESSING THAN YOU LET ON?
NO, DANA, LOOK, SOME OF THESE FAMILIES CAN'T DEAL WITH--
JESUS. I TOLD YOU ABOUT MY SISTER. I TOLD A GUY WORKING FOR A REVIVER PRISON CAMP THAT MY SISTER IS A REVIVER.
THAT SHE CAN BE-- DIFFICULT.
YOU LET ME TRUST YOU. YOU LET ME GET... CLOSE TO YOU.
WHAT ELSE HAVE YOU BEEN HIDING?
HNF!!
HNF... HEH.

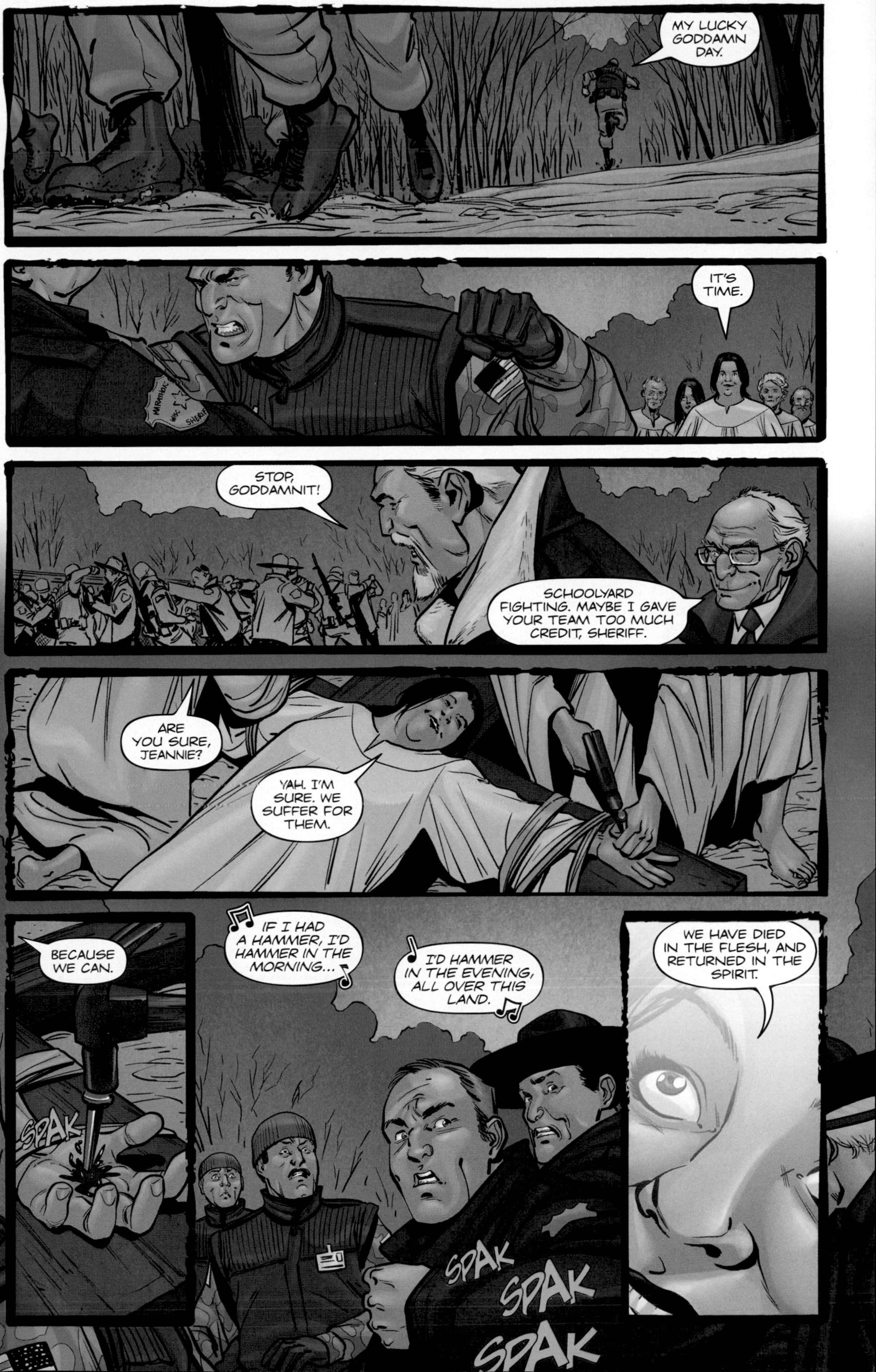
MY LUCKY GODDAMN DAY.
IT'S TIME.
MARATHON WISC SHERIFF
STOP, GODDAMNIT!
SCHOOLYARD FIGHTING. MAYBE I GAVE YOUR TEAM TOO MUCH CREDIT, SHERIFF.
ARE YOU SURE, JEANNIE?
YAH. I'M SURE. WE SUFFER FOR THEM.
BECAUSE WE CAN.
SPAK
IF I HAD A HAMMER, I'D HAMMER IN THE MORNING...
I'D HAMMER IN THE EVENING, ALL OVER THIS LAND.
WE HAVE DIED IN THE FLESH, AND RETURNED IN THE SPIRIT.
SPAK
SPAK
SPAK

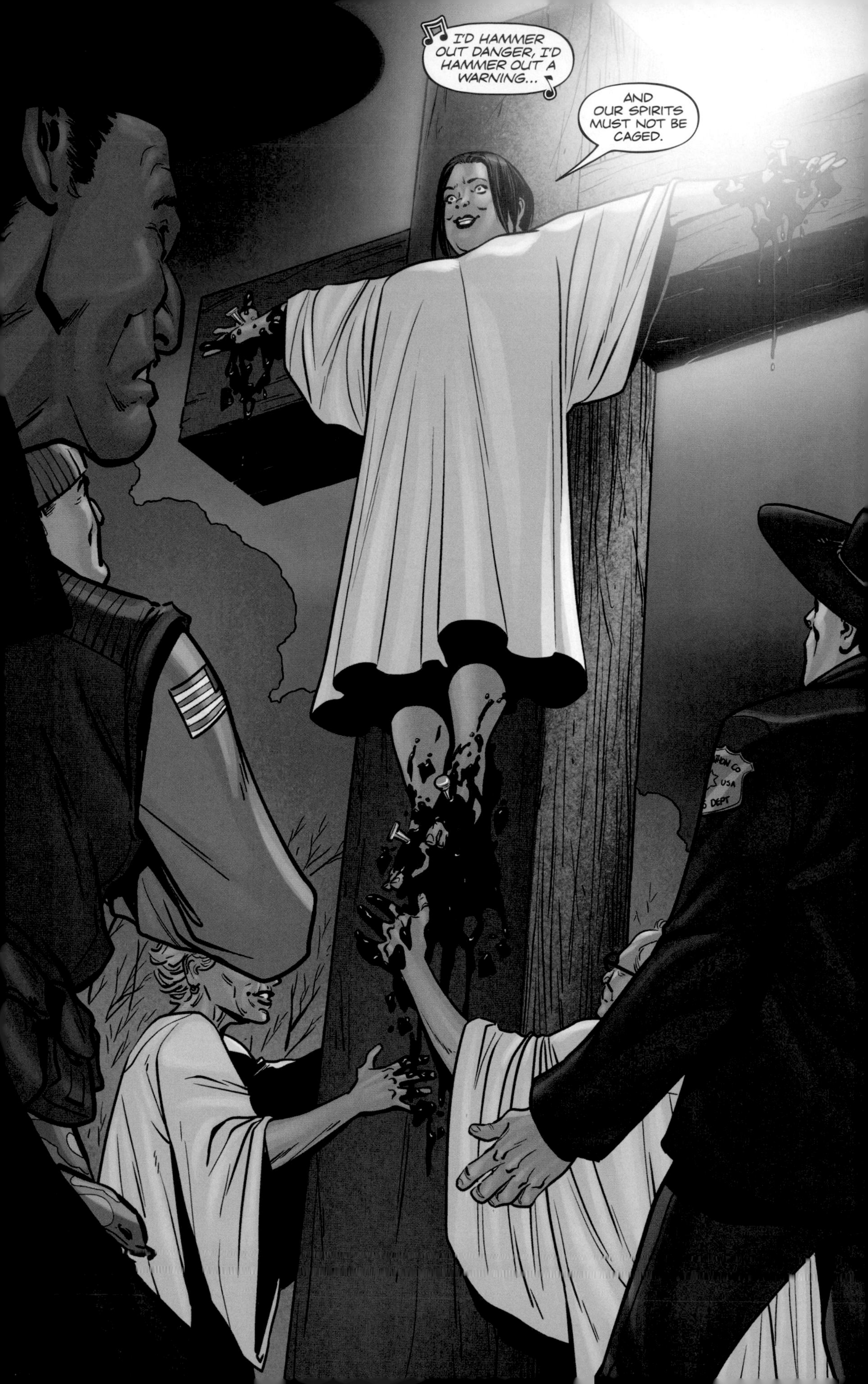
I'D HAMMER OUT DANGER, I'D HAMMER OUT A WARNING...
AND OUR SPIRITS MUST NOT BE CAGED.

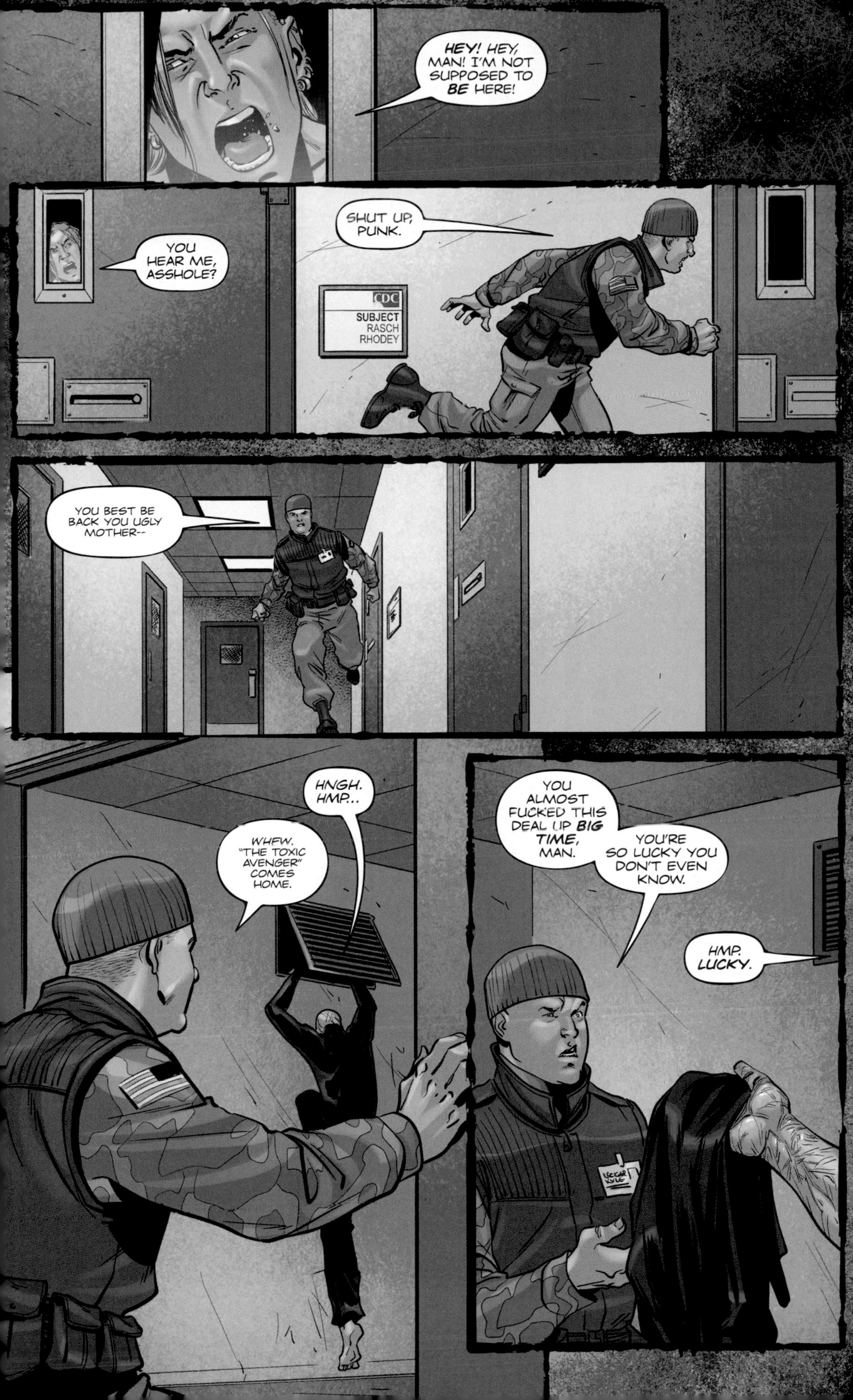

HEY! HEY, MAN! I'M NOT SUPPOSED TO BE HERE!
YOU HEAR ME, ASSHOLE?
SHUT UP, PUNK.
CDC
SUBJECT
RASCH
RHODEY
YOU BEST BE BACK YOU UGLY MOTHER--
HNGH. HMP...
WHFW. "THE TOXIC AVENGER" COMES HOME.
YOU ALMOST FUCKED THIS DEAL UP BIG TIME, MAN.
YOU'RE SO LUCKY YOU DON'T EVEN KNOW.
HMP. LUCKY.

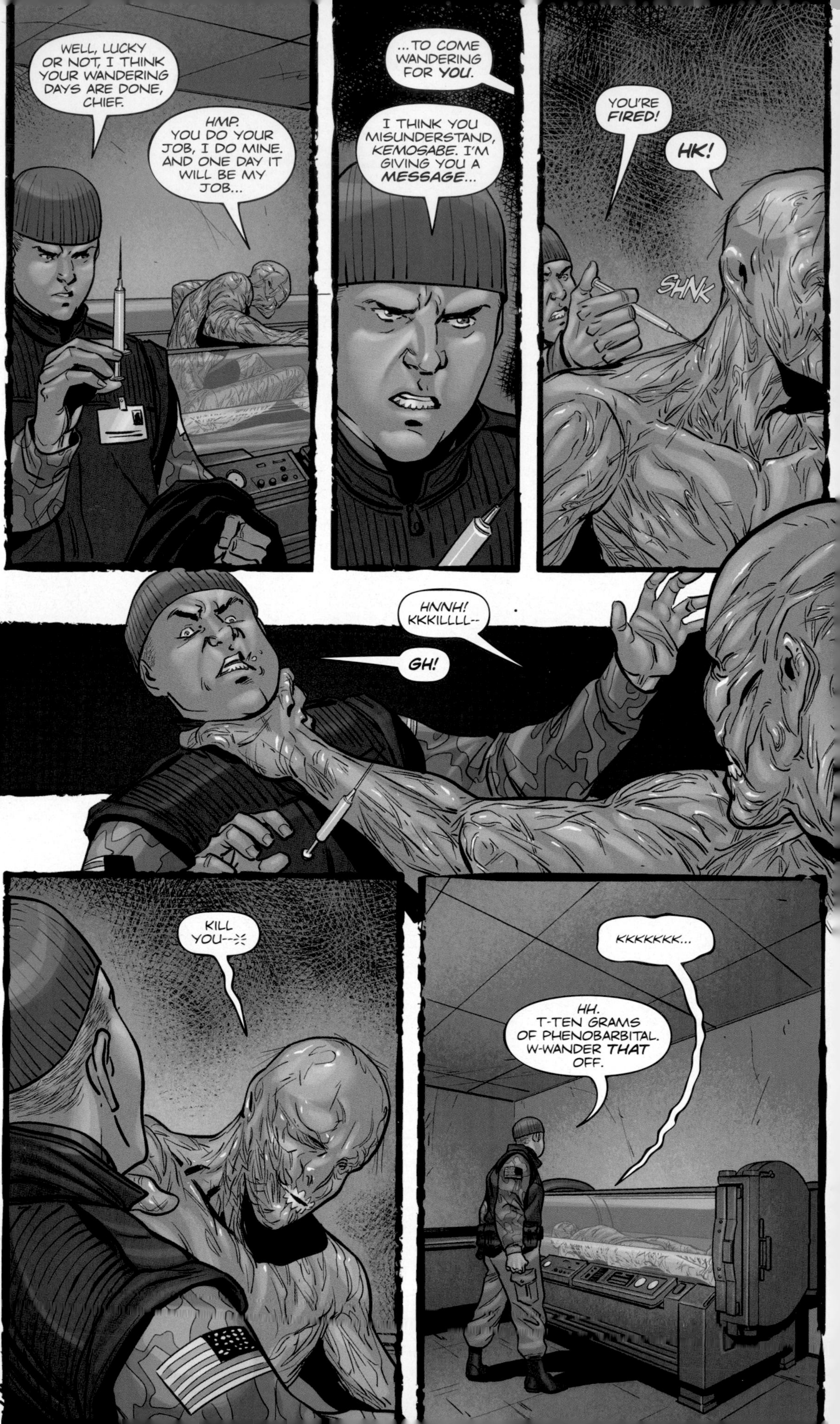
WELL, LUCKY OR NOT, I THINK YOUR WANDERING DAYS ARE DONE, CHIEF.
HMP. YOU DO YOUR JOB, I DO MINE. AND ONE DAY IT WILL BE MY JOB...
...TO COME WANDERING FOR YOU.
I THINK YOU MISUNDERSTAND, KEMOSABE. I'M GIVING YOU A MESSAGE...
YOU'RE FIRED!
HK!
SHNK
HNNH! KKKILLLL--
GH!
KILL YOU--
KKKKKKK...
HH. T-TEN GRAMS OF PHENOBARBITAL. W-WANDER THAT OFF.

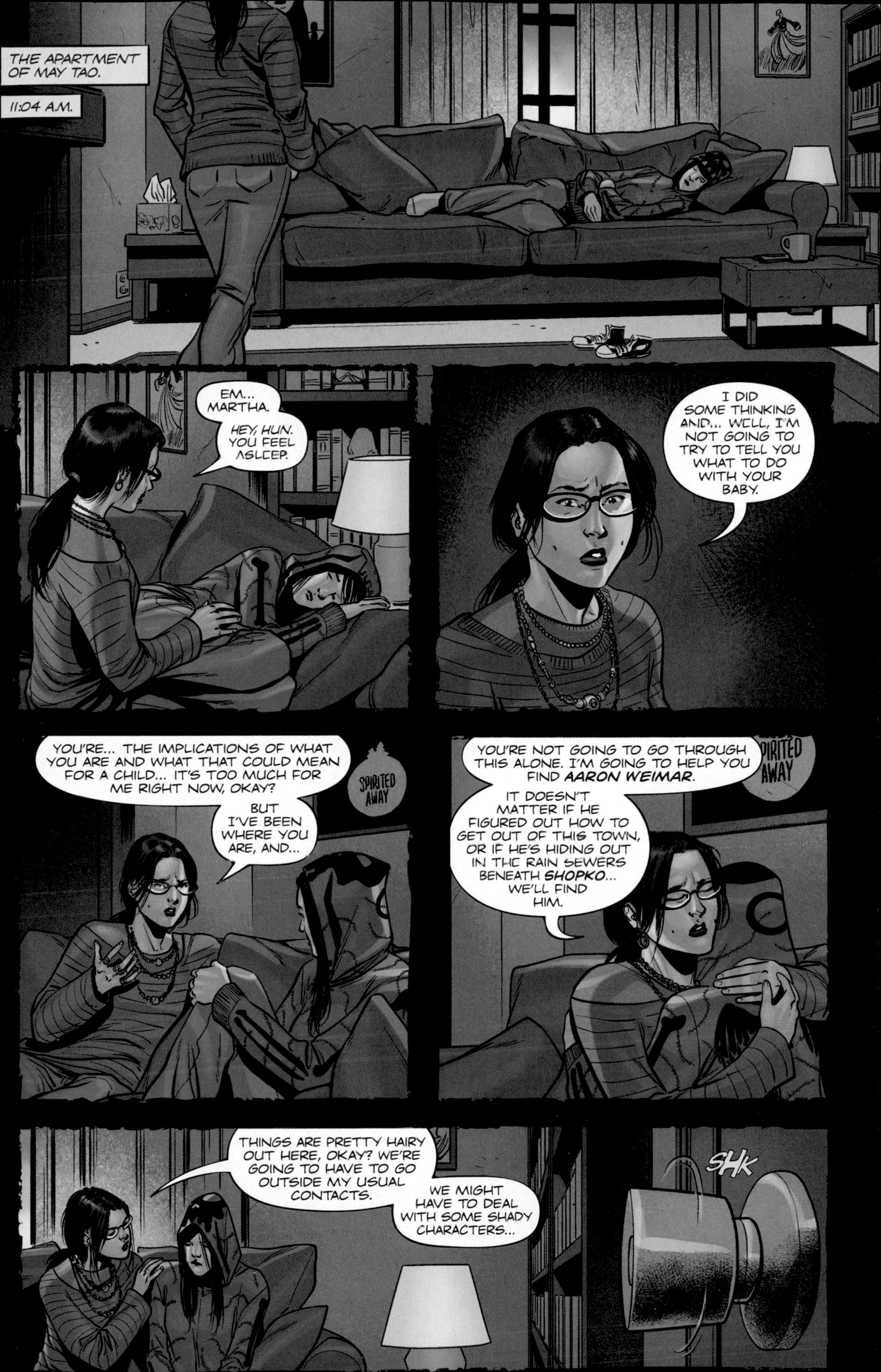
THE APARTMENT OF MAY TAO.
11:04 A.M.
EM... MARTHA.
HEY, HUN. YOU FELL ASLEEP.
I DID SOME THINKING AND... WELL, I'M NOT GOING TO TRY TO TELL YOU WHAT TO DO WITH YOUR BABY.
YOU'RE... THE IMPLICATIONS OF WHAT YOU ARE AND WHAT THAT COULD MEAN FOR A CHILD... IT'S TOO MUCH FOR ME RIGHT NOW, OKAY?
SPIRITED AWAY
BUT I'VE BEEN WHERE YOU ARE, AND...
YOU'RE NOT GOING TO GO THROUGH THIS ALONE. I'M GOING TO HELP YOU FIND AARON WEIMAR.
SPIRITED AWAY
IT DOESN'T MATTER IF HE FIGURED OUT HOW TO GET OUT OF THIS TOWN, OR IF HE'S HIDING OUT IN THE RAIN SEWERS BENEATH SHOPKO... WE'LL FIND HIM.
THINGS ARE PRETTY HAIRY OUT HERE, OKAY? WE'RE GOING TO HAVE TO GO OUTSIDE MY USUAL CONTACTS.
WE MIGHT HAVE TO DEAL WITH SOME SHADY CHARACTERS...
SHK

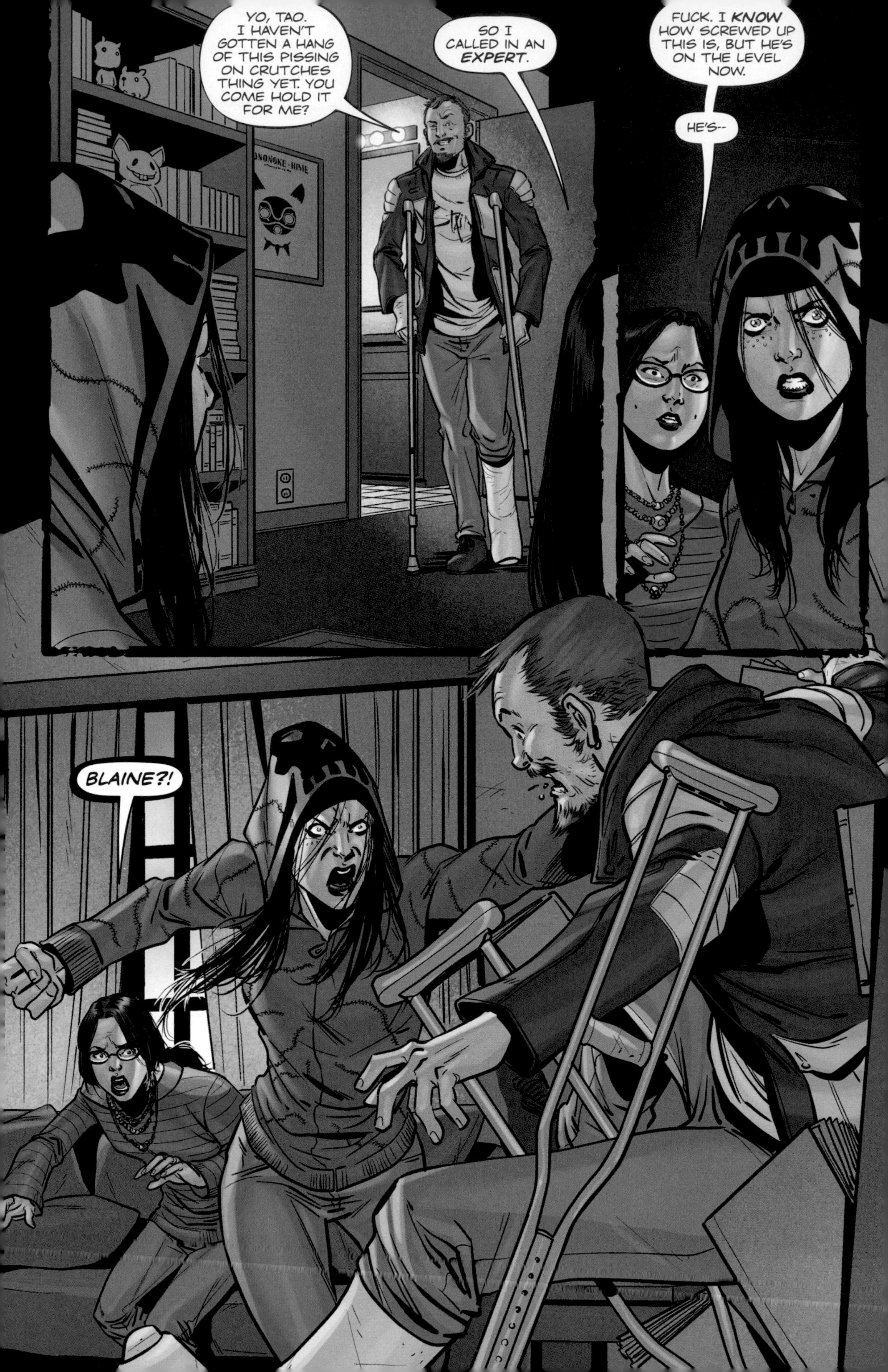
YO, TAO. I HAVEN'T GOTTEN A HANG OF THIS PISSING ON CRUTCHES THING YET. YOU COME HOLD IT FOR ME?
SO I CALLED IN AN **EXPERT**.
FUCK. I **KNOW** HOW SCREWED UP THIS IS, BUT HE'S ON THE LEVEL NOW.
HE'S--
ONONOKE-HIME
BLAINE?!

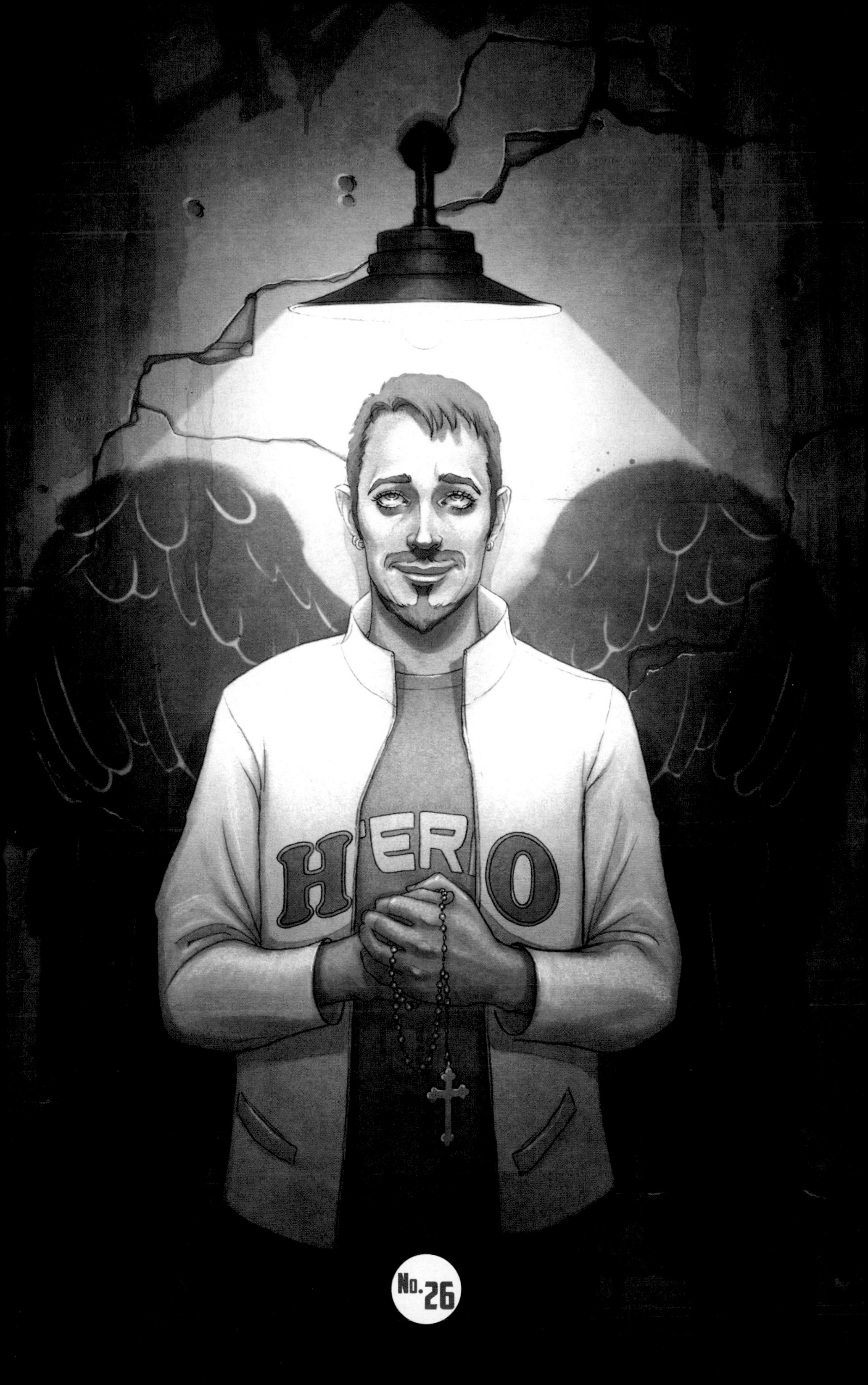
No. 26

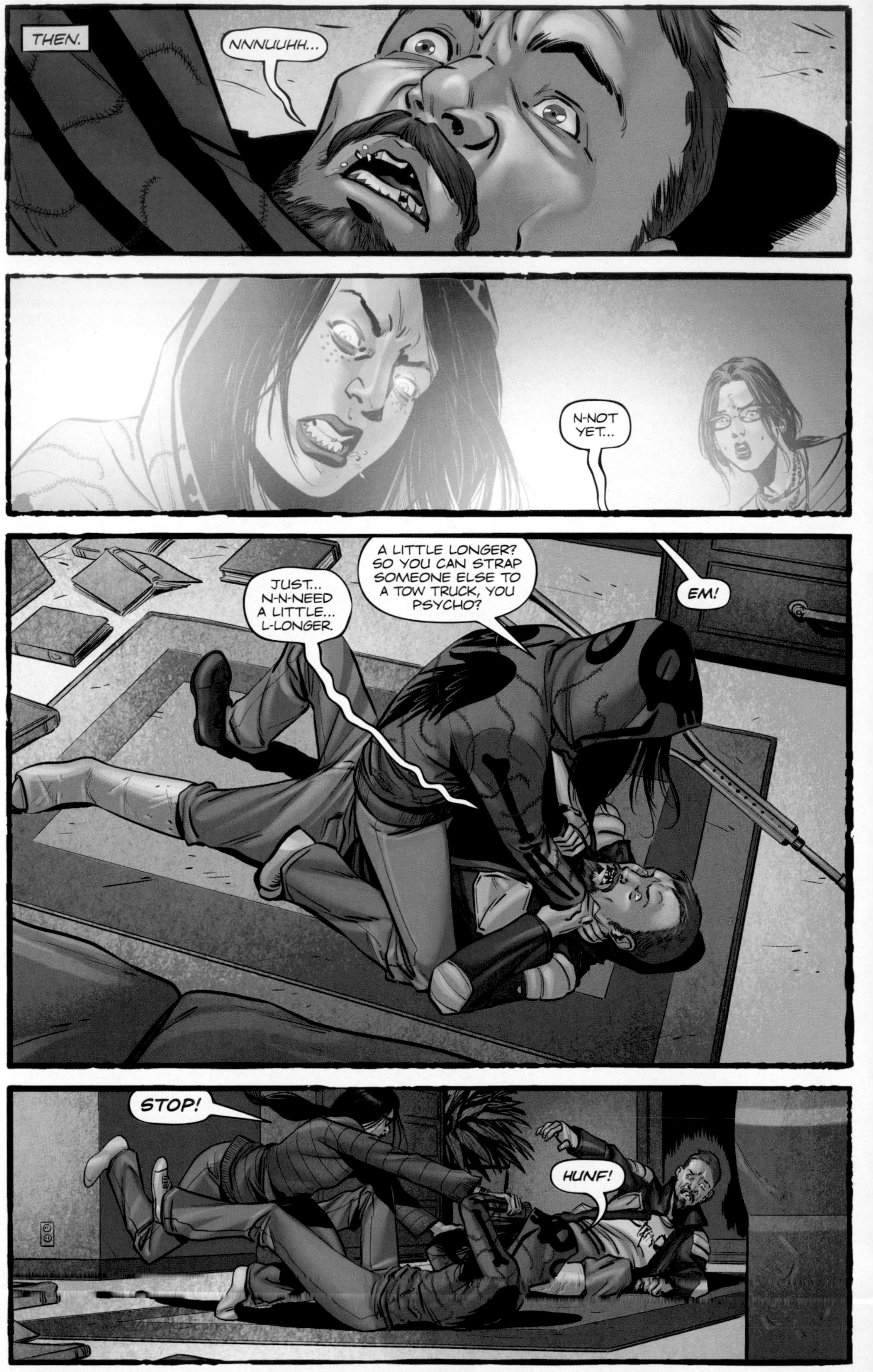
THEN.
NNNUUHH...
N-NOT YET...
JUST... N-N-NEED A LITTLE... L-LONGER.
A LITTLE LONGER? SO YOU CAN STRAP SOMEONE ELSE TO A TOW TRUCK, YOU PSYCHO?
EM!
STOP!
HUNF!

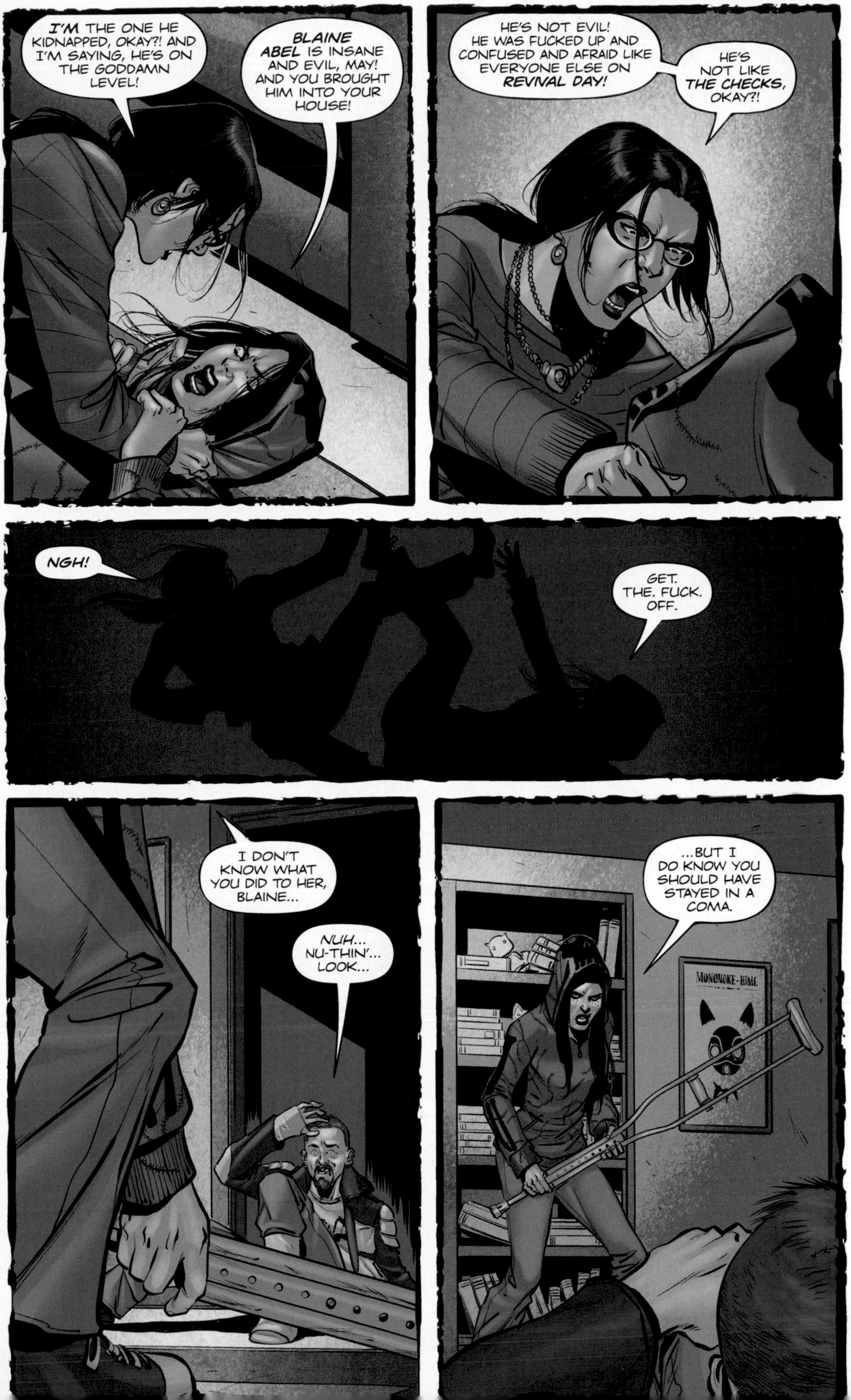
I'M THE ONE HE KIDNAPPED, OKAY?! AND I'M SAYING, HE'S ON THE GODDAMN LEVEL!
BLAINE ABEL IS INSANE AND EVIL, MAY! AND YOU BROUGHT HIM INTO YOUR HOUSE!
HE'S NOT EVIL! HE WAS FUCKED UP AND CONFUSED AND AFRAID LIKE EVERYONE ELSE ON REVIVAL DAY!
HE'S NOT LIKE THE CHECKS, OKAY?!
NGH!
GET. THE. FUCK. OFF.
I DON'T KNOW WHAT YOU DID TO HER, BLAINE...
NUH... NU-THIN'... LOOK...
...BUT I DO KNOW YOU SHOULD HAVE STAYED IN A COMA.
MONONOKE-HIME

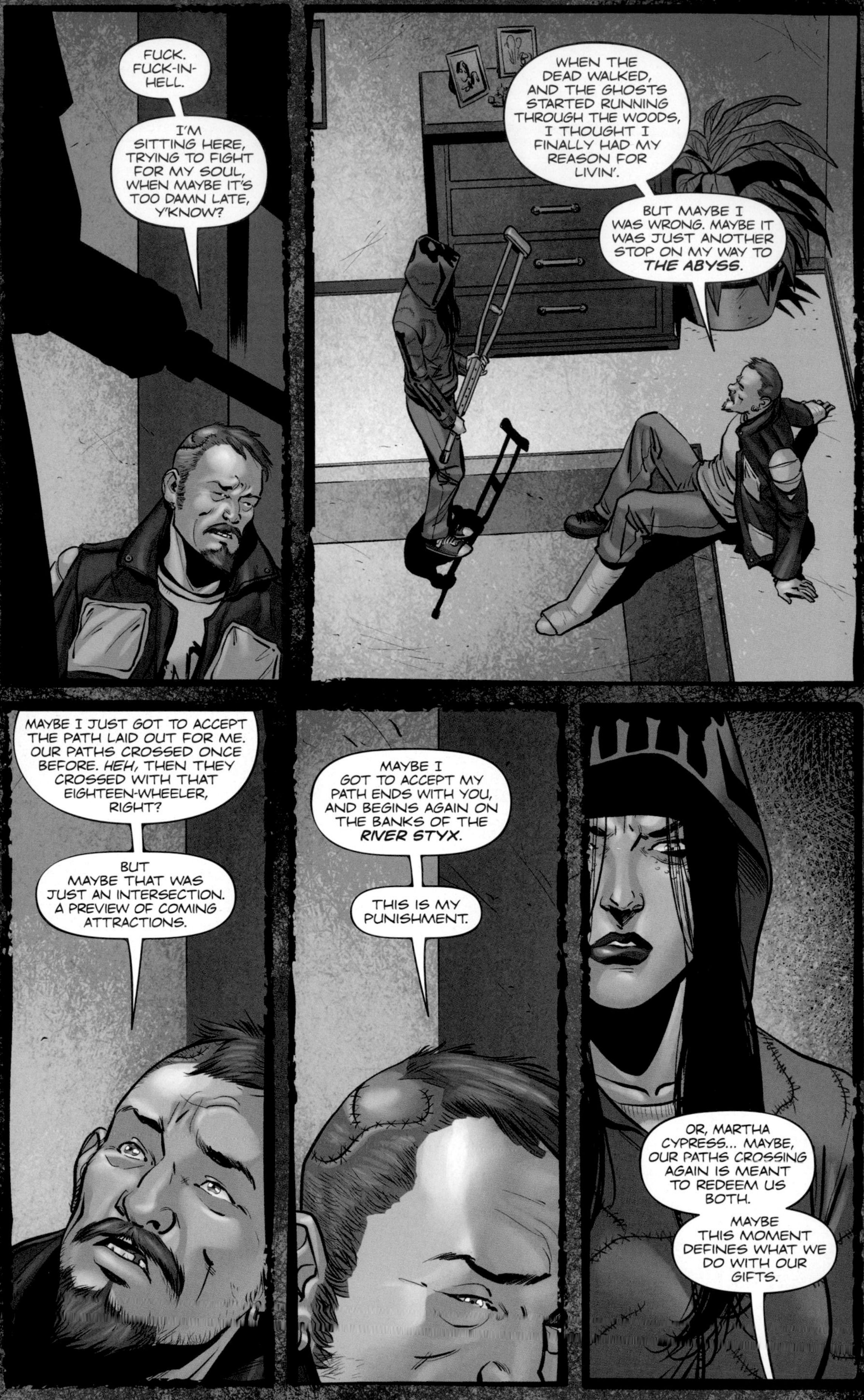
FUCK. FUCK-IN-HELL.
I'M SITTING HERE, TRYING TO FIGHT FOR MY SOUL, WHEN MAYBE IT'S TOO DAMN LATE, Y'KNOW?
WHEN THE DEAD WALKED, AND THE GHOSTS STARTED RUNNING THROUGH THE WOODS, I THOUGHT I FINALLY HAD MY REASON FOR LIVIN'.
BUT MAYBE I WAS WRONG. MAYBE IT WAS JUST ANOTHER STOP ON MY WAY TO THE ABYSS.
MAYBE I JUST GOT TO ACCEPT THE PATH LAID OUT FOR ME. OUR PATHS CROSSED ONCE BEFORE. HEH, THEN THEY CROSSED WITH THAT EIGHTEEN-WHEELER, RIGHT?
BUT MAYBE THAT WAS JUST AN INTERSECTION. A PREVIEW OF COMING ATTRACTIONS.
MAYBE I GOT TO ACCEPT MY PATH ENDS WITH YOU, AND BEGINS AGAIN ON THE BANKS OF THE RIVER STYX.
THIS IS MY PUNISHMENT.
OR, MARTHA CYPRESS... MAYBE, OUR PATHS CROSSING AGAIN IS MEANT TO REDEEM US BOTH.
MAYBE THIS MOMENT DEFINES WHAT WE DO WITH OUR GIFTS.

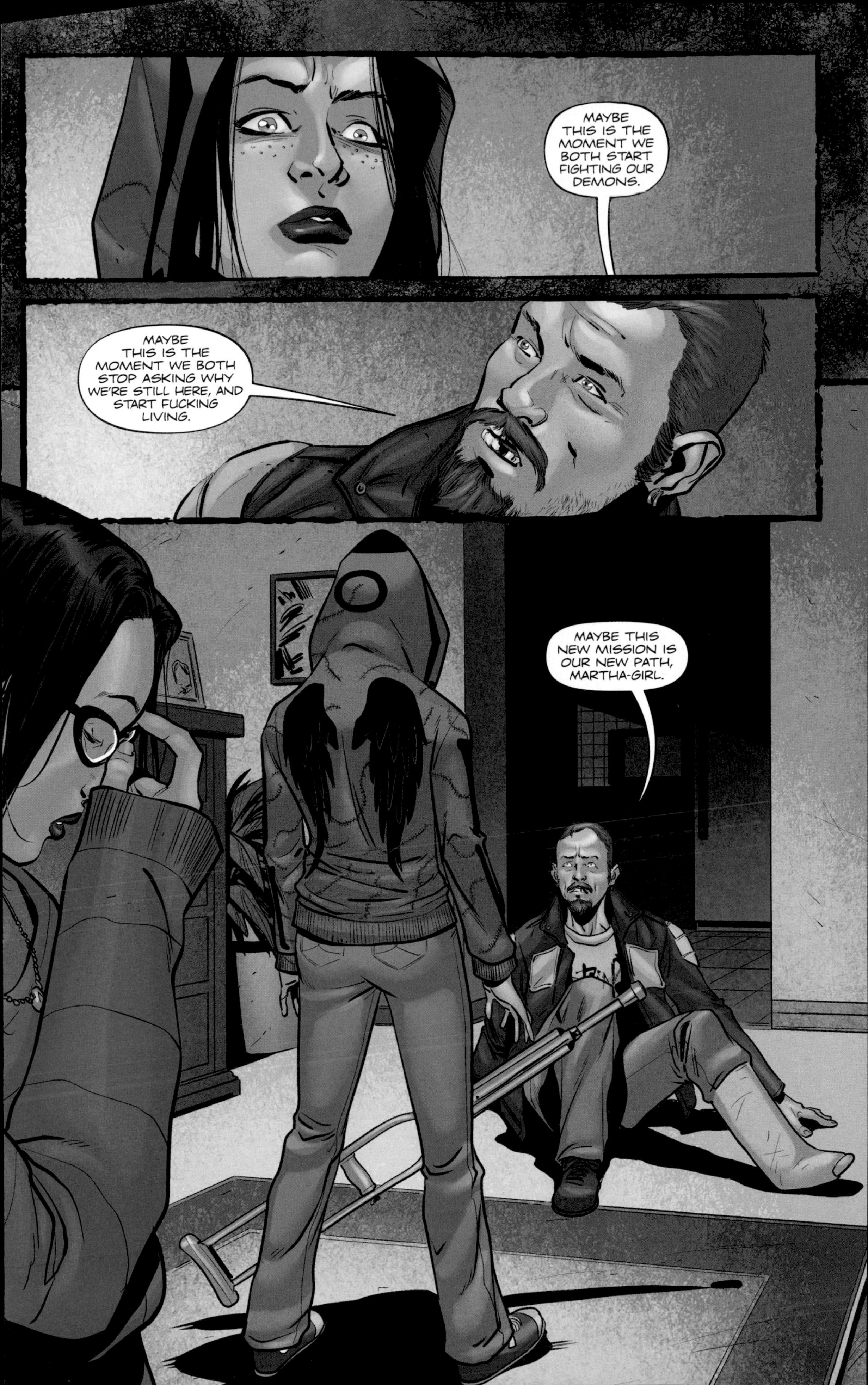
MAYBE THIS IS THE MOMENT WE BOTH START FIGHTING OUR DEMONS.
MAYBE THIS IS THE MOMENT WE BOTH STOP ASKING WHY WE'RE STILL HERE, AND START FUCKING LIVING.
MAYBE THIS NEW MISSION IS OUR NEW PATH, MARTHA-GIRL.

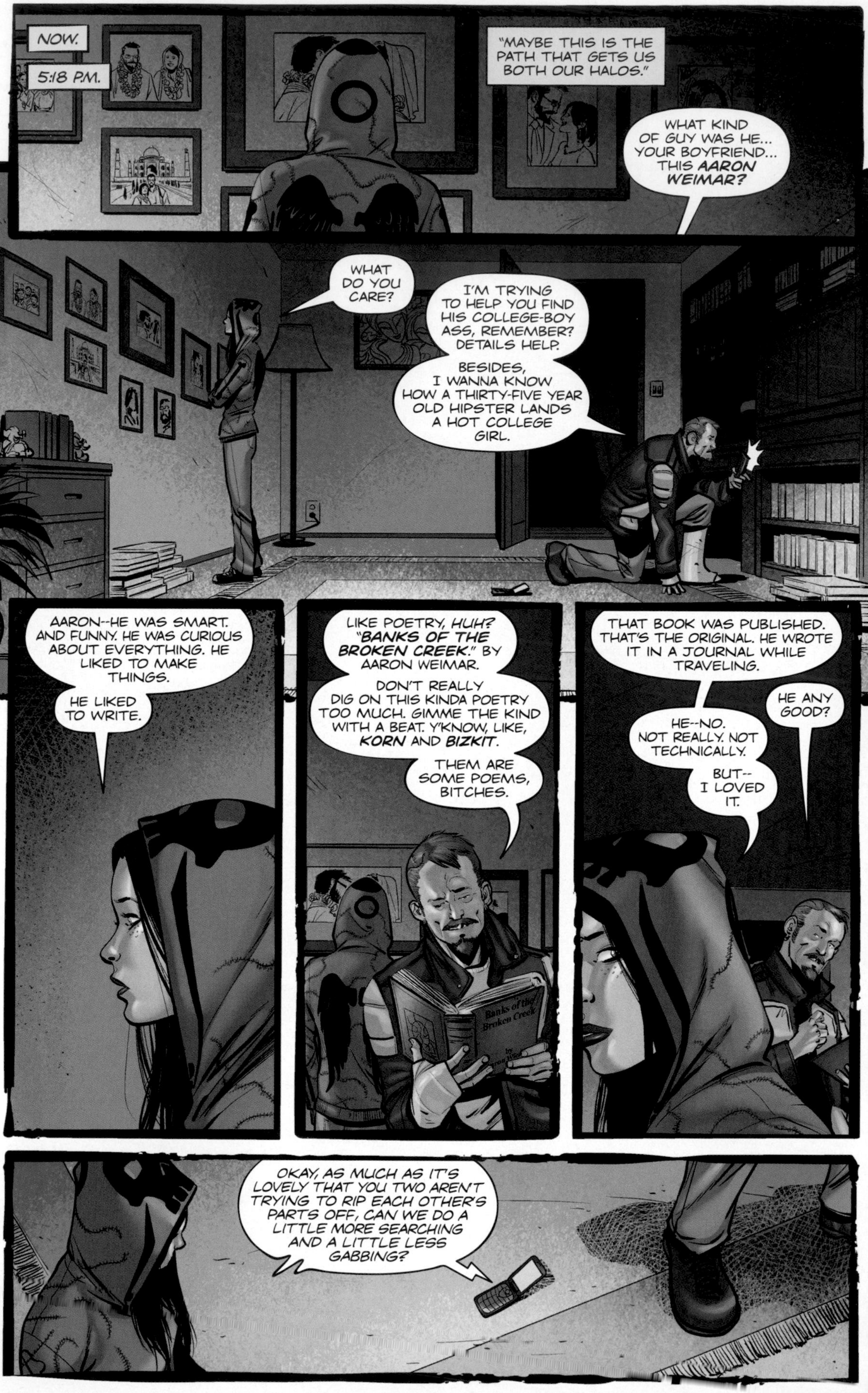
NOW.
5:18 P.M.
"MAYBE THIS IS THE PATH THAT GETS US BOTH OUR HALOS."
WHAT KIND OF GUY WAS HE... YOUR BOYFRIEND... THIS **AARON WEIMAR?**
WHAT DO YOU CARE?
I'M TRYING TO HELP YOU FIND HIS COLLEGE-BOY ASS, REMEMBER? DETAILS HELP.
BESIDES, I WANNA KNOW HOW A THIRTY-FIVE YEAR OLD HIPSTER LANDS A HOT COLLEGE GIRL.
AARON--HE WAS SMART. AND FUNNY. HE WAS CURIOUS ABOUT EVERYTHING. HE LIKED TO MAKE THINGS.
HE LIKED TO WRITE.
LIKE POETRY, *HUH?* "***BANKS OF THE BROKEN CREEK.***" BY AARON WEIMAR.
DON'T REALLY DIG ON THIS KINDA POETRY TOO MUCH. GIMME THE KIND WITH A BEAT. Y'KNOW, LIKE, ***KORN*** AND ***BIZKIT***.
THEM ARE SOME POEMS, BITCHES.
Banks of the Broken Creek
THAT BOOK WAS PUBLISHED. THAT'S THE ORIGINAL. HE WROTE IT IN A JOURNAL WHILE TRAVELING.
HE ANY GOOD?
HE--NO. NOT REALLY. NOT TECHNICALLY.
BUT-- I LOVED IT.
OKAY, AS MUCH AS IT'S LOVELY THAT YOU TWO AREN'T TRYING TO RIP EACH OTHER'S PARTS OFF, CAN WE DO A LITTLE MORE SEARCHING AND A LITTLE LESS GABBING?

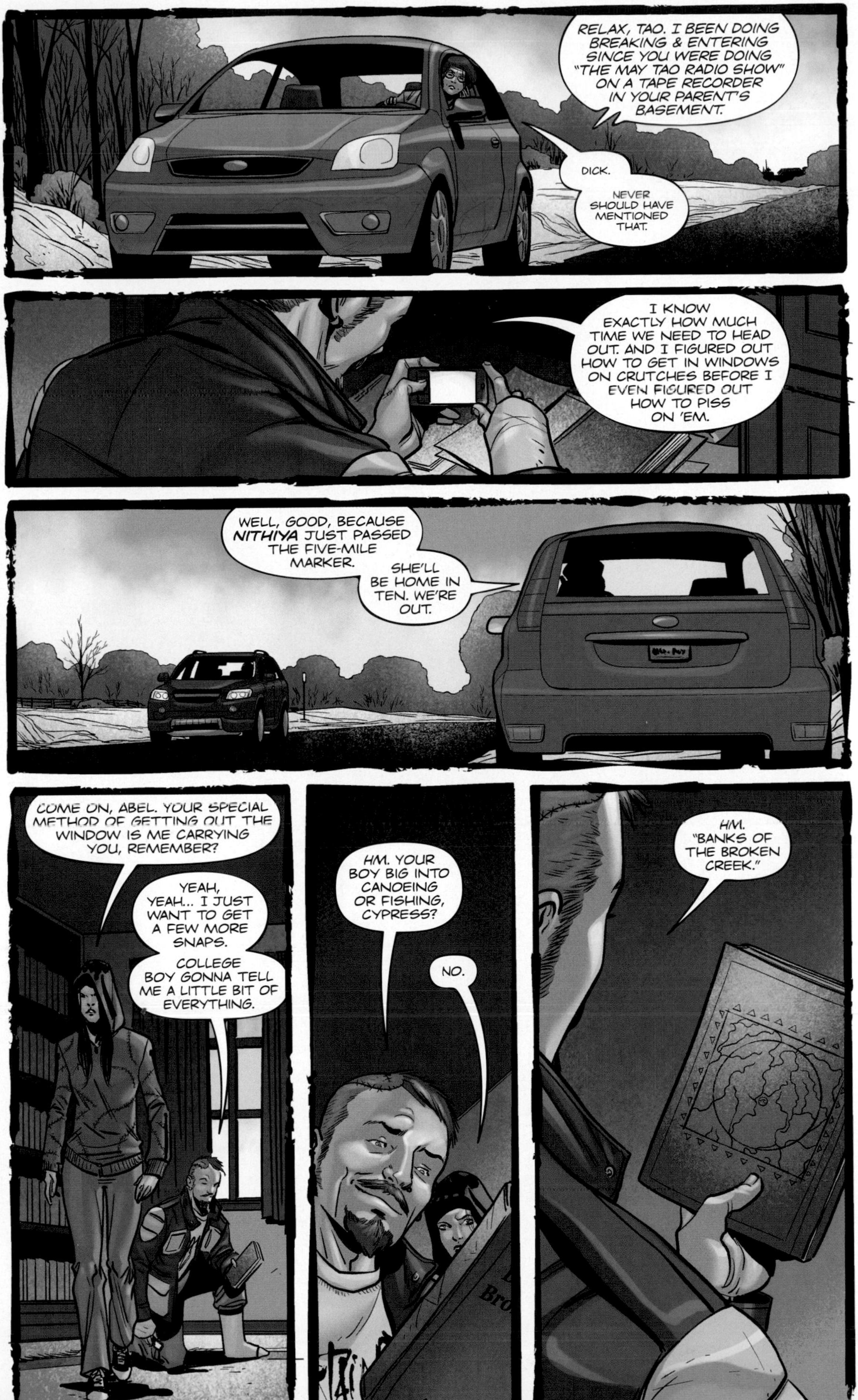
RELAX, TAO. I BEEN DOING BREAKING & ENTERING SINCE YOU WERE DOING "THE MAY TAO RADIO SHOW" ON A TAPE RECORDER IN YOUR PARENT'S BASEMENT.
DICK.
NEVER SHOULD HAVE MENTIONED THAT.
I KNOW EXACTLY HOW MUCH TIME WE NEED TO HEAD OUT. AND I FIGURED OUT HOW TO GET IN WINDOWS ON CRUTCHES BEFORE I EVEN FIGURED OUT HOW TO PISS ON 'EM.
WELL, GOOD, BECAUSE NITHIYA JUST PASSED THE FIVE-MILE MARKER.
SHE'LL BE HOME IN TEN. WE'RE OUT.
COME ON, ABEL. YOUR SPECIAL METHOD OF GETTING OUT THE WINDOW IS ME CARRYING YOU, REMEMBER?
YEAH, YEAH... I JUST WANT TO GET A FEW MORE SNAPS.
COLLEGE BOY GONNA TELL ME A LITTLE BIT OF EVERYTHING.
HM. YOUR BOY BIG INTO CANOEING OR FISHING, CYPRESS?
NO.
HM. "BANKS OF THE BROKEN CREEK."

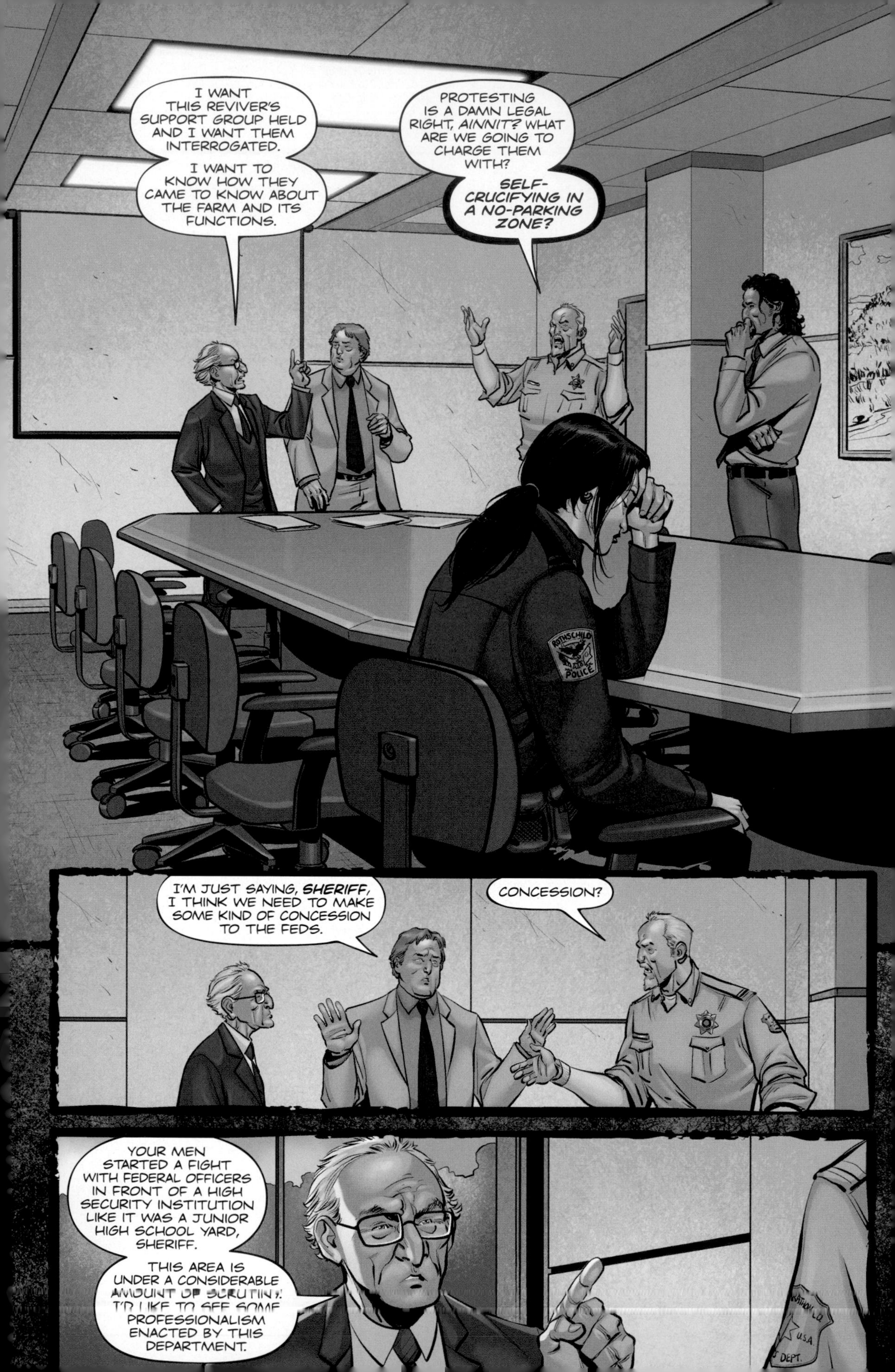
I WANT THIS REVIVER'S SUPPORT GROUP HELD AND I WANT THEM INTERROGATED.
I WANT TO KNOW HOW THEY CAME TO KNOW ABOUT THE FARM AND ITS FUNCTIONS.
PROTESTING IS A DAMN LEGAL RIGHT, AINNIT? WHAT ARE WE GOING TO CHARGE THEM WITH?
SELF-CRUCIFYING IN A NO-PARKING ZONE?
I'M JUST SAYING, SHERIFF, I THINK WE NEED TO MAKE SOME KIND OF CONCESSION TO THE FEDS.
CONCESSION?
YOUR MEN STARTED A FIGHT WITH FEDERAL OFFICERS IN FRONT OF A HIGH SECURITY INSTITUTION LIKE IT WAS A JUNIOR HIGH SCHOOL YARD, SHERIFF.
THIS AREA IS UNDER A CONSIDERABLE AMOUNT OF SCRUTINY. I'D LIKE TO SEE SOME PROFESSIONALISM ENACTED BY THIS DEPARTMENT.

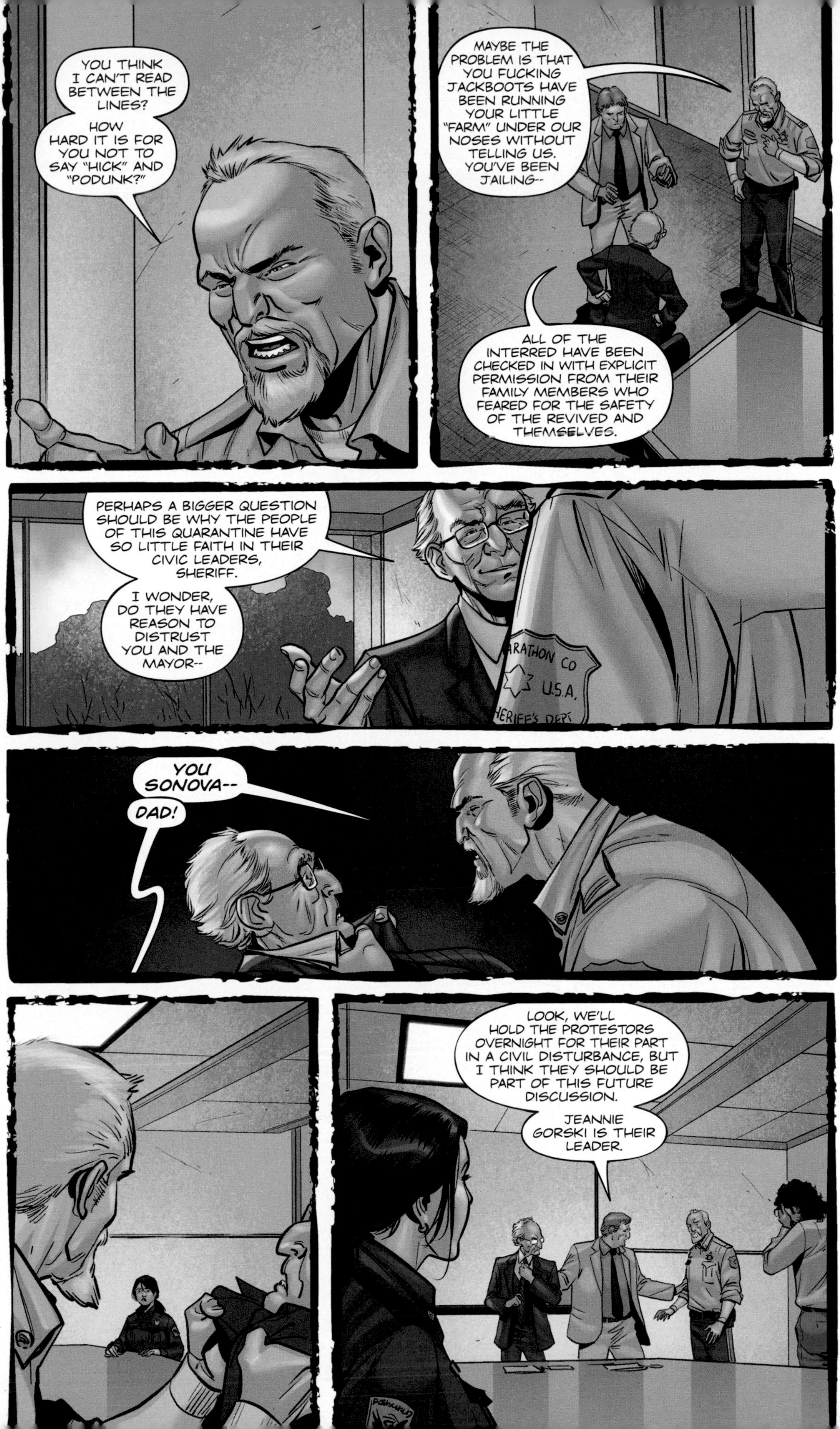

YOU THINK I CAN'T READ BETWEEN THE LINES?
HOW HARD IT IS FOR YOU NOT TO SAY "HICK" AND "PODUNK?"
MAYBE THE PROBLEM IS THAT YOU FUCKING JACKBOOTS HAVE BEEN RUNNING YOUR LITTLE "FARM" UNDER OUR NOSES WITHOUT TELLING US. YOU'VE BEEN JAILING--
ALL OF THE INTERRED HAVE BEEN CHECKED IN WITH EXPLICIT PERMISSION FROM THEIR FAMILY MEMBERS WHO FEARED FOR THE SAFETY OF THE REVIVED AND THEMSELVES.
PERHAPS A BIGGER QUESTION SHOULD BE WHY THE PEOPLE OF THIS QUARANTINE HAVE SO LITTLE FAITH IN THEIR CIVIC LEADERS, SHERIFF.
I WONDER, DO THEY HAVE REASON TO DISTRUST YOU AND THE MAYOR--
YOU SONOVA--
DAD!
LOOK, WE'LL HOLD THE PROTESTORS OVERNIGHT FOR THEIR PART IN A CIVIL DISTURBANCE, BUT I THINK THEY SHOULD BE PART OF THIS FUTURE DISCUSSION.
JEANNIE GORSKI IS THEIR LEADER.

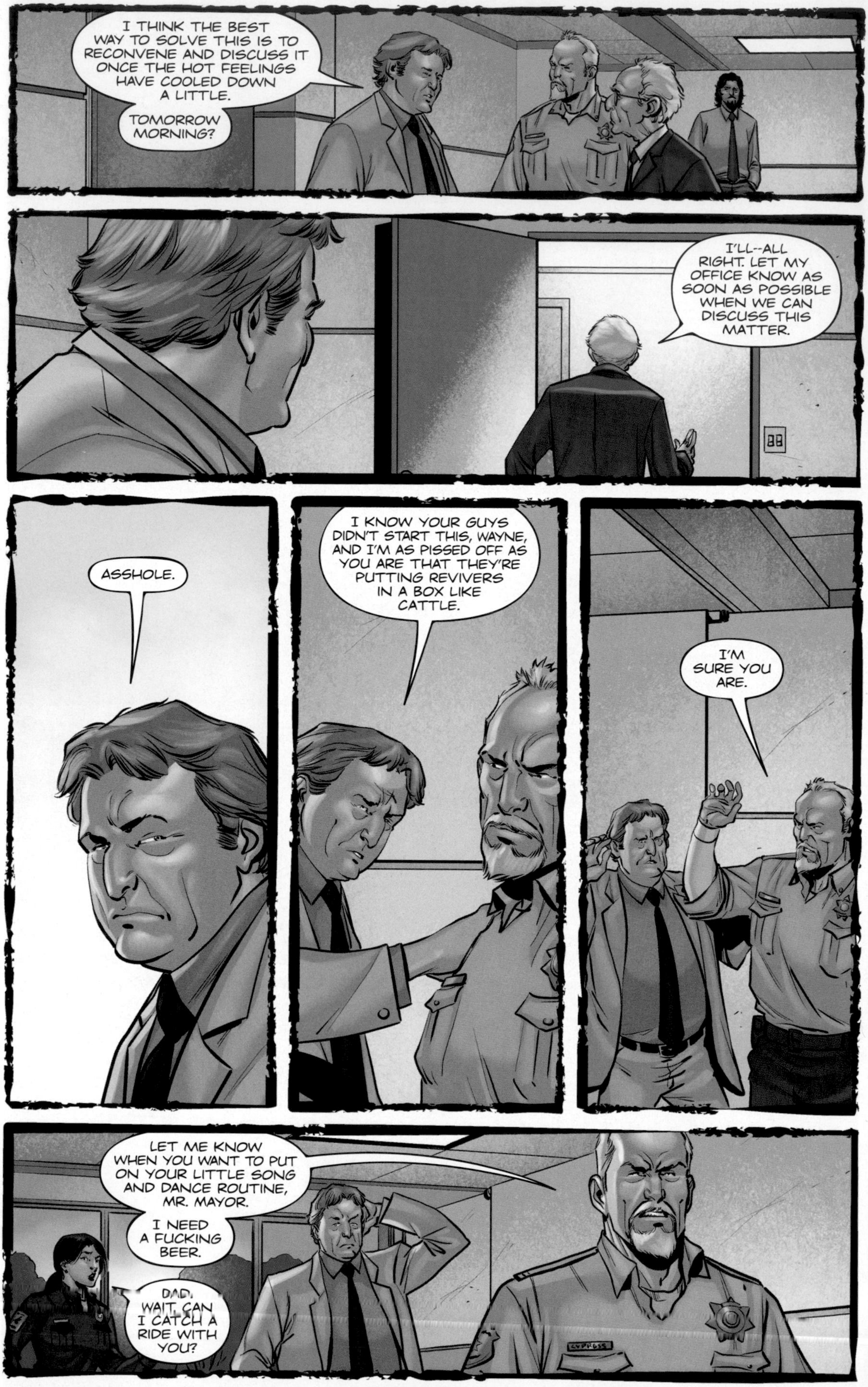
I THINK THE BEST WAY TO SOLVE THIS IS TO RECONVENE AND DISCUSS IT ONCE THE HOT FEELINGS HAVE COOLED DOWN A LITTLE.
TOMORROW MORNING?
I'LL--ALL RIGHT. LET MY OFFICE KNOW AS SOON AS POSSIBLE WHEN WE CAN DISCUSS THIS MATTER.
ASSHOLE.
I KNOW YOUR GUYS DIDN'T START THIS, WAYNE, AND I'M AS PISSED OFF AS YOU ARE THAT THEY'RE PUTTING REVIVERS IN A BOX LIKE CATTLE.
I'M SURE YOU ARE.
LET ME KNOW WHEN YOU WANT TO PUT ON YOUR LITTLE SONG AND DANCE ROUTINE, MR. MAYOR.
I NEED A FUCKING BEER.
DAD, WAIT. CAN I CATCH A RIDE WITH YOU?

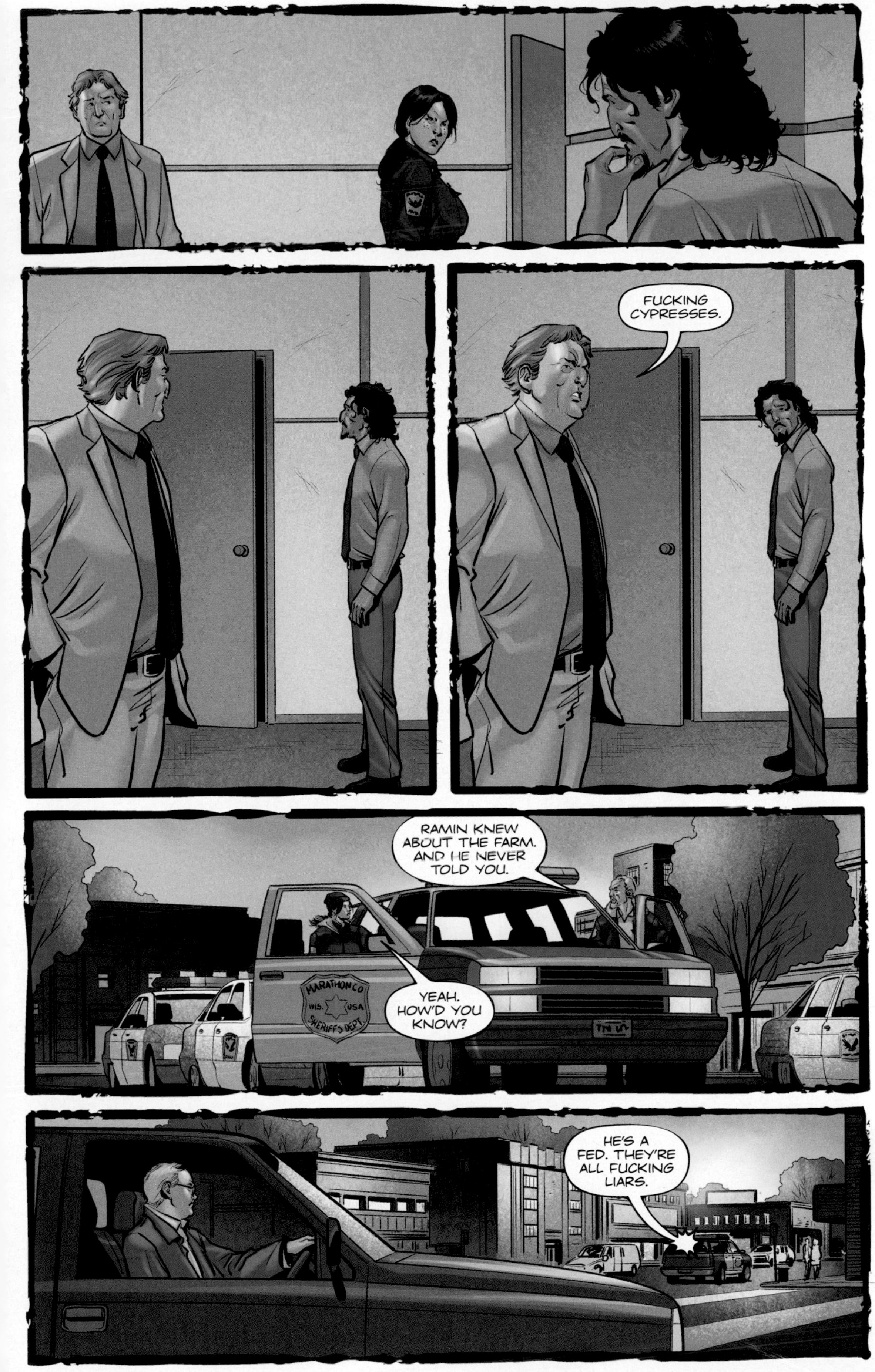
FUCKING CYPRESSES.
RAMIN KNEW ABOUT THE FARM. AND HE NEVER TOLD YOU.
MARATHON CO. WIS. USA SHERIFFS DEPT.
YEAH. HOW'D YOU KNOW?
HE'S A FED. THEY'RE ALL FUCKING LIARS.

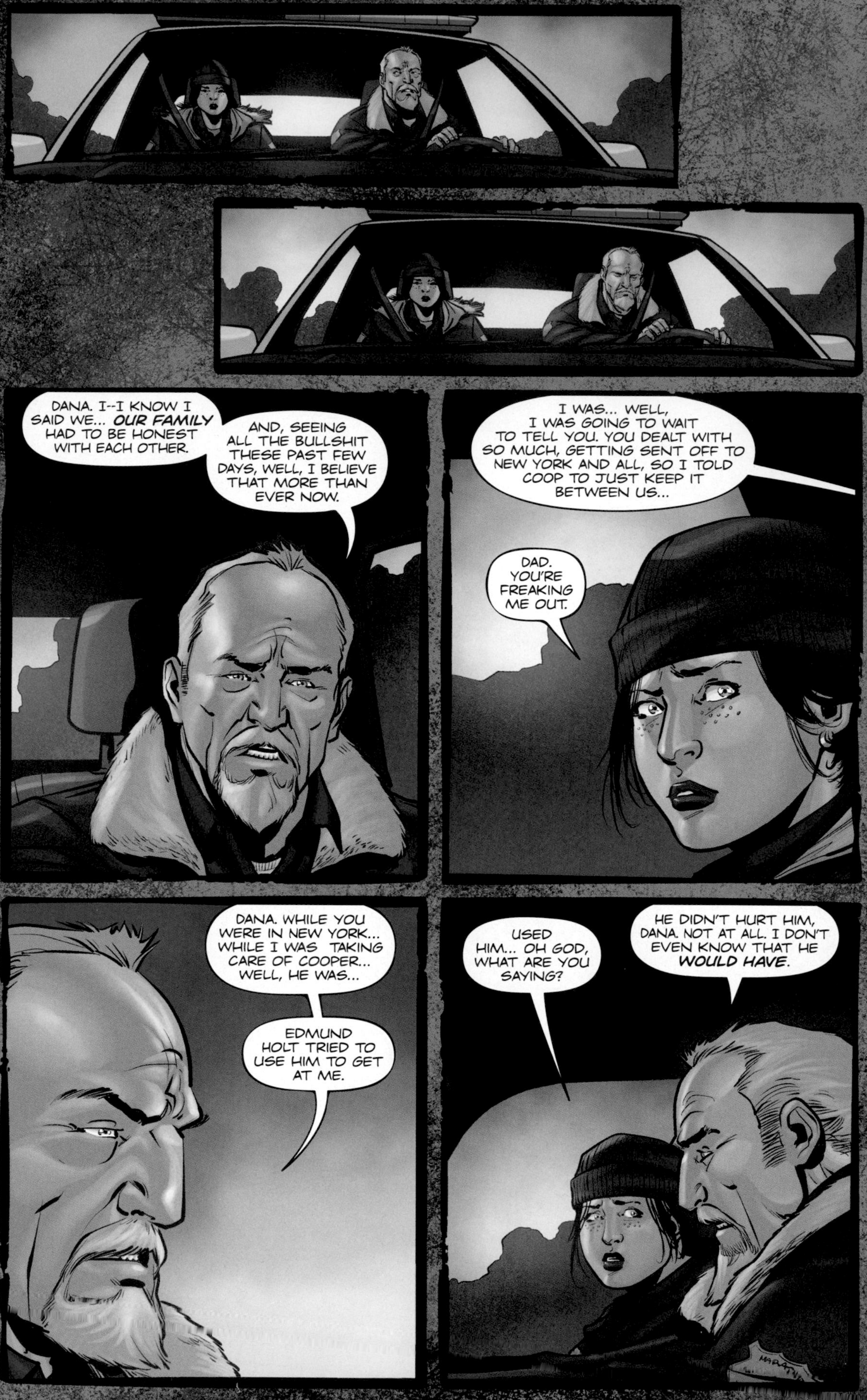
DANA. I--I KNOW I SAID WE... OUR FAMILY HAD TO BE HONEST WITH EACH OTHER.
AND, SEEING ALL THE BULLSHIT THESE PAST FEW DAYS, WELL, I BELIEVE THAT MORE THAN EVER NOW.
I WAS... WELL, I WAS GOING TO WAIT TO TELL YOU. YOU DEALT WITH SO MUCH, GETTING SENT OFF TO NEW YORK AND ALL, SO I TOLD COOP TO JUST KEEP IT BETWEEN US...
DAD. YOU'RE FREAKING ME OUT.
DANA. WHILE YOU WERE IN NEW YORK... WHILE I WAS TAKING CARE OF COOPER... WELL, HE WAS...
EDMUND HOLT TRIED TO USE HIM TO GET AT ME.
USED HIM... OH GOD, WHAT ARE YOU SAYING?
HE DIDN'T HURT HIM, DANA. NOT AT ALL. I DON'T EVEN KNOW THAT HE WOULD HAVE.

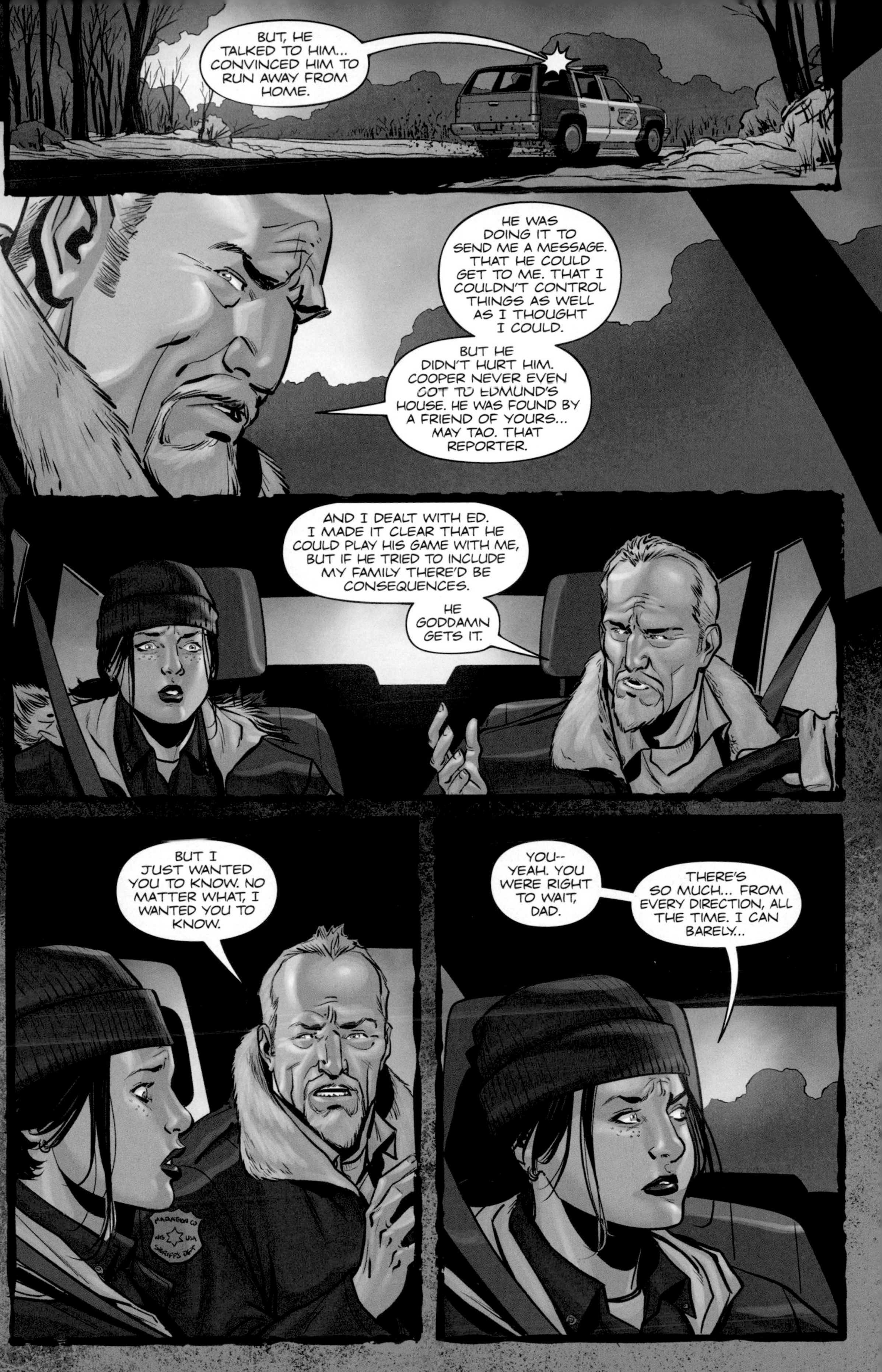
BUT, HE TALKED TO HIM... CONVINCED HIM TO RUN AWAY FROM HOME.
HE WAS DOING IT TO SEND ME A MESSAGE. THAT HE COULD GET TO ME. THAT I COULDN'T CONTROL THINGS AS WELL AS I THOUGHT I COULD.
BUT HE DIDN'T HURT HIM. COOPER NEVER EVEN GOT TO EDMUND'S HOUSE. HE WAS FOUND BY A FRIEND OF YOURS... MAY TAO. THAT REPORTER.
AND I DEALT WITH ED. I MADE IT CLEAR THAT HE COULD PLAY HIS GAME WITH ME, BUT IF HE TRIED TO INCLUDE MY FAMILY THERE'D BE CONSEQUENCES.
HE GODDAMN GETS IT.
BUT I JUST WANTED YOU TO KNOW. NO MATTER WHAT, I WANTED YOU TO KNOW.
YOU-- YEAH. YOU WERE RIGHT TO WAIT, DAD.
THERE'S SO MUCH... FROM EVERY DIRECTION, ALL THE TIME. I CAN BARELY...

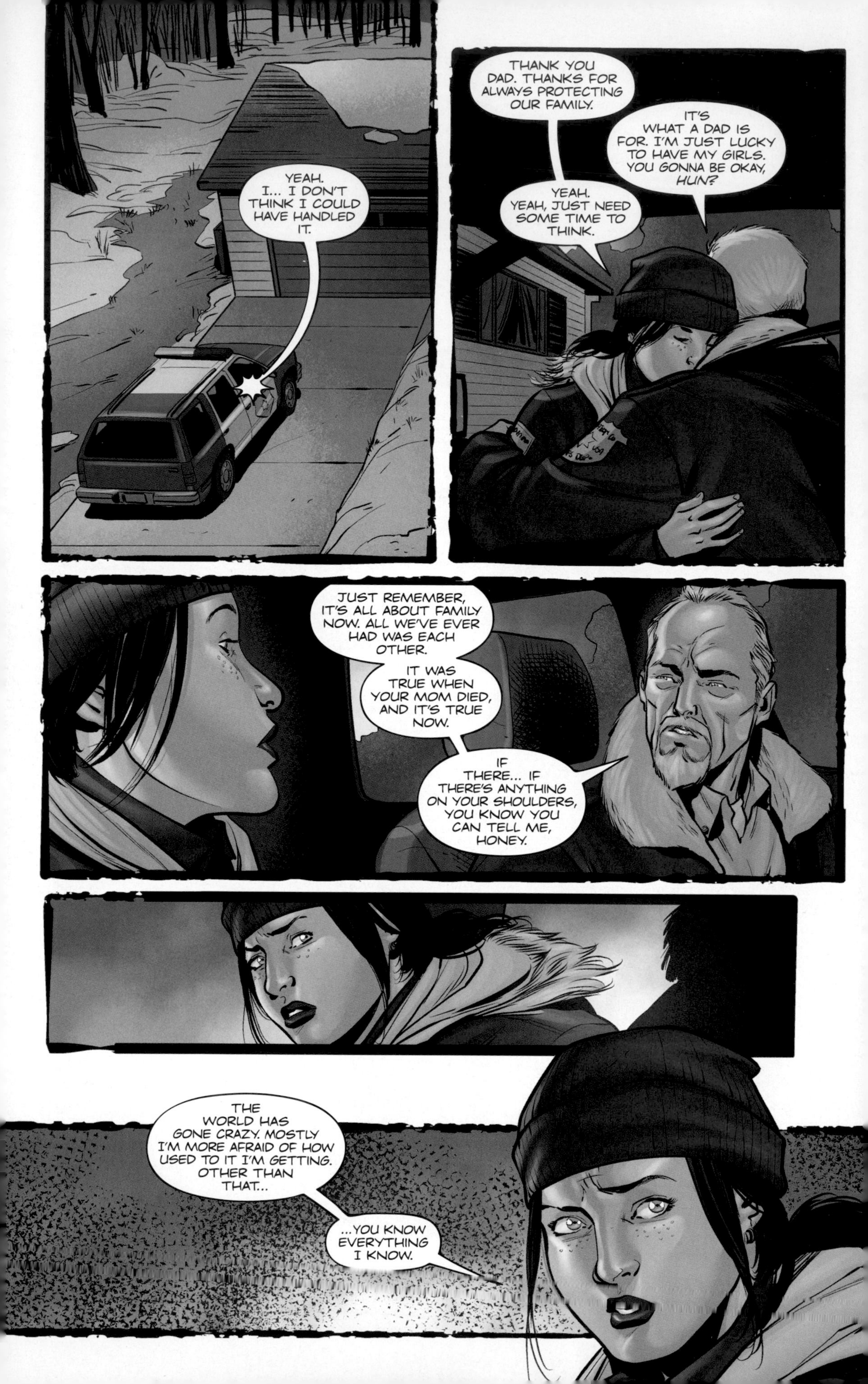
YEAH. I... I DON'T THINK I COULD HAVE HANDLED IT.
THANK YOU DAD. THANKS FOR ALWAYS PROTECTING OUR FAMILY.
IT'S WHAT A DAD IS FOR. I'M JUST LUCKY TO HAVE MY GIRLS. YOU GONNA BE OKAY, HUN?
YEAH. YEAH, JUST NEED SOME TIME TO THINK.
JUST REMEMBER, IT'S ALL ABOUT FAMILY NOW. ALL WE'VE EVER HAD WAS EACH OTHER.
IT WAS TRUE WHEN YOUR MOM DIED, AND IT'S TRUE NOW.
IF THERE... IF THERE'S ANYTHING ON YOUR SHOULDERS, YOU KNOW YOU CAN TELL ME, HONEY.
THE WORLD HAS GONE CRAZY. MOSTLY I'M MORE AFRAID OF HOW USED TO IT I'M GETTING. OTHER THAN THAT...
...YOU KNOW EVERYTHING I KNOW.

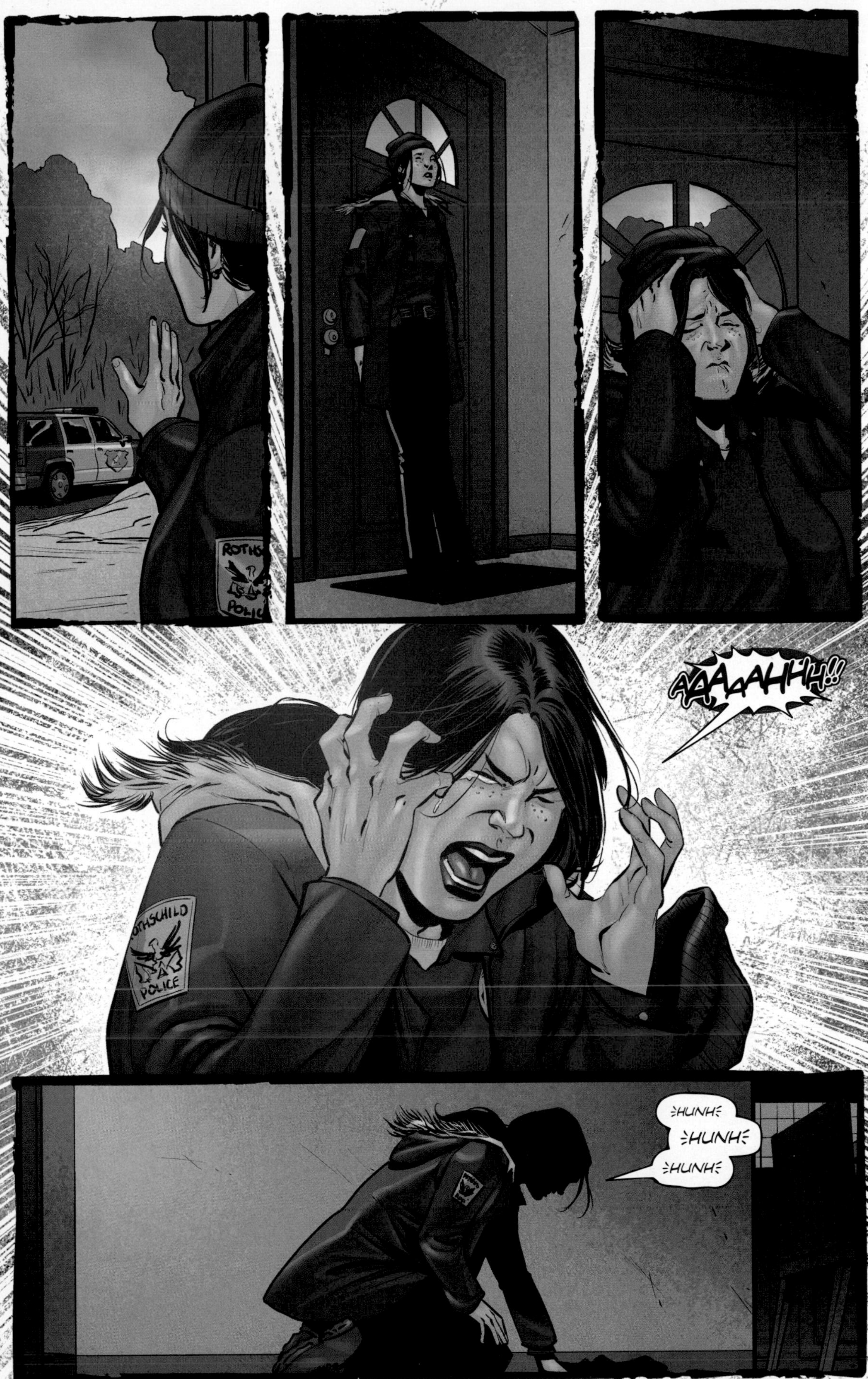
ROTHS
POLICE
ROTHSCHILD
POLICE
AAAAAHHH!!
HUNH
HUNH
HUNH

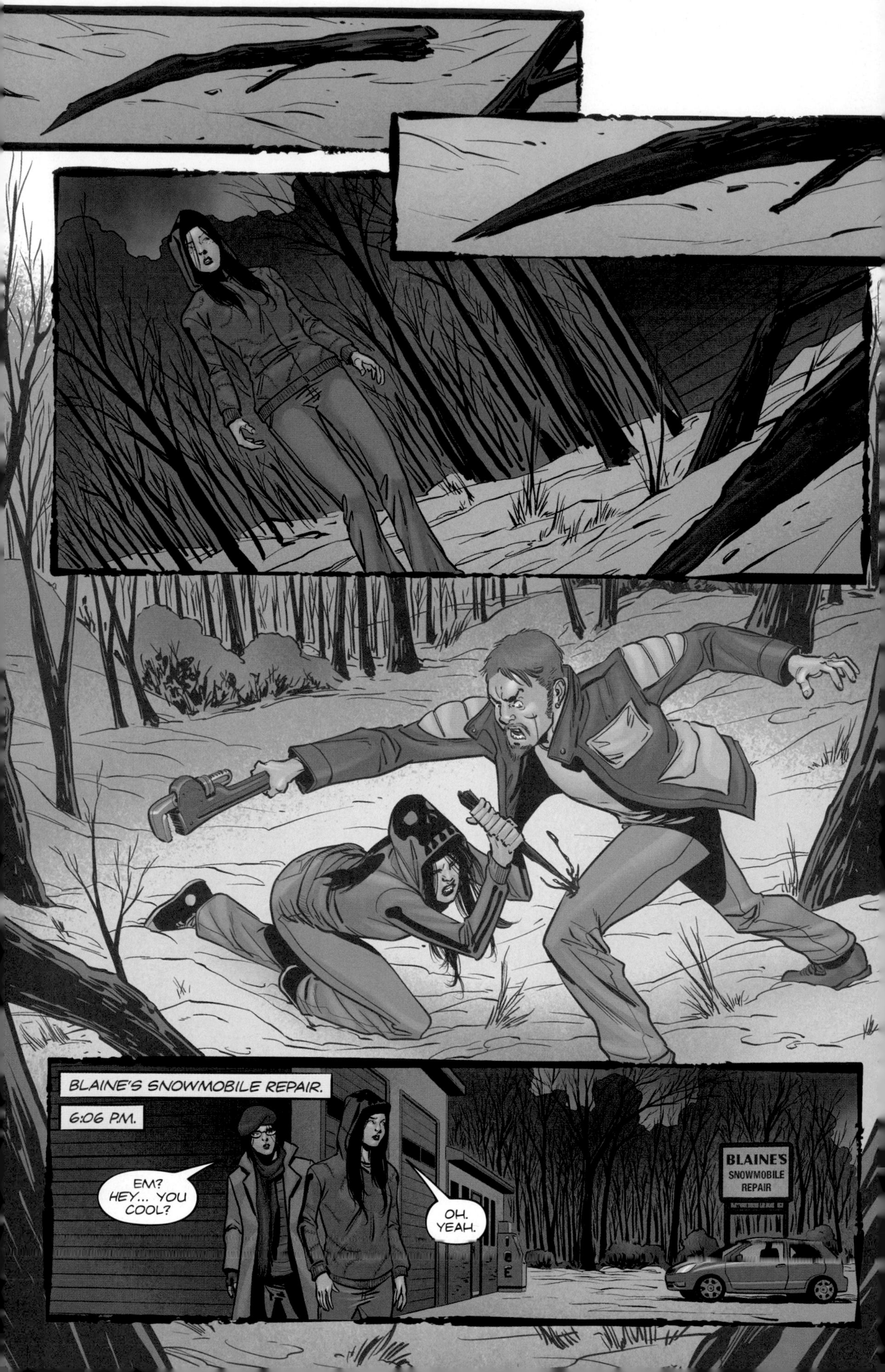
BLAINE'S SNOWMOBILE REPAIR.
6:06 P.M.
EM? HEY... YOU COOL?
OH. YEAH.
BLAINE'S SNOWMOBILE REPAIR

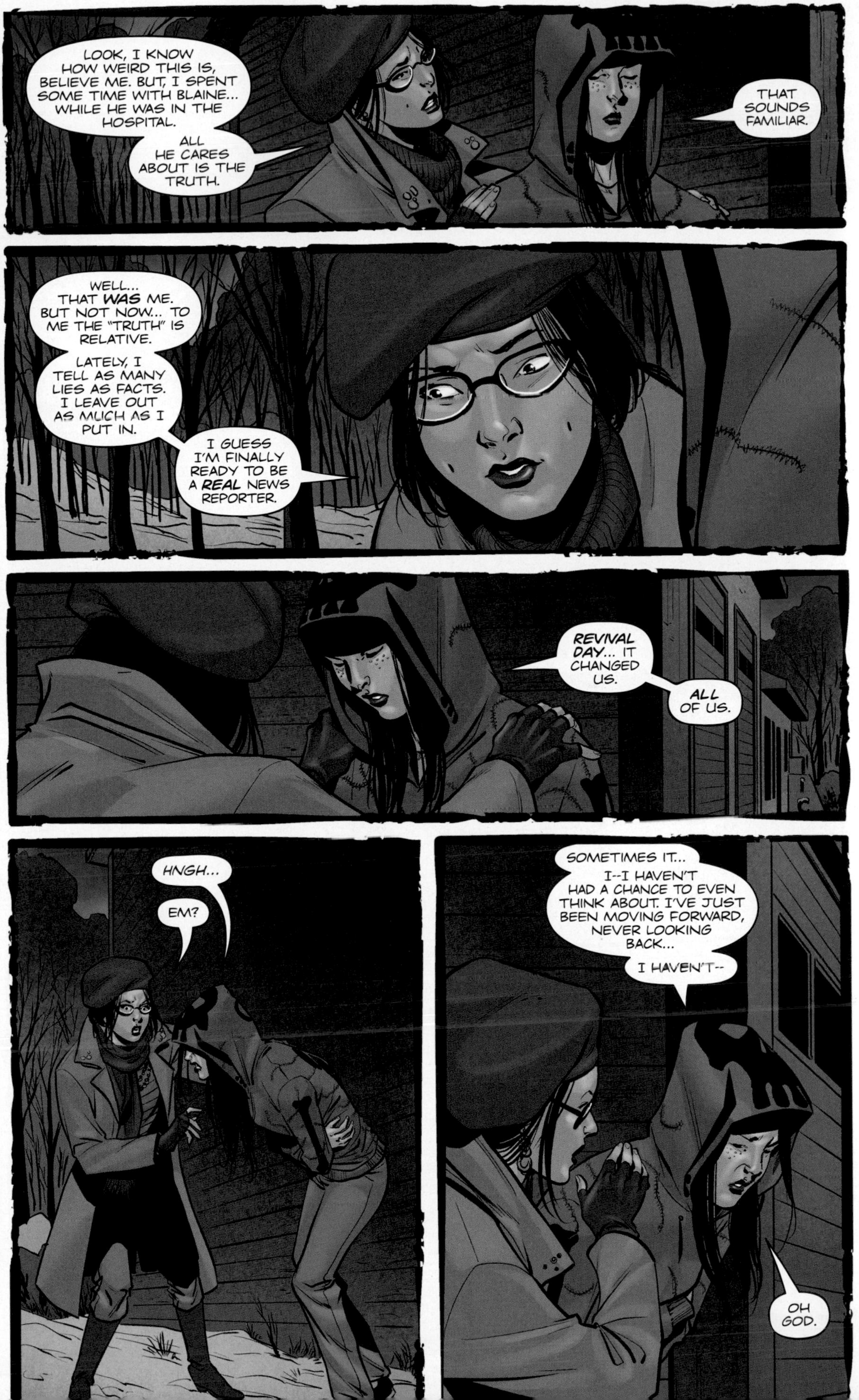
LOOK, I KNOW HOW WEIRD THIS IS, BELIEVE ME. BUT, I SPENT SOME TIME WITH BLAINE... WHILE HE WAS IN THE HOSPITAL.
ALL HE CARES ABOUT IS THE TRUTH.
THAT SOUNDS FAMILIAR.
WELL... THAT **WAS** ME. BUT NOT NOW... TO ME THE "TRUTH" IS RELATIVE.
LATELY, I TELL AS MANY LIES AS FACTS. I LEAVE OUT AS MUCH AS I PUT IN.
I GUESS I'M FINALLY READY TO BE A ***REAL*** NEWS REPORTER.
REVIVAL DAY... IT CHANGED US.
ALL OF US.
HNGH...
EM?
SOMETIMES IT...
I--I HAVEN'T HAD A CHANCE TO EVEN THINK ABOUT. I'VE JUST BEEN MOVING FORWARD, NEVER LOOKING BACK...
I HAVEN'T--
OH GOD.

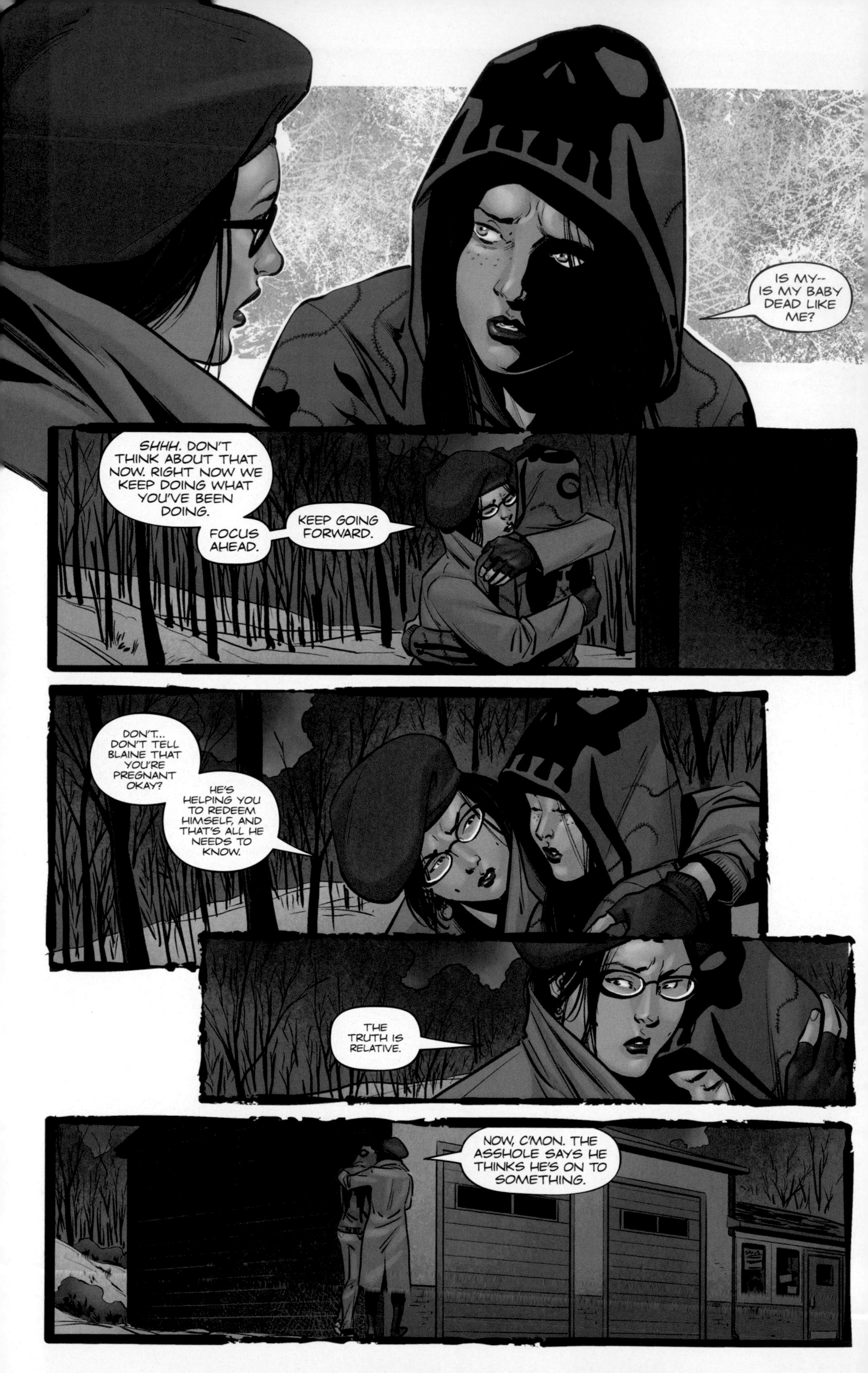
IS MY-- IS MY BABY DEAD LIKE ME?
SHHH. DON'T THINK ABOUT THAT NOW. RIGHT NOW WE KEEP DOING WHAT YOU'VE BEEN DOING.
FOCUS AHEAD.
KEEP GOING FORWARD.
DON'T... DON'T TELL BLAINE THAT YOU'RE PREGNANT OKAY?
HE'S HELPING YOU TO REDEEM HIMSELF, AND THAT'S ALL HE NEEDS TO KNOW.
THE TRUTH IS RELATIVE.
NOW, C'MON. THE ASSHOLE SAYS HE THINKS HE'S ON TO SOMETHING.

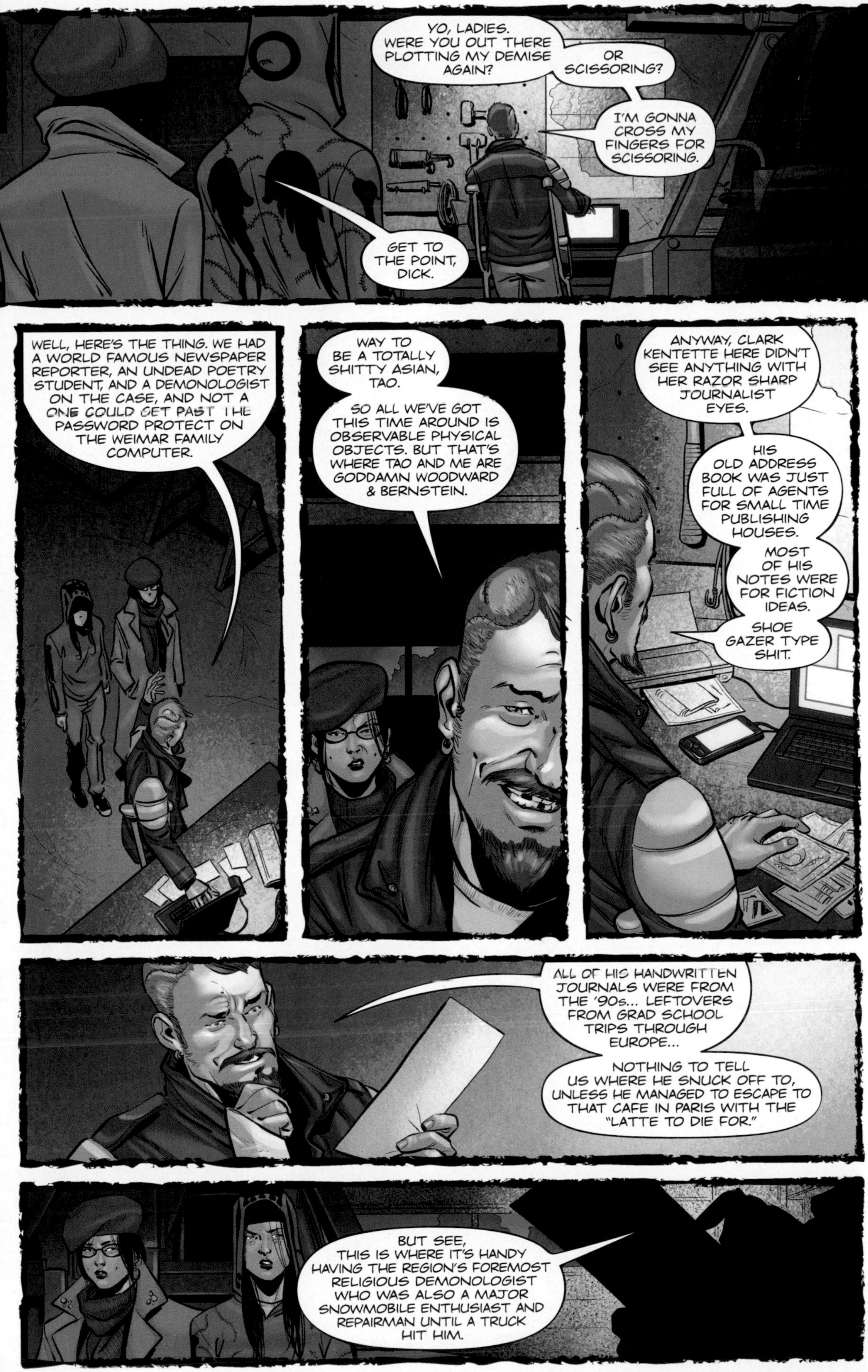
YO, LADIES. WERE YOU OUT THERE PLOTTING MY DEMISE AGAIN?
OR SCISSORING?
I'M GONNA CROSS MY FINGERS FOR SCISSORING.
GET TO THE POINT, DICK.
WELL, HERE'S THE THING. WE HAD A WORLD FAMOUS NEWSPAPER REPORTER, AN UNDEAD POETRY STUDENT, AND A DEMONOLOGIST ON THE CASE, AND NOT A ONE COULD GET PAST THE PASSWORD PROTECT ON THE WEIMAR FAMILY COMPUTER.
WAY TO BE A TOTALLY SHITTY ASIAN, TAO.
SO ALL WE'VE GOT THIS TIME AROUND IS OBSERVABLE PHYSICAL OBJECTS. BUT THAT'S WHERE TAO AND ME ARE GODDAMN WOODWARD & BERNSTEIN.
ANYWAY, CLARK KENTETTE HERE DIDN'T SEE ANYTHING WITH HER RAZOR SHARP JOURNALIST EYES.
HIS OLD ADDRESS BOOK WAS JUST FULL OF AGENTS FOR SMALL TIME PUBLISHING HOUSES.
MOST OF HIS NOTES WERE FOR FICTION IDEAS.
SHOE GAZER TYPE SHIT.
ALL OF HIS HANDWRITTEN JOURNALS WERE FROM THE '90s... LEFTOVERS FROM GRAD SCHOOL TRIPS THROUGH EUROPE...
NOTHING TO TELL US WHERE HE SNUCK OFF TO, UNLESS HE MANAGED TO ESCAPE TO THAT CAFE IN PARIS WITH THE "LATTE TO DIE FOR."
BUT SEE, THIS IS WHERE IT'S HANDY HAVING THE REGION'S FOREMOST RELIGIOUS DEMONOLOGIST WHO WAS ALSO A MAJOR SNOWMOBILE ENTHUSIAST AND REPAIRMAN UNTIL A TRUCK HIT HIM.

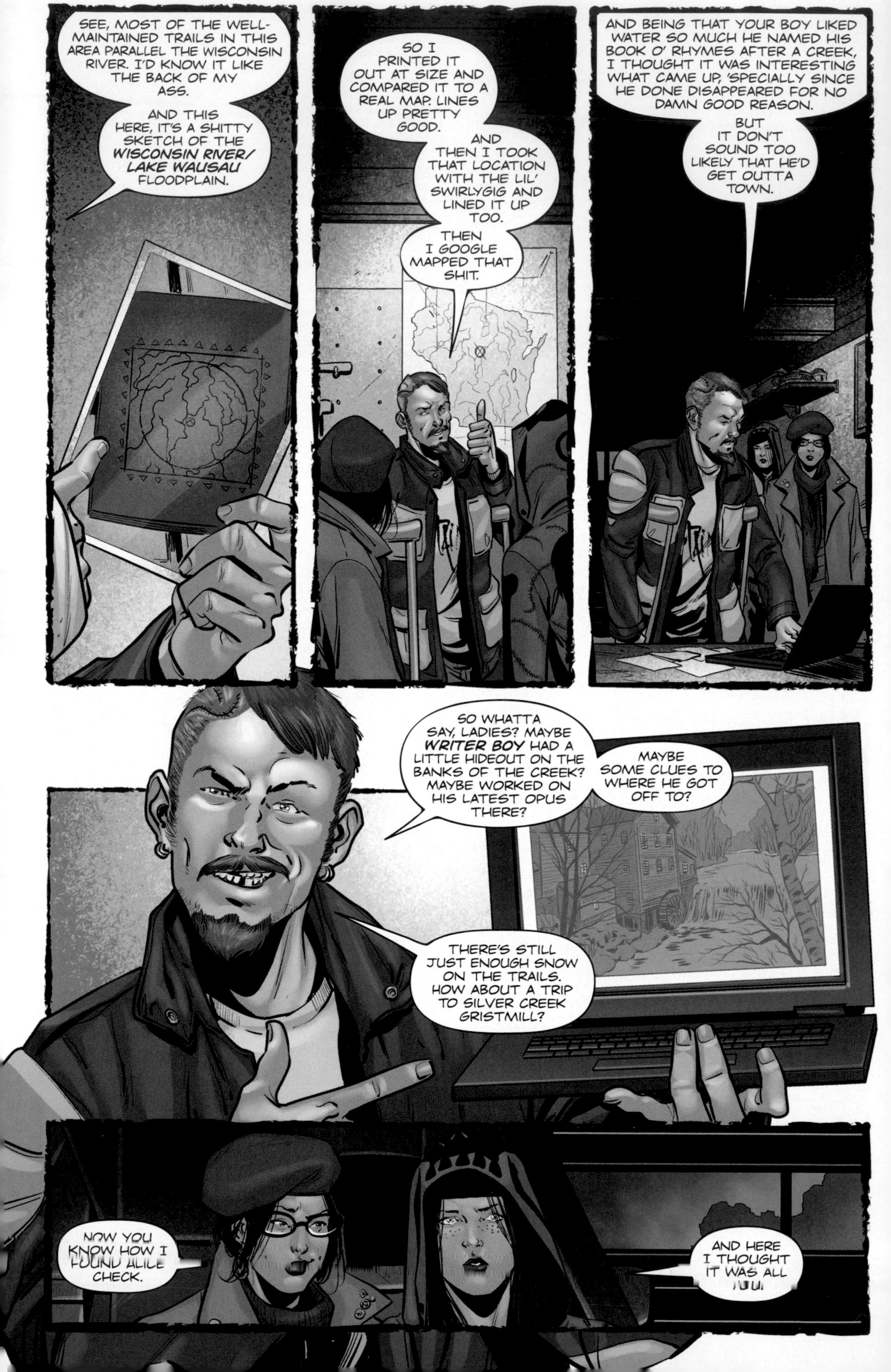
SEE, MOST OF THE WELL-MAINTAINED TRAILS IN THIS AREA PARALLEL THE WISCONSIN RIVER. I'D KNOW IT LIKE THE BACK OF MY ASS.
AND THIS HERE, IT'S A SHITTY SKETCH OF THE **WISCONSIN RIVER/ LAKE WAUSAU** FLOODPLAIN.
SO I PRINTED IT OUT AT SIZE AND COMPARED IT TO A REAL MAP. LINES UP PRETTY GOOD.
AND THEN I TOOK THAT LOCATION WITH THE LIL' SWIRLYGIG AND LINED IT UP TOO.
THEN I GOOGLE MAPPED THAT SHIT.
AND BEING THAT YOUR BOY LIKED WATER SO MUCH HE NAMED HIS BOOK O' RHYMES AFTER A CREEK, I THOUGHT IT WAS INTERESTING WHAT CAME UP, 'SPECIALLY SINCE HE DONE DISAPPEARED FOR NO DAMN GOOD REASON.
BUT IT DON'T SOUND TOO LIKELY THAT HE'D GET OUTTA TOWN.
SO WHATTA SAY, LADIES? MAYBE **WRITER BOY** HAD A LITTLE HIDEOUT ON THE BANKS OF THE CREEK? MAYBE WORKED ON HIS LATEST OPUS THERE?
MAYBE SOME CLUES TO WHERE HE GOT OFF TO?
THERE'S STILL JUST ENOUGH SNOW ON THE TRAILS. HOW ABOUT A TRIP TO SILVER CREEK GRISTMILL?
NOW YOU KNOW HOW I
CHECK.
AND HERE I THOUGHT IT WAS ALL

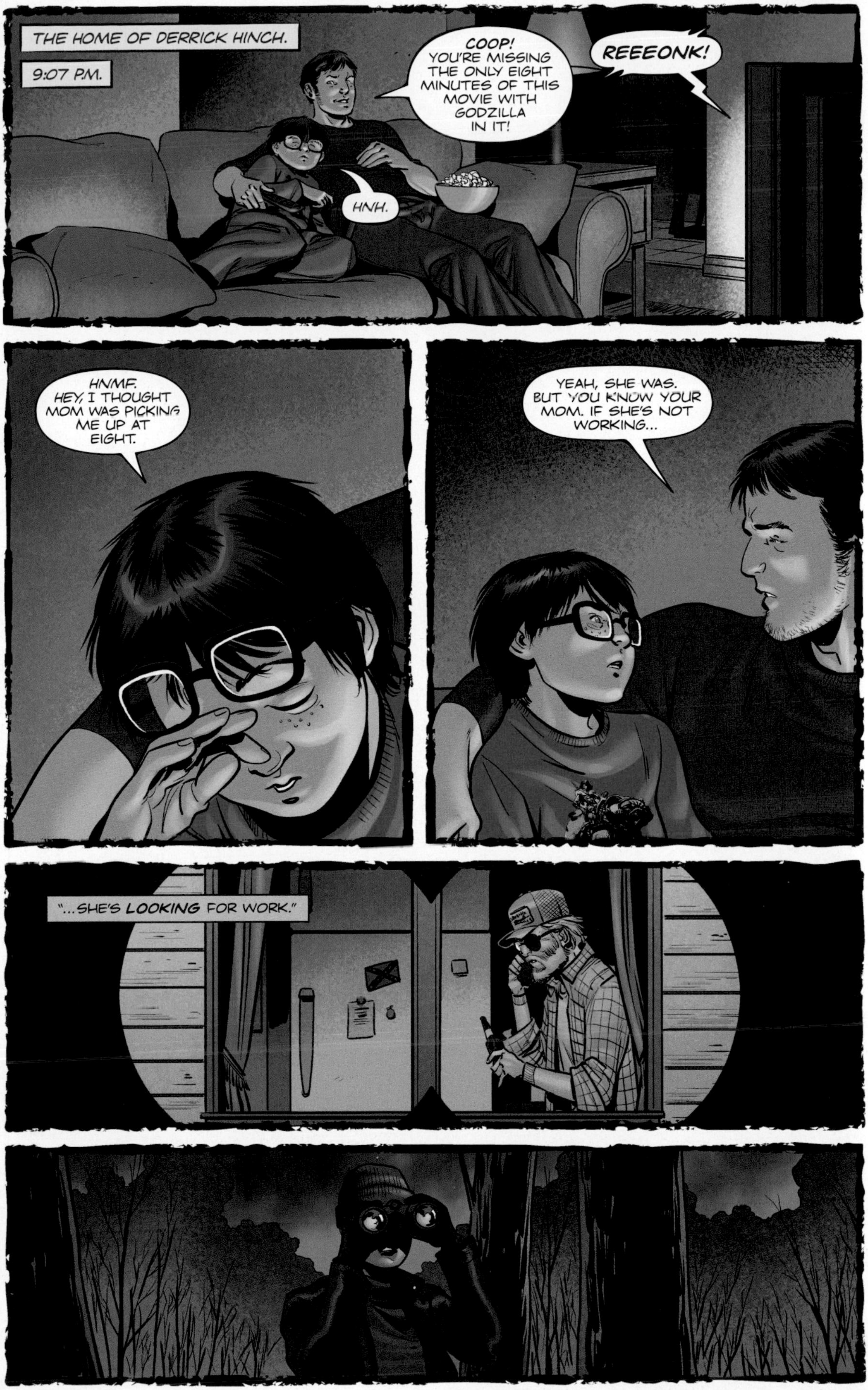
THE HOME OF DERRICK HINCH.
9:07 P.M.
COOP! YOU'RE MISSING THE ONLY EIGHT MINUTES OF THIS MOVIE WITH GODZILLA IN IT!
REEEONK!
HNH.
HNMF. HEY, I THOUGHT MOM WAS PICKING ME UP AT EIGHT.
YEAH, SHE WAS. BUT YOU KNOW YOUR MOM. IF SHE'S NOT WORKING...
"...SHE'S LOOKING FOR WORK."

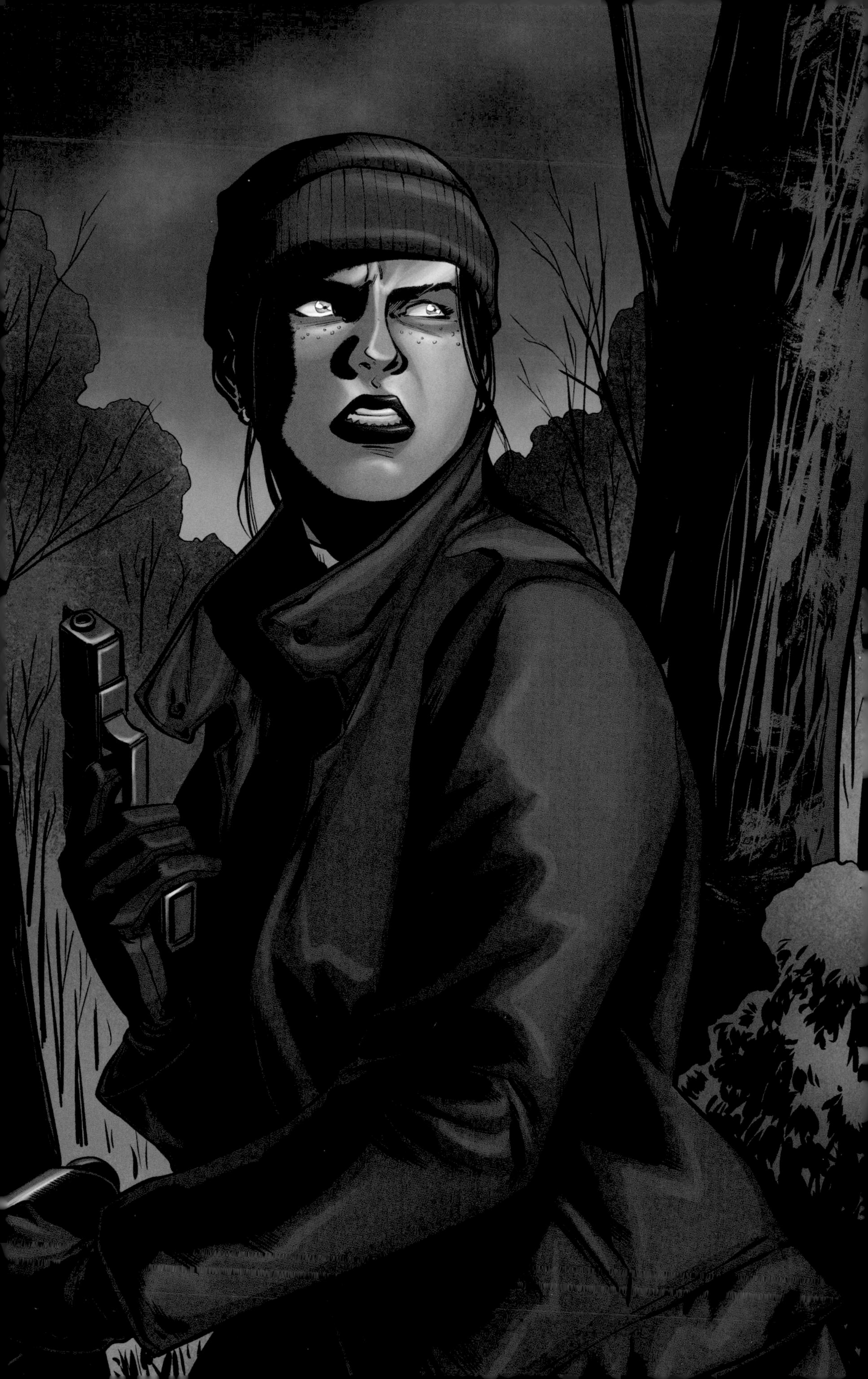

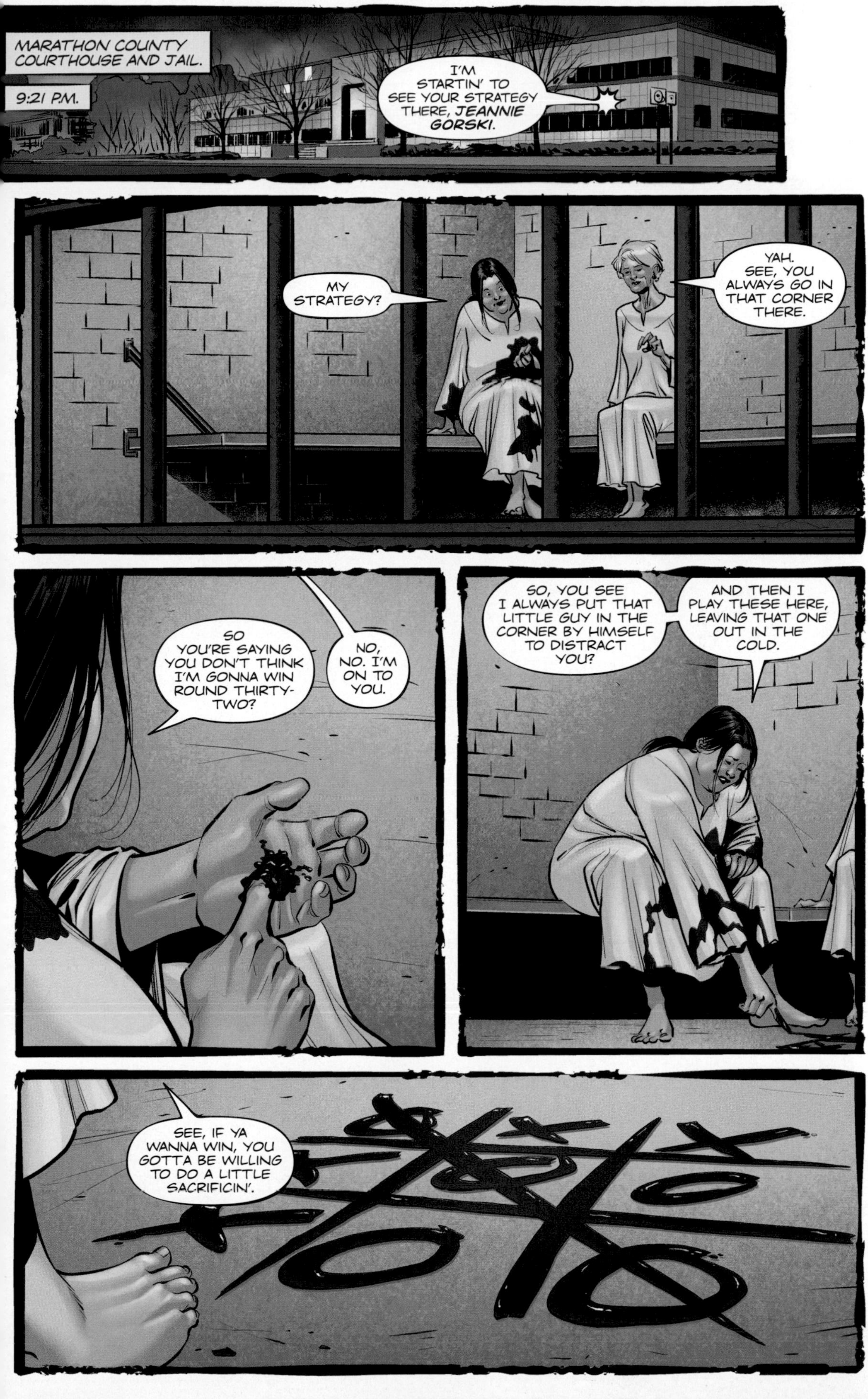
MARATHON COUNTY COURTHOUSE AND JAIL.
9:21 P.M.
I'M STARTIN' TO SEE YOUR STRATEGY THERE, JEANNIE GORSKI.
MY STRATEGY?
YAH. SEE, YOU ALWAYS GO IN THAT CORNER THERE.
SO YOU'RE SAYING YOU DON'T THINK I'M GONNA WIN ROUND THIRTY-TWO?
NO, NO. I'M ON TO YOU.
SO, YOU SEE I ALWAYS PUT THAT LITTLE GUY IN THE CORNER BY HIMSELF TO DISTRACT YOU?
AND THEN I PLAY THESE HERE, LEAVING THAT ONE OUT IN THE COLD.
SEE, IF YA WANNA WIN, YOU GOTTA BE WILLING TO DO A LITTLE SACRIFICIN'.

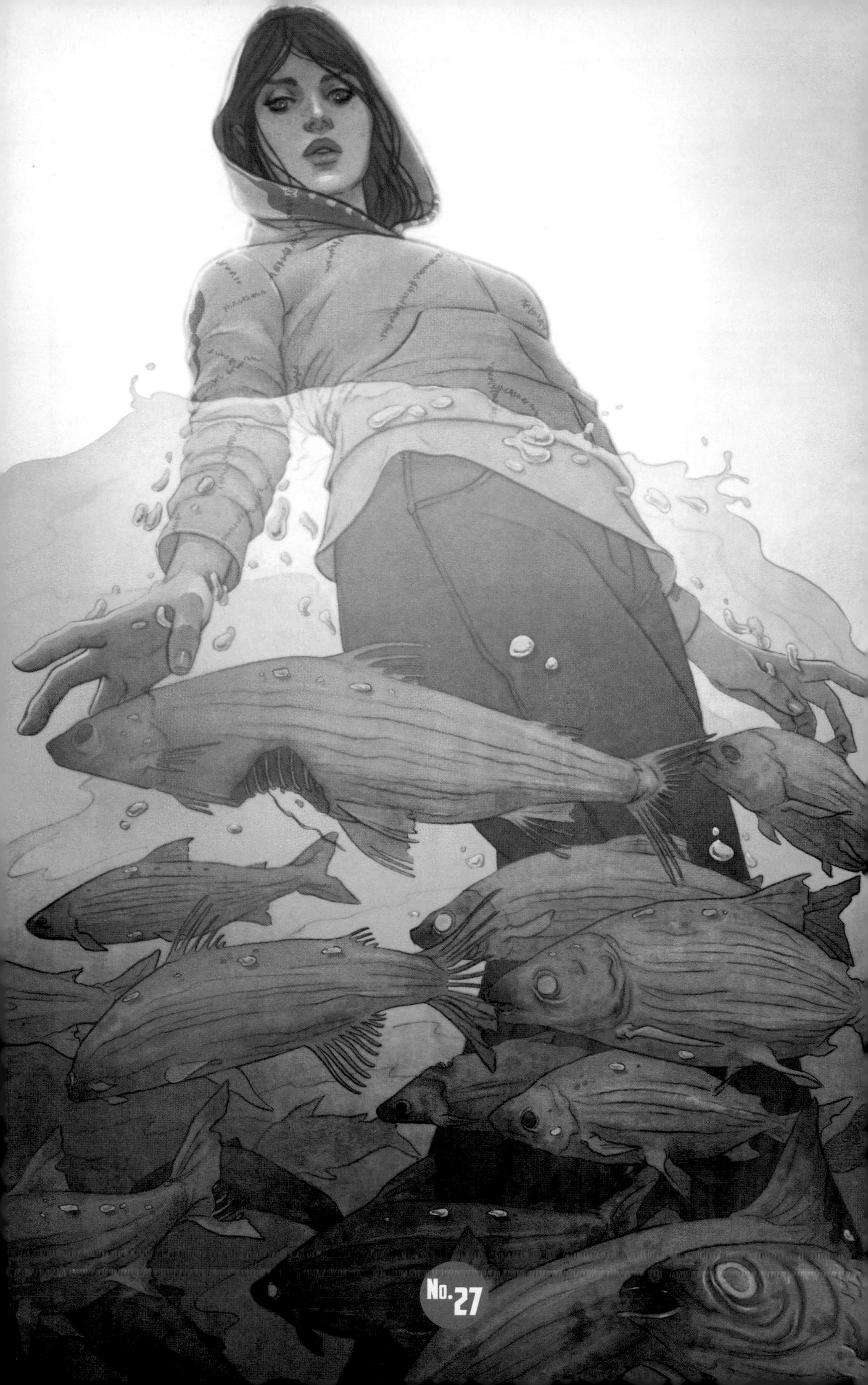
No. 27

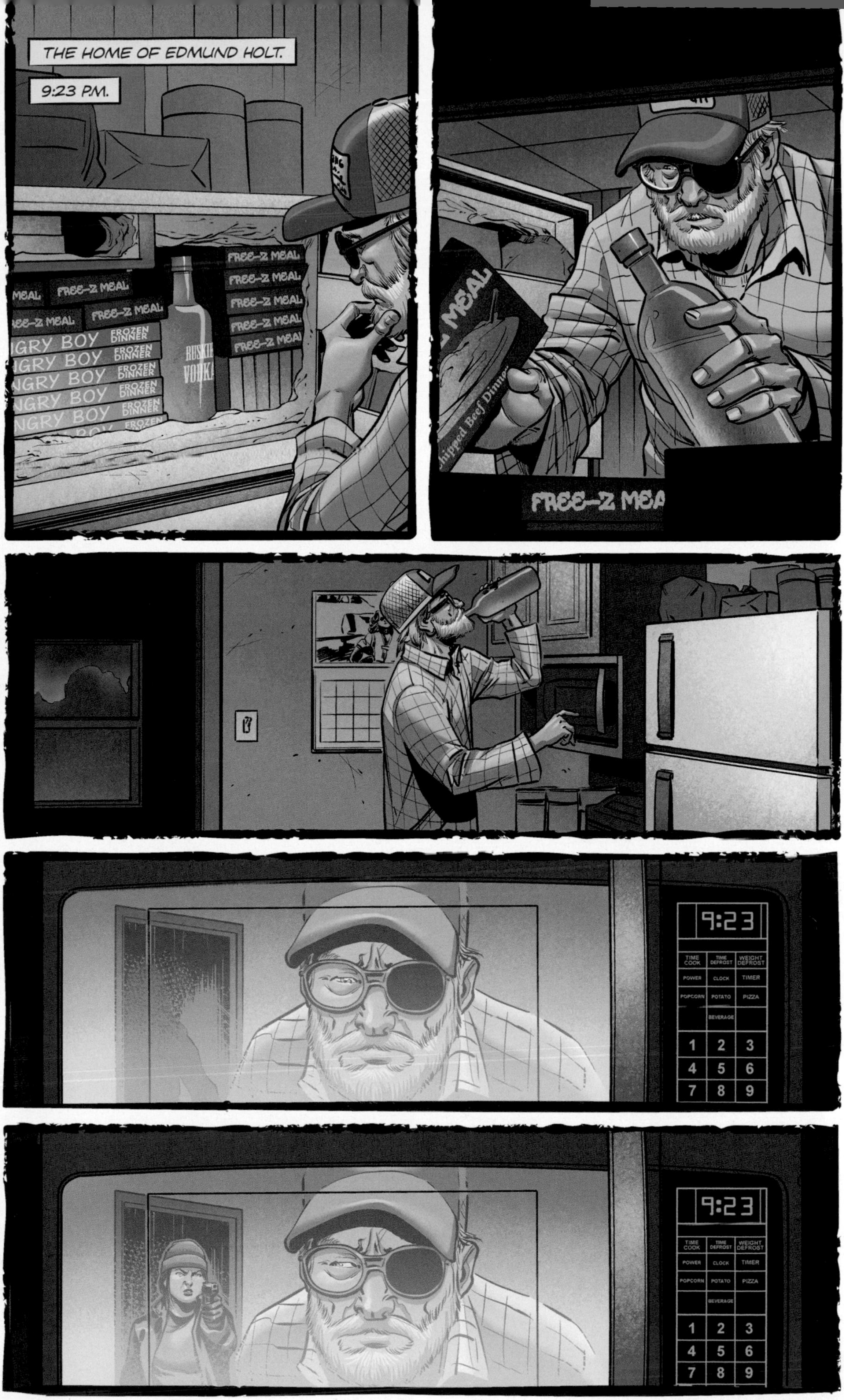

THE HOME OF EDMUND HOLT.
9:23 P.M.
FREE-Z MEAL
FROZEN DINNER
RUSKIE VODKA
FREE-Z MEAL
9:23
TIME COOK
TIME DEFROST
WEIGHT DEFROST
POWER
CLOCK
TIMER
POPCORN
POTATO
PIZZA
BEVERAGE
1 2 3
4 5 6
7 8 9

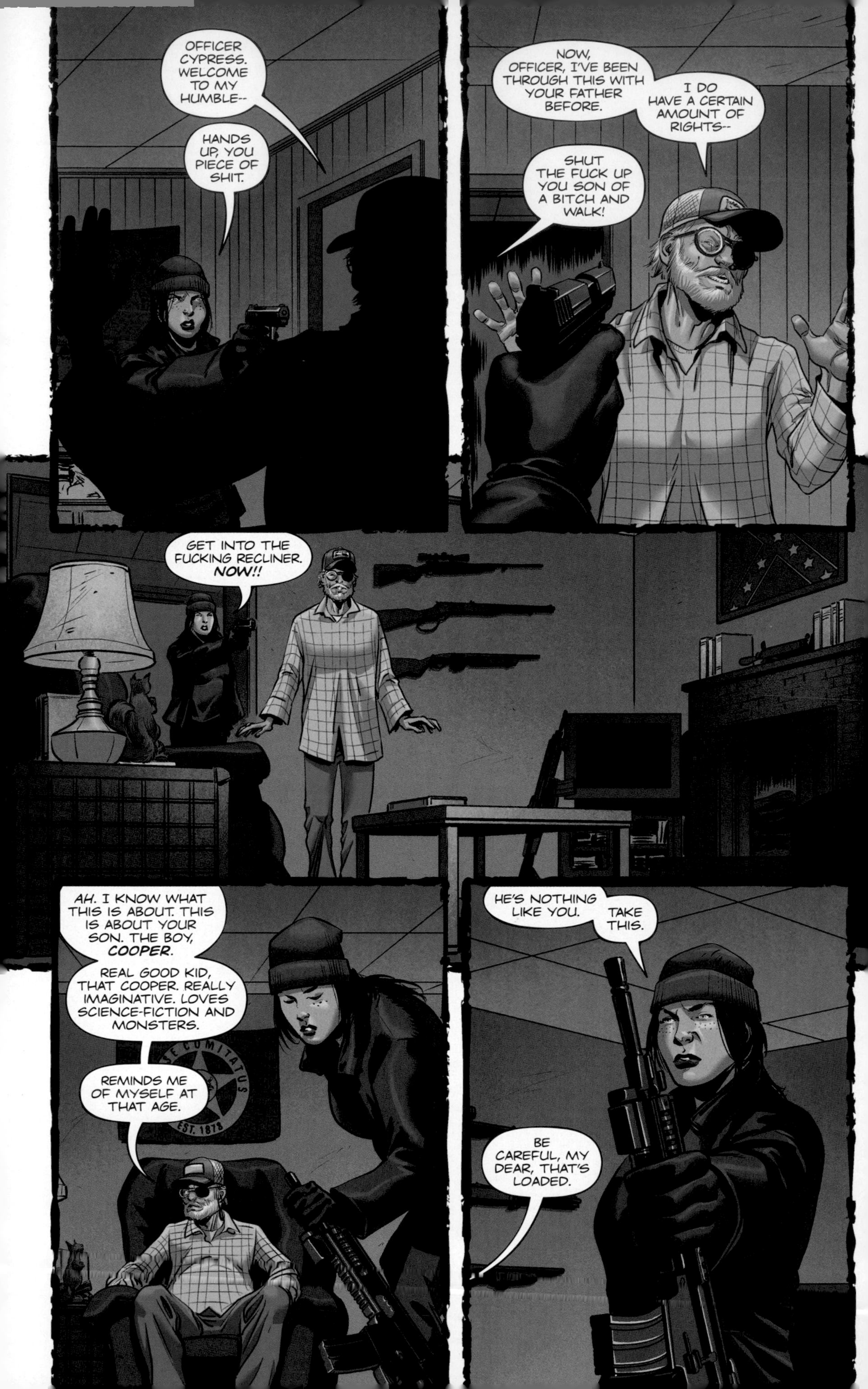
OFFICER CYPRESS. WELCOME TO MY HUMBLE--
HANDS UP, YOU PIECE OF SHIT.
NOW, OFFICER, I'VE BEEN THROUGH THIS WITH YOUR FATHER BEFORE.
I DO HAVE A CERTAIN AMOUNT OF RIGHTS--
SHUT THE FUCK UP YOU SON OF A BITCH AND WALK!
GET INTO THE FUCKING RECLINER. NOW!!
AH. I KNOW WHAT THIS IS ABOUT. THIS IS ABOUT YOUR SON. THE BOY, COOPER.
REAL GOOD KID, THAT COOPER. REALLY IMAGINATIVE. LOVES SCIENCE-FICTION AND MONSTERS.
REMINDS ME OF MYSELF AT THAT AGE.
EST. 1878
HE'S NOTHING LIKE YOU.
TAKE THIS.
BE CAREFUL, MY DEAR, THAT'S LOADED.

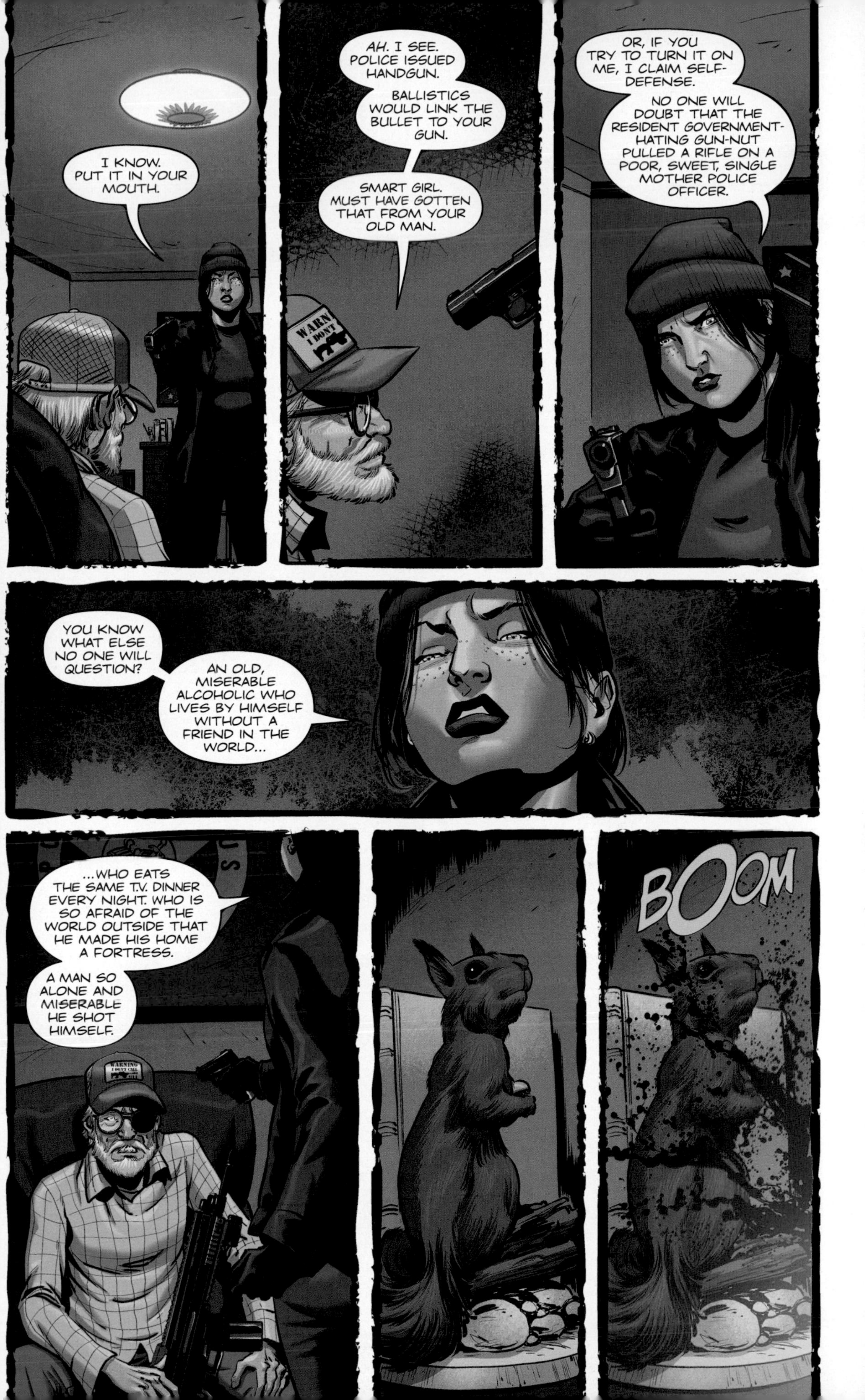
I KNOW. PUT IT IN YOUR MOUTH.
AH. I SEE. POLICE ISSUED HANDGUN.
BALLISTICS WOULD LINK THE BULLET TO YOUR GUN.
SMART GIRL. MUST HAVE GOTTEN THAT FROM YOUR OLD MAN.
OR, IF YOU TRY TO TURN IT ON ME, I CLAIM SELF-DEFENSE.
NO ONE WILL DOUBT THAT THE RESIDENT GOVERNMENT-HATING GUN-NUT PULLED A RIFLE ON A POOR, SWEET, SINGLE MOTHER POLICE OFFICER.
YOU KNOW WHAT ELSE NO ONE WILL QUESTION?
AN OLD, MISERABLE ALCOHOLIC WHO LIVES BY HIMSELF WITHOUT A FRIEND IN THE WORLD...
...WHO EATS THE SAME T.V. DINNER EVERY NIGHT. WHO IS SO AFRAID OF THE WORLD OUTSIDE THAT HE MADE HIS HOME A FORTRESS.
A MAN SO ALONE AND MISERABLE HE SHOT HIMSELF.
BOOM

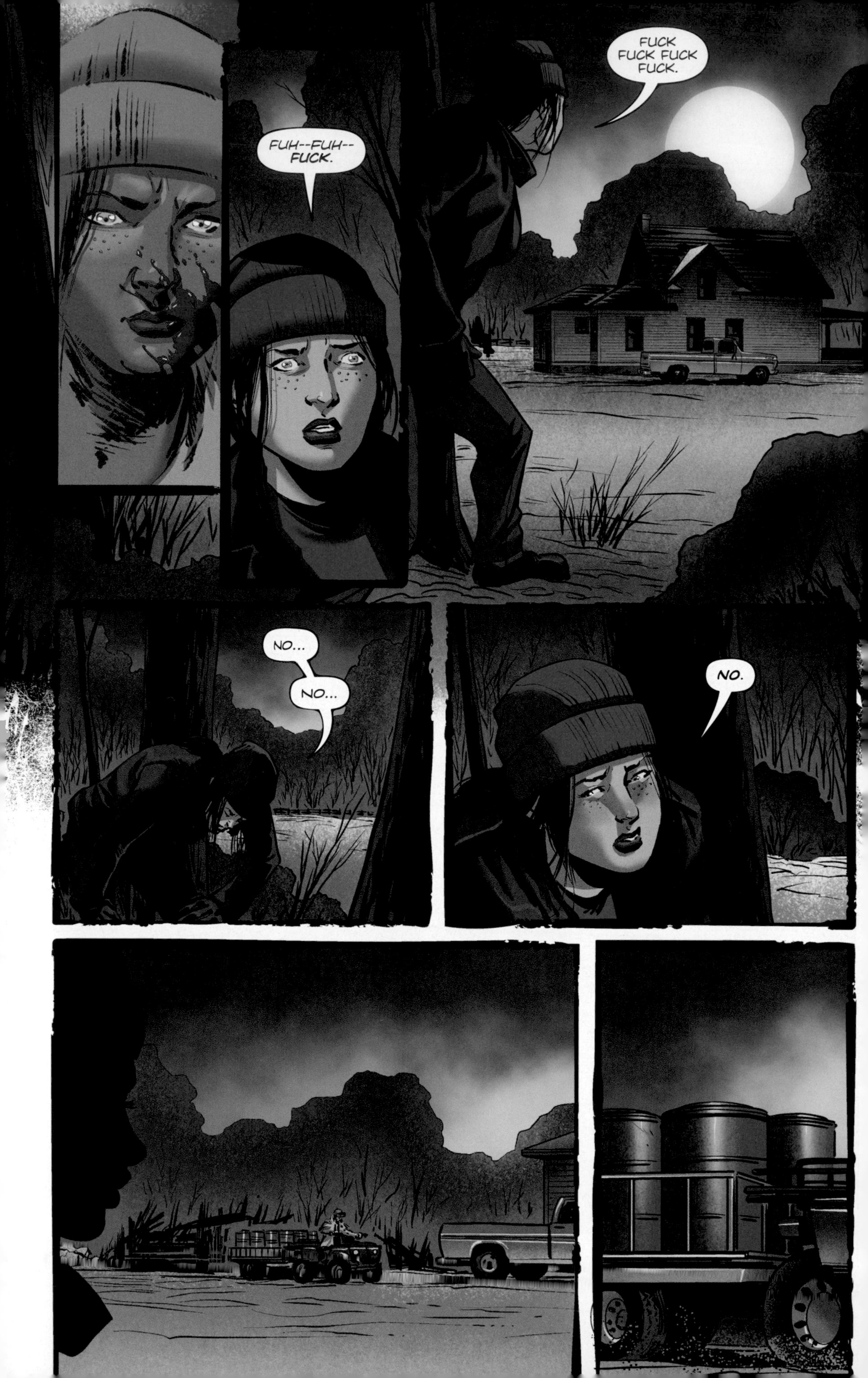
FUH--FUH--
FUCK.
FUCK
FUCK FUCK FUCK
FUCK.
NO...
NO...
NO.

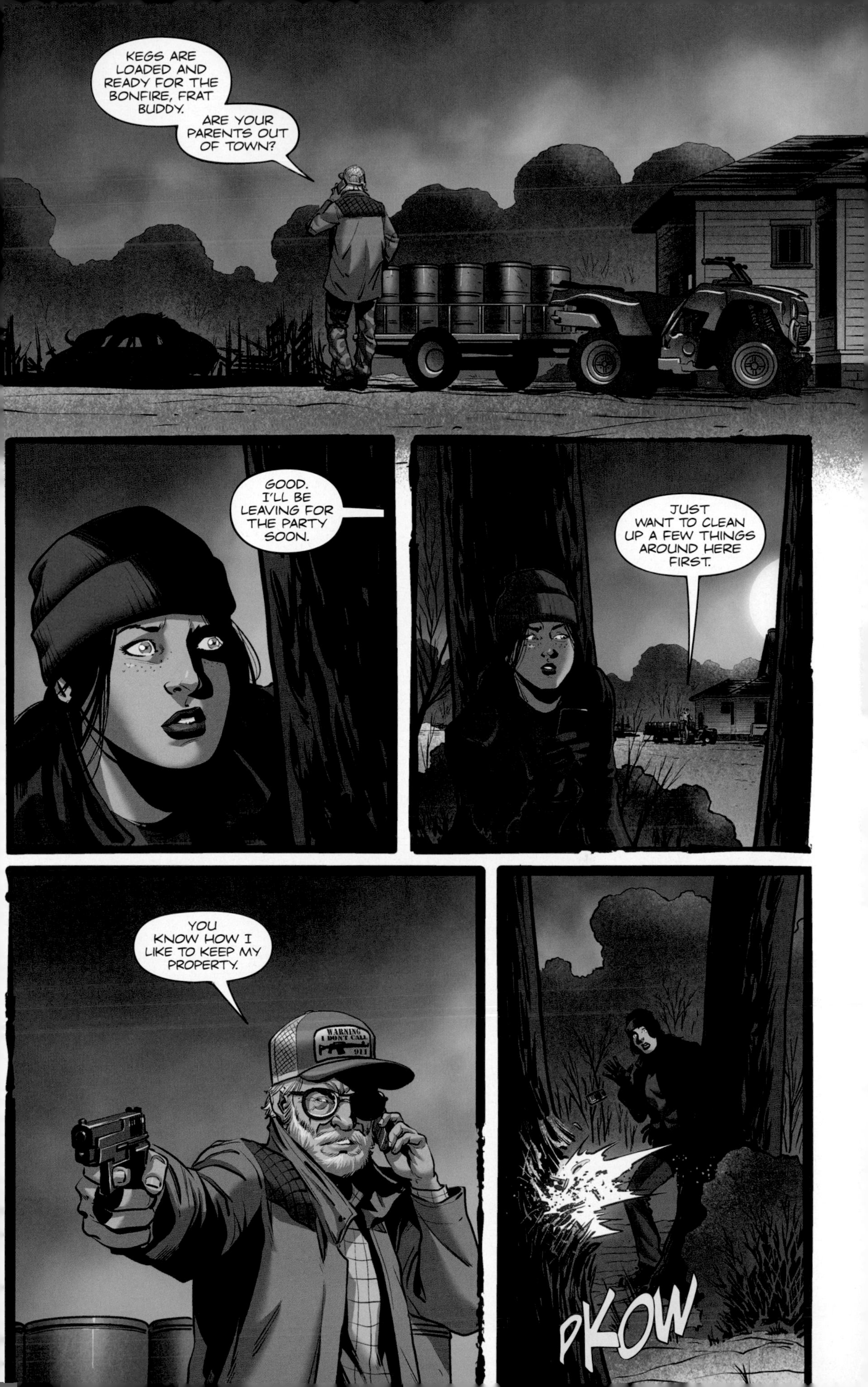

KEGS ARE LOADED AND READY FOR THE BONFIRE, FRAT BUDDY.
ARE YOUR PARENTS OUT OF TOWN?
GOOD. I'LL BE LEAVING FOR THE PARTY SOON.
JUST WANT TO CLEAN UP A FEW THINGS AROUND HERE FIRST.
YOU KNOW HOW I LIKE TO KEEP MY PROPERTY.
WARNING I DON'T CALL 911
PKOW

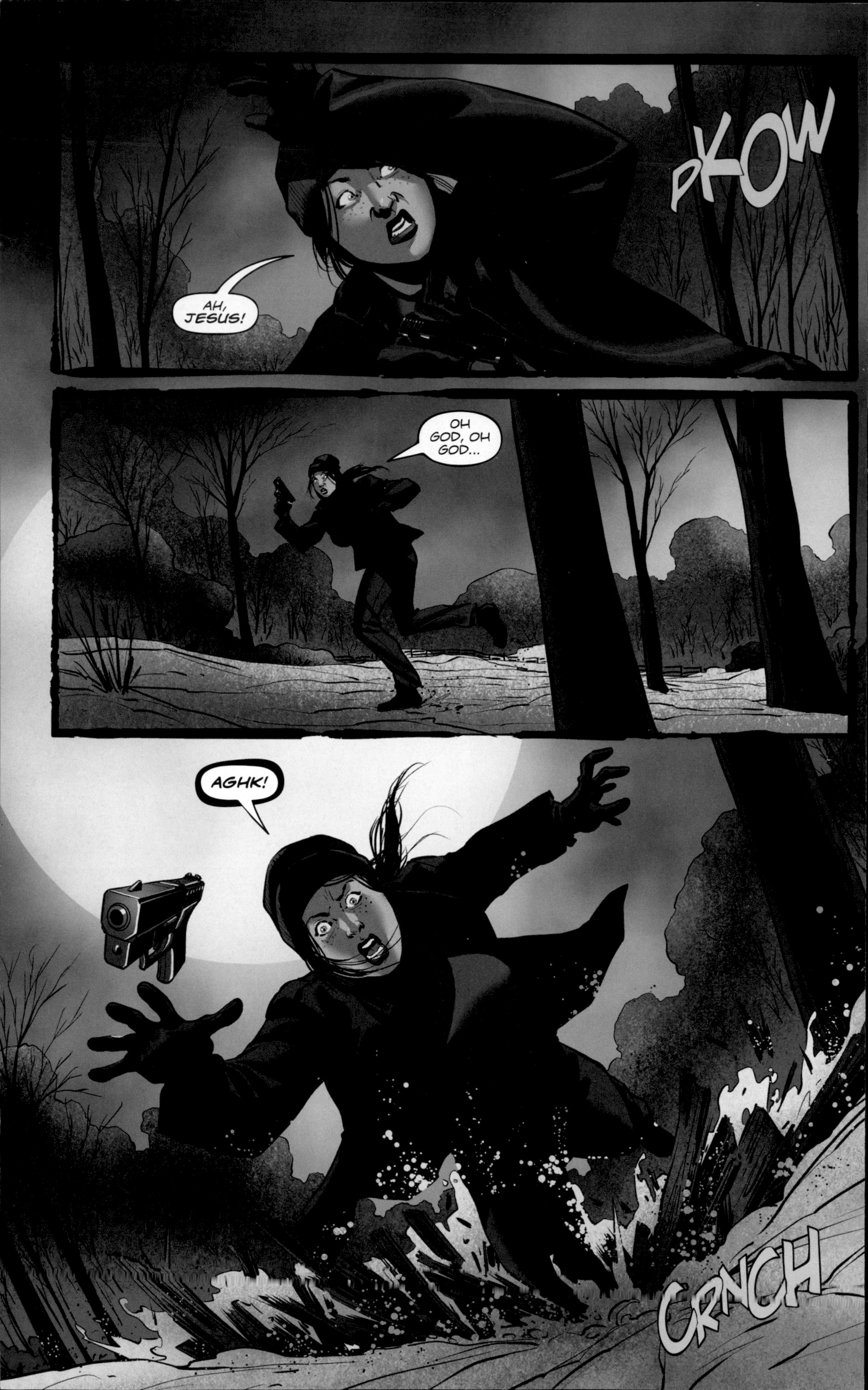
PKOW
AH, JESUS!
OH GOD, OH GOD...
AGHK!
CRNCH

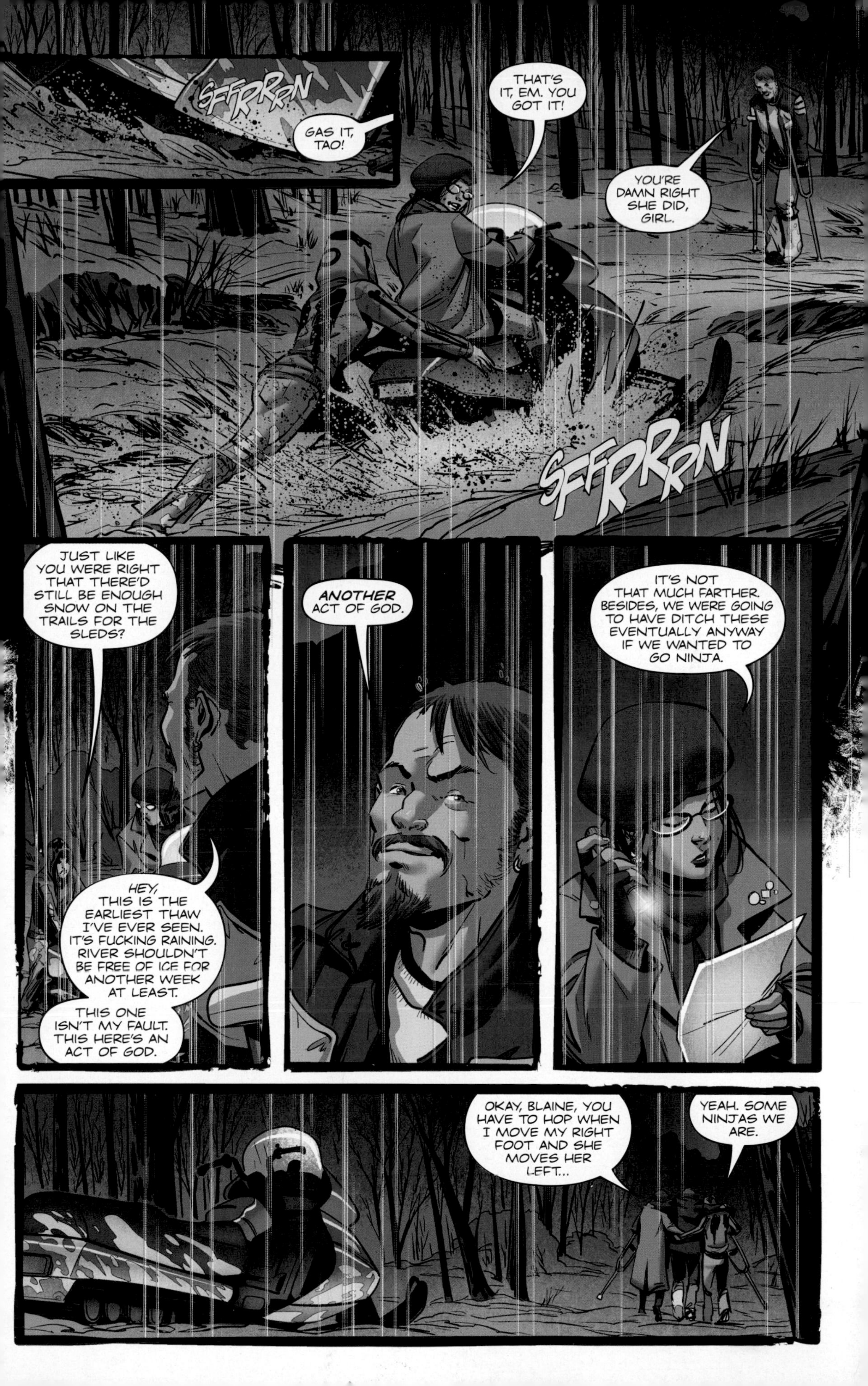
SFFRRRN
GAS IT, TAO!
THAT'S IT, EM. YOU GOT IT!
YOU'RE DAMN RIGHT SHE DID, GIRL.
SFFRRRN
JUST LIKE YOU WERE RIGHT THAT THERE'D STILL BE ENOUGH SNOW ON THE TRAILS FOR THE SLEDS?
HEY, THIS IS THE EARLIEST THAW I'VE EVER SEEN. IT'S FUCKING RAINING. RIVER SHOULDN'T BE FREE OF ICE FOR ANOTHER WEEK AT LEAST.
THIS ONE ISN'T MY FAULT. THIS HERE'S AN ACT OF GOD.
ANOTHER ACT OF GOD.
IT'S NOT THAT MUCH FARTHER. BESIDES, WE WERE GOING TO HAVE DITCH THESE EVENTUALLY ANYWAY IF WE WANTED TO GO NINJA.
OKAY, BLAINE, YOU HAVE TO HOP WHEN I MOVE MY RIGHT FOOT AND SHE MOVES HER LEFT...
YEAH. SOME NINJAS WE ARE.

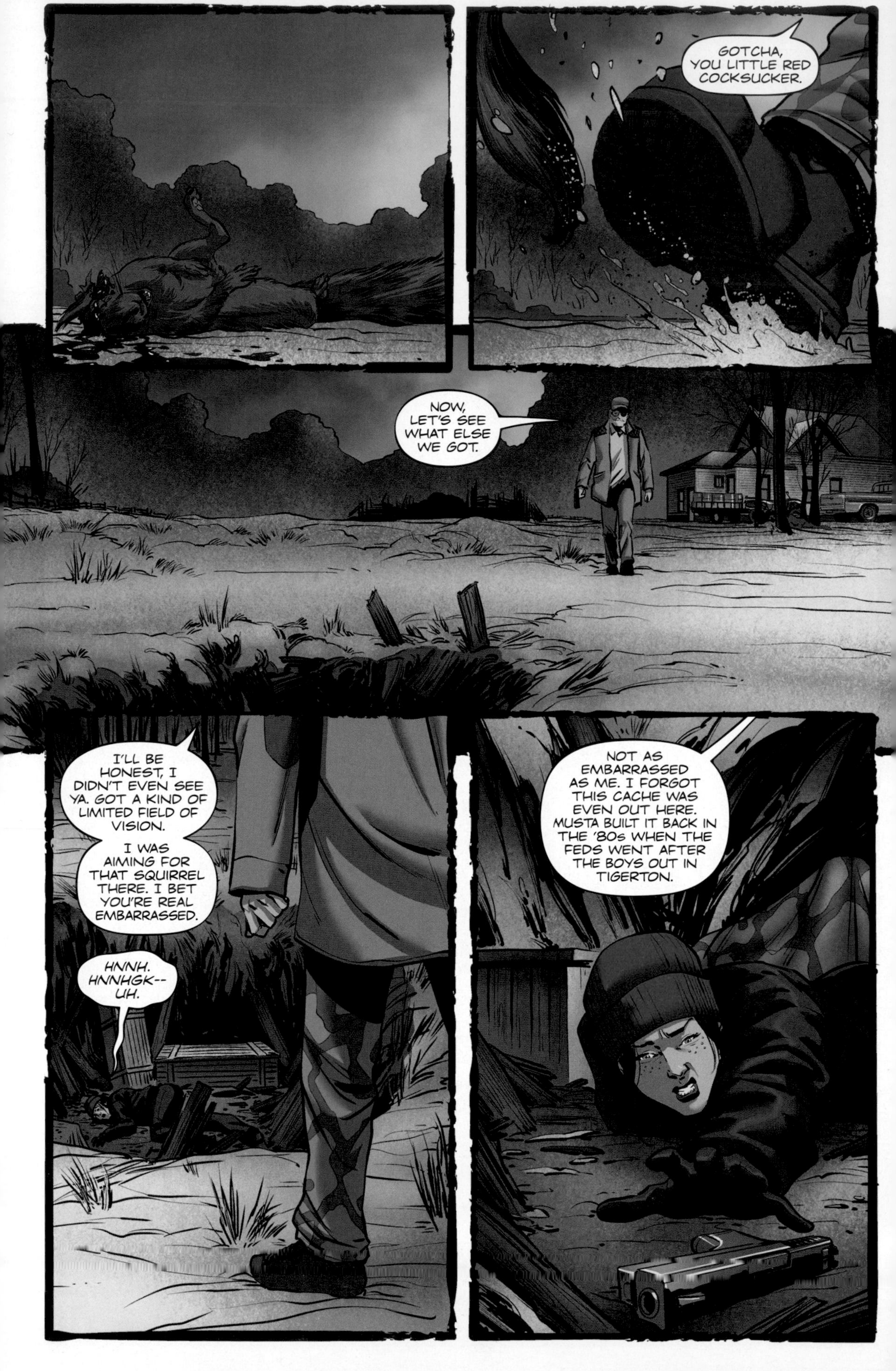
GOTCHA, YOU LITTLE RED COCKSUCKER.
NOW, LET'S SEE WHAT ELSE WE GOT.
I'LL BE HONEST, I DIDN'T EVEN SEE YA. GOT A KIND OF LIMITED FIELD OF VISION.
I WAS AIMING FOR THAT SQUIRREL THERE. I BET YOU'RE REAL EMBARRASSED.
HNNH. HNNHGK-- UH.
NOT AS EMBARRASSED AS ME. I FORGOT THIS CACHE WAS EVEN OUT HERE. MUSTA BUILT IT BACK IN THE '80s WHEN THE FEDS WENT AFTER THE BOYS OUT IN TIGERTON.

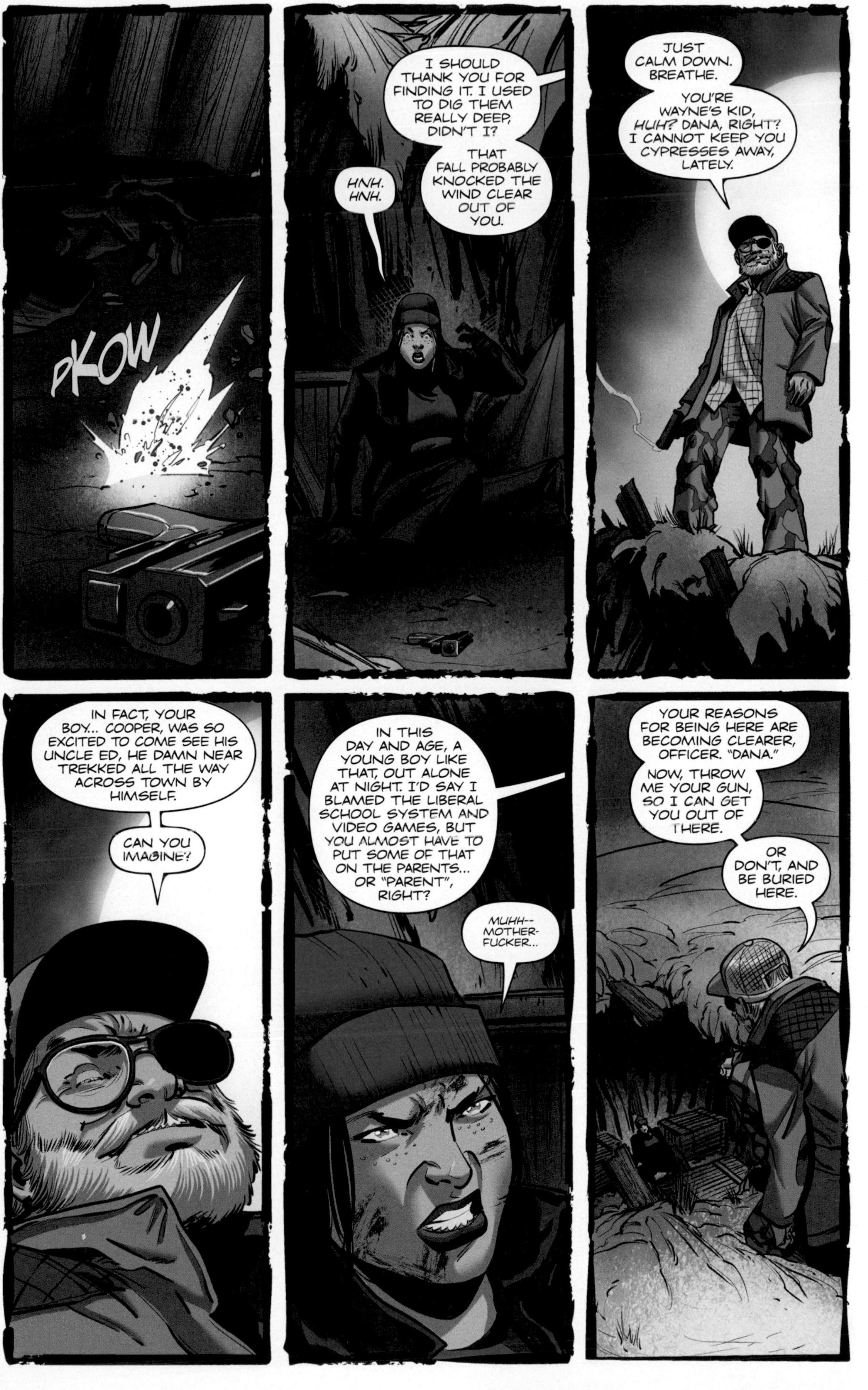
PKOW
I SHOULD THANK YOU FOR FINDING IT. I USED TO DIG THEM REALLY DEEP, DIDN'T I?
THAT FALL PROBABLY KNOCKED THE WIND CLEAR OUT OF YOU.
HNH. HNH.
JUST CALM DOWN. BREATHE.
YOU'RE WAYNE'S KID, HUH? DANA, RIGHT? I CANNOT KEEP YOU CYPRESSES AWAY, LATELY.
IN FACT, YOUR BOY... COOPER, WAS SO EXCITED TO COME SEE HIS UNCLE ED, HE DAMN NEAR TREKKED ALL THE WAY ACROSS TOWN BY HIMSELF.
CAN YOU IMAGINE?
IN THIS DAY AND AGE, A YOUNG BOY LIKE THAT, OUT ALONE AT NIGHT. I'D SAY I BLAMED THE LIBERAL SCHOOL SYSTEM AND VIDEO GAMES, BUT YOU ALMOST HAVE TO PUT SOME OF THAT ON THE PARENTS... OR "PARENT", RIGHT?
MUHH-- MOTHER-FUCKER...
YOUR REASONS FOR BEING HERE ARE BECOMING CLEARER, OFFICER. "DANA."
NOW, THROW ME YOUR GUN, SO I CAN GET YOU OUT OF THERE.
OR DON'T, AND BE BURIED HERE.

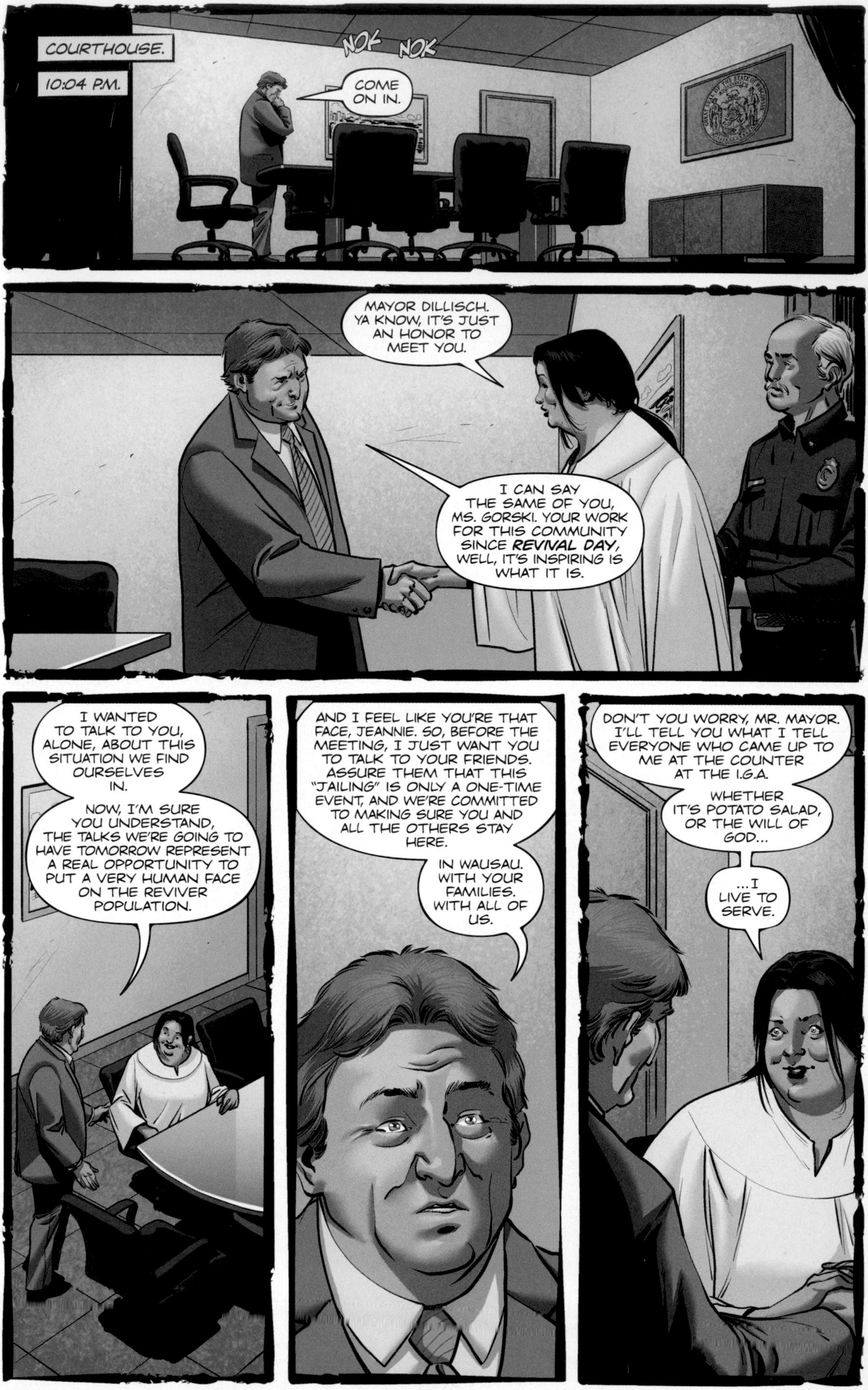
COURTHOUSE.
10:04 P.M.
NOK NOK
COME ON IN.
MAYOR DILLISCH. YA KNOW, IT'S JUST AN HONOR TO MEET YOU.
I CAN SAY THE SAME OF YOU, MS. GORSKI. YOUR WORK FOR THIS COMMUNITY SINCE REVIVAL DAY, WELL, IT'S INSPIRING IS WHAT IT IS.
I WANTED TO TALK TO YOU, ALONE, ABOUT THIS SITUATION WE FIND OURSELVES IN.
NOW, I'M SURE YOU UNDERSTAND, THE TALKS WE'RE GOING TO HAVE TOMORROW REPRESENT A REAL OPPORTUNITY TO PUT A VERY HUMAN FACE ON THE REVIVER POPULATION.
AND I FEEL LIKE YOU'RE THAT FACE, JEANNIE. SO, BEFORE THE MEETING, I JUST WANT YOU TO TALK TO YOUR FRIENDS. ASSURE THEM THAT THIS "JAILING" IS ONLY A ONE-TIME EVENT, AND WE'RE COMMITTED TO MAKING SURE YOU AND ALL THE OTHERS STAY HERE.
IN WAUSAU. WITH YOUR FAMILIES. WITH ALL OF US.
DON'T YOU WORRY, MR. MAYOR. I'LL TELL YOU WHAT I TELL EVERYONE WHO CAME UP TO ME AT THE COUNTER AT THE I.G.A.
WHETHER IT'S POTATO SALAD, OR THE WILL OF GOD...
...I LIVE TO SERVE.

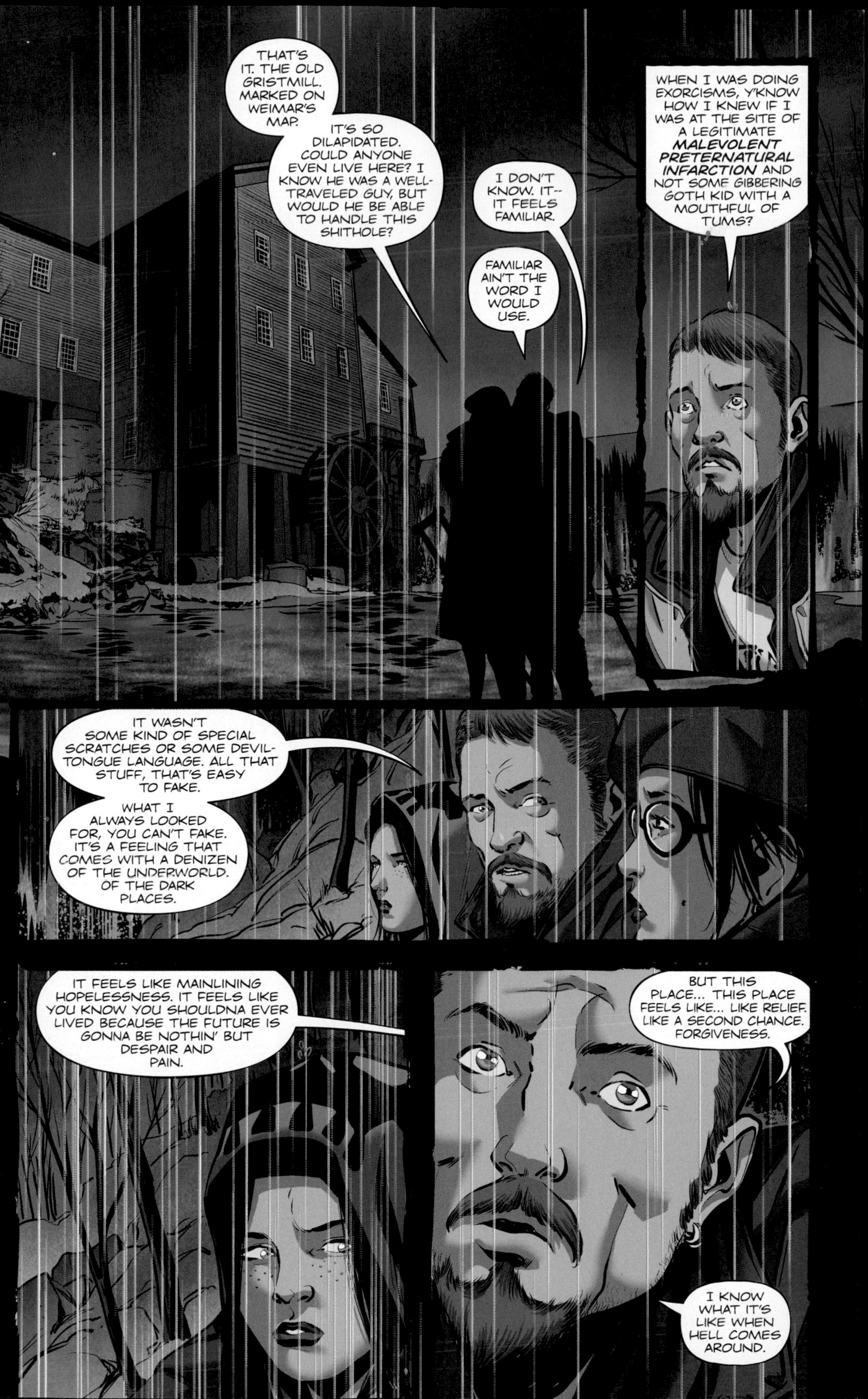
THAT'S IT. THE OLD GRISTMILL. MARKED ON WEIMAR'S MAP.
IT'S SO DILAPIDATED. COULD ANYONE EVEN LIVE HERE? I KNOW HE WAS A WELL-TRAVELED GUY, BUT WOULD HE BE ABLE TO HANDLE THIS SHITHOLE?
I DON'T KNOW. IT-- IT FEELS FAMILIAR.
FAMILIAR AIN'T THE WORD I WOULD USE.
WHEN I WAS DOING EXORCISMS, Y'KNOW HOW I KNEW IF I WAS AT THE SITE OF A LEGITIMATE ***MALEVOLENT PRETERNATURAL INFARCTION*** AND NOT SOME GIBBERING GOTH KID WITH A MOUTHFUL OF TUMS?
IT WASN'T SOME KIND OF SPECIAL SCRATCHES OR SOME DEVIL-TONGUE LANGUAGE. ALL THAT STUFF, THAT'S EASY TO FAKE.
WHAT I ALWAYS LOOKED FOR, YOU CAN'T FAKE. IT'S A FEELING THAT COMES WITH A DENIZEN OF THE UNDERWORLD. OF THE DARK PLACES.
IT FEELS LIKE MAINLINING HOPELESSNESS. IT FEELS LIKE YOU KNOW YOU SHOULDNA EVER LIVED BECAUSE THE FUTURE IS GONNA BE NOTHIN' BUT DESPAIR AND PAIN.
BUT THIS PLACE... THIS PLACE FEELS LIKE... LIKE RELIEF. LIKE A SECOND CHANCE. FORGIVENESS.
I KNOW WHAT IT'S LIKE WHEN HELL COMES AROUND.

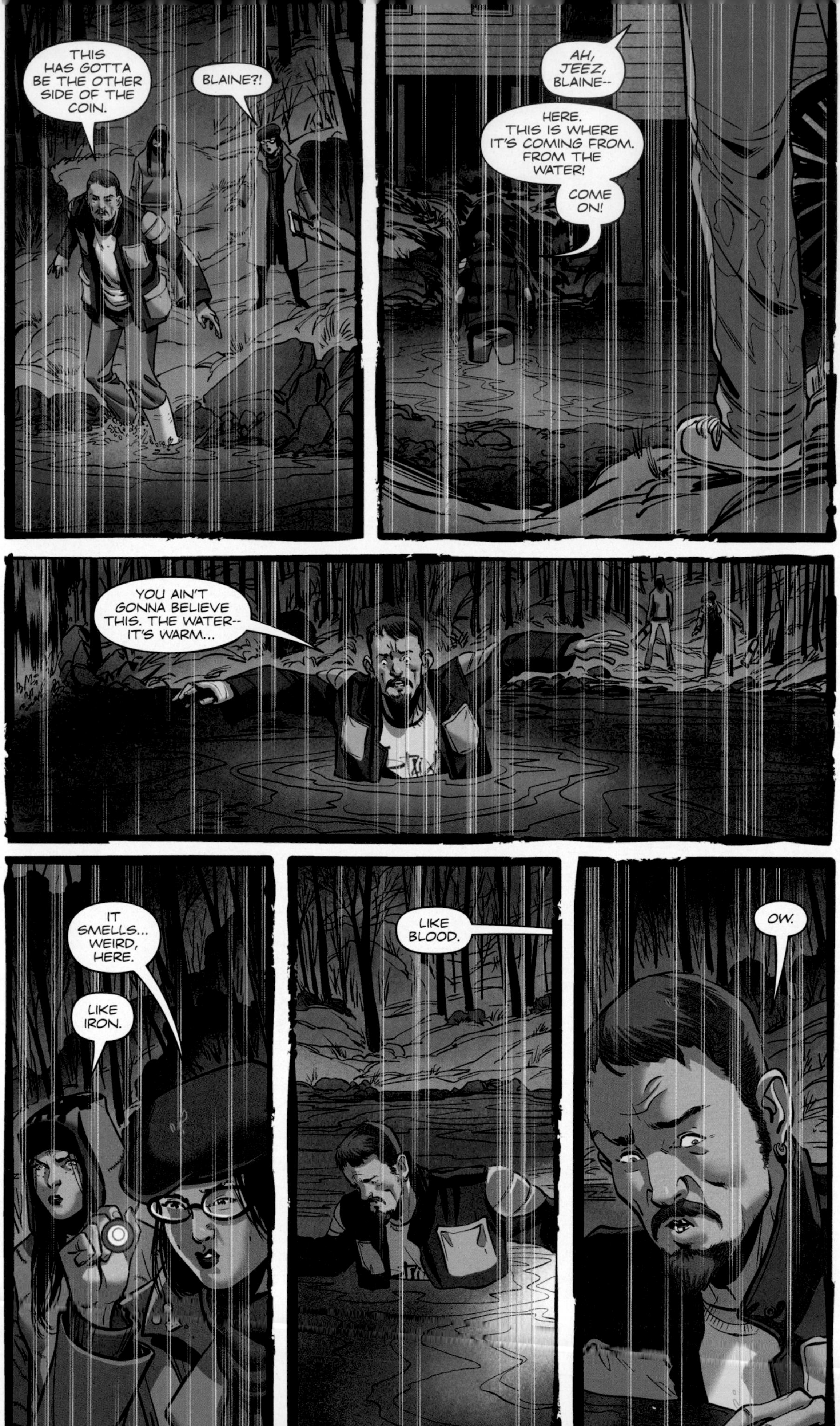
THIS HAS GOTTA BE THE OTHER SIDE OF THE COIN.
BLAINE?!
AH, JEEZ, BLAINE--
HERE. THIS IS WHERE IT'S COMING FROM. FROM THE WATER!
COME ON!
YOU AIN'T GONNA BELIEVE THIS. THE WATER-- IT'S WARM...
IT SMELLS... WEIRD, HERE.
LIKE IRON.
LIKE BLOOD.
OW.

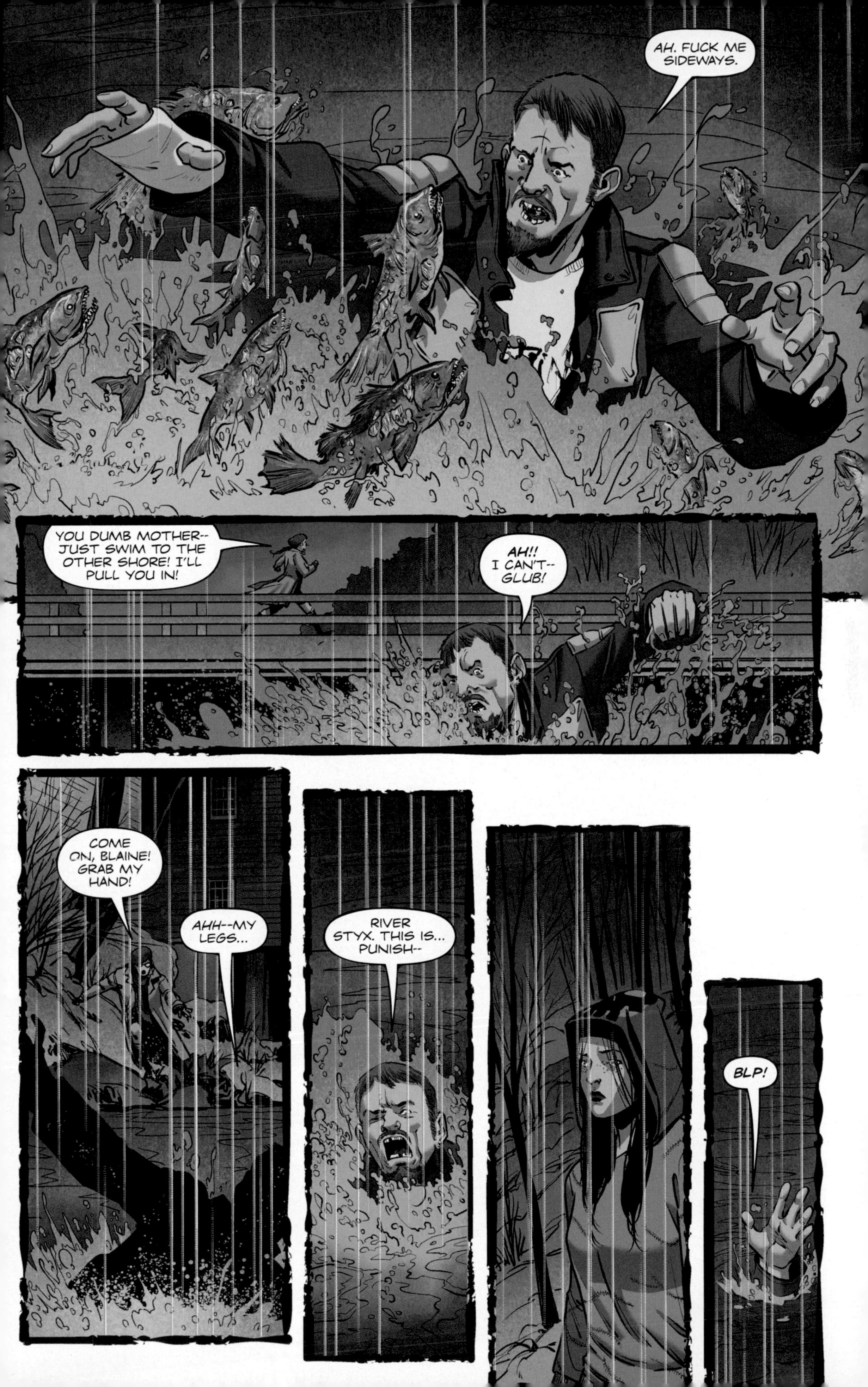

AH. FUCK ME SIDEWAYS.
YOU DUMB MOTHER-- JUST SWIM TO THE OTHER SHORE! I'LL PULL YOU IN!
AH!! I CAN'T-- GLUB!
COME ON, BLAINE! GRAB MY HAND!
AHH--MY LEGS...
RIVER STYX. THIS IS... PUNISH--
BLP!

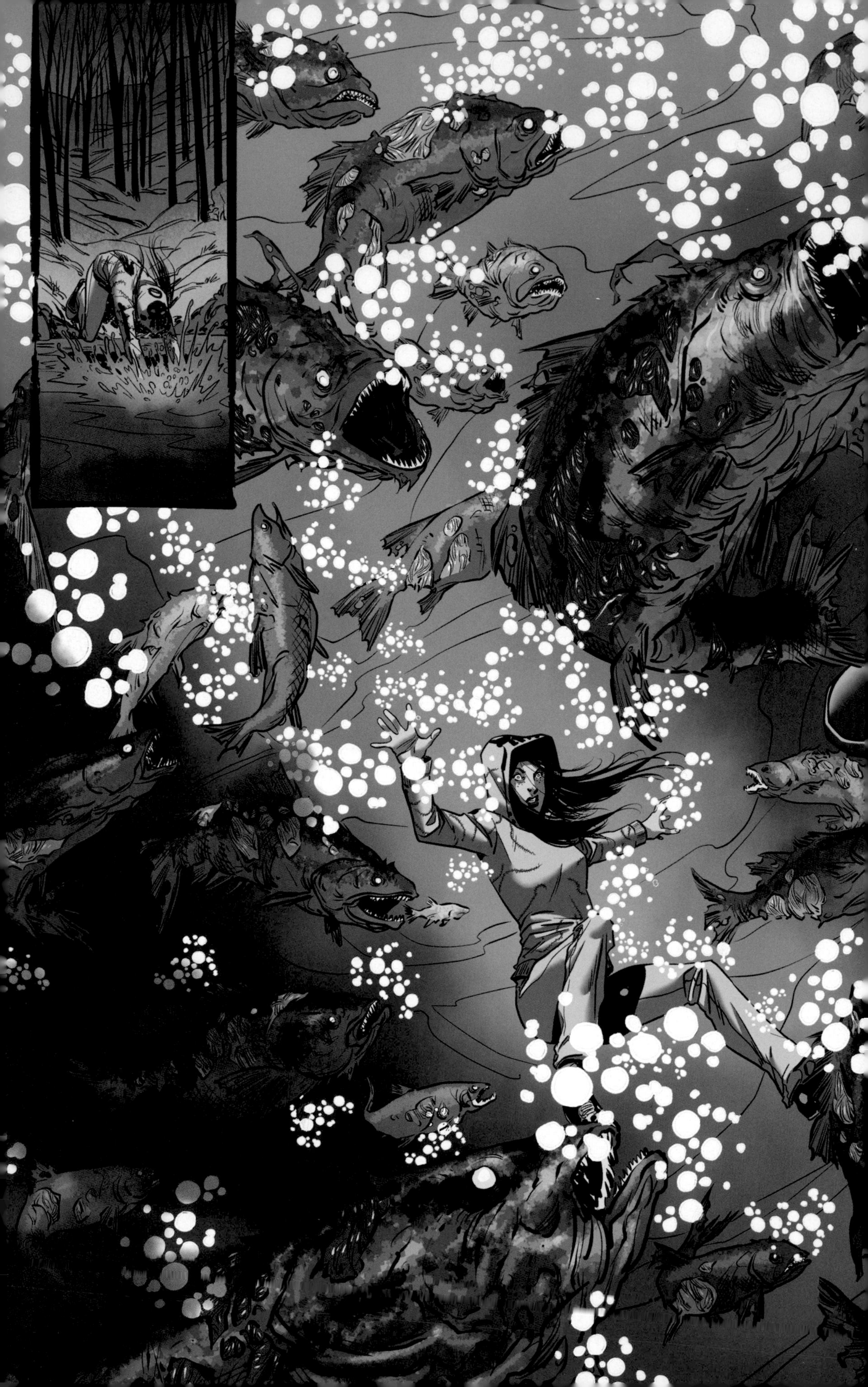

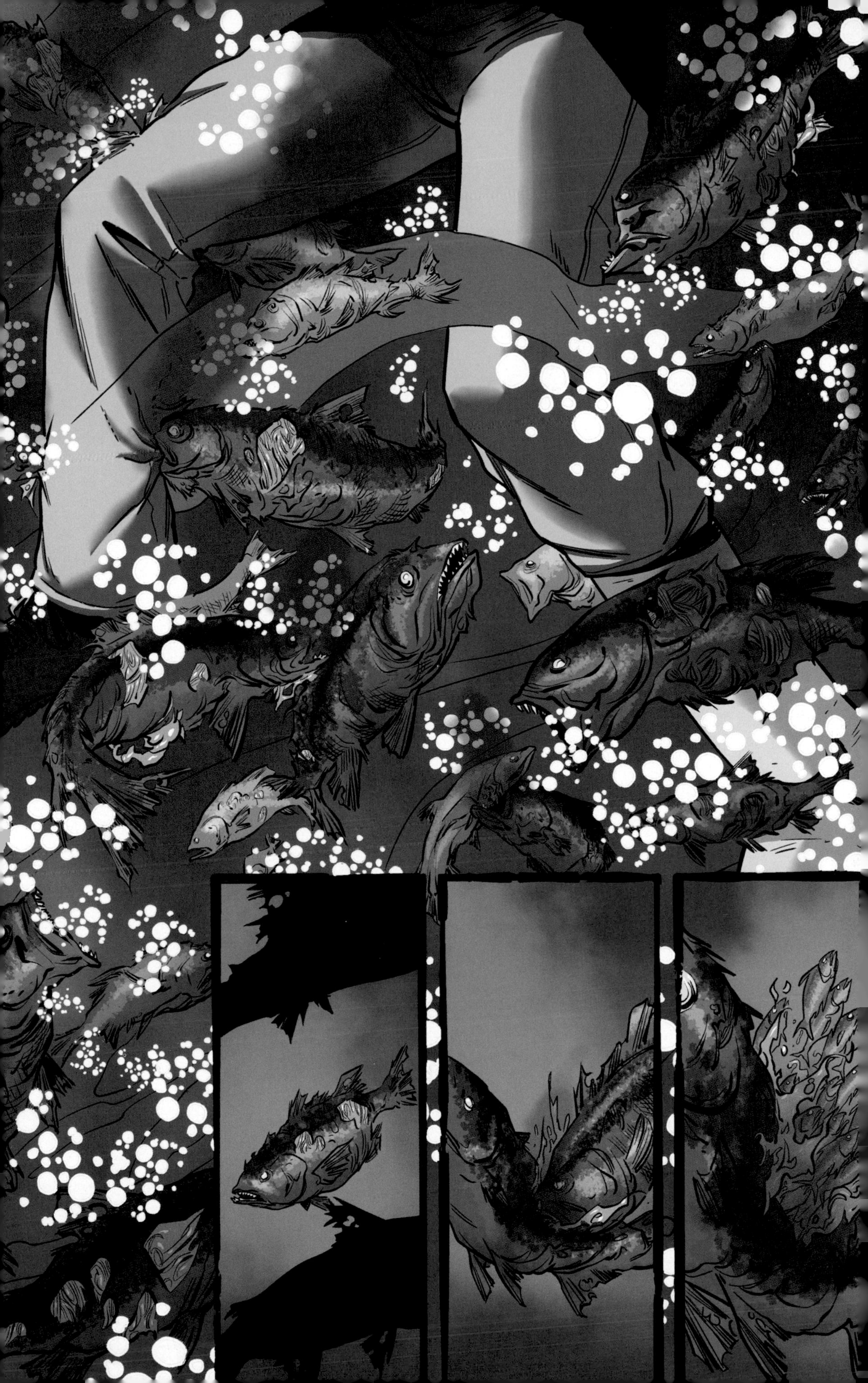

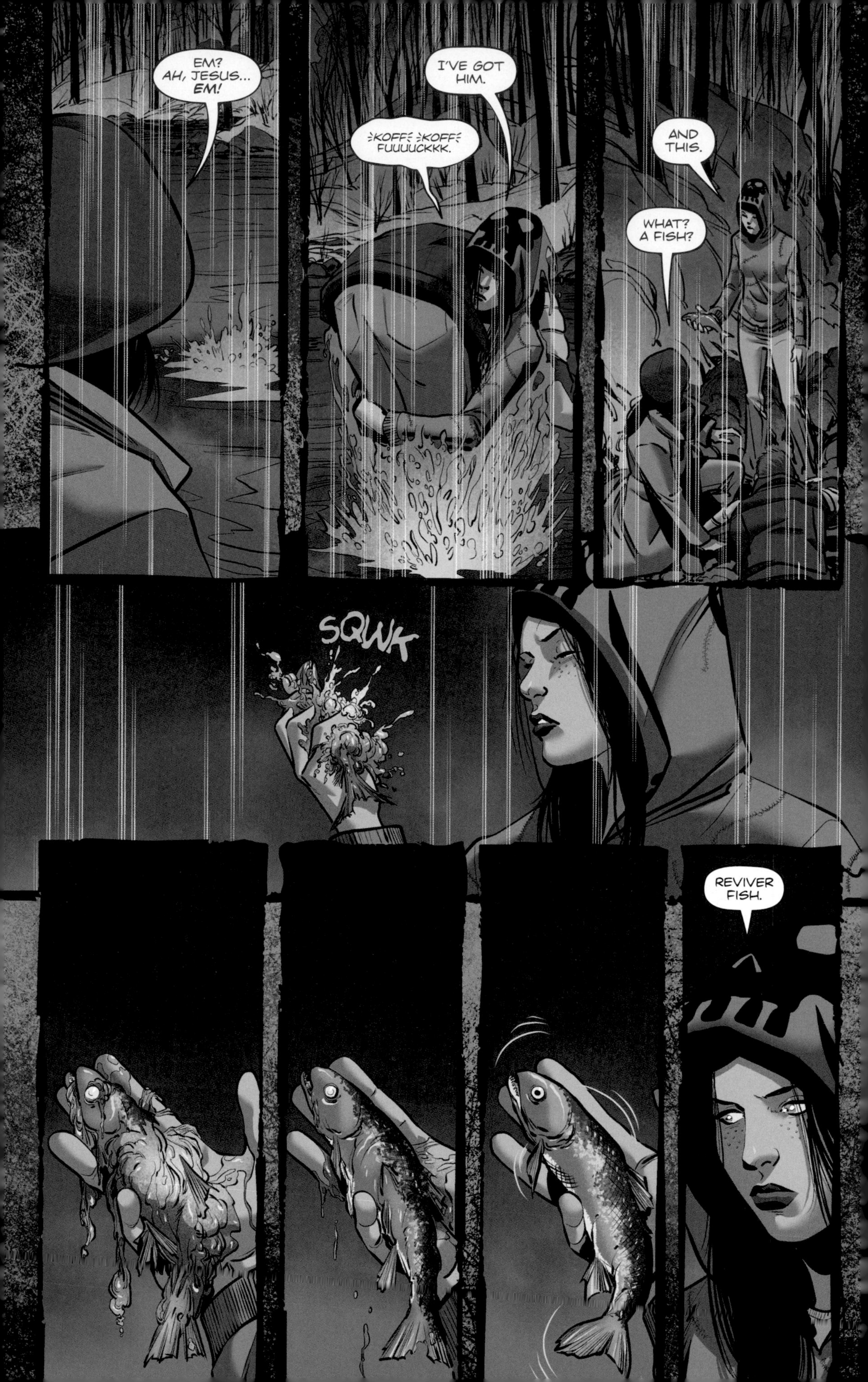
EM? AH, JESUS... EM!
I'VE GOT HIM.
KOFF *KOFF* FUUUUCKKK.
AND THIS.
WHAT? A FISH?
SQWK
REVIVER FISH.

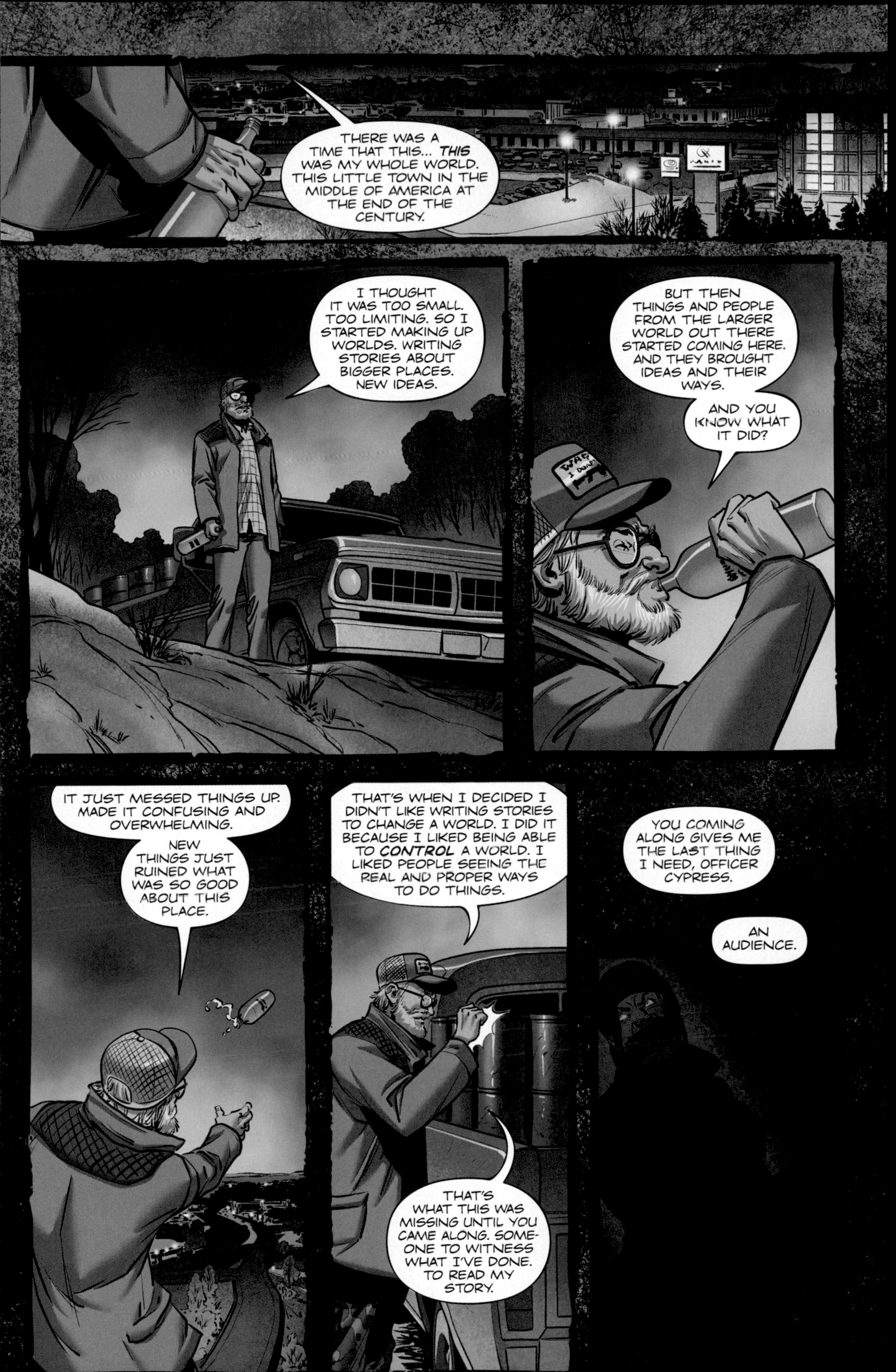
THERE WAS A TIME THAT THIS... THIS WAS MY WHOLE WORLD. THIS LITTLE TOWN IN THE MIDDLE OF AMERICA AT THE END OF THE CENTURY.
I THOUGHT IT WAS TOO SMALL. TOO LIMITING. SO I STARTED MAKING UP WORLDS. WRITING STORIES ABOUT BIGGER PLACES. NEW IDEAS.
BUT THEN THINGS AND PEOPLE FROM THE LARGER WORLD OUT THERE STARTED COMING HERE. AND THEY BROUGHT IDEAS AND THEIR WAYS.
AND YOU KNOW WHAT IT DID?
IT JUST MESSED THINGS UP. MADE IT CONFUSING AND OVERWHELMING.
NEW THINGS JUST RUINED WHAT WAS SO GOOD ABOUT THIS PLACE.
THAT'S WHEN I DECIDED I DIDN'T LIKE WRITING STORIES TO CHANGE A WORLD. I DID IT BECAUSE I LIKED BEING ABLE TO CONTROL A WORLD. I LIKED PEOPLE SEEING THE REAL AND PROPER WAYS TO DO THINGS.
THAT'S WHAT THIS WAS MISSING UNTIL YOU CAME ALONG. SOME-ONE TO WITNESS WHAT I'VE DONE. TO READ MY STORY.
YOU COMING ALONG GIVES ME THE LAST THING I NEED, OFFICER CYPRESS.
AN AUDIENCE.

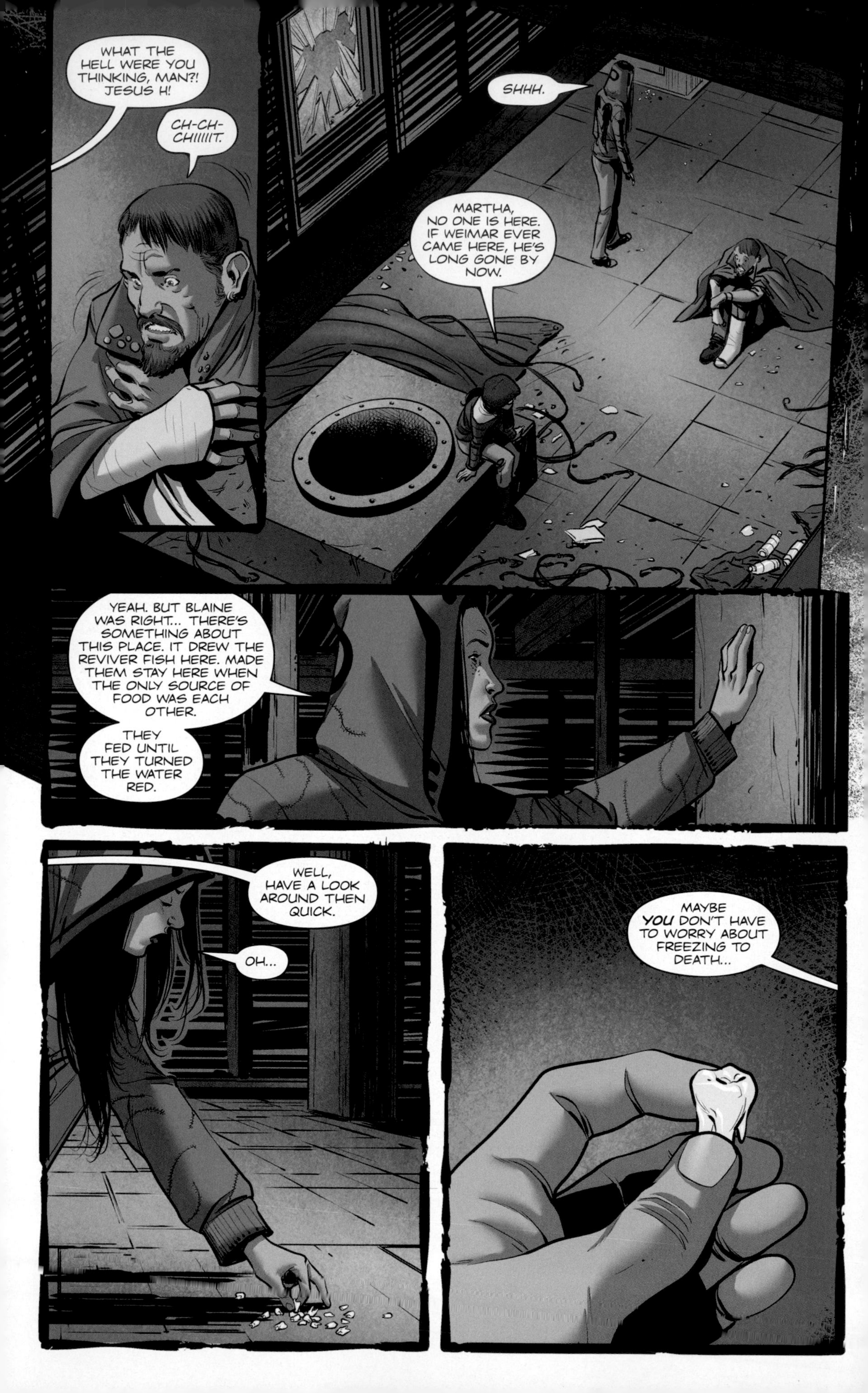
WHAT THE HELL WERE YOU THINKING, MAN?! JESUS H!
CH-CH-CHIIIIIT.
SHHH.
MARTHA, NO ONE IS HERE. IF WEIMAR EVER CAME HERE, HE'S LONG GONE BY NOW.
YEAH. BUT BLAINE WAS RIGHT... THERE'S SOMETHING ABOUT THIS PLACE. IT DREW THE REVIVER FISH HERE. MADE THEM STAY HERE WHEN THE ONLY SOURCE OF FOOD WAS EACH OTHER.
THEY FED UNTIL THEY TURNED THE WATER RED.
WELL, HAVE A LOOK AROUND THEN QUICK.
OH...
MAYBE YOU DON'T HAVE TO WORRY ABOUT FREEZING TO DEATH...

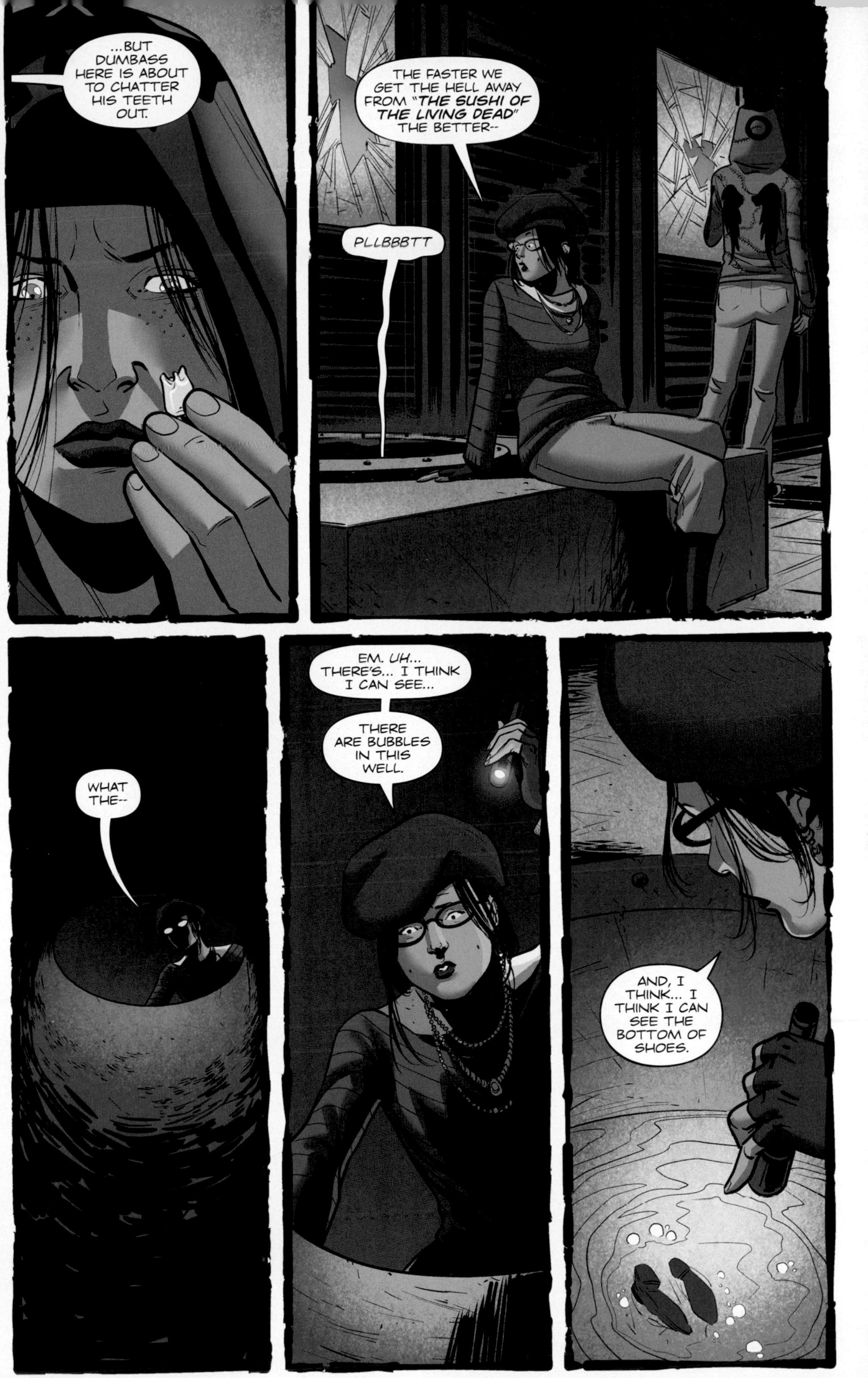
...BUT DUMBASS HERE IS ABOUT TO CHATTER HIS TEETH OUT.
THE FASTER WE GET THE HELL AWAY FROM "THE SUSHI OF THE LIVING DEAD" THE BETTER--
PLLBBBTT
WHAT THE--
EM. UH... THERE'S... I THINK I CAN SEE...
THERE ARE BUBBLES IN THIS WELL.
AND, I THINK... I THINK I CAN SEE THE BOTTOM OF SHOES.

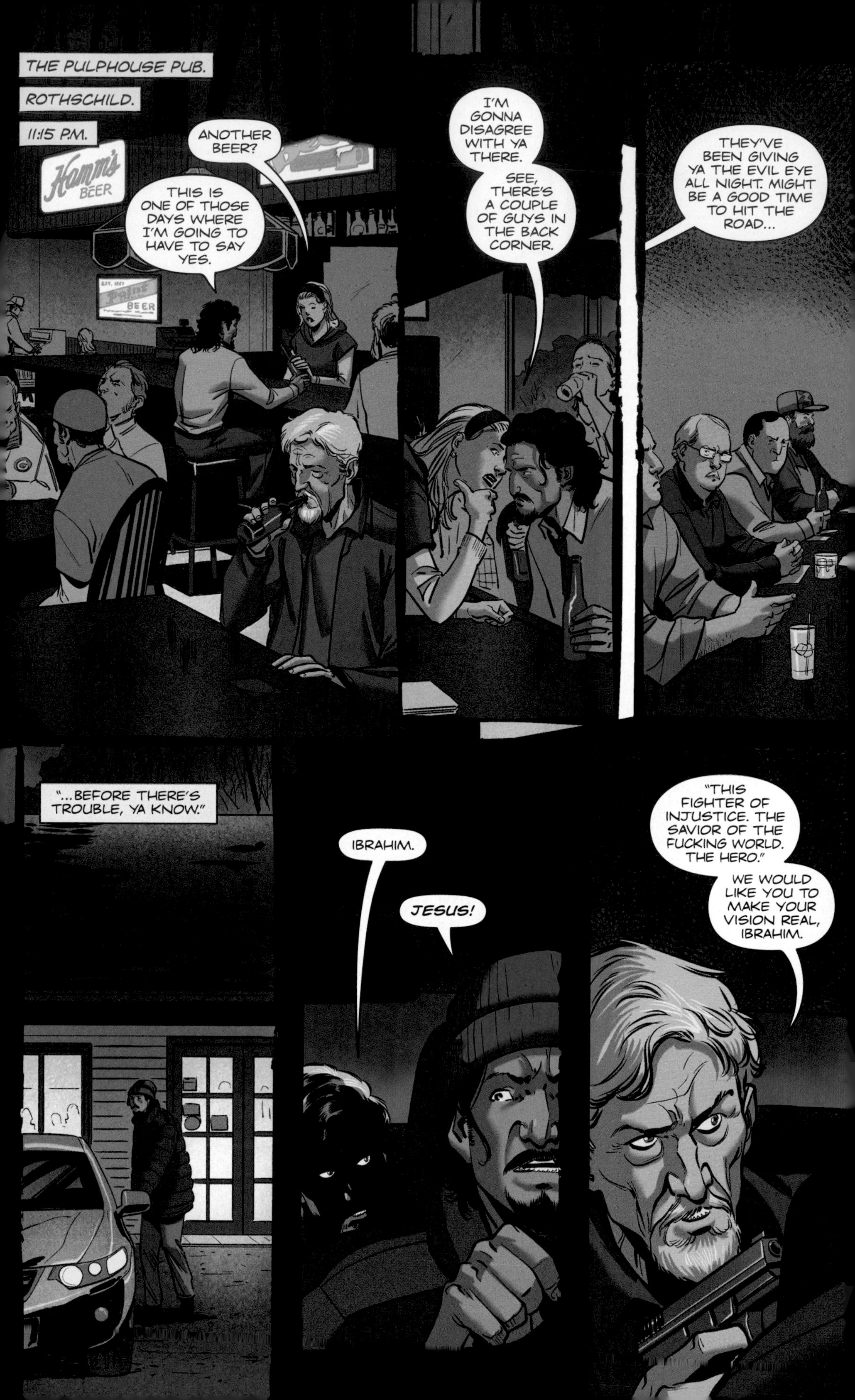

THE PULPHOUSE PUB.
ROTHSCHILD.
11:15 P.M.
Hamm's BEER
ANOTHER BEER?
THIS IS ONE OF THOSE DAYS WHERE I'M GOING TO HAVE TO SAY YES.
Point BEER
I'M GONNA DISAGREE WITH YA THERE.
SEE, THERE'S A COUPLE OF GUYS IN THE BACK CORNER.
THEY'VE BEEN GIVING YA THE EVIL EYE ALL NIGHT. MIGHT BE A GOOD TIME TO HIT THE ROAD...
"...BEFORE THERE'S TROUBLE, YA KNOW."
IBRAHIM.
JESUS!
"THIS FIGHTER OF INJUSTICE. THE SAVIOR OF THE FUCKING WORLD. THE HERO."
WE WOULD LIKE YOU TO MAKE YOUR VISION REAL, IBRAHIM.

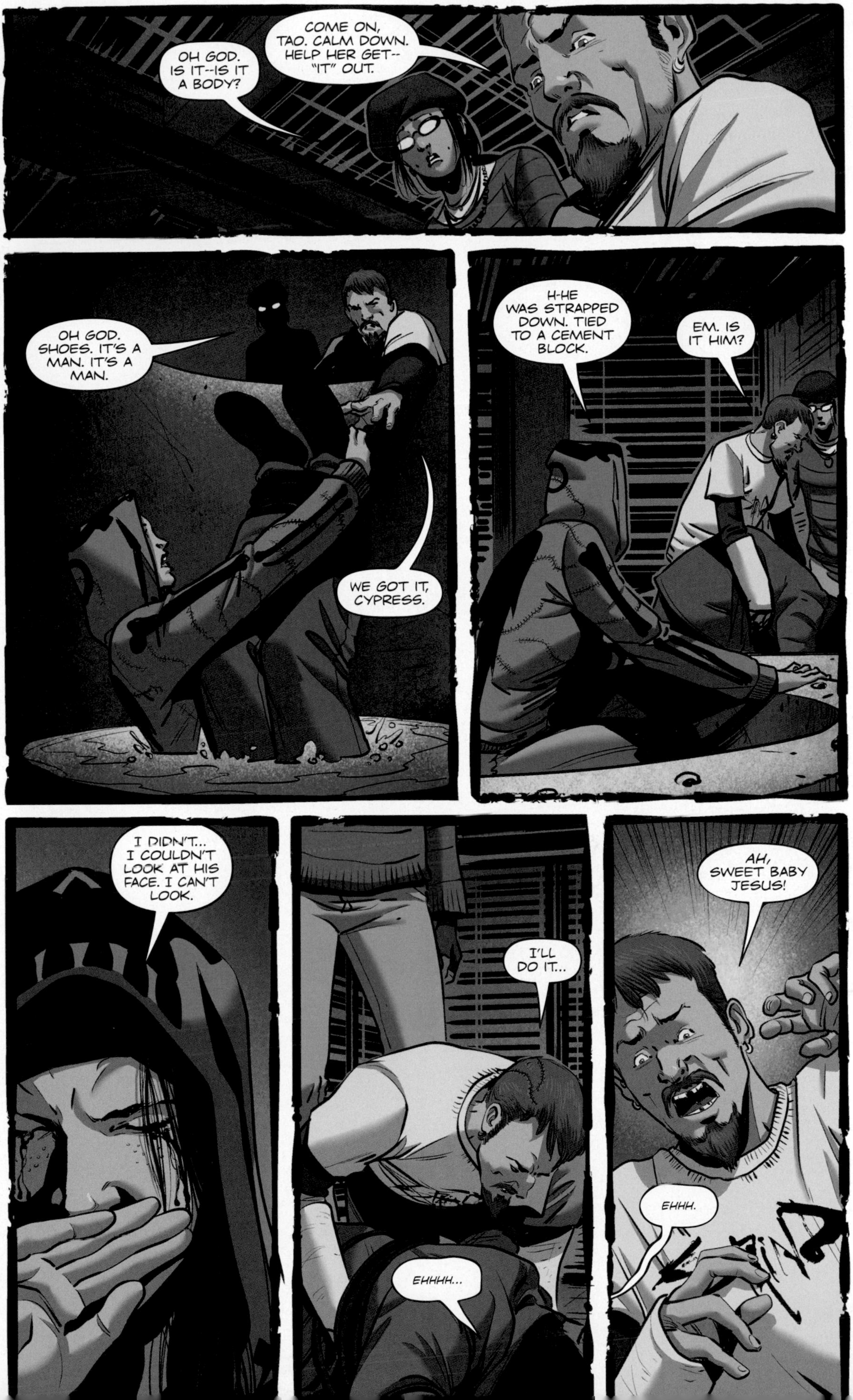
OH GOD. IS IT--IS IT A BODY?
COME ON, TAO. CALM DOWN. HELP HER GET-- "IT" OUT.
OH GOD. SHOES. IT'S A MAN. IT'S A MAN.
WE GOT IT, CYPRESS.
H-HE WAS STRAPPED DOWN. TIED TO A CEMENT BLOCK.
EM. IS IT HIM?
I DIDN'T... I COULDN'T LOOK AT HIS FACE. I CAN'T LOOK.
I'LL DO IT...
EHHHH...
AH, SWEET BABY JESUS!
EHHH.

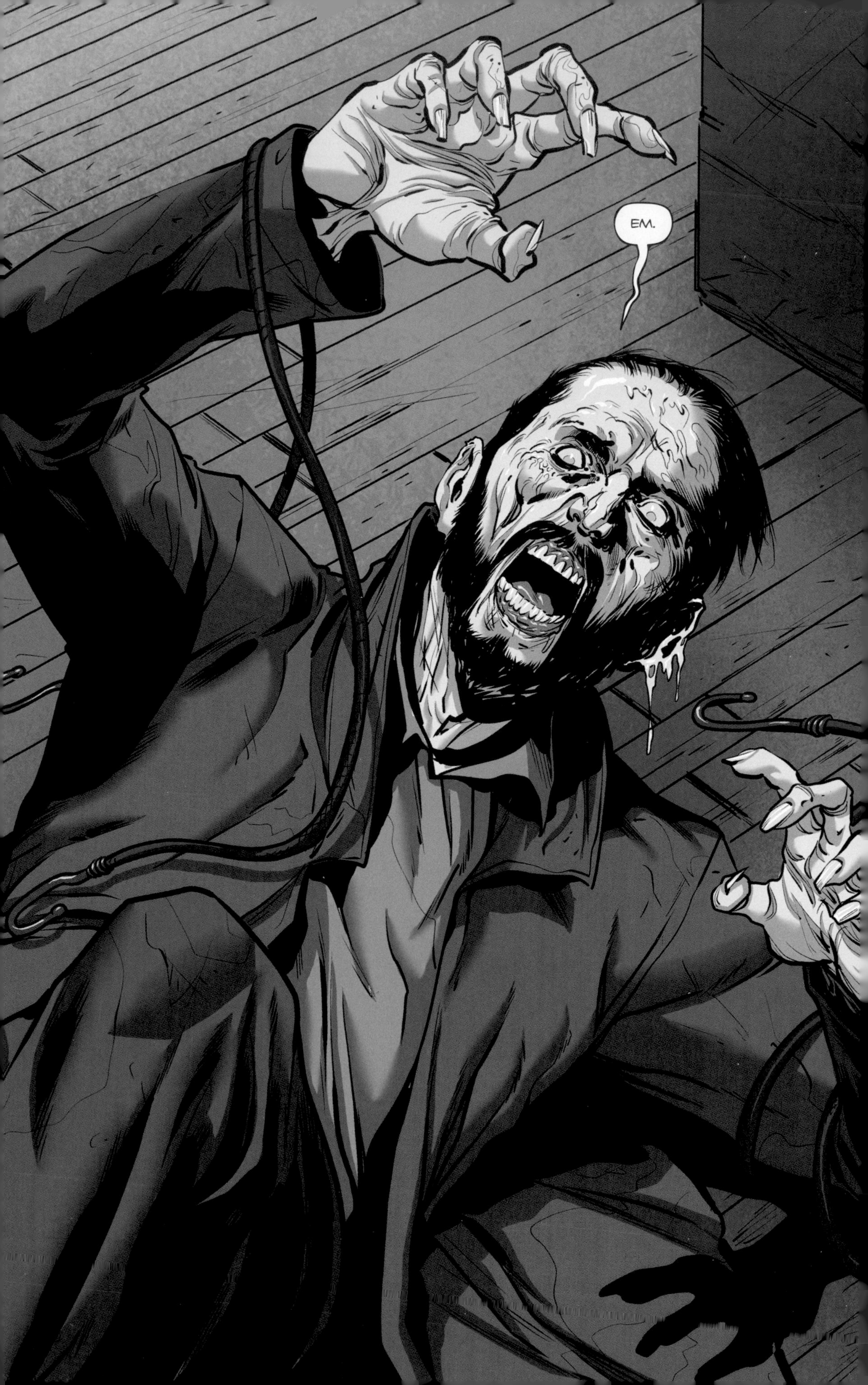
EM.

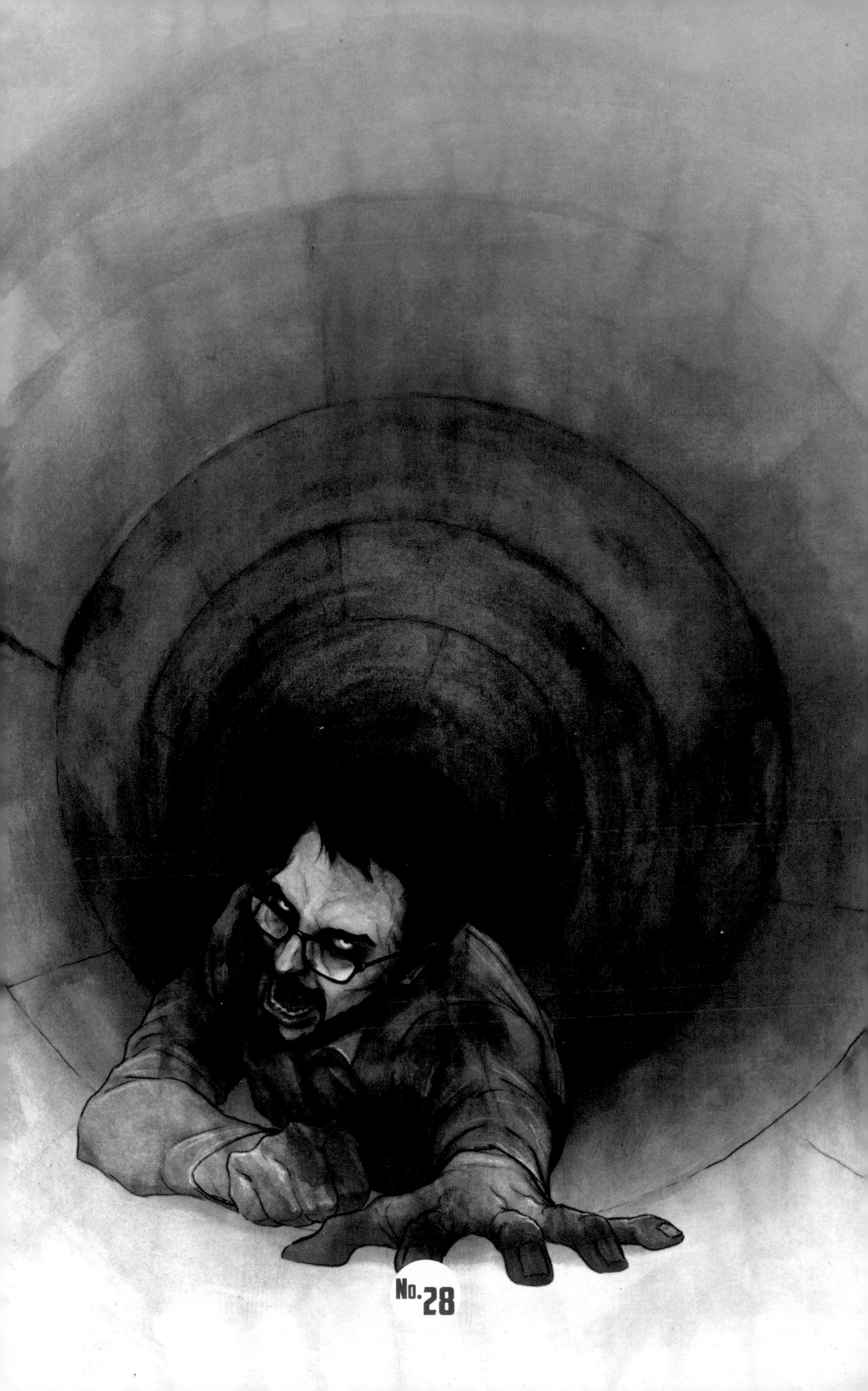
No.28

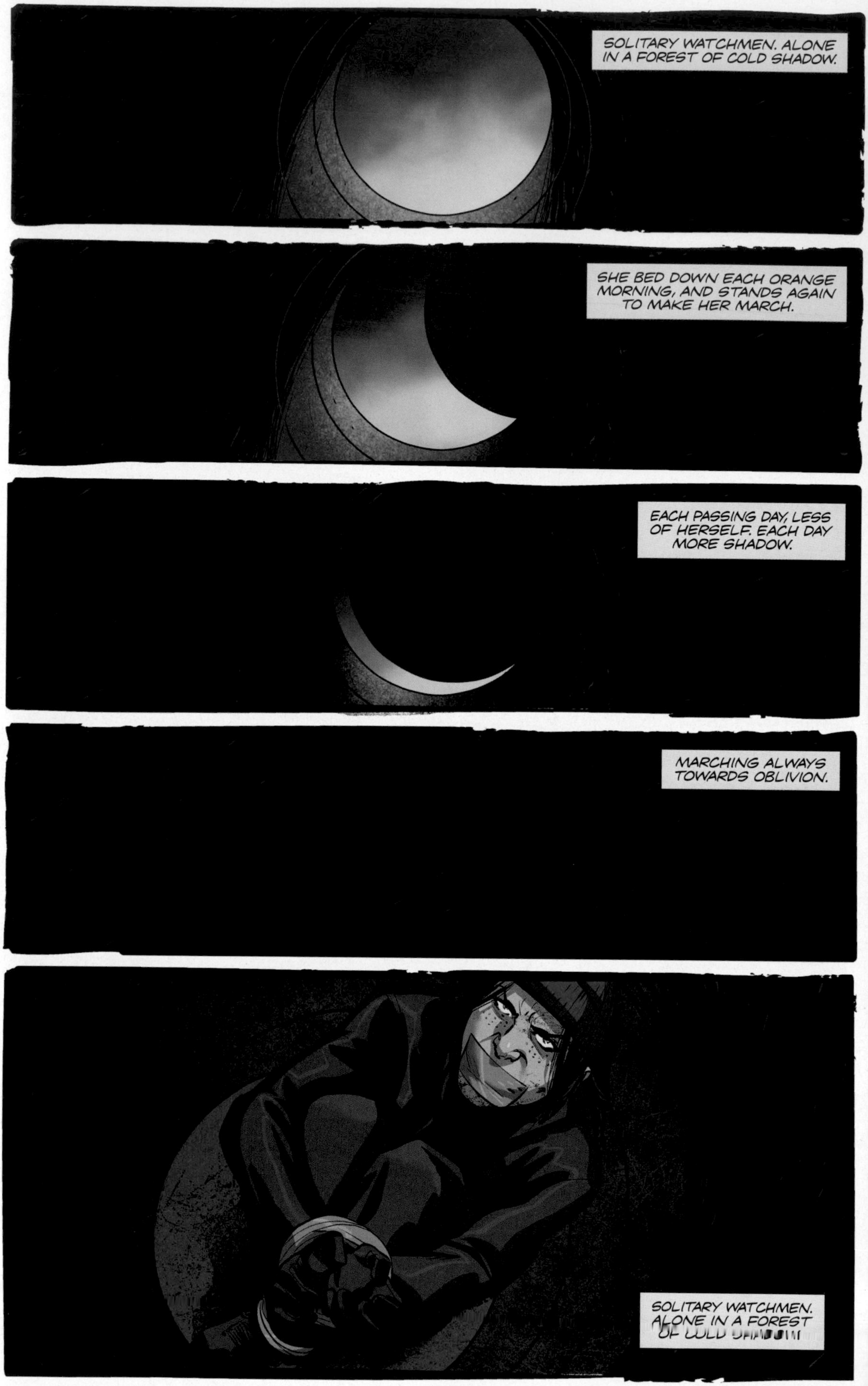
SOLITARY WATCHMEN. ALONE IN A FOREST OF COLD SHADOW.
SHE BED DOWN EACH ORANGE MORNING, AND STANDS AGAIN TO MAKE HER MARCH.
EACH PASSING DAY, LESS OF HERSELF. EACH DAY MORE SHADOW.
MARCHING ALWAYS TOWARDS OBLIVION.
SOLITARY WATCHMEN. ALONE IN A FOREST

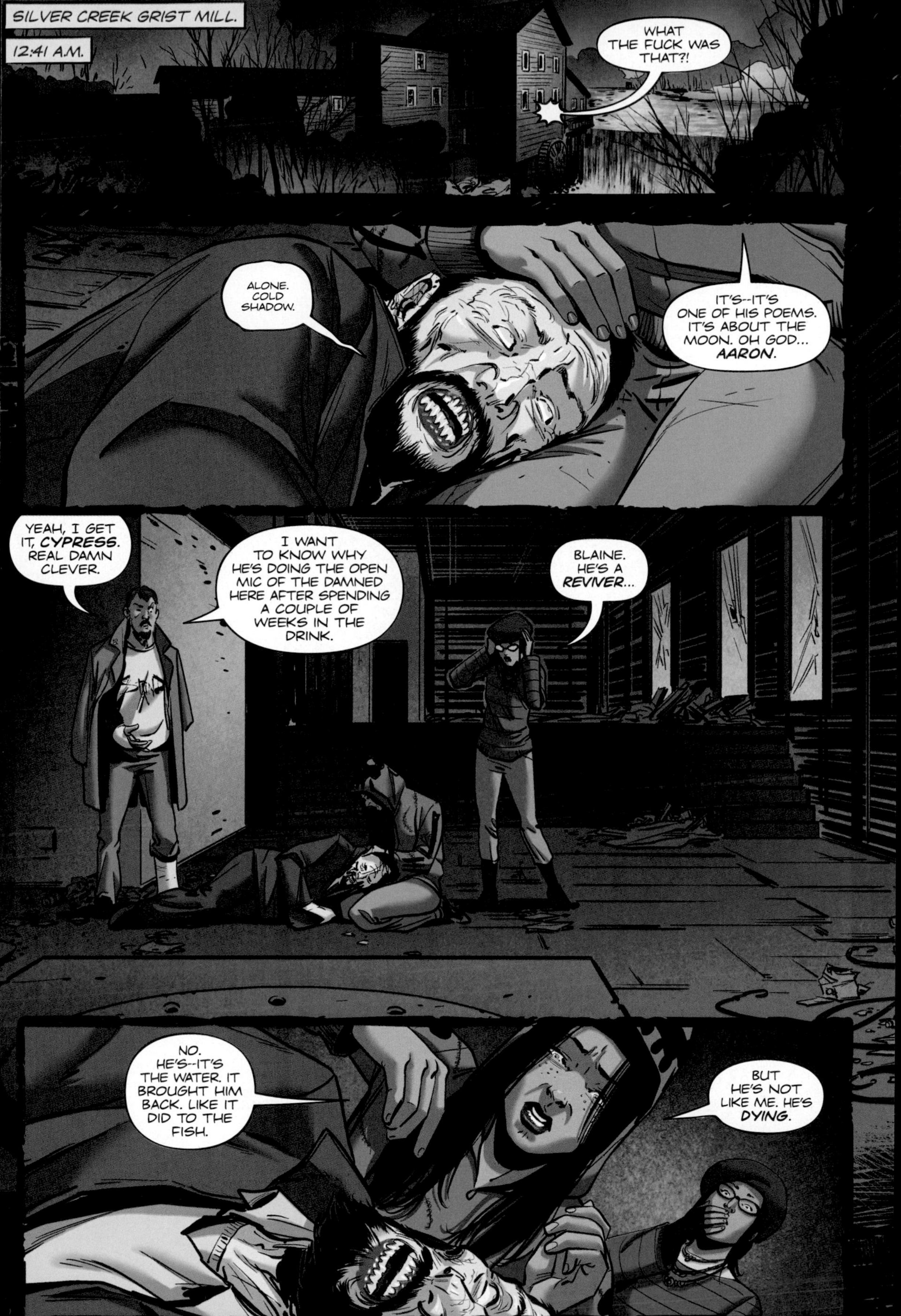
SILVER CREEK GRIST MILL.
12:41 A.M.
WHAT THE FUCK WAS THAT?!
ALONE. COLD SHADOW.
IT'S--IT'S ONE OF HIS POEMS. IT'S ABOUT THE MOON. OH GOD... AARON.
YEAH, I GET IT, CYPRESS. REAL DAMN CLEVER.
I WANT TO KNOW WHY HE'S DOING THE OPEN MIC OF THE DAMNED HERE AFTER SPENDING A COUPLE OF WEEKS IN THE DRINK.
BLAINE. HE'S A REVIVER...
NO. HE'S--IT'S THE WATER. IT BROUGHT HIM BACK. LIKE IT DID TO THE FISH.
BUT HE'S NOT LIKE ME. HE'S DYING.

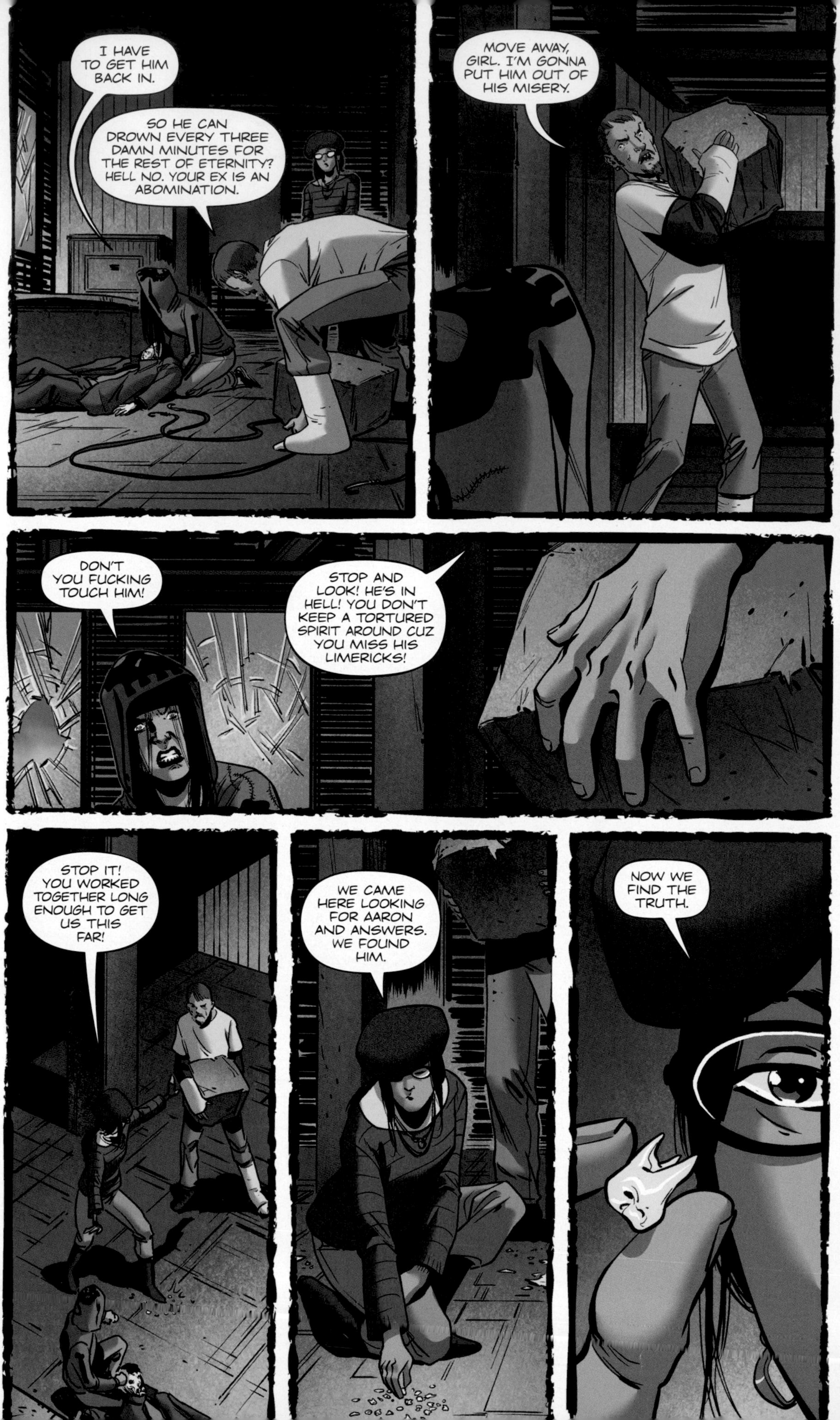
I HAVE TO GET HIM BACK IN.
SO HE CAN DROWN EVERY THREE DAMN MINUTES FOR THE REST OF ETERNITY? HELL NO. YOUR EX IS AN ABOMINATION.
MOVE AWAY, GIRL. I'M GONNA PUT HIM OUT OF HIS MISERY.
DON'T YOU FUCKING TOUCH HIM!
STOP AND LOOK! HE'S IN HELL! YOU DON'T KEEP A TORTURED SPIRIT AROUND CUZ YOU MISS HIS LIMERICKS!
STOP IT! YOU WORKED TOGETHER LONG ENOUGH TO GET US THIS FAR!
WE CAME HERE LOOKING FOR AARON AND ANSWERS. WE FOUND HIM.
NOW WE FIND THE TRUTH.

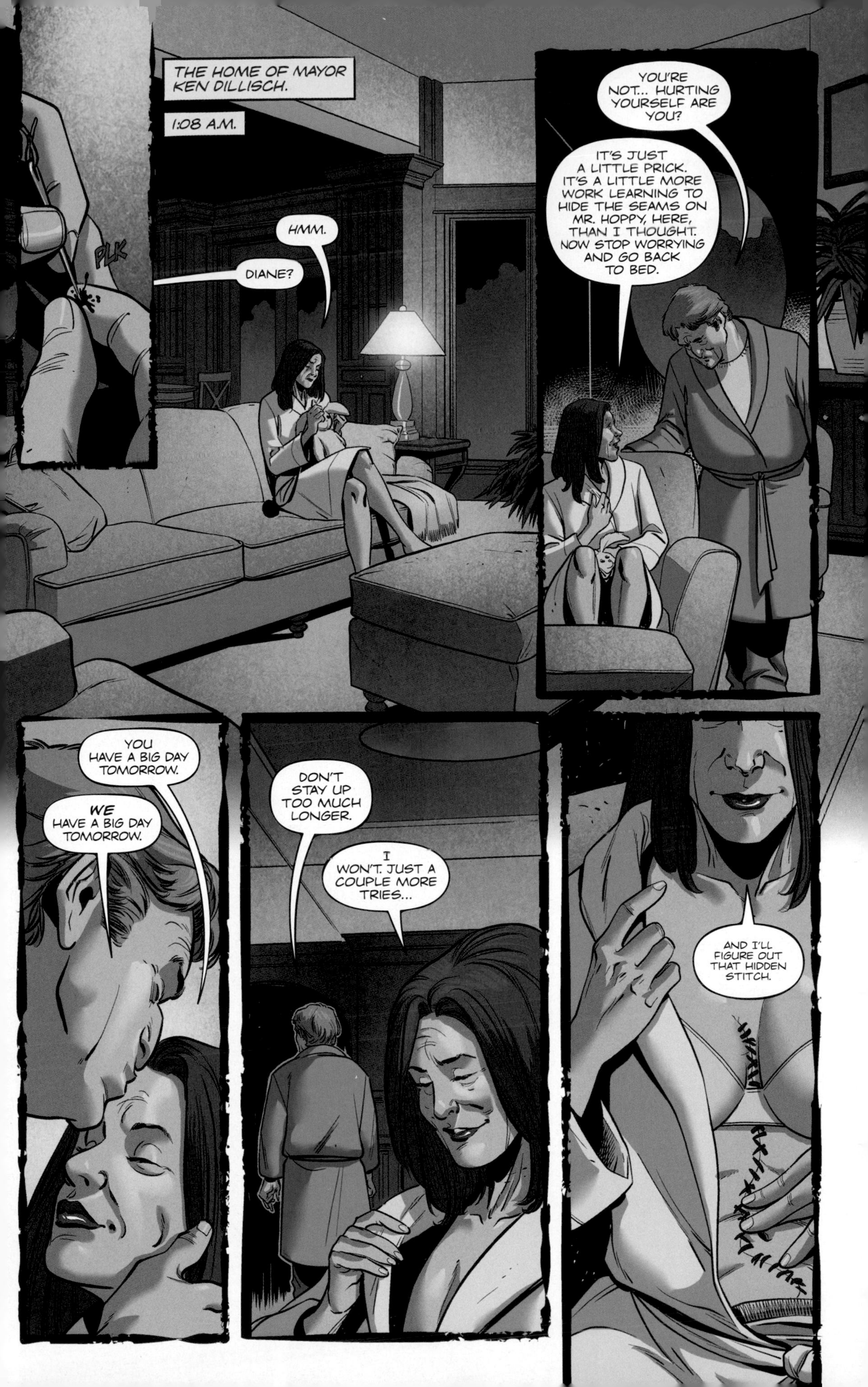
THE HOME OF MAYOR KEN DILLISCH.
1:08 A.M.
PLK
DIANE?
HMM.
YOU'RE NOT... HURTING YOURSELF ARE YOU?
IT'S JUST A LITTLE PRICK. IT'S A LITTLE MORE WORK LEARNING TO HIDE THE SEAMS ON MR. HOPPY, HERE, THAN I THOUGHT. NOW STOP WORRYING AND GO BACK TO BED.
YOU HAVE A BIG DAY TOMORROW.
WE HAVE A BIG DAY TOMORROW.
DON'T STAY UP TOO MUCH LONGER.
I WON'T. JUST A COUPLE MORE TRIES...
AND I'LL FIGURE OUT THAT HIDDEN STITCH.

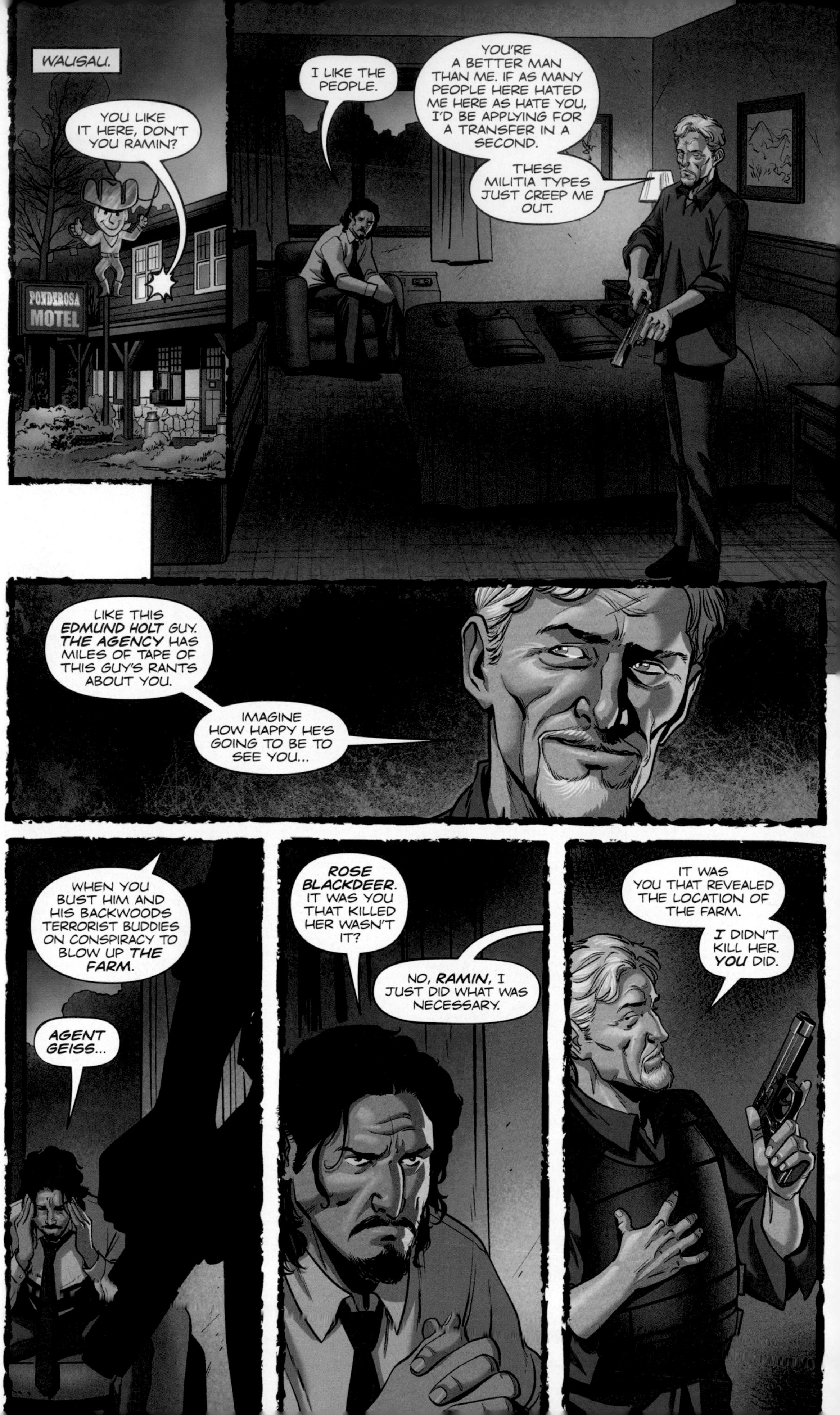
WAUSAU.
YOU LIKE IT HERE, DON'T YOU RAMIN?
PONDEROSA MOTEL
I LIKE THE PEOPLE.
YOU'RE A BETTER MAN THAN ME. IF AS MANY PEOPLE HERE HATED ME HERE AS HATE YOU, I'D BE APPLYING FOR A TRANSFER IN A SECOND.
THESE MILITIA TYPES JUST CREEP ME OUT.
LIKE THIS EDMUND HOLT GUY. THE AGENCY HAS MILES OF TAPE OF THIS GUY'S RANTS ABOUT YOU.
IMAGINE HOW HAPPY HE'S GOING TO BE TO SEE YOU...
WHEN YOU BUST HIM AND HIS BACKWOODS TERRORIST BUDDIES ON CONSPIRACY TO BLOW UP THE FARM.
AGENT GEISS...
ROSE BLACKDEER. IT WAS YOU THAT KILLED HER WASN'T IT?
NO, RAMIN, I JUST DID WHAT WAS NECESSARY.
IT WAS YOU THAT REVEALED THE LOCATION OF THE FARM.
I DIDN'T KILL HER. YOU DID.

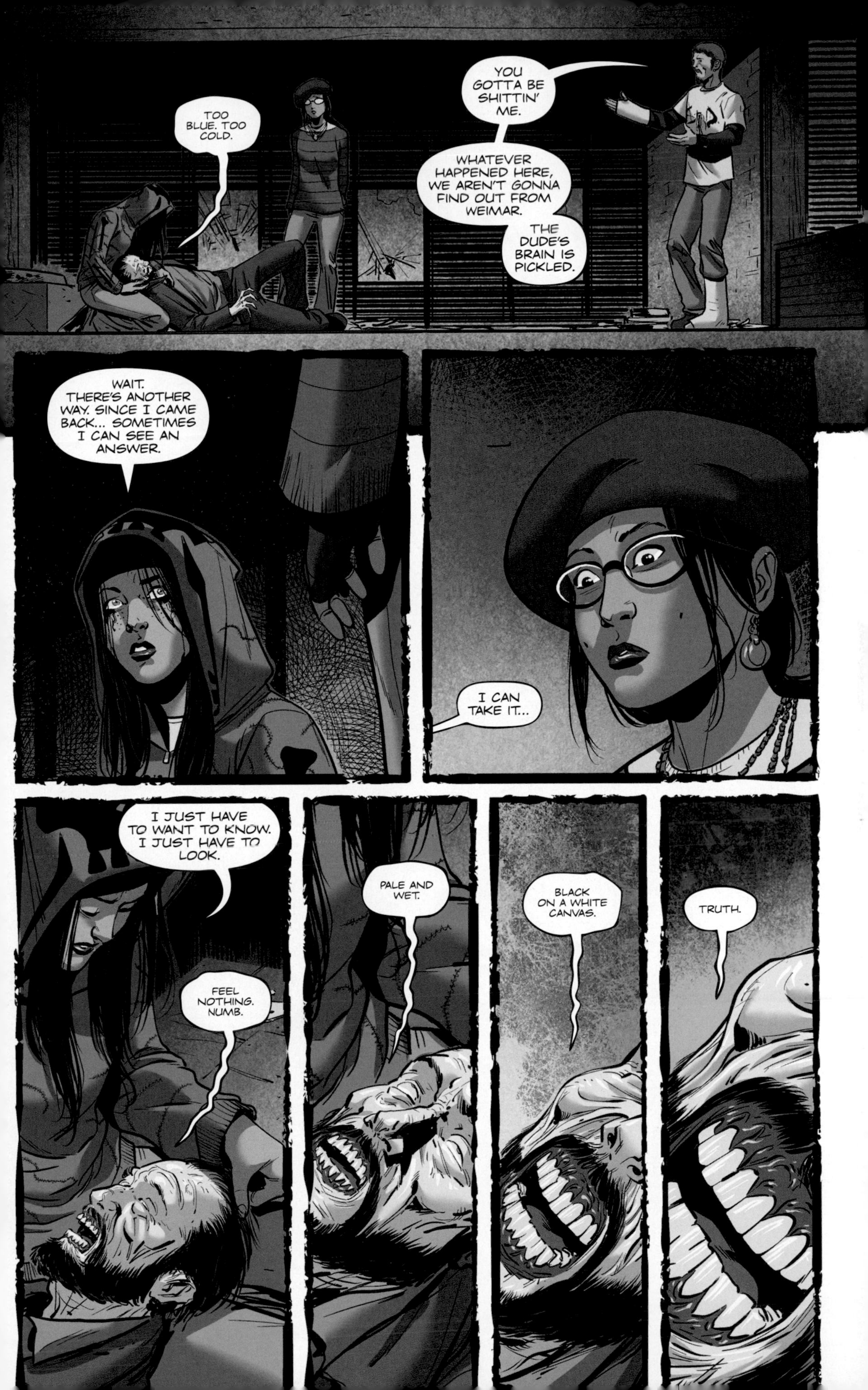
TOO BLUE. TOO COLD.
YOU GOTTA BE SHITTIN' ME.
WHATEVER HAPPENED HERE, WE AREN'T GONNA FIND OUT FROM WEIMAR.
THE DUDE'S BRAIN IS PICKLED.
WAIT. THERE'S ANOTHER WAY. SINCE I CAME BACK... SOMETIMES I CAN SEE AN ANSWER.
I CAN TAKE IT...
I JUST HAVE TO WANT TO KNOW. I JUST HAVE TO LOOK.
FEEL NOTHING. NUMB.
PALE AND WET.
BLACK ON A WHITE CANVAS.
TRUTH.

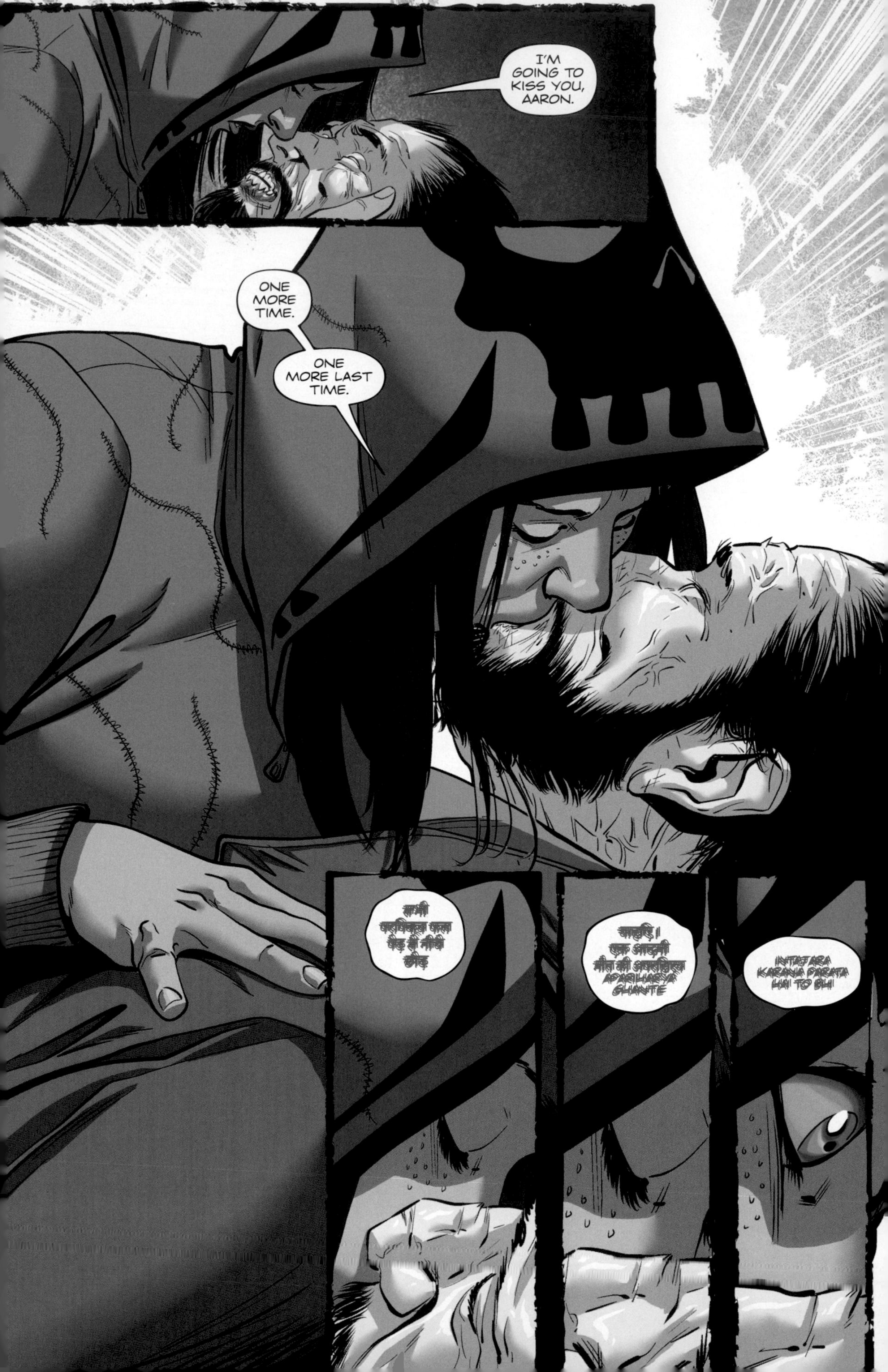
I'M GOING TO KISS YOU, AARON.
ONE MORE TIME.
ONE MORE LAST TIME.
APARIHARYA GHANTE
INTAJARA KARANA PARATA HAI TO BHI

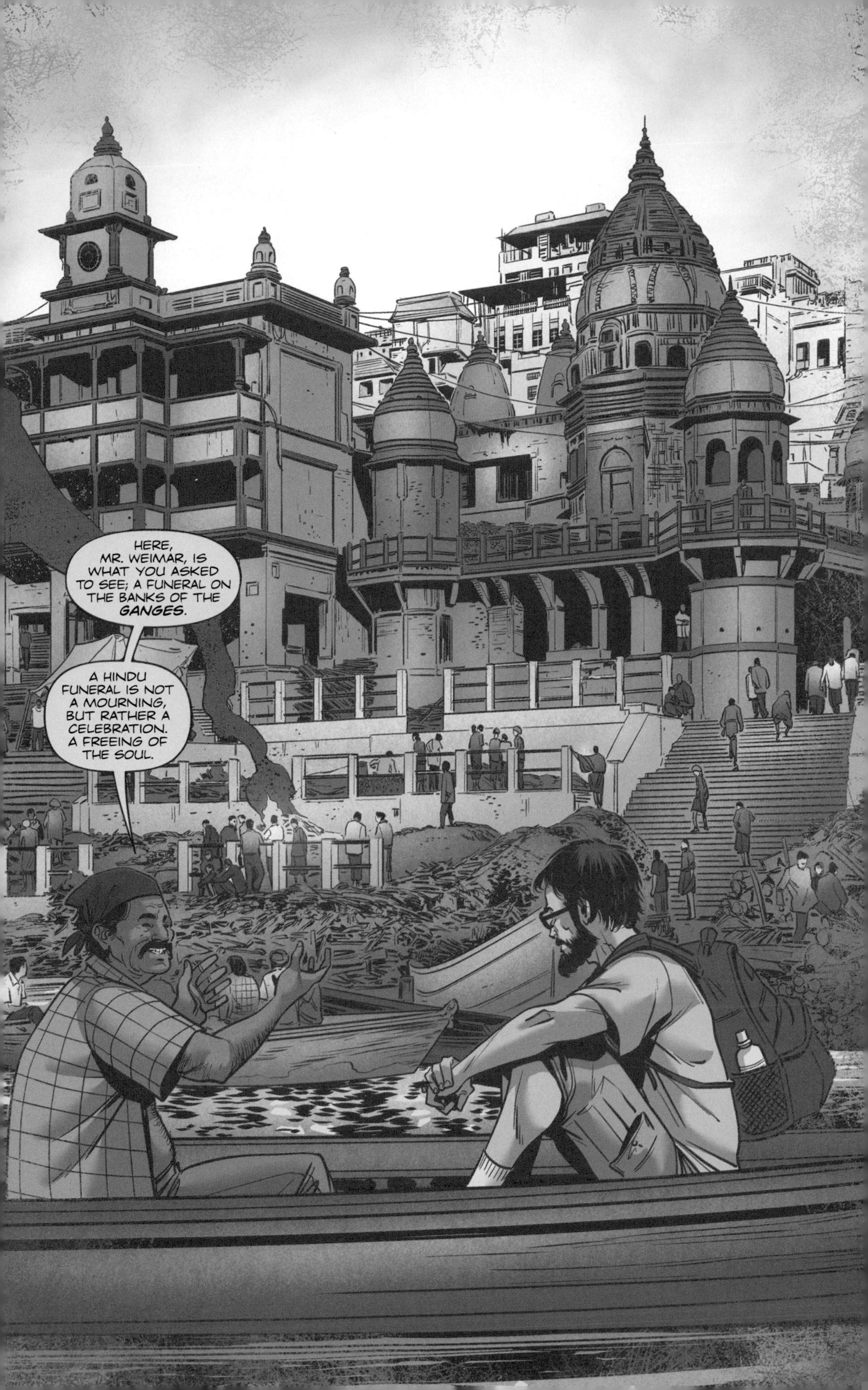
HERE, MR. WEIMAR, IS WHAT YOU ASKED TO SEE; A FUNERAL ON THE BANKS OF THE *GANGES*.
A HINDU FUNERAL IS NOT A MOURNING, BUT RATHER A CELEBRATION. A FREEING OF THE SOUL.

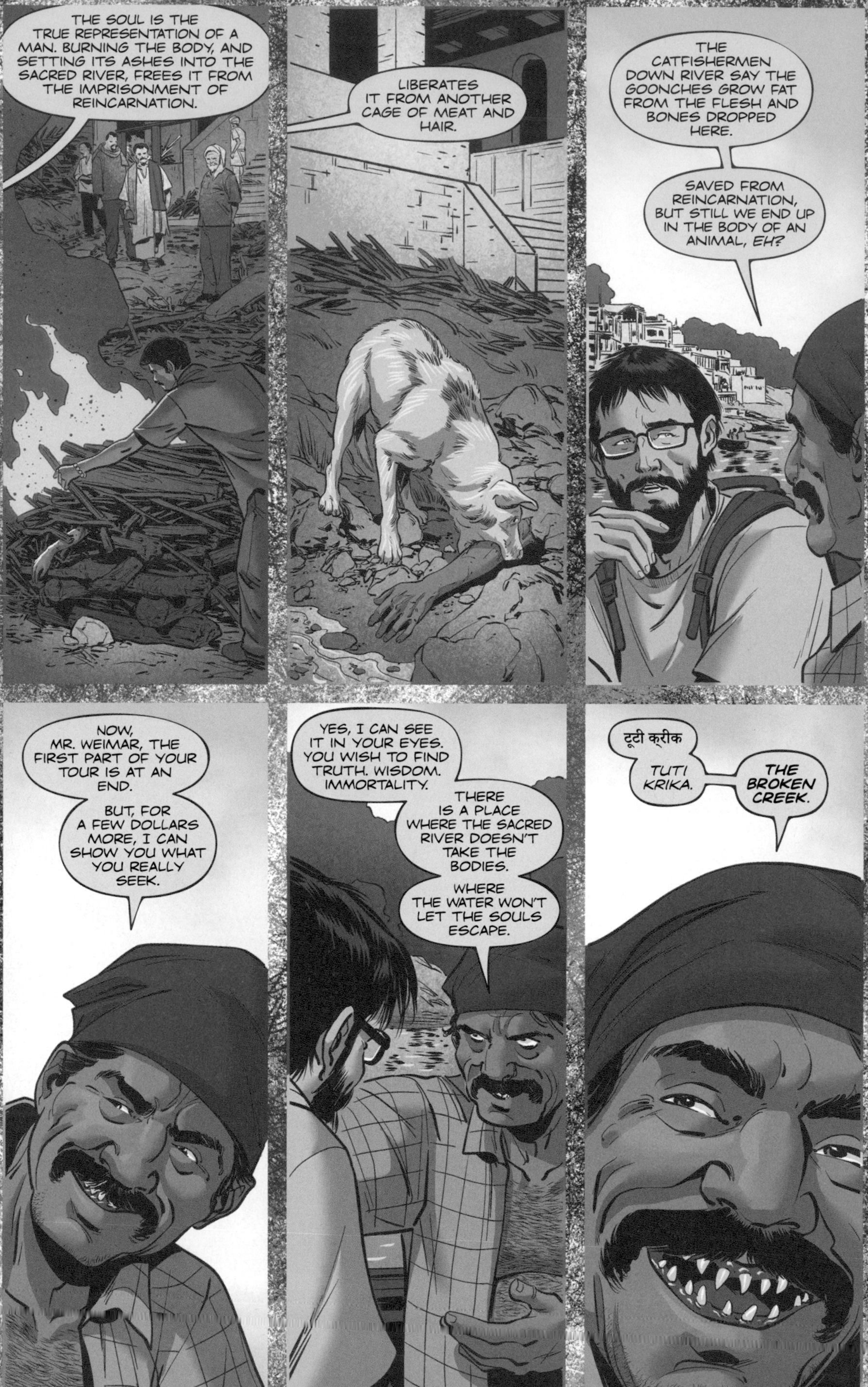
THE SOUL IS THE TRUE REPRESENTATION OF A MAN. BURNING THE BODY, AND SETTING ITS ASHES INTO THE SACRED RIVER, FREES IT FROM THE IMPRISONMENT OF REINCARNATION.
LIBERATES IT FROM ANOTHER CAGE OF MEAT AND HAIR.
THE CATFISHERMEN DOWN RIVER SAY THE GOONCHES GROW FAT FROM THE FLESH AND BONES DROPPED HERE.
SAVED FROM REINCARNATION, BUT STILL WE END UP IN THE BODY OF AN ANIMAL, *EH?*
NOW, MR. WEIMAR, THE FIRST PART OF YOUR TOUR IS AT AN END.
BUT, FOR A FEW DOLLARS MORE, I CAN SHOW YOU WHAT YOU REALLY SEEK.
YES, I CAN SEE IT IN YOUR EYES. YOU WISH TO FIND TRUTH. WISDOM. IMMORTALITY.
THERE IS A PLACE WHERE THE SACRED RIVER DOESN'T TAKE THE BODIES.
WHERE THE WATER WON'T LET THE SOULS ESCAPE.
टूटी क्रीक
TUTI KRIKA.
THE BROKEN CREEK.

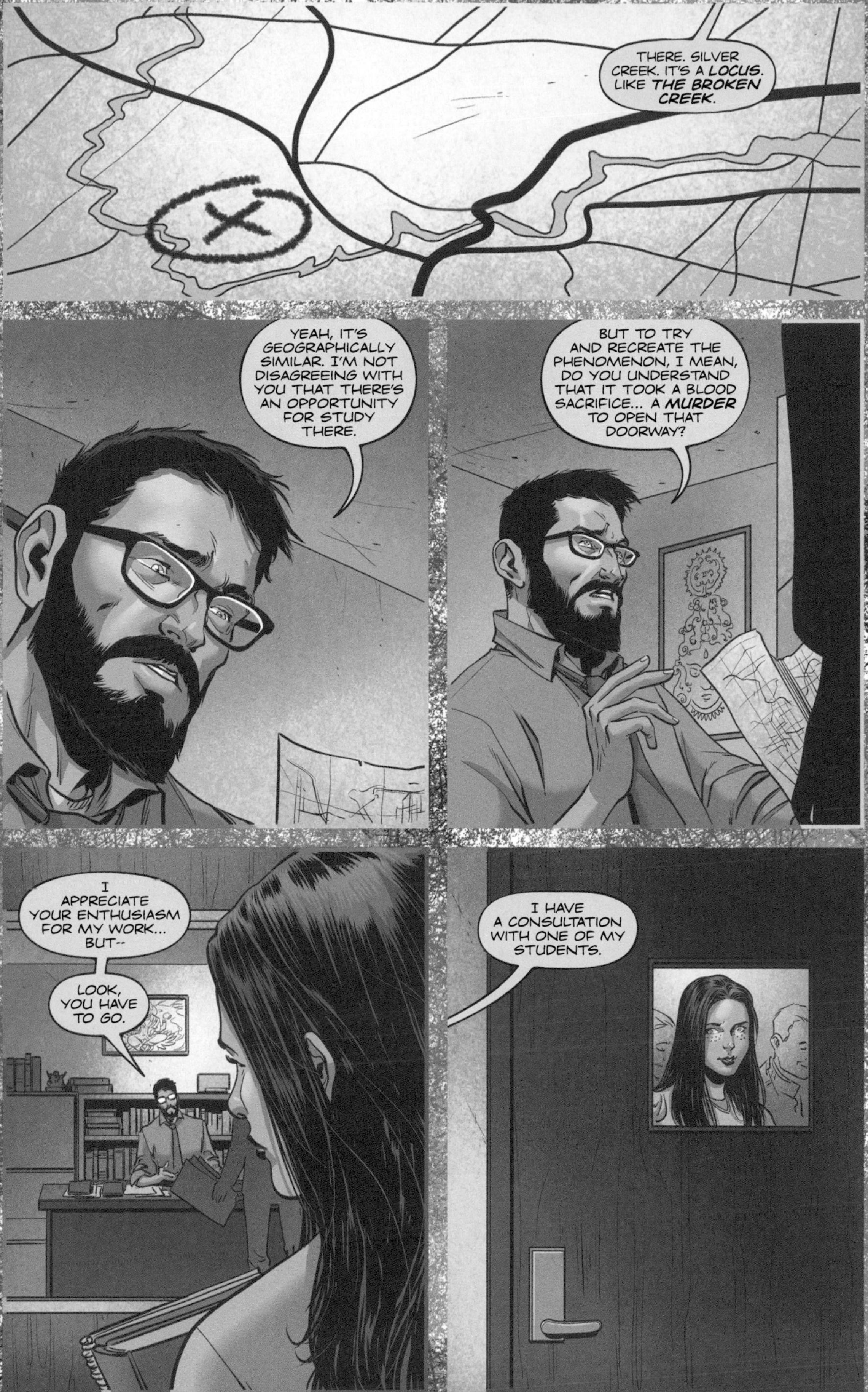
THERE. SILVER CREEK. IT'S A *LOCUS*. LIKE ***THE BROKEN CREEK***.
YEAH, IT'S GEOGRAPHICALLY SIMILAR. I'M NOT DISAGREEING WITH YOU THAT THERE'S AN OPPORTUNITY FOR STUDY THERE.
BUT TO TRY AND RECREATE THE PHENOMENON, I MEAN, DO YOU UNDERSTAND THAT IT TOOK A BLOOD SACRIFICE... A ***MURDER*** TO OPEN THAT DOORWAY?
I APPRECIATE YOUR ENTHUSIASM FOR MY WORK... BUT--
LOOK, YOU HAVE TO GO.
I HAVE A CONSULTATION WITH ONE OF MY STUDENTS.

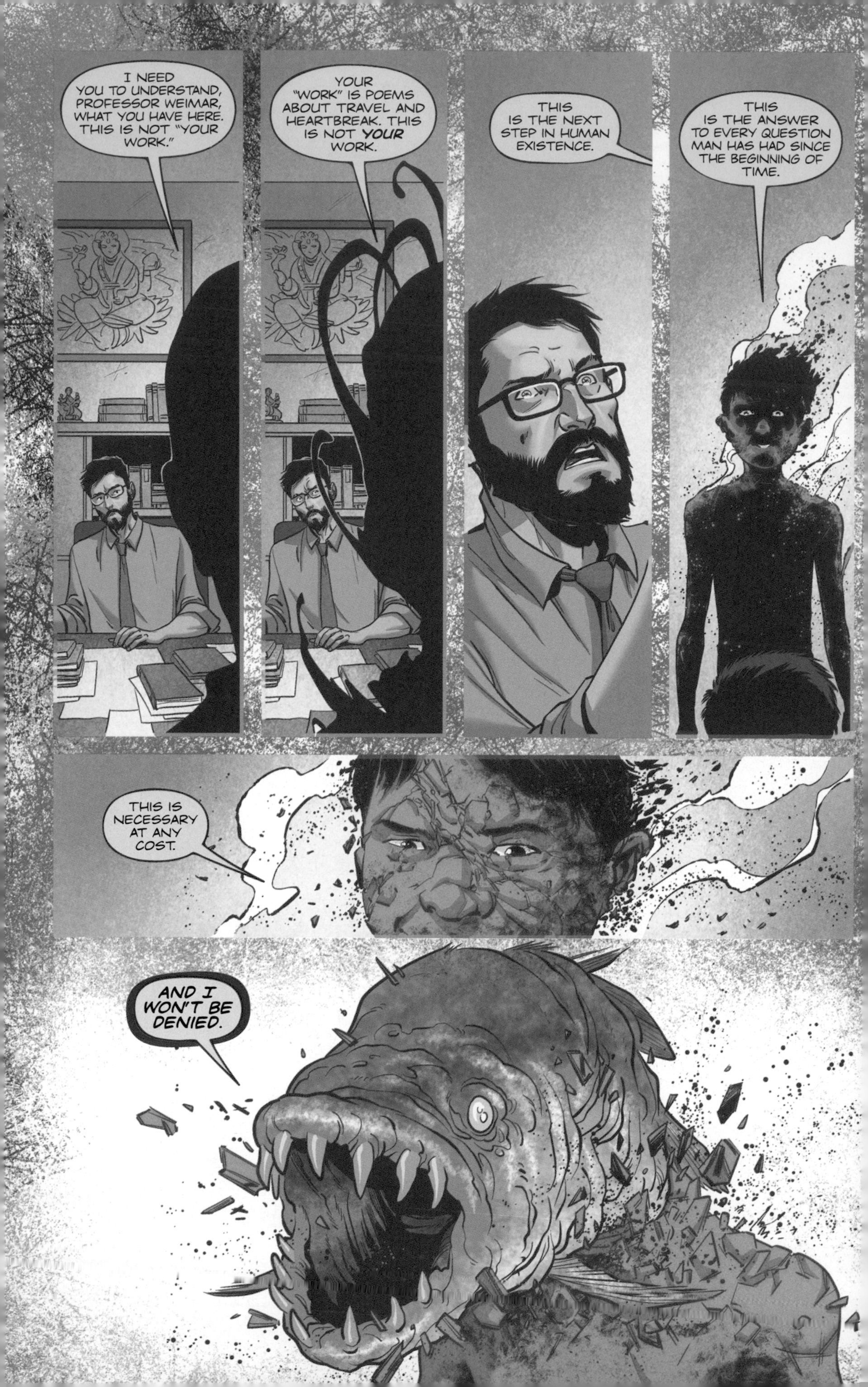
I NEED YOU TO UNDERSTAND, PROFESSOR WEIMAR, WHAT YOU HAVE HERE. THIS IS NOT "YOUR WORK."
YOUR "WORK" IS POEMS ABOUT TRAVEL AND HEARTBREAK. THIS IS NOT *YOUR* WORK.
THIS IS THE NEXT STEP IN HUMAN EXISTENCE.
THIS IS THE ANSWER TO EVERY QUESTION MAN HAS HAD SINCE THE BEGINNING OF TIME.
THIS IS NECESSARY AT ANY COST.
AND I WON'T BE DENIED.

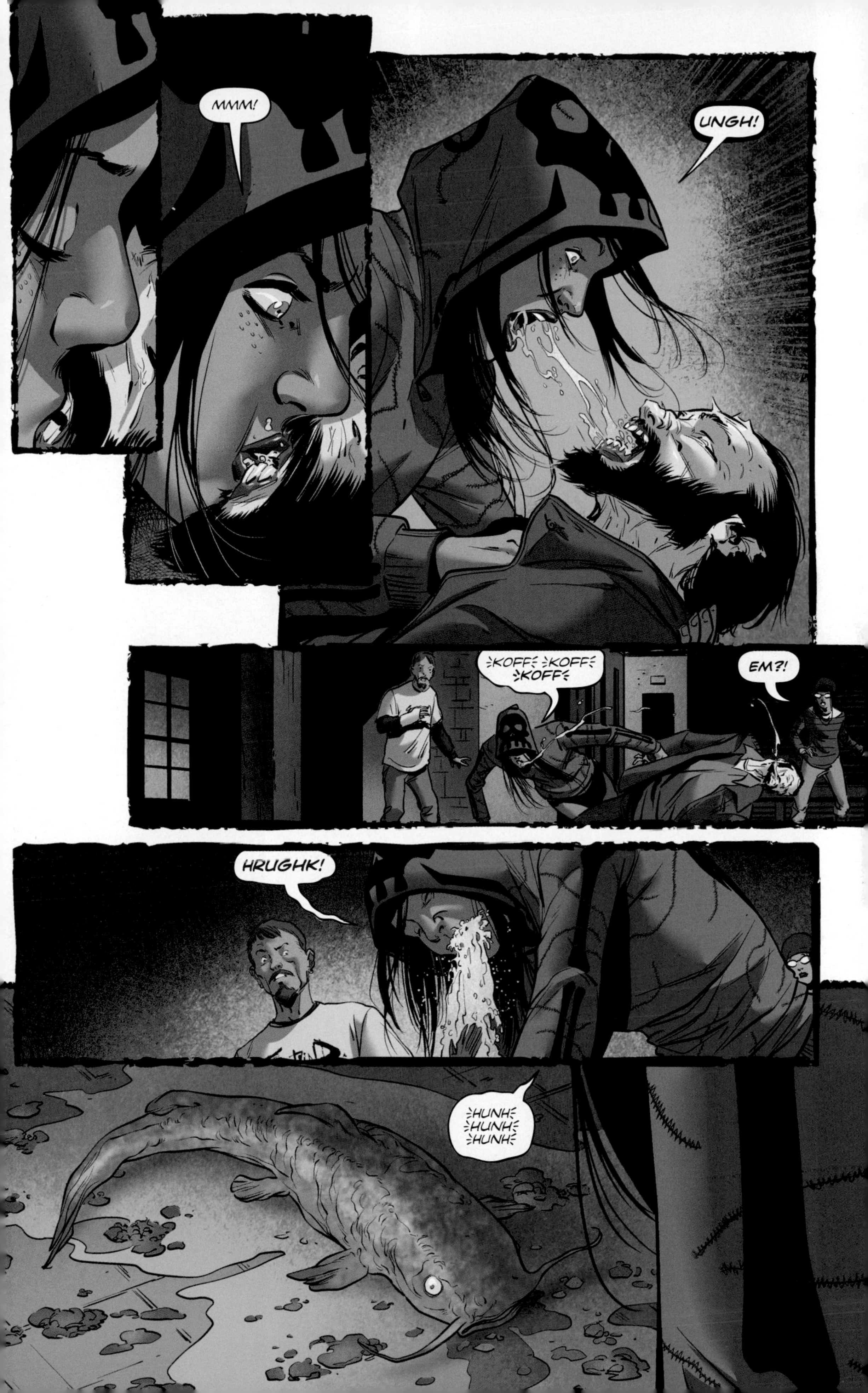
MMM!
UNGH!
KOFF KOFF KOFF
EM?!
HRUGHK!
HUNH HUNH HUNH

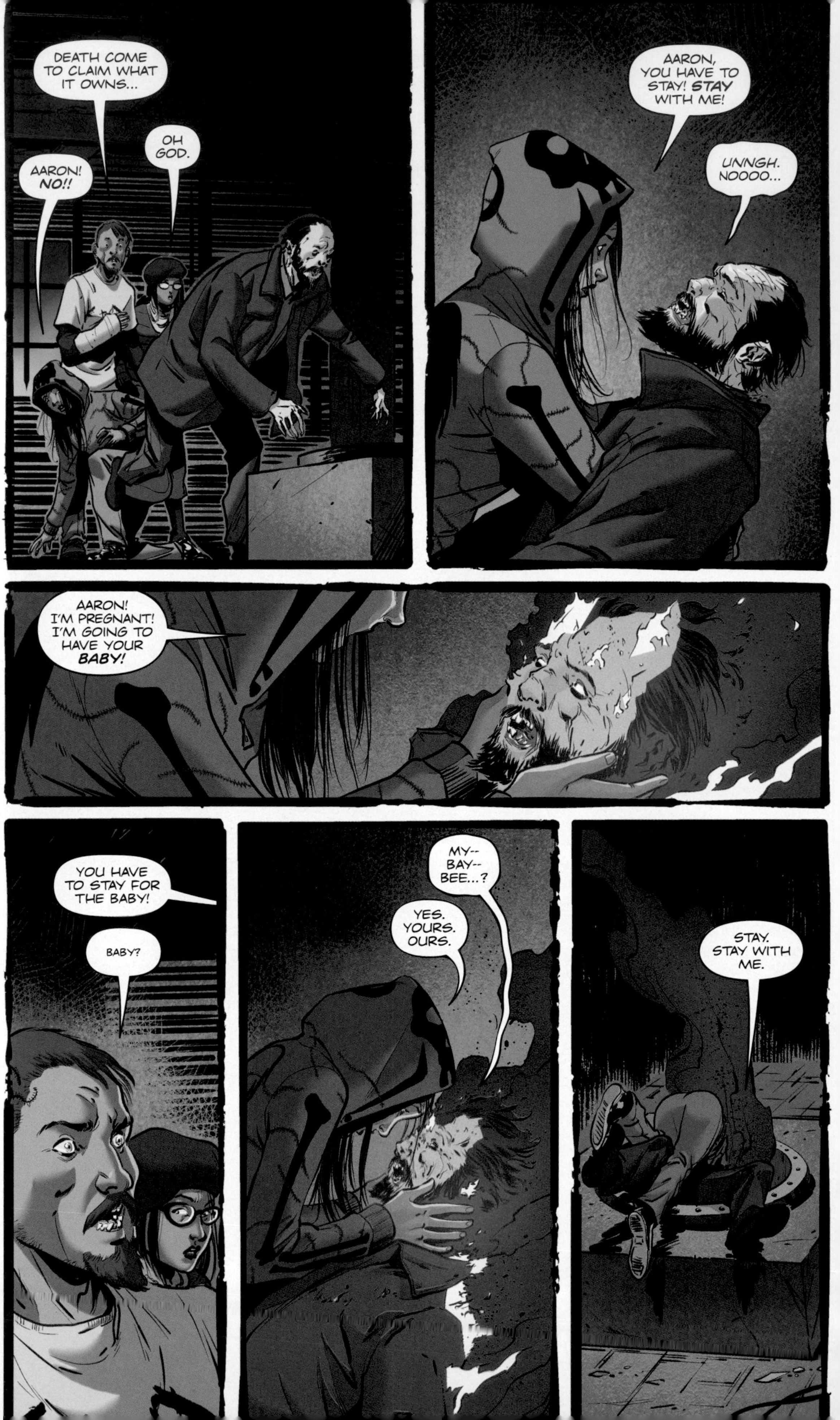
DEATH COME TO CLAIM WHAT IT OWNS...
AARON! NO!!
OH GOD.
AARON, YOU HAVE TO STAY! STAY WITH ME!
UNNGH. NOOOO...
AARON! I'M PREGNANT! I'M GOING TO HAVE YOUR BABY!
YOU HAVE TO STAY FOR THE BABY!
BABY?
MY-- BAY-- BEE...?
YES. YOURS. OURS.
STAY. STAY WITH ME.

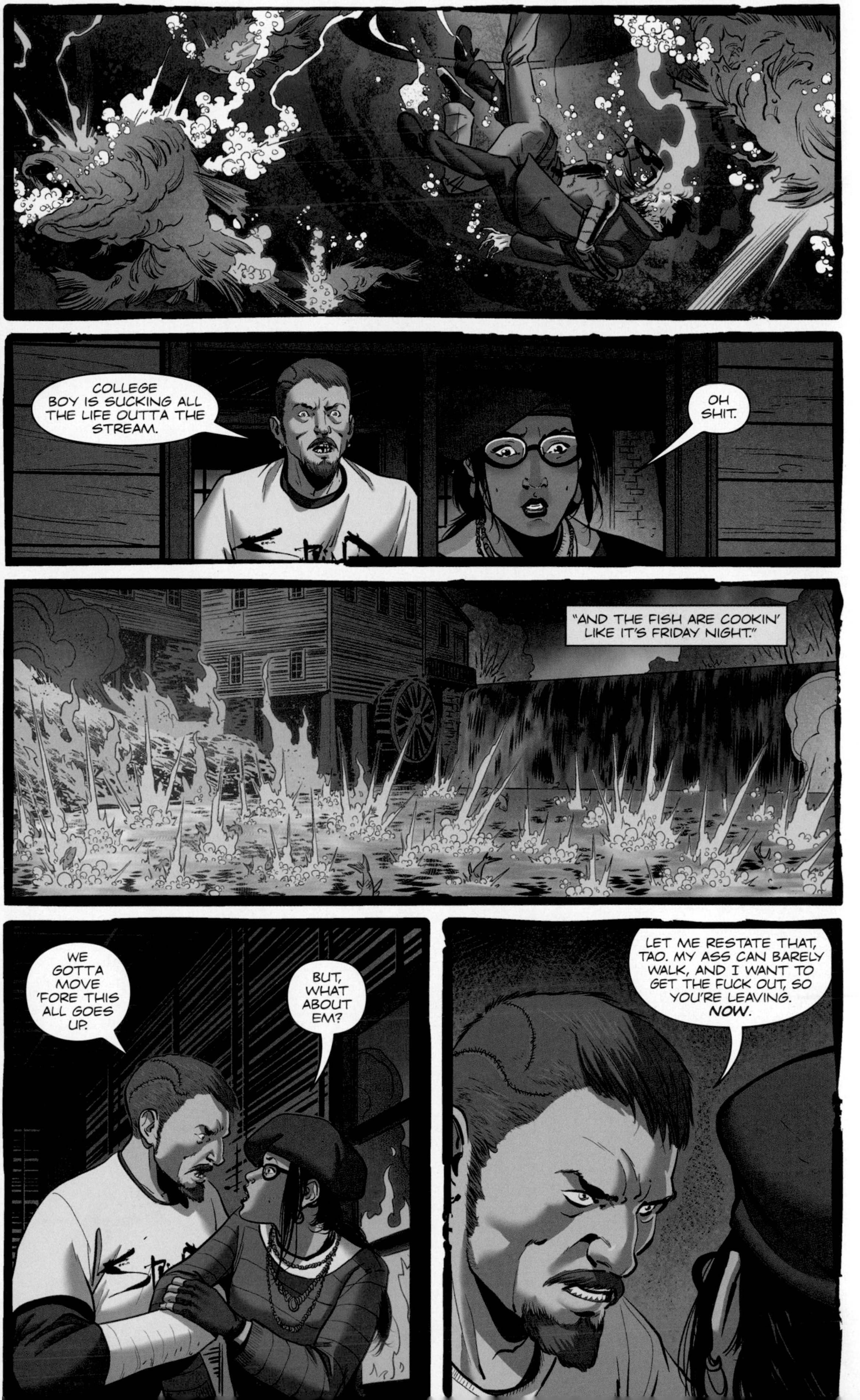
COLLEGE BOY IS SUCKING ALL THE LIFE OUTTA THE STREAM.
OH SHIT.
"AND THE FISH ARE COOKIN' LIKE IT'S FRIDAY NIGHT."
WE GOTTA MOVE 'FORE THIS ALL GOES UP.
BUT, WHAT ABOUT EM?
LET ME RESTATE THAT, TAO. MY ASS CAN BARELY WALK, AND I WANT TO GET THE FUCK OUT, SO YOU'RE LEAVING. **NOW**.

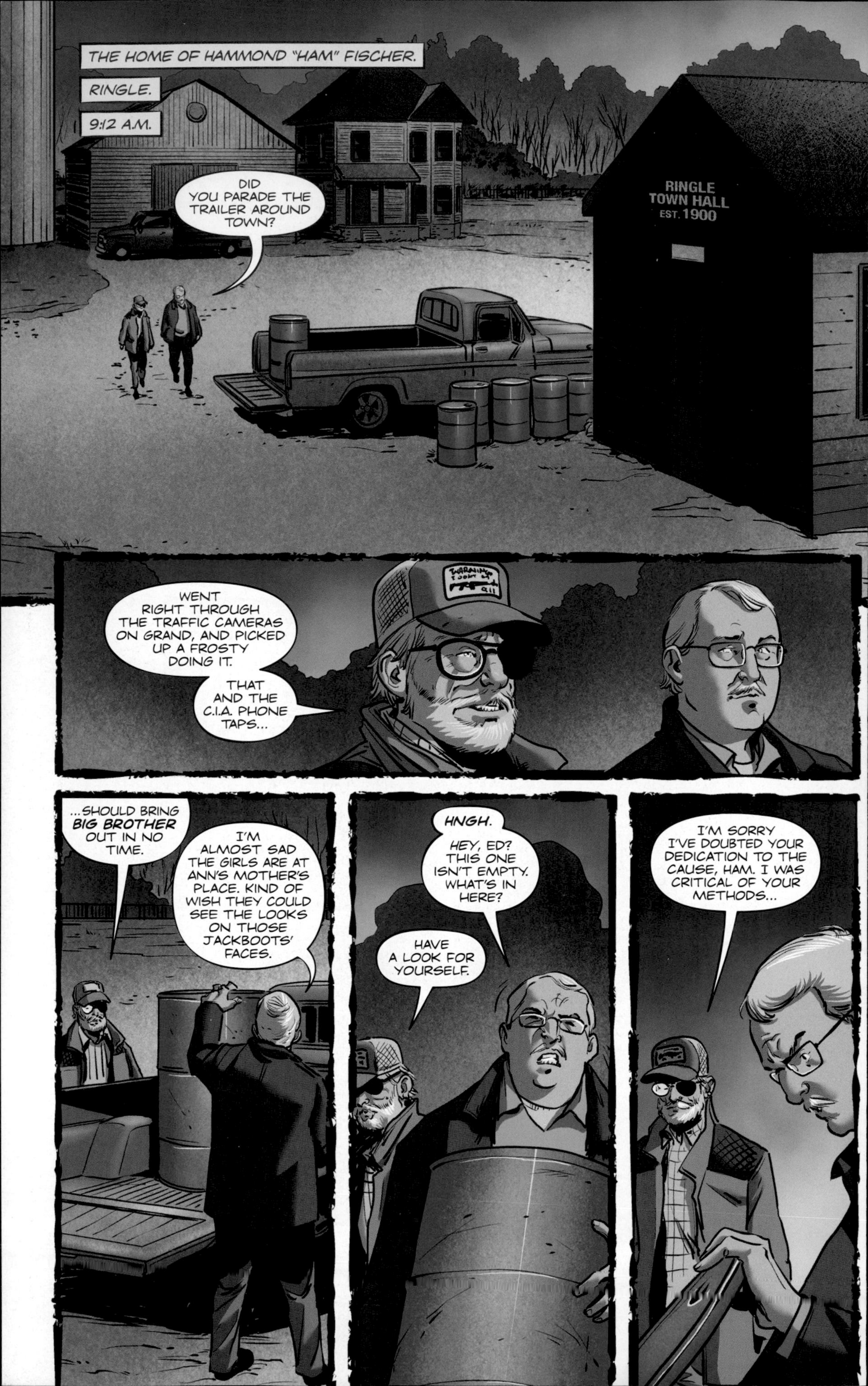
THE HOME OF HAMMOND "HAM" FISCHER.
RINGLE.
9:12 A.M.
DID YOU PARADE THE TRAILER AROUND TOWN?
RINGLE TOWN HALL EST. 1900
WENT RIGHT THROUGH THE TRAFFIC CAMERAS ON GRAND, AND PICKED UP A FROSTY DOING IT.
THAT AND THE C.I.A. PHONE TAPS...
...SHOULD BRING **BIG BROTHER** OUT IN NO TIME.
I'M ALMOST SAD THE GIRLS ARE AT ANN'S MOTHER'S PLACE. KIND OF WISH THEY COULD SEE THE LOOKS ON THOSE JACKBOOTS' FACES.
HNGH.
HEY, ED? THIS ONE ISN'T EMPTY. WHAT'S IN HERE?
HAVE A LOOK FOR YOURSELF.
I'M SORRY I'VE DOUBTED YOUR DEDICATION TO THE CAUSE, HAM. I WAS CRITICAL OF YOUR METHODS...

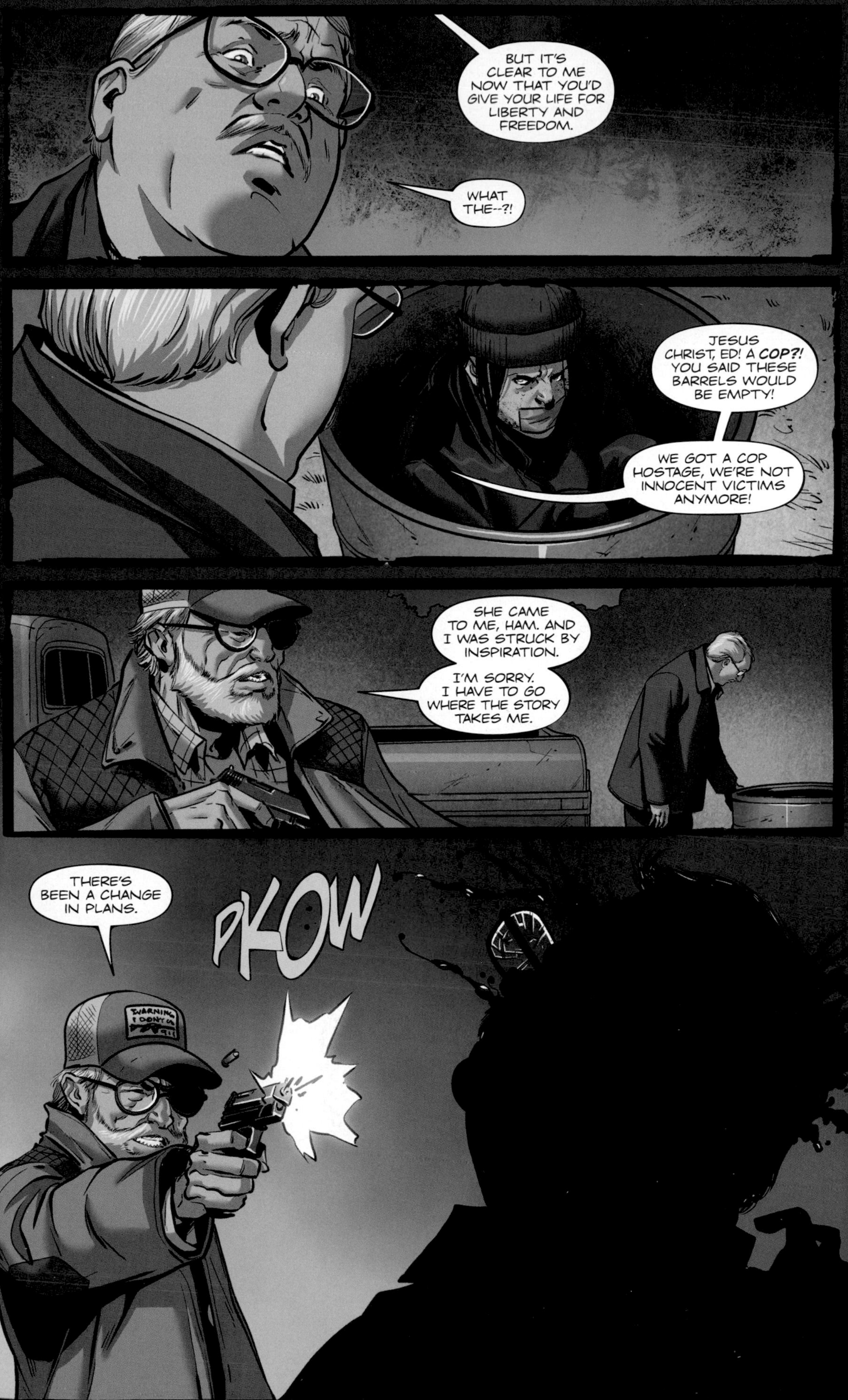
BUT IT'S CLEAR TO ME NOW THAT YOU'D GIVE YOUR LIFE FOR LIBERTY AND FREEDOM.
WHAT THE--?!
JESUS CHRIST, ED! A COP?! YOU SAID THESE BARRELS WOULD BE EMPTY!
WE GOT A COP HOSTAGE, WE'RE NOT INNOCENT VICTIMS ANYMORE!
SHE CAME TO ME, HAM. AND I WAS STRUCK BY INSPIRATION.
I'M SORRY. I HAVE TO GO WHERE THE STORY TAKES ME.
THERE'S BEEN A CHANGE IN PLANS.
PKOW

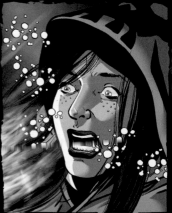

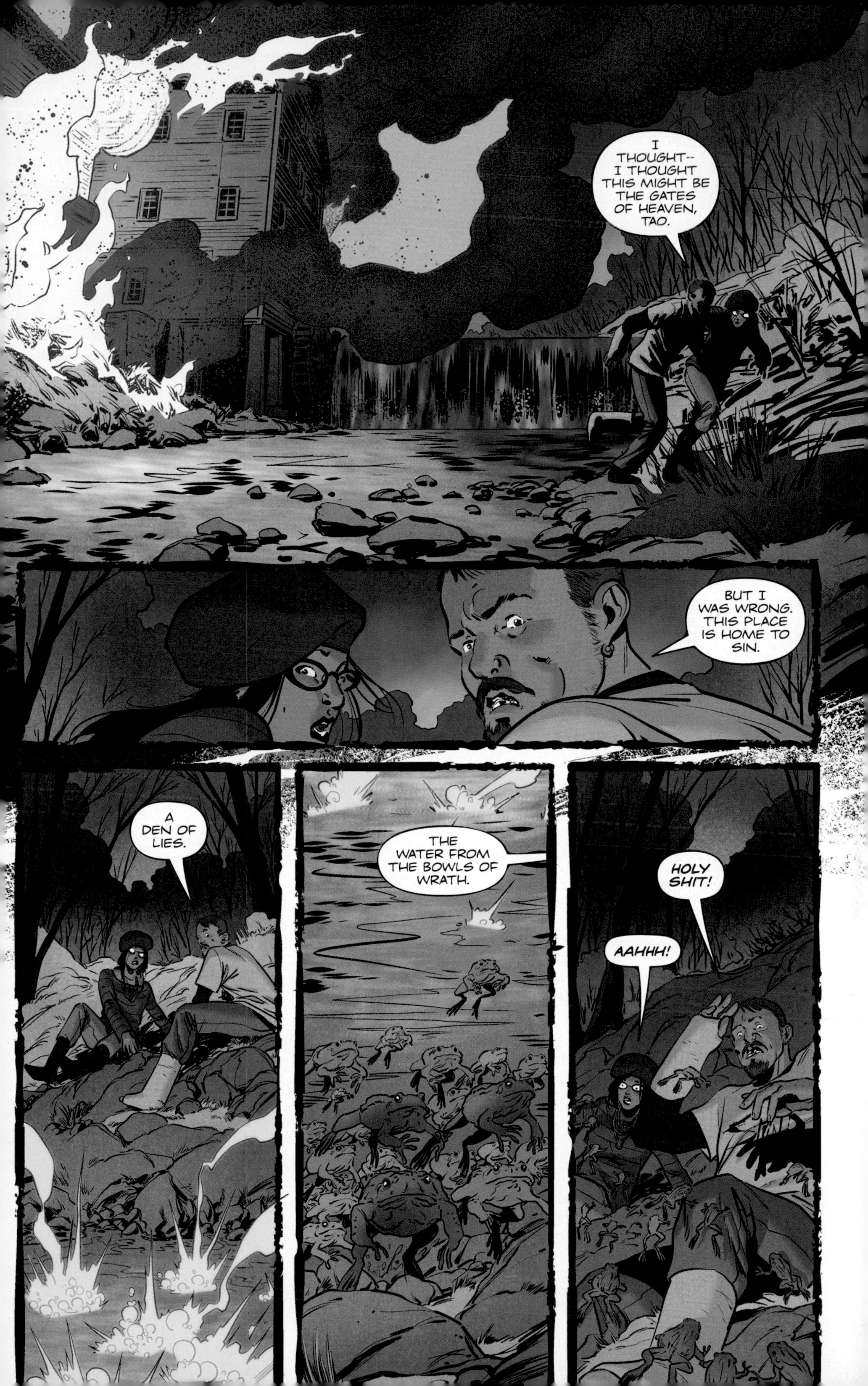
I THOUGHT-- I THOUGHT THIS MIGHT BE THE GATES OF HEAVEN, TAO.
BUT I WAS WRONG. THIS PLACE IS HOME TO SIN.
A DEN OF LIES.
THE WATER FROM THE BOWLS OF WRATH.
HOLY SHIT!
AAHHH!

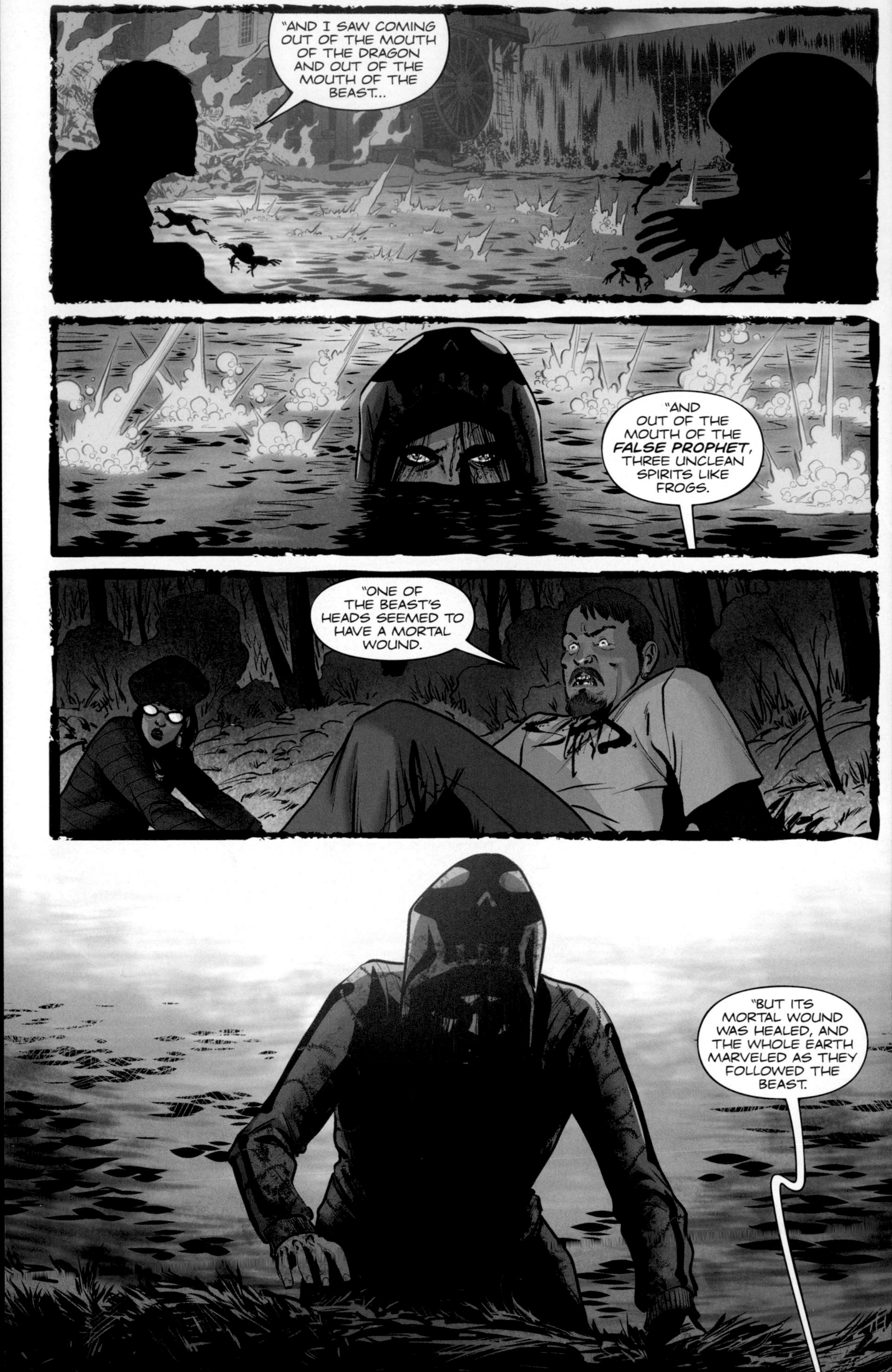
"AND I SAW COMING OUT OF THE MOUTH OF THE DRAGON AND OUT OF THE MOUTH OF THE BEAST...
"AND OUT OF THE MOUTH OF THE FALSE PROPHET, THREE UNCLEAN SPIRITS LIKE FROGS.
"ONE OF THE BEAST'S HEADS SEEMED TO HAVE A MORTAL WOUND.
"BUT ITS MORTAL WOUND WAS HEALED, AND THE WHOLE EARTH MARVELED AS THEY FOLLOWED THE BEAST.

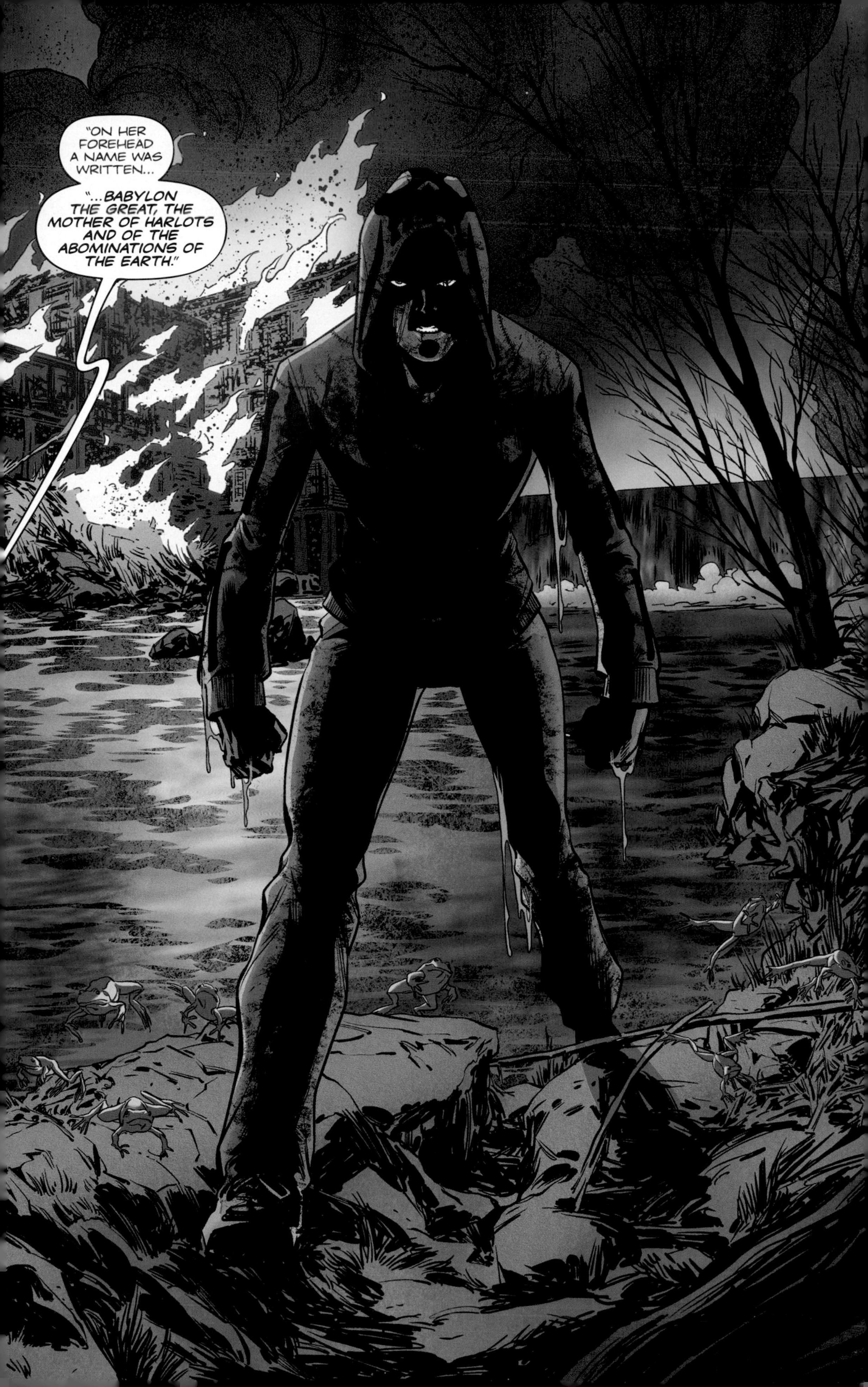
"ON HER FOREHEAD A NAME WAS WRITTEN...
"...BABYLON THE GREAT, THE MOTHER OF HARLOTS AND OF THE ABOMINATIONS OF THE EARTH."

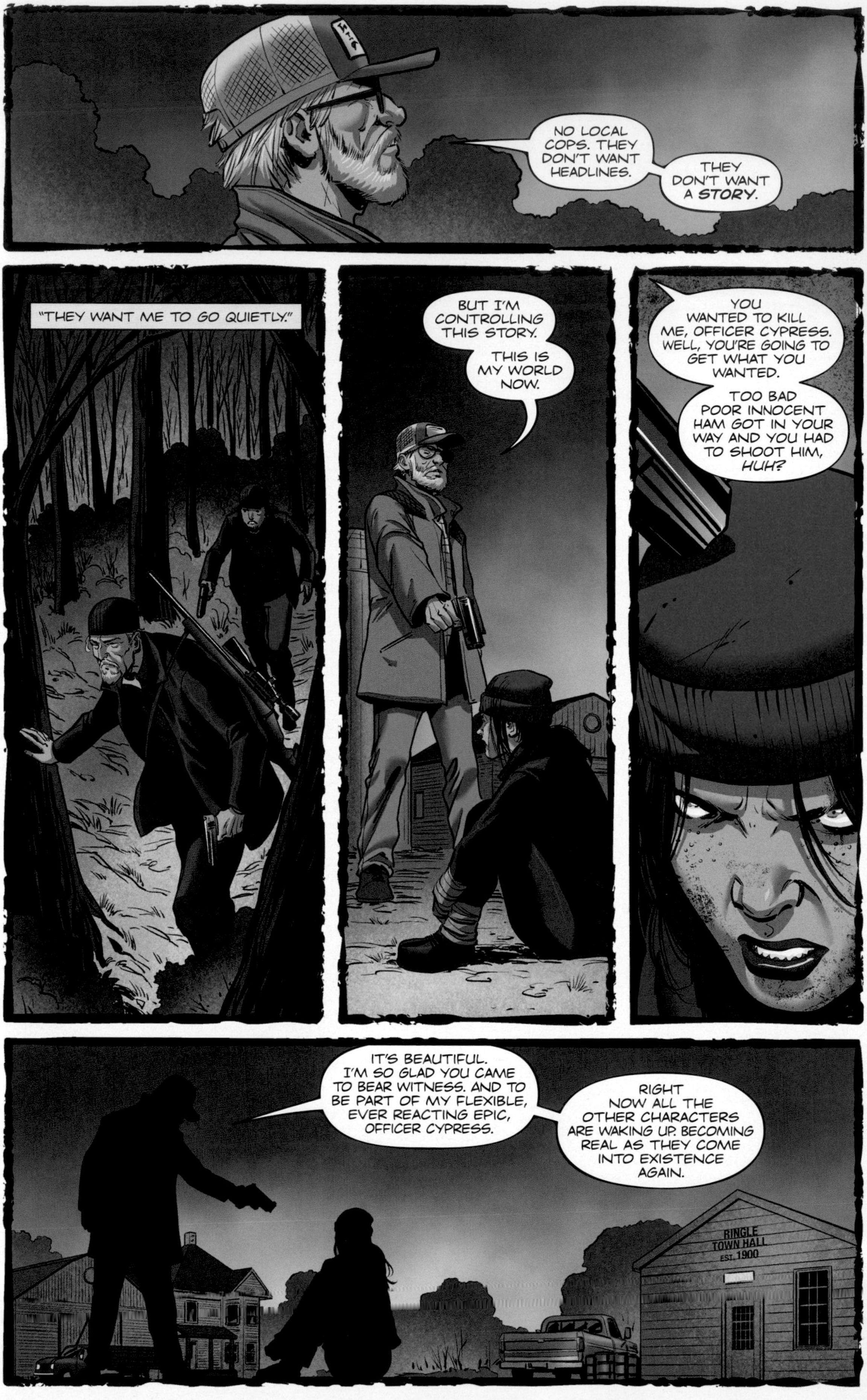
NO LOCAL COPS. THEY DON'T WANT HEADLINES.
THEY DON'T WANT A STORY.
"THEY WANT ME TO GO QUIETLY."
BUT I'M CONTROLLING THIS STORY.
THIS IS MY WORLD NOW.
YOU WANTED TO KILL ME, OFFICER CYPRESS. WELL, YOU'RE GOING TO GET WHAT YOU WANTED.
TOO BAD POOR INNOCENT HAM GOT IN YOUR WAY AND YOU HAD TO SHOOT HIM, HUH?
IT'S BEAUTIFUL. I'M SO GLAD YOU CAME TO BEAR WITNESS. AND TO BE PART OF MY FLEXIBLE, EVER REACTING EPIC, OFFICER CYPRESS.
RIGHT NOW ALL THE OTHER CHARACTERS ARE WAKING UP. BECOMING REAL AS THEY COME INTO EXISTENCE AGAIN.
RINGLE TOWN HALL EST. 1900

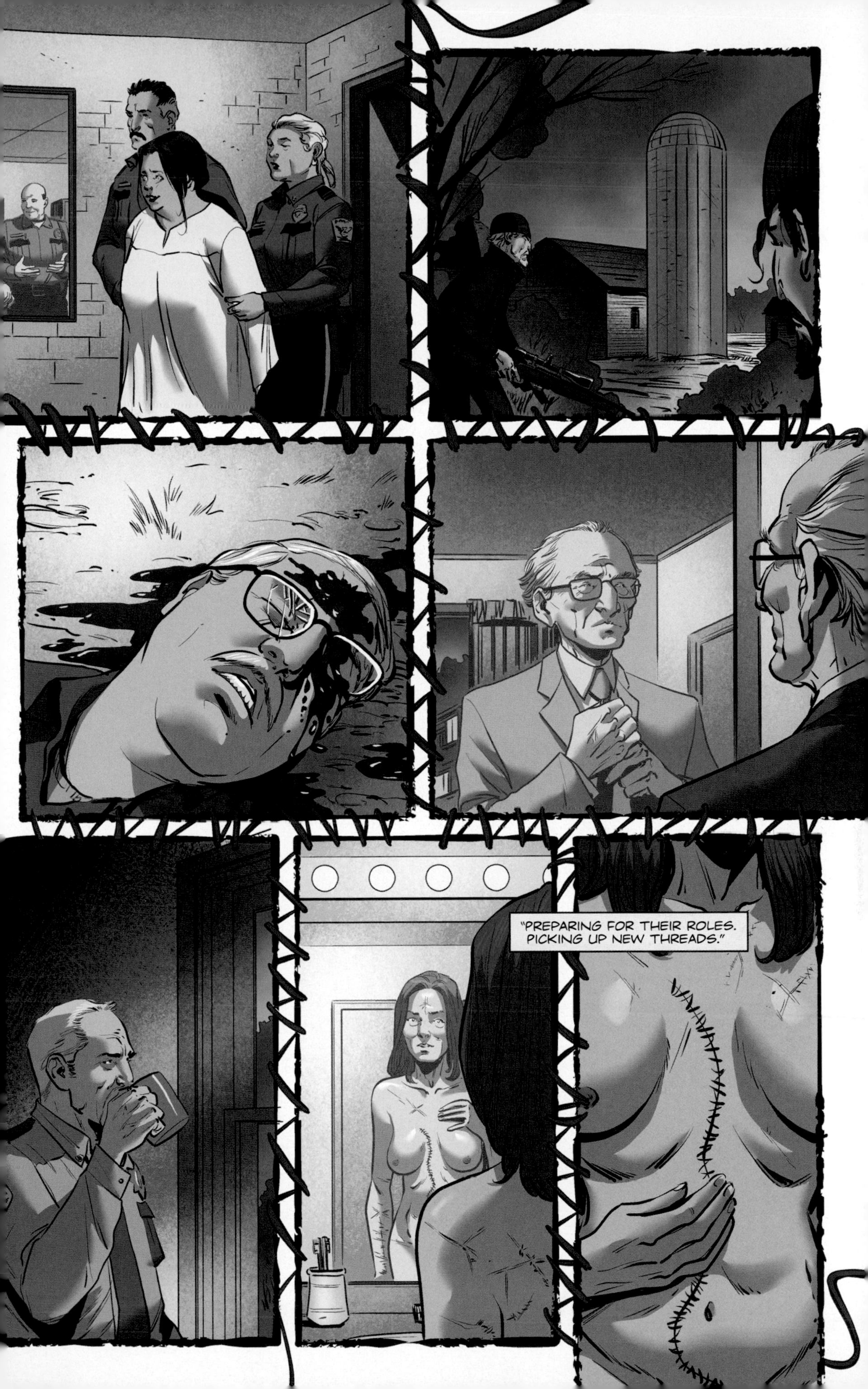
"PREPARING FOR THEIR ROLES. PICKING UP NEW THREADS."

No. 29

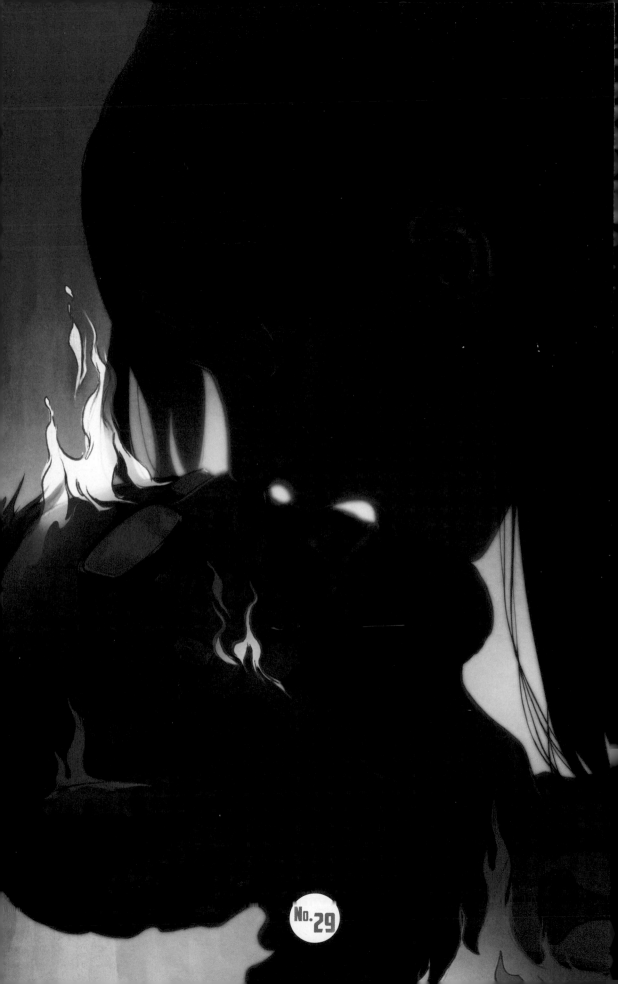

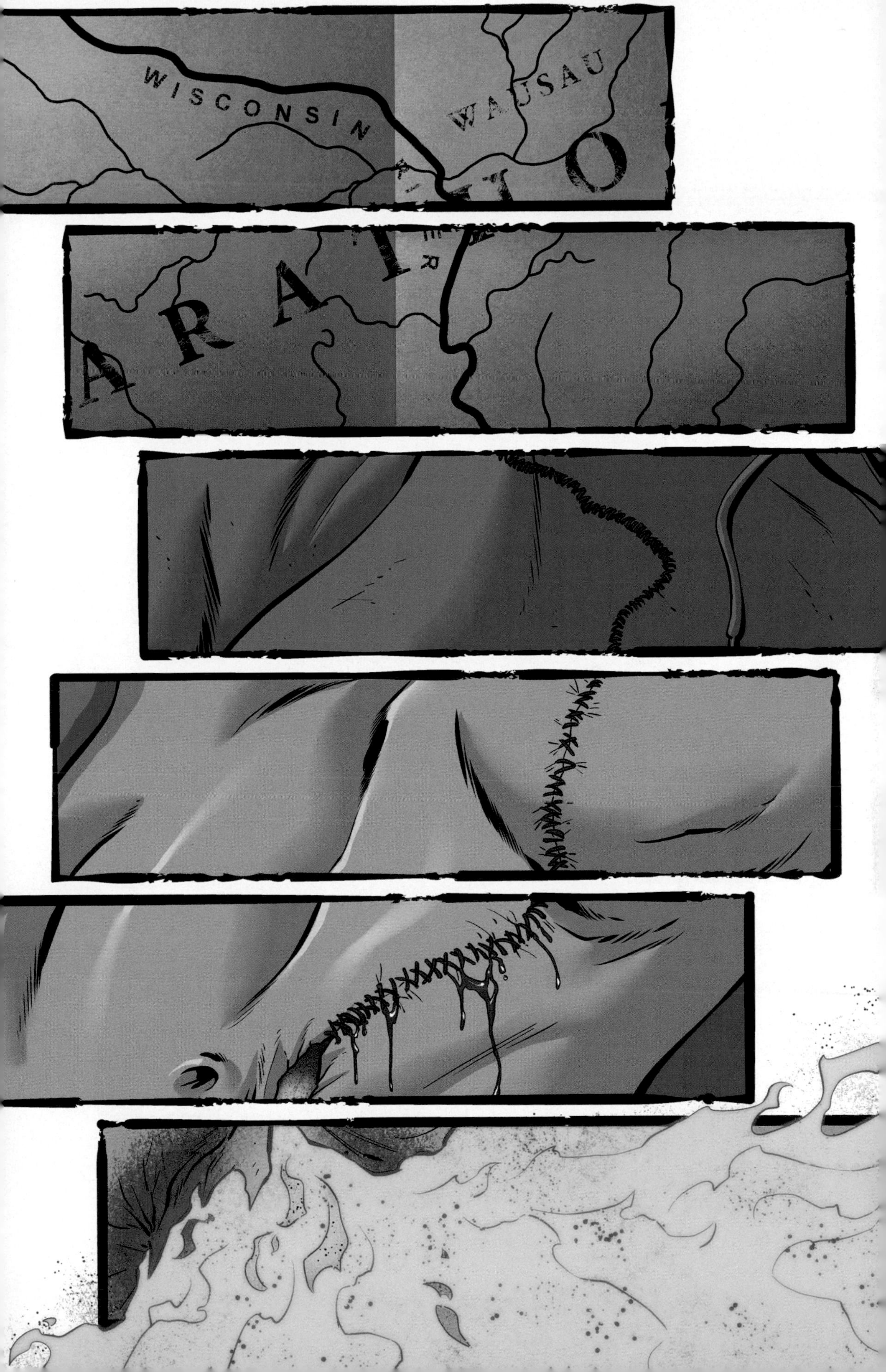
WISCONSIN
WAUSAU

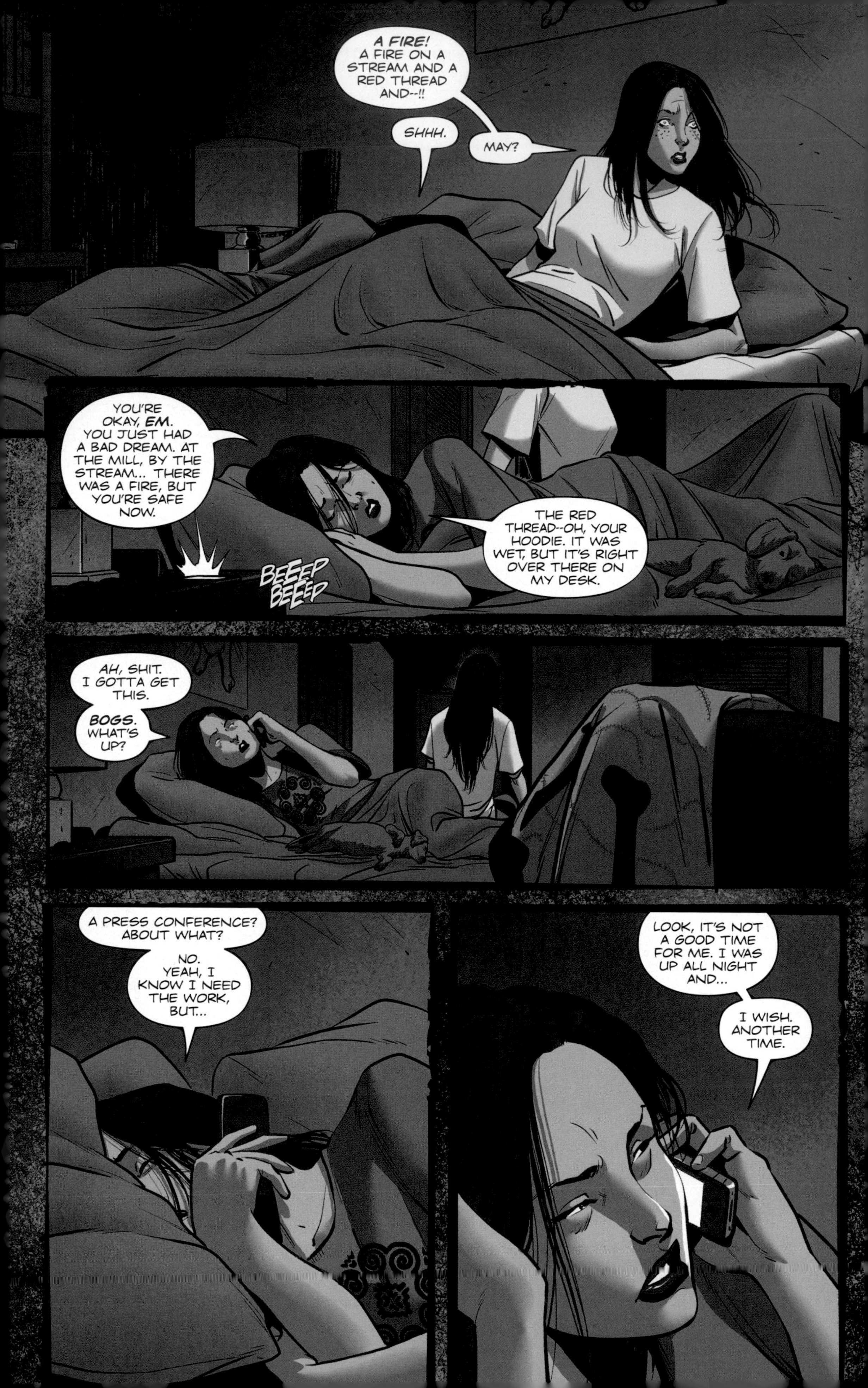
A FIRE! A FIRE ON A STREAM AND A RED THREAD AND--!!
MAY?
SHHH.
YOU'RE OKAY, EM. YOU JUST HAD A BAD DREAM. AT THE MILL, BY THE STREAM... THERE WAS A FIRE, BUT YOU'RE SAFE NOW.
THE RED THREAD--OH, YOUR HOODIE. IT WAS WET, BUT IT'S RIGHT OVER THERE ON MY DESK.
BEEEP BEEEP
AH, SHIT. I GOTTA GET THIS.
BOGS. WHAT'S UP?
A PRESS CONFERENCE? ABOUT WHAT?
NO. YEAH, I KNOW I NEED THE WORK, BUT...
LOOK, IT'S NOT A GOOD TIME FOR ME. I WAS UP ALL NIGHT AND...
I WISH. ANOTHER TIME.

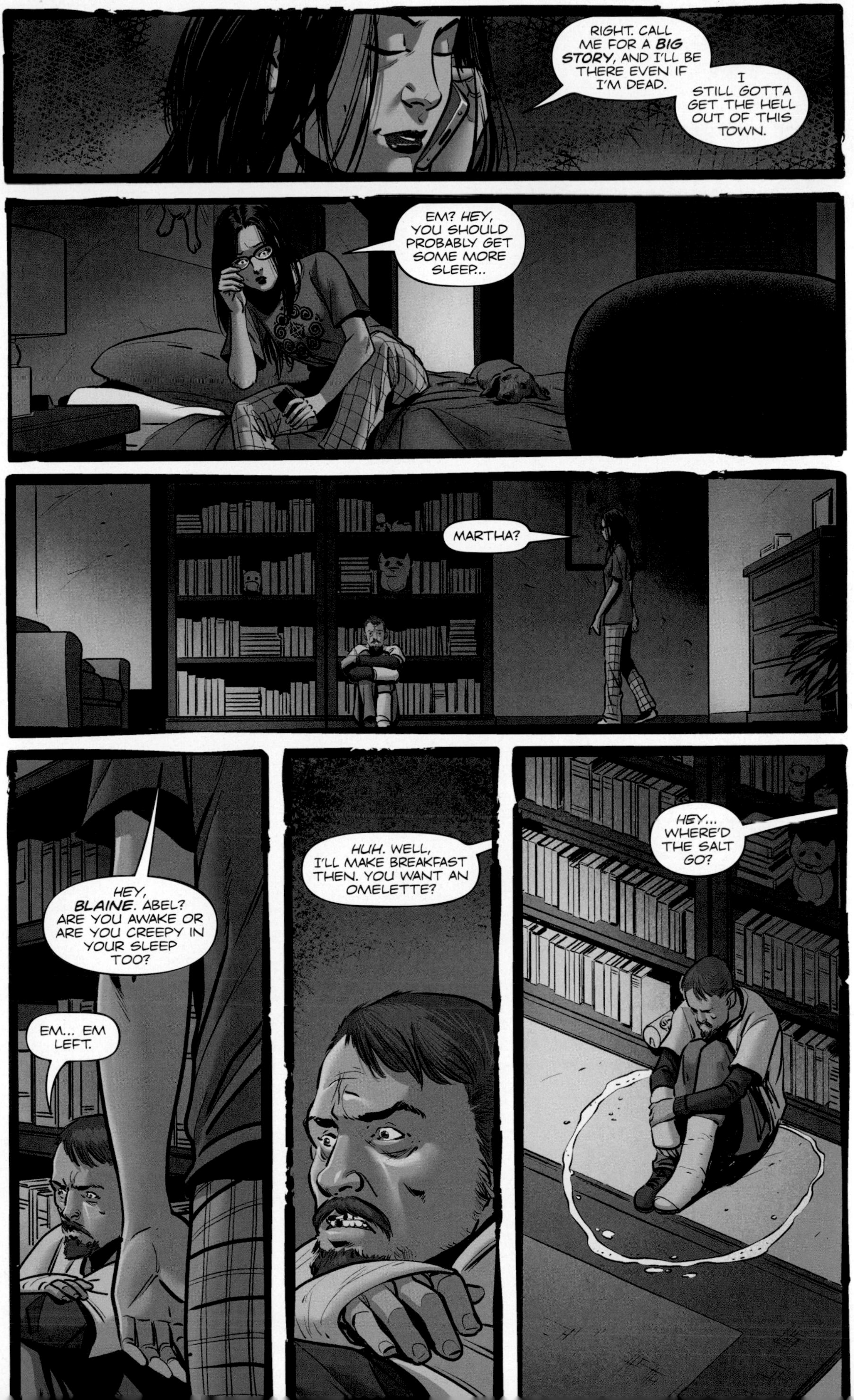
RIGHT. CALL ME FOR A BIG STORY, AND I'LL BE THERE EVEN IF I'M DEAD.
I STILL GOTTA GET THE HELL OUT OF THIS TOWN.
EM? HEY, YOU SHOULD PROBABLY GET SOME MORE SLEEP...
MARTHA?
HEY, BLAINE. ABEL? ARE YOU AWAKE OR ARE YOU CREEPY IN YOUR SLEEP TOO?
EM... EM LEFT.
HUH. WELL, I'LL MAKE BREAKFAST THEN. YOU WANT AN OMELETTE?
HEY... WHERE'D THE SALT GO?

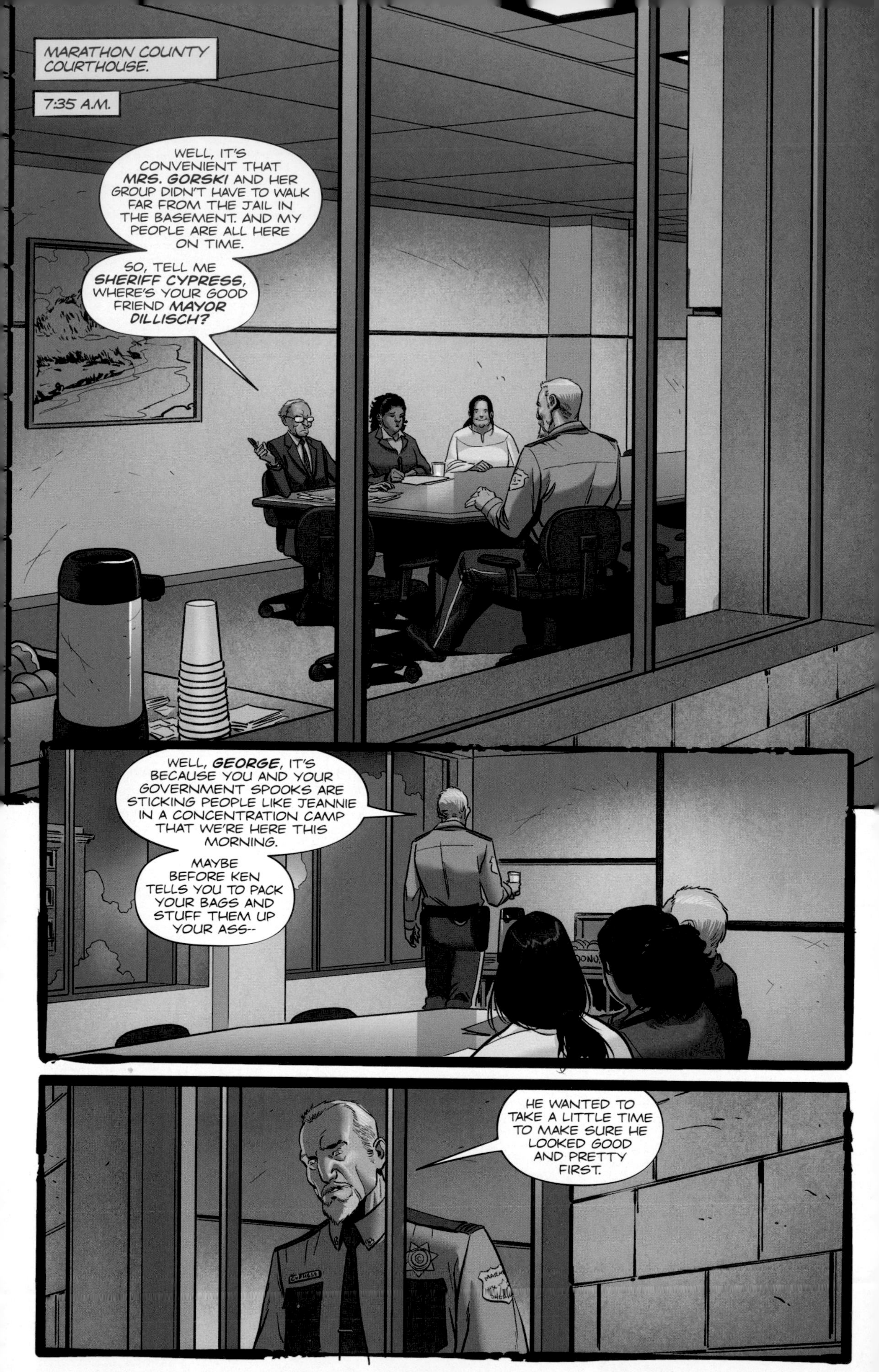
MARATHON COUNTY COURTHOUSE.
7:35 A.M.
WELL, IT'S CONVENIENT THAT MRS. GORSKI AND HER GROUP DIDN'T HAVE TO WALK FAR FROM THE JAIL IN THE BASEMENT. AND MY PEOPLE ARE ALL HERE ON TIME.
SO, TELL ME SHERIFF CYPRESS, WHERE'S YOUR GOOD FRIEND MAYOR DILLISCH?
WELL, GEORGE, IT'S BECAUSE YOU AND YOUR GOVERNMENT SPOOKS ARE STICKING PEOPLE LIKE JEANNIE IN A CONCENTRATION CAMP THAT WE'RE HERE THIS MORNING.
MAYBE BEFORE KEN TELLS YOU TO PACK YOUR BAGS AND STUFF THEM UP YOUR ASS--
HE WANTED TO TAKE A LITTLE TIME TO MAKE SURE HE LOOKED GOOD AND PRETTY FIRST.

I'M A LITTLE LATE EVERYONE...

"...THE PARKING LOT WAS FULL."

I'M SO GLAD EVERYONE COULD MAKE IT TODAY.

THE CONVERSATION ABOUT WHAT TO DO WITH "PROBLEM REVIVERS" IS IMPORTANT, BECAUSE IT SETS A PRECEDENT AND A TONE FOR HOW WE'LL TREAT ALL OUR NEWLY REVIVED CITIZENS.

SOMETIMES I THINK EVEN HAVING THAT TALK TELLS US HOW FAR WE'VE COME SINCE REVIVAL DAY ONLY A FEW SHORT MONTHS AGO.

YOU SLY SONOVA-BITCH.

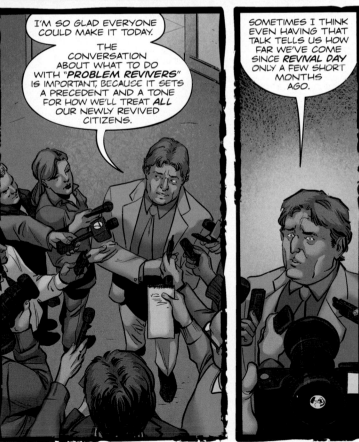

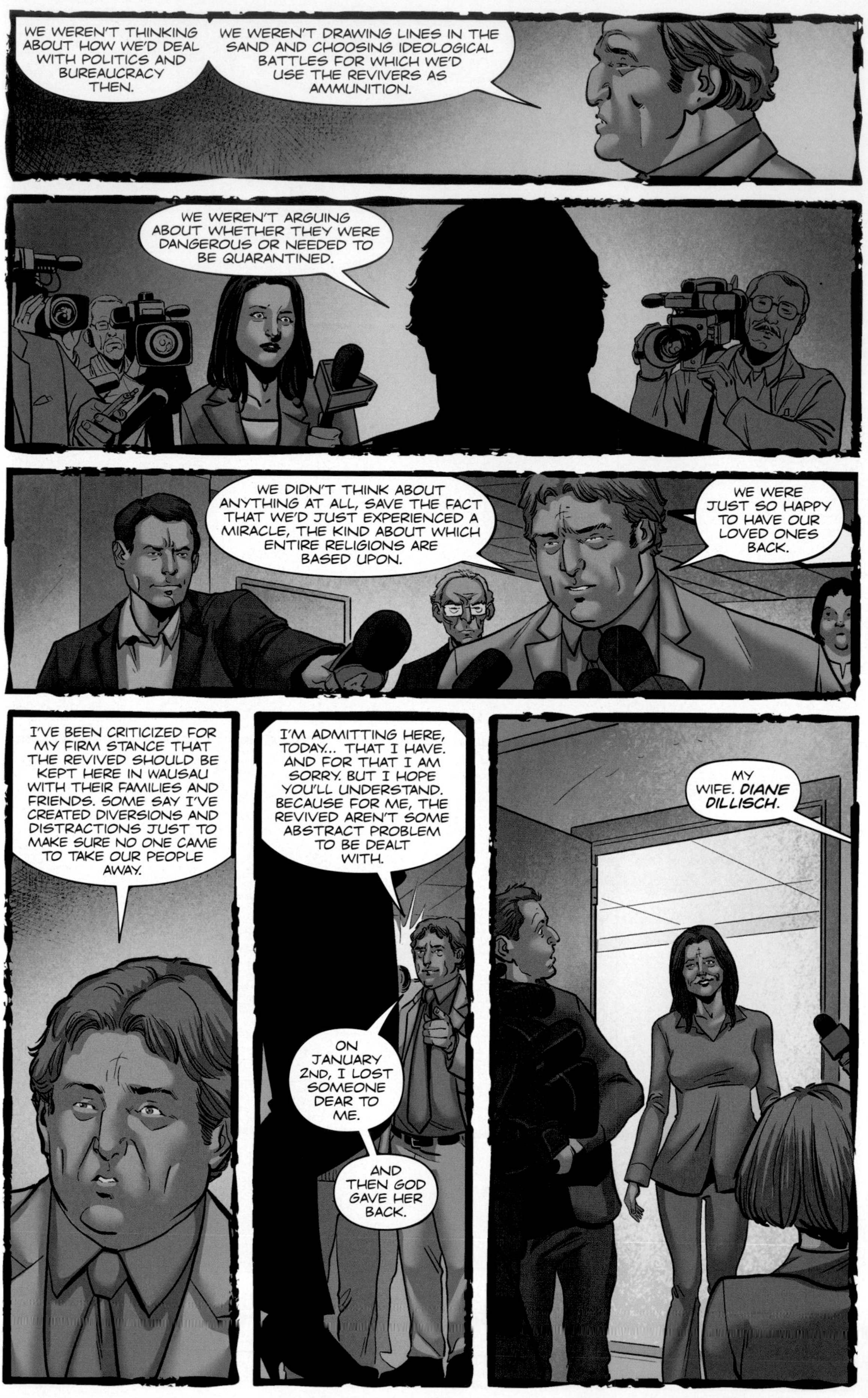
WE WEREN'T THINKING ABOUT HOW WE'D DEAL WITH POLITICS AND BUREAUCRACY THEN.
WE WEREN'T DRAWING LINES IN THE SAND AND CHOOSING IDEOLOGICAL BATTLES FOR WHICH WE'D USE THE REVIVERS AS AMMUNITION.
WE WEREN'T ARGUING ABOUT WHETHER THEY WERE DANGEROUS OR NEEDED TO BE QUARANTINED.
WE DIDN'T THINK ABOUT ANYTHING AT ALL, SAVE THE FACT THAT WE'D JUST EXPERIENCED A MIRACLE, THE KIND ABOUT WHICH ENTIRE RELIGIONS ARE BASED UPON.
WE WERE JUST SO HAPPY TO HAVE OUR LOVED ONES BACK.
I'VE BEEN CRITICIZED FOR MY FIRM STANCE THAT THE REVIVED SHOULD BE KEPT HERE IN WAUSAU WITH THEIR FAMILIES AND FRIENDS. SOME SAY I'VE CREATED DIVERSIONS AND DISTRACTIONS JUST TO MAKE SURE NO ONE CAME TO TAKE OUR PEOPLE AWAY.
I'M ADMITTING HERE, TODAY... THAT I HAVE. AND FOR THAT I AM SORRY. BUT I HOPE YOU'LL UNDERSTAND. BECAUSE FOR ME, THE REVIVED AREN'T SOME ABSTRACT PROBLEM TO BE DEALT WITH.
ON JANUARY 2ND, I LOST SOMEONE DEAR TO ME.
AND THEN GOD GAVE HER BACK.
MY WIFE. *DIANE DILLISCH*.

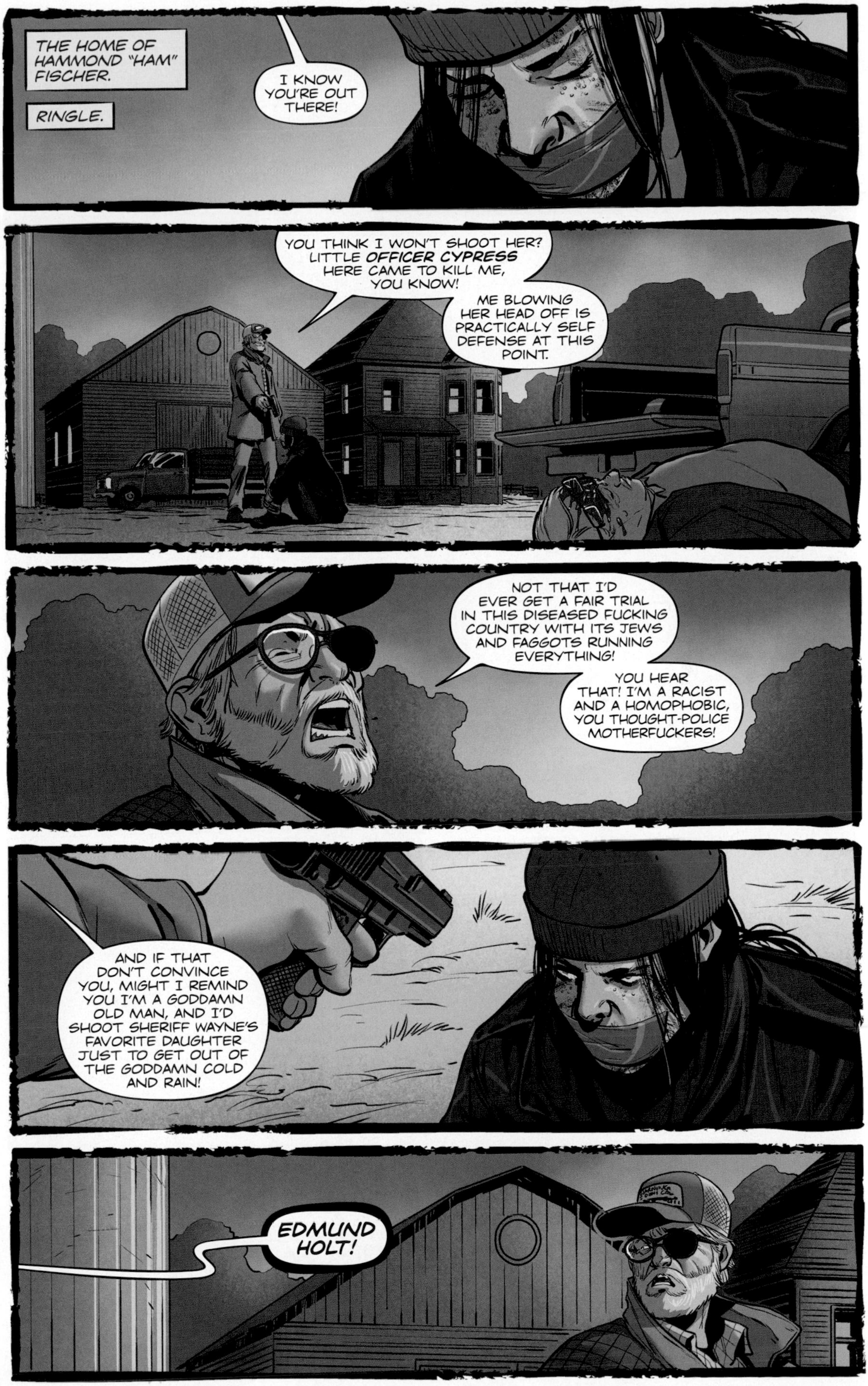
THE HOME OF HAMMOND "HAM" FISCHER.
RINGLE.
I KNOW YOU'RE OUT THERE!
YOU THINK I WON'T SHOOT HER? LITTLE **OFFICER CYPRESS** HERE CAME TO KILL ME, YOU KNOW!
ME BLOWING HER HEAD OFF IS PRACTICALLY SELF DEFENSE AT THIS POINT.
NOT THAT I'D EVER GET A FAIR TRIAL IN THIS DISEASED FUCKING COUNTRY WITH ITS JEWS AND FAGGOTS RUNNING EVERYTHING!
YOU HEAR THAT! I'M A RACIST AND A HOMOPHOBIC, YOU THOUGHT-POLICE MOTHERFUCKERS!
AND IF THAT DON'T CONVINCE YOU, MIGHT I REMIND YOU I'M A GODDAMN OLD MAN, AND I'D SHOOT SHERIFF WAYNE'S FAVORITE DAUGHTER JUST TO GET OUT OF THE GODDAMN COLD AND RAIN!
EDMUND HOLT!

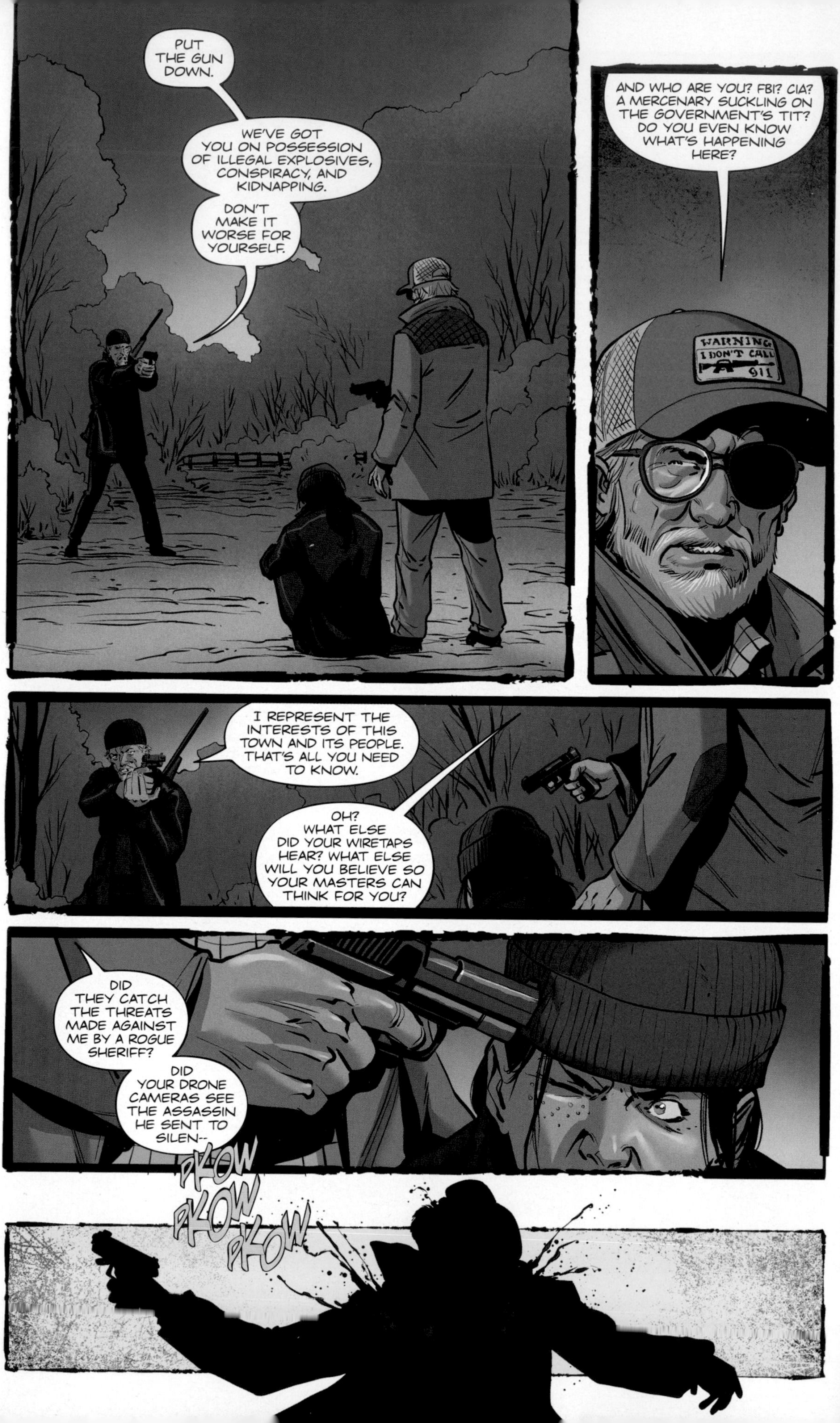
PUT THE GUN DOWN.
WE'VE GOT YOU ON POSSESSION OF ILLEGAL EXPLOSIVES, CONSPIRACY, AND KIDNAPPING.
DON'T MAKE IT WORSE FOR YOURSELF.
AND WHO ARE YOU? FBI? CIA? A MERCENARY SUCKLING ON THE GOVERNMENT'S TIT? DO YOU EVEN KNOW WHAT'S HAPPENING HERE?
WARNING I DON'T CALL 911
I REPRESENT THE INTERESTS OF THIS TOWN AND ITS PEOPLE. THAT'S ALL YOU NEED TO KNOW.
OH? WHAT ELSE DID YOUR WIRETAPS HEAR? WHAT ELSE WILL YOU BELIEVE SO YOUR MASTERS CAN THINK FOR YOU?
DID THEY CATCH THE THREATS MADE AGAINST ME BY A ROGUE SHERIFF?
DID YOUR DRONE CAMERAS SEE THE ASSASSIN HE SENT TO SILEN--
PKOW PKOW PKOW

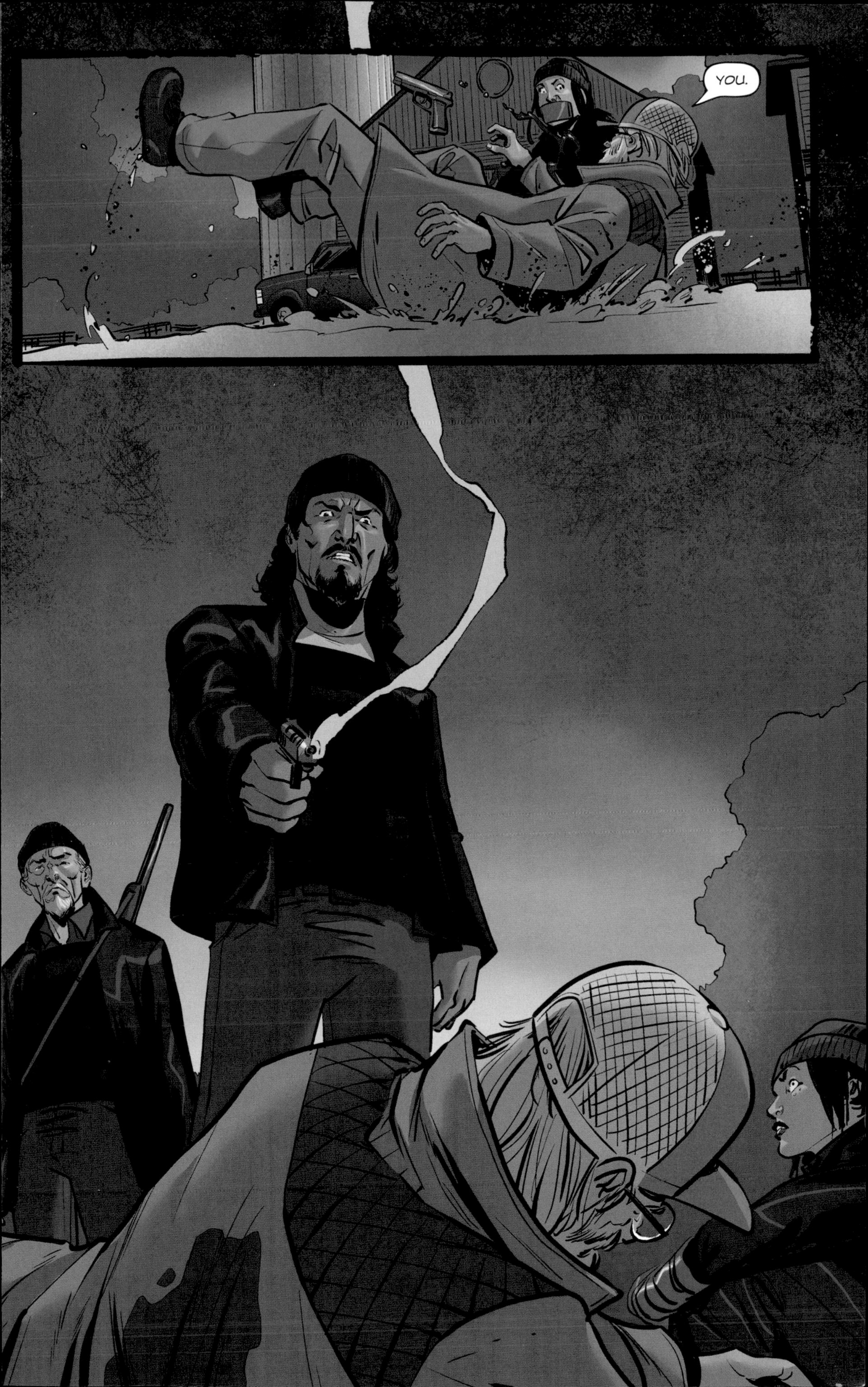
YOU.

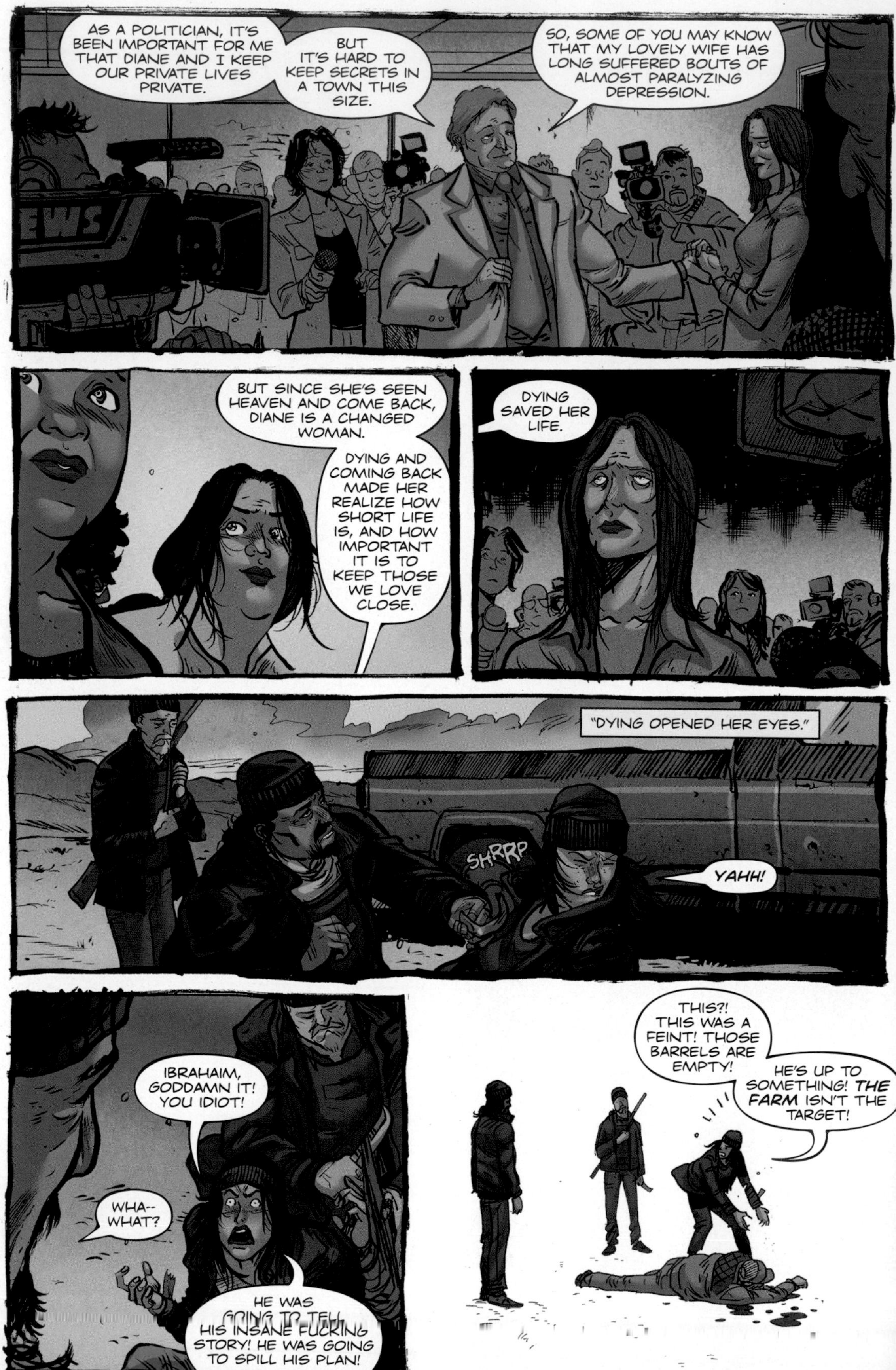
AS A POLITICIAN, IT'S BEEN IMPORTANT FOR ME THAT DIANE AND I KEEP OUR PRIVATE LIVES PRIVATE.
BUT IT'S HARD TO KEEP SECRETS IN A TOWN THIS SIZE.
SO, SOME OF YOU MAY KNOW THAT MY LOVELY WIFE HAS LONG SUFFERED BOUTS OF ALMOST PARALYZING DEPRESSION.
EWS
BUT SINCE SHE'S SEEN HEAVEN AND COME BACK, DIANE IS A CHANGED WOMAN.
DYING AND COMING BACK MADE HER REALIZE HOW SHORT LIFE IS, AND HOW IMPORTANT IT IS TO KEEP THOSE WE LOVE CLOSE.
DYING SAVED HER LIFE.
"DYING OPENED HER EYES."
SHRRP
YAHH!
IBRAHAIM, GODDAMN IT! YOU IDIOT!
WHA-- WHAT?
HE WAS GOING TO TELL HIS INSANE FUCKING STORY! HE WAS GOING TO SPILL HIS PLAN!
THIS?! THIS WAS A FEINT! THOSE BARRELS ARE EMPTY!
HE'S UP TO SOMETHING! THE FARM ISN'T THE TARGET!

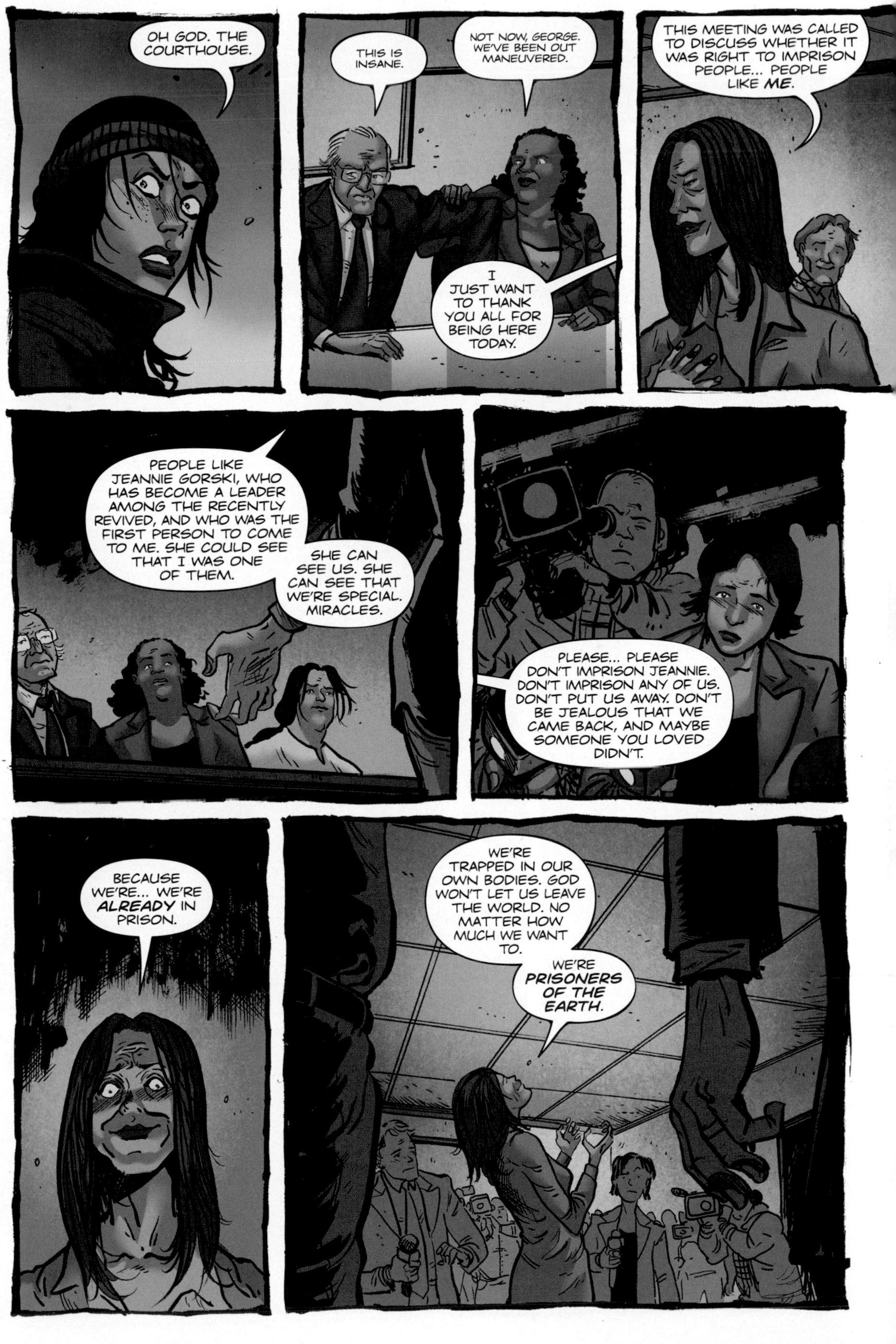
OH GOD. THE COURTHOUSE.
THIS IS INSANE.
NOT NOW, GEORGE. WE'VE BEEN OUT MANEUVERED.
I JUST WANT TO THANK YOU ALL FOR BEING HERE TODAY.
THIS MEETING WAS CALLED TO DISCUSS WHETHER IT WAS RIGHT TO IMPRISON PEOPLE... PEOPLE LIKE *ME*.
PEOPLE LIKE JEANNIE GORSKI, WHO HAS BECOME A LEADER AMONG THE RECENTLY REVIVED, AND WHO WAS THE FIRST PERSON TO COME TO ME. SHE COULD SEE THAT I WAS ONE OF THEM.
SHE CAN SEE US. SHE CAN SEE THAT WE'RE SPECIAL. MIRACLES.
PLEASE... PLEASE DON'T IMPRISON JEANNIE. DON'T IMPRISON ANY OF US. DON'T PUT US AWAY. DON'T BE JEALOUS THAT WE CAME BACK, AND MAYBE SOMEONE YOU LOVED DIDN'T.
BECAUSE WE'RE... WE'RE *ALREADY* IN PRISON.
WE'RE TRAPPED IN OUR OWN BODIES. GOD WON'T LET US LEAVE THE WORLD. NO MATTER HOW MUCH WE WANT TO.
WE'RE *PRISONERS OF THE EARTH*.

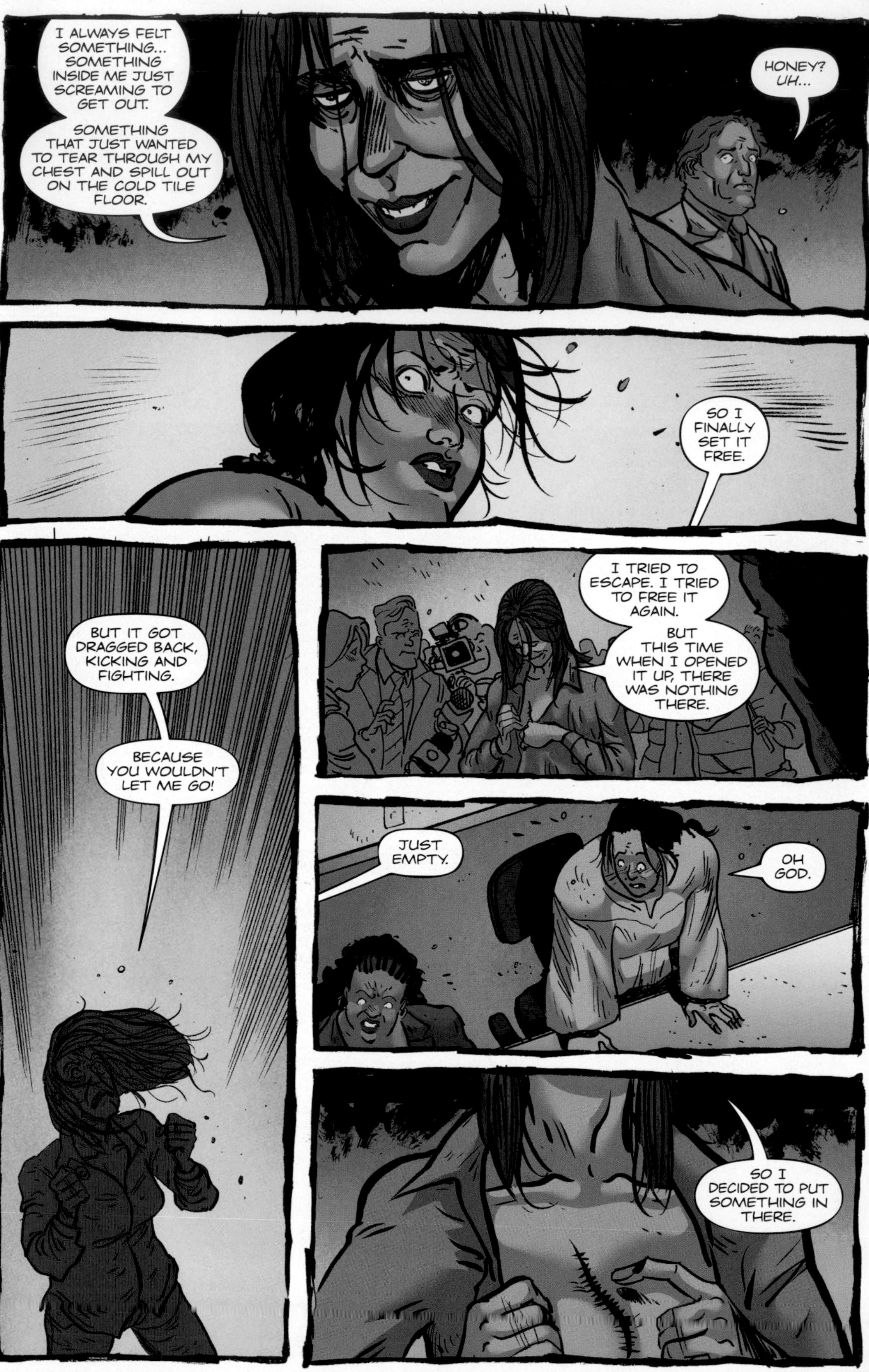
I ALWAYS FELT SOMETHING... SOMETHING INSIDE ME JUST SCREAMING TO GET OUT.
SOMETHING THAT JUST WANTED TO TEAR THROUGH MY CHEST AND SPILL OUT ON THE COLD TILE FLOOR.
HONEY? UH...
SO I FINALLY SET IT FREE.
BUT IT GOT DRAGGED BACK, KICKING AND FIGHTING.
BECAUSE YOU WOULDN'T LET ME GO!
I TRIED TO ESCAPE. I TRIED TO FREE IT AGAIN.
BUT THIS TIME WHEN I OPENED IT UP, THERE WAS NOTHING THERE.
JUST EMPTY.
OH GOD.
SO I DECIDED TO PUT SOMETHING IN THERE.

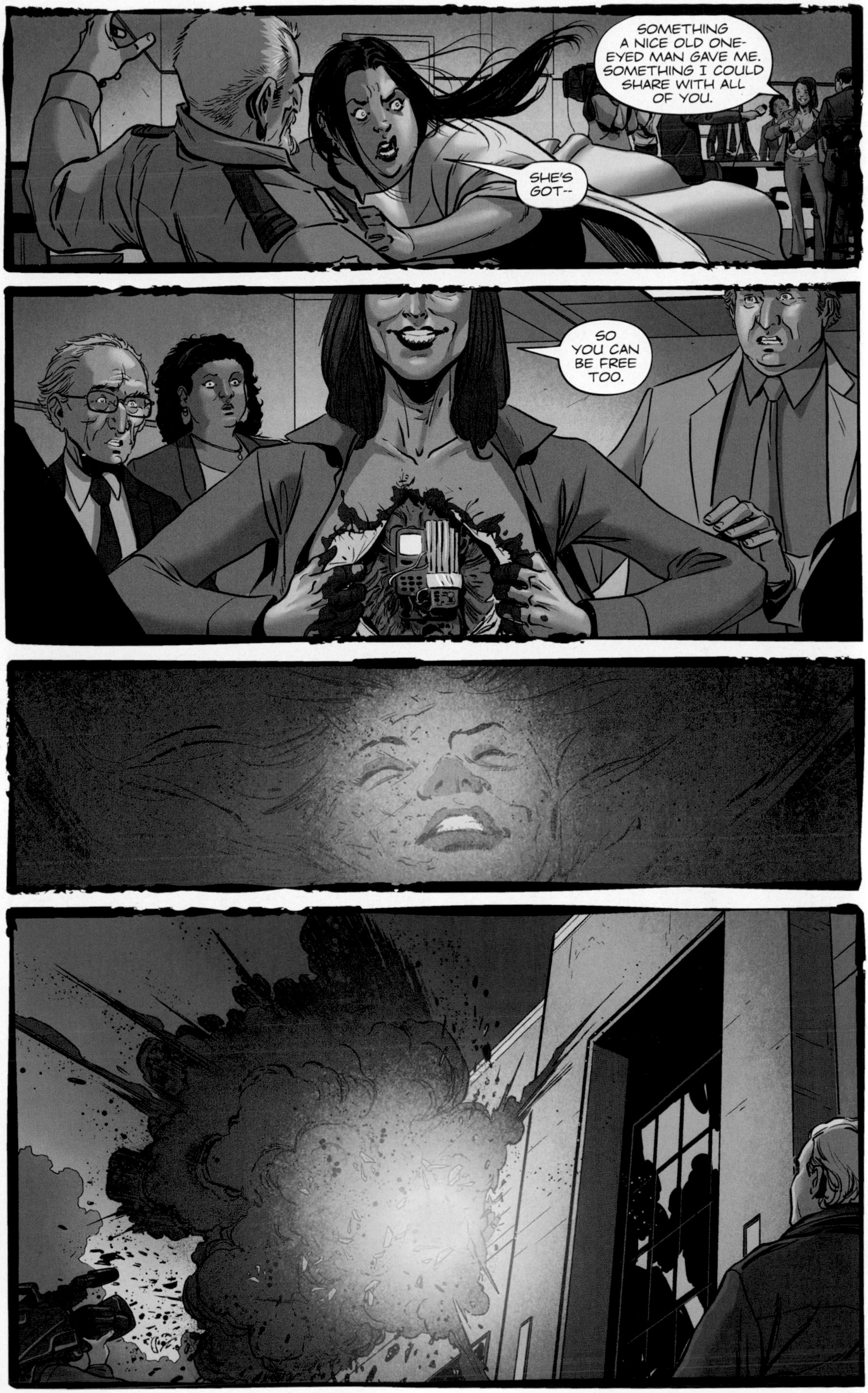
SOMETHING A NICE OLD ONE-EYED MAN GAVE ME. SOMETHING I COULD SHARE WITH ALL OF YOU.
SHE'S GOT--
SO YOU CAN BE FREE TOO.

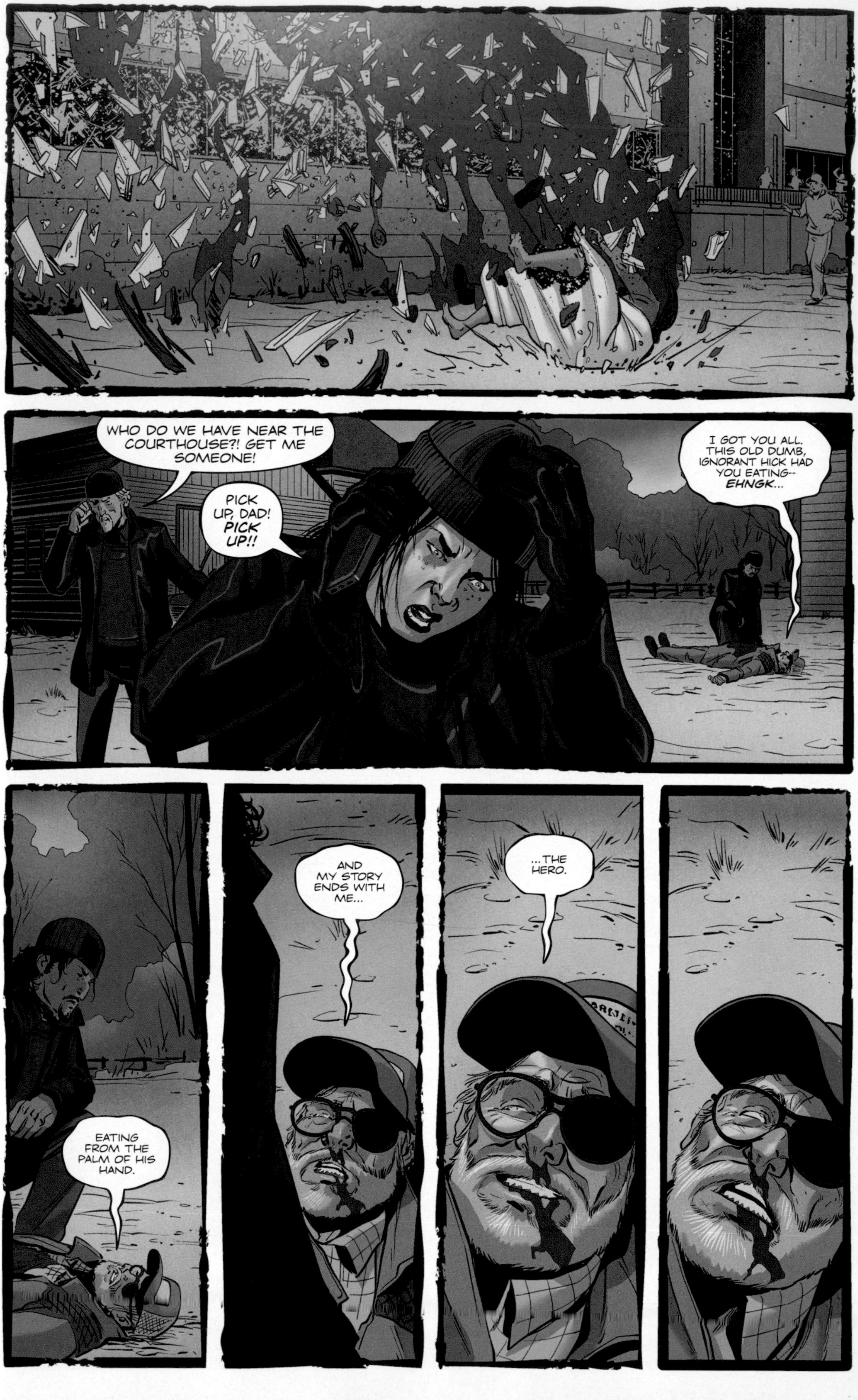
WHO DO WE HAVE NEAR THE COURTHOUSE?! GET ME SOMEONE!
PICK UP, DAD! PICK UP!!
I GOT YOU ALL. THIS OLD DUMB, IGNORANT HICK HAD YOU EATING-- EHNGK...
EATING FROM THE PALM OF HIS HAND.
AND MY STORY ENDS WITH ME...
...THE HERO.

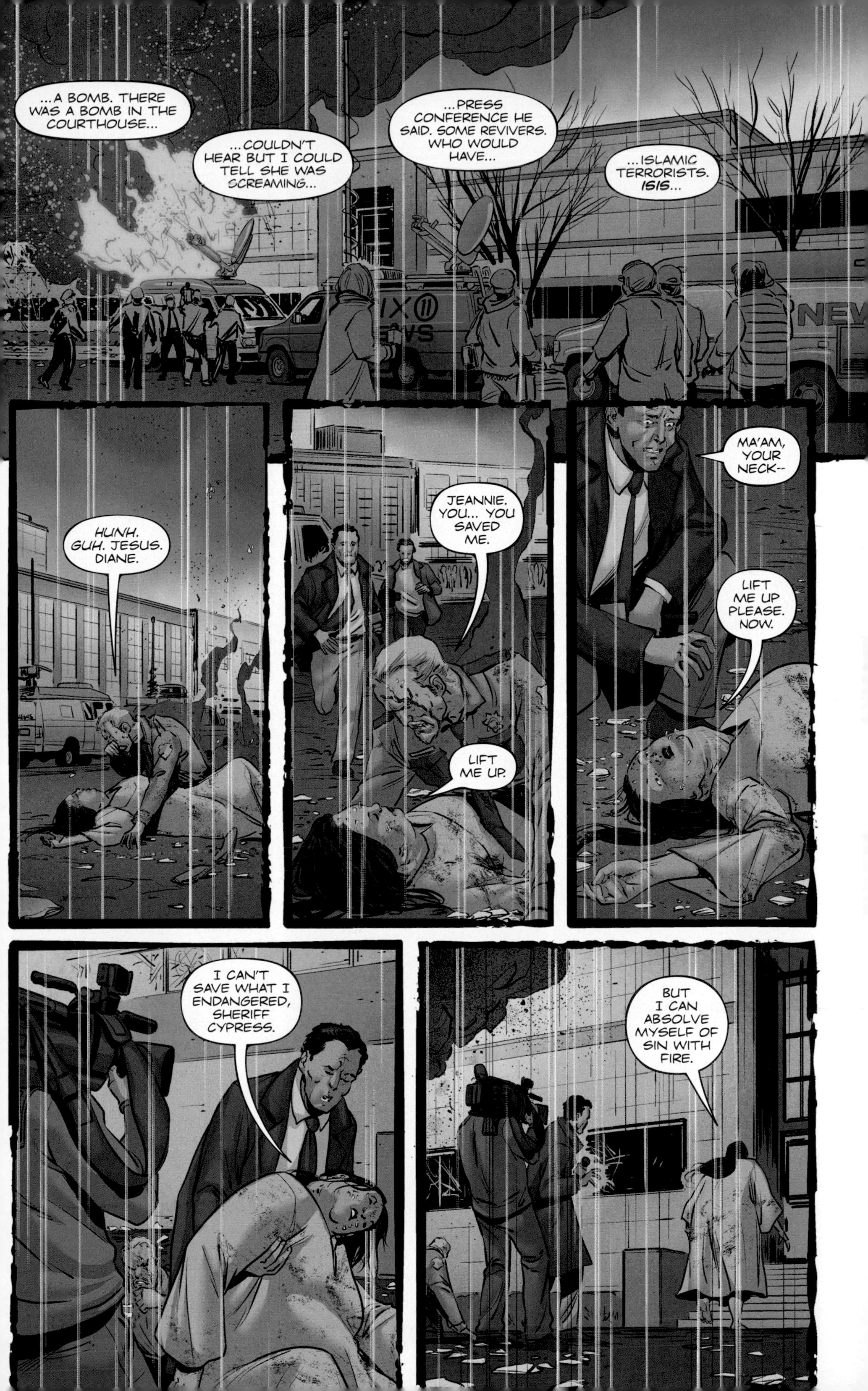
...A BOMB. THERE WAS A BOMB IN THE COURTHOUSE...
...COULDN'T HEAR BUT I COULD TELL SHE WAS SCREAMING...
...PRESS CONFERENCE HE SAID. SOME REVIVERS. WHO WOULD HAVE...
...ISLAMIC TERRORISTS. ISIS...
HUNH. GUH. JESUS. DIANE.
JEANNIE. YOU... YOU SAVED ME.
LIFT ME UP.
MA'AM, YOUR NECK--
LIFT ME UP PLEASE. NOW.
I CAN'T SAVE WHAT I ENDANGERED, SHERIFF CYPRESS.
BUT I CAN ABSOLVE MYSELF OF SIN WITH FIRE.

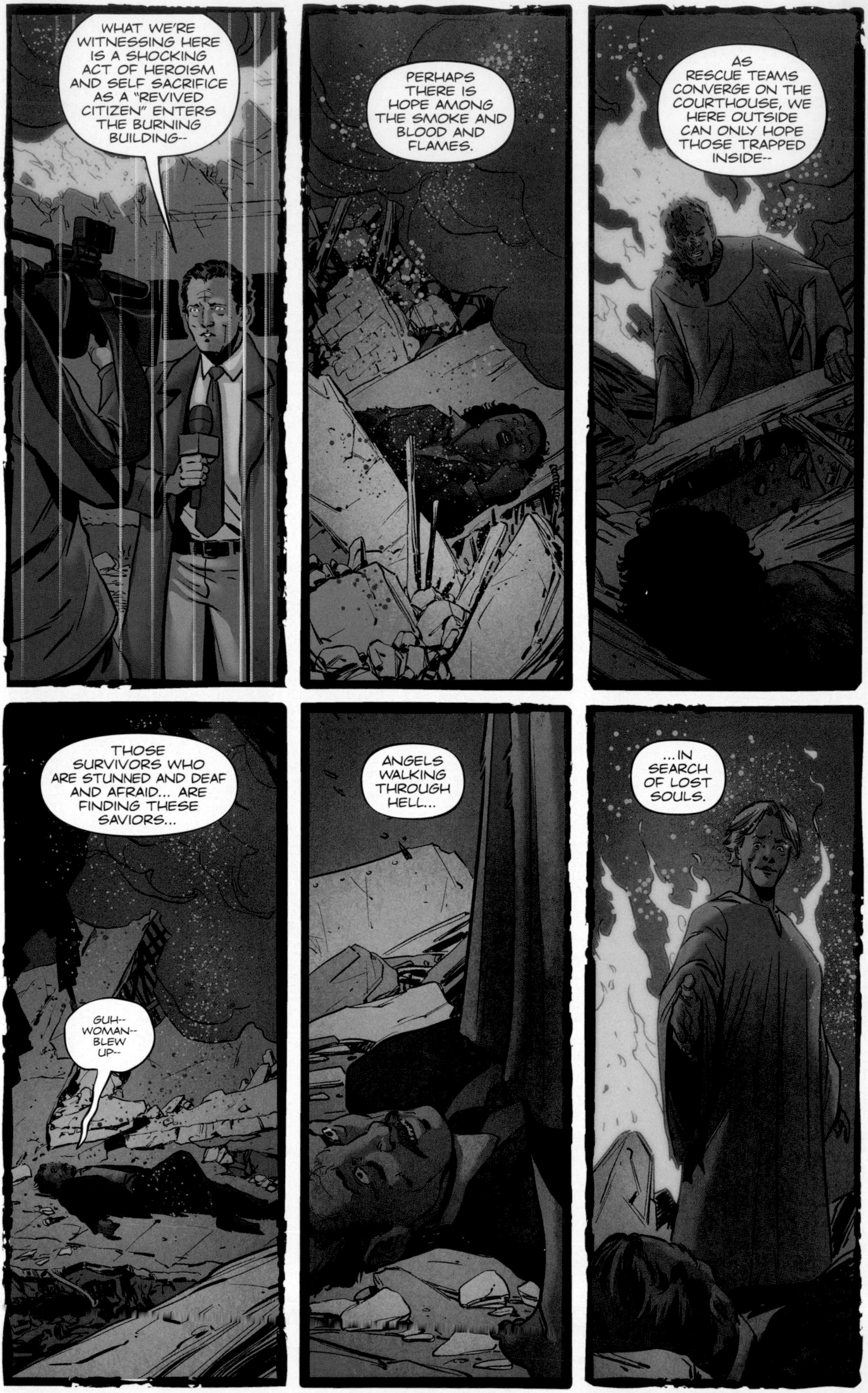
WHAT WE'RE WITNESSING HERE IS A SHOCKING ACT OF HEROISM AND SELF SACRIFICE AS A "REVIVED CITIZEN" ENTERS THE BURNING BUILDING--
PERHAPS THERE IS HOPE AMONG THE SMOKE AND BLOOD AND FLAMES.
AS RESCUE TEAMS CONVERGE ON THE COURTHOUSE, WE HERE OUTSIDE CAN ONLY HOPE THOSE TRAPPED INSIDE--
THOSE SURVIVORS WHO ARE STUNNED AND DEAF AND AFRAID... ARE FINDING THESE SAVIORS...
GUH-- WOMAN-- BLEW UP--
ANGELS WALKING THROUGH HELL...
...IN SEARCH OF LOST SOULS.

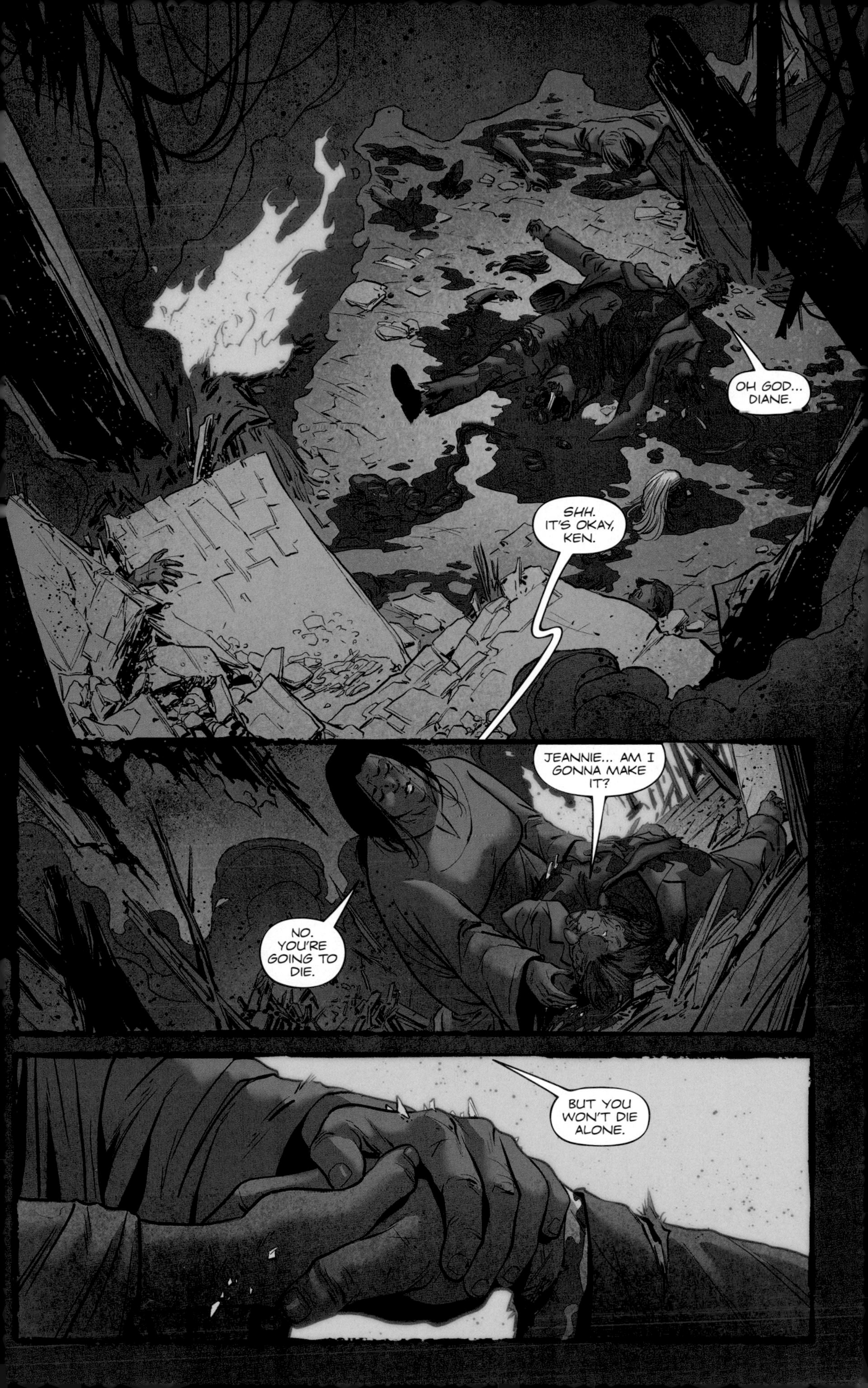
OH GOD... DIANE.
SHH. IT'S OKAY, KEN.
JEANNIE... AM I GONNA MAKE IT?
NO. YOU'RE GOING TO DIE.
BUT YOU WON'T DIE ALONE.

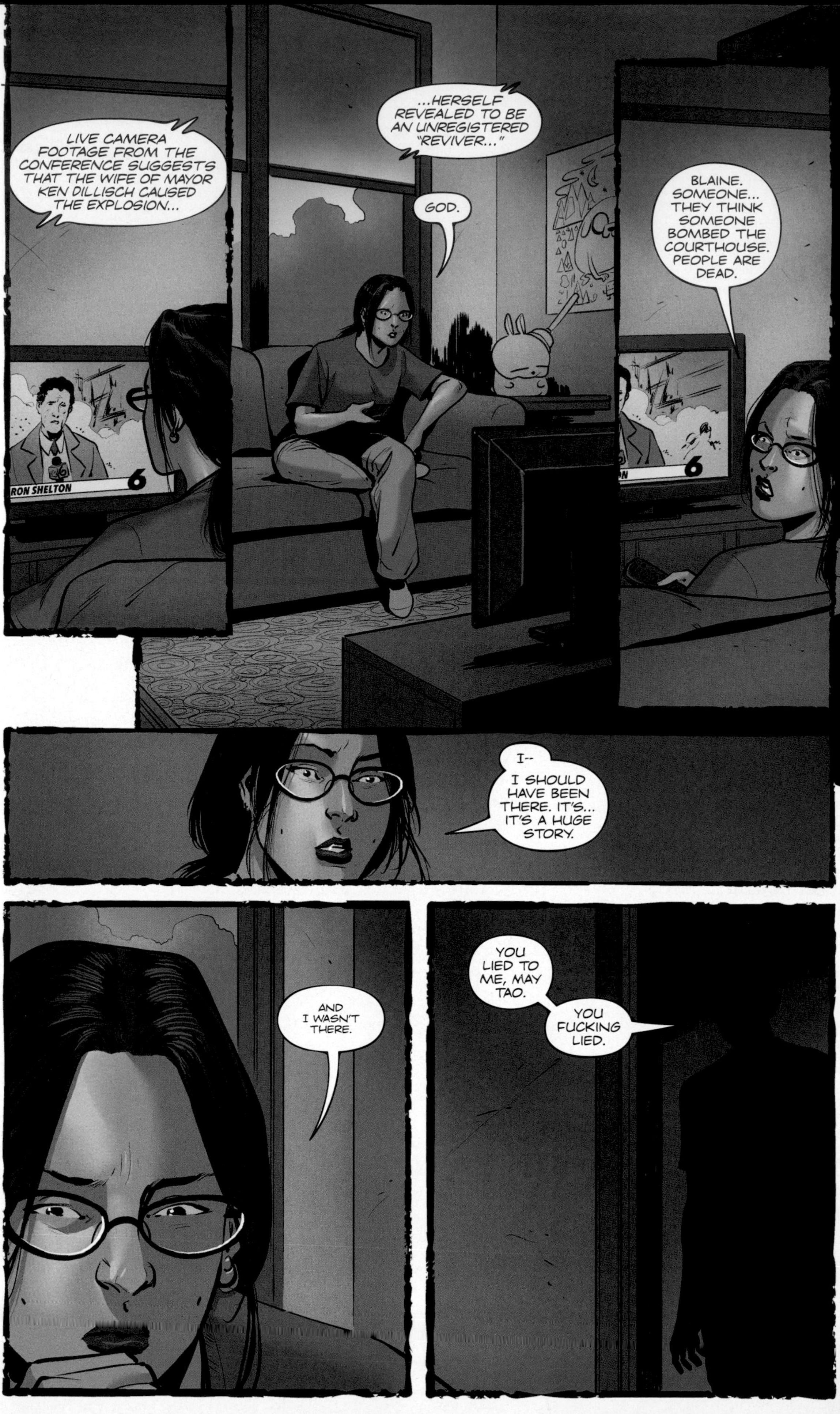
LIVE CAMERA FOOTAGE FROM THE CONFERENCE SUGGESTS THAT THE WIFE OF MAYOR KEN DILLISCH CAUSED THE EXPLOSION...
...HERSELF REVEALED TO BE AN UNREGISTERED "REVIVER..."
GOD.
BLAINE. SOMEONE... THEY THINK SOMEONE BOMBED THE COURTHOUSE. PEOPLE ARE DEAD.
RON SHELTON
6
I--
I SHOULD HAVE BEEN THERE. IT'S... IT'S A HUGE STORY.
AND I WASN'T THERE.
YOU LIED TO ME, MAY TAO.
YOU FUCKING LIED.

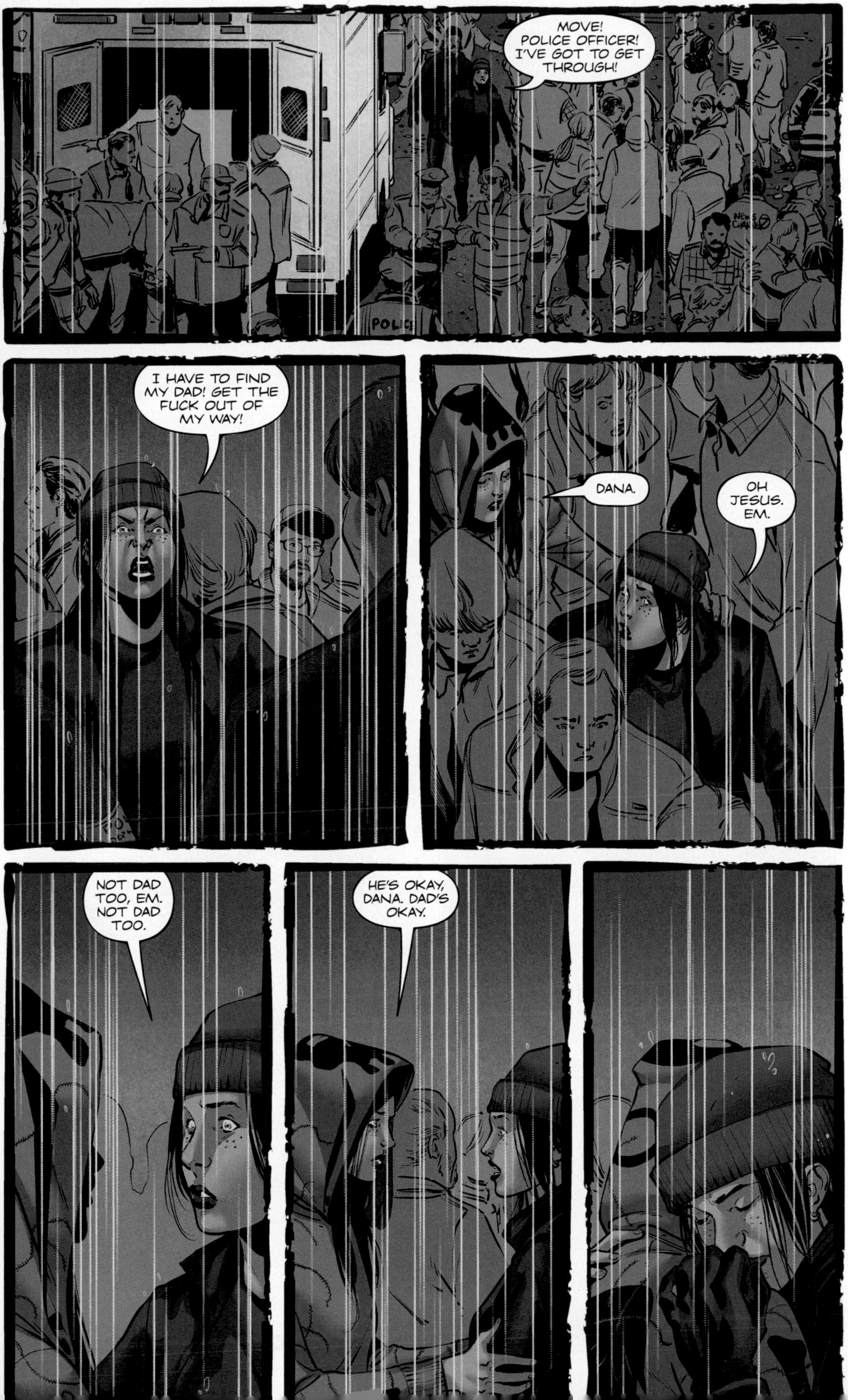
MOVE! POLICE OFFICER! I'VE GOT TO GET THROUGH!
NEWS CHANNEL
POLICE
I HAVE TO FIND MY DAD! GET THE FUCK OUT OF MY WAY!
DANA.
OH JESUS. EM.
NOT DAD TOO, EM. NOT DAD TOO.
HE'S OKAY, DANA. DAD'S OKAY.

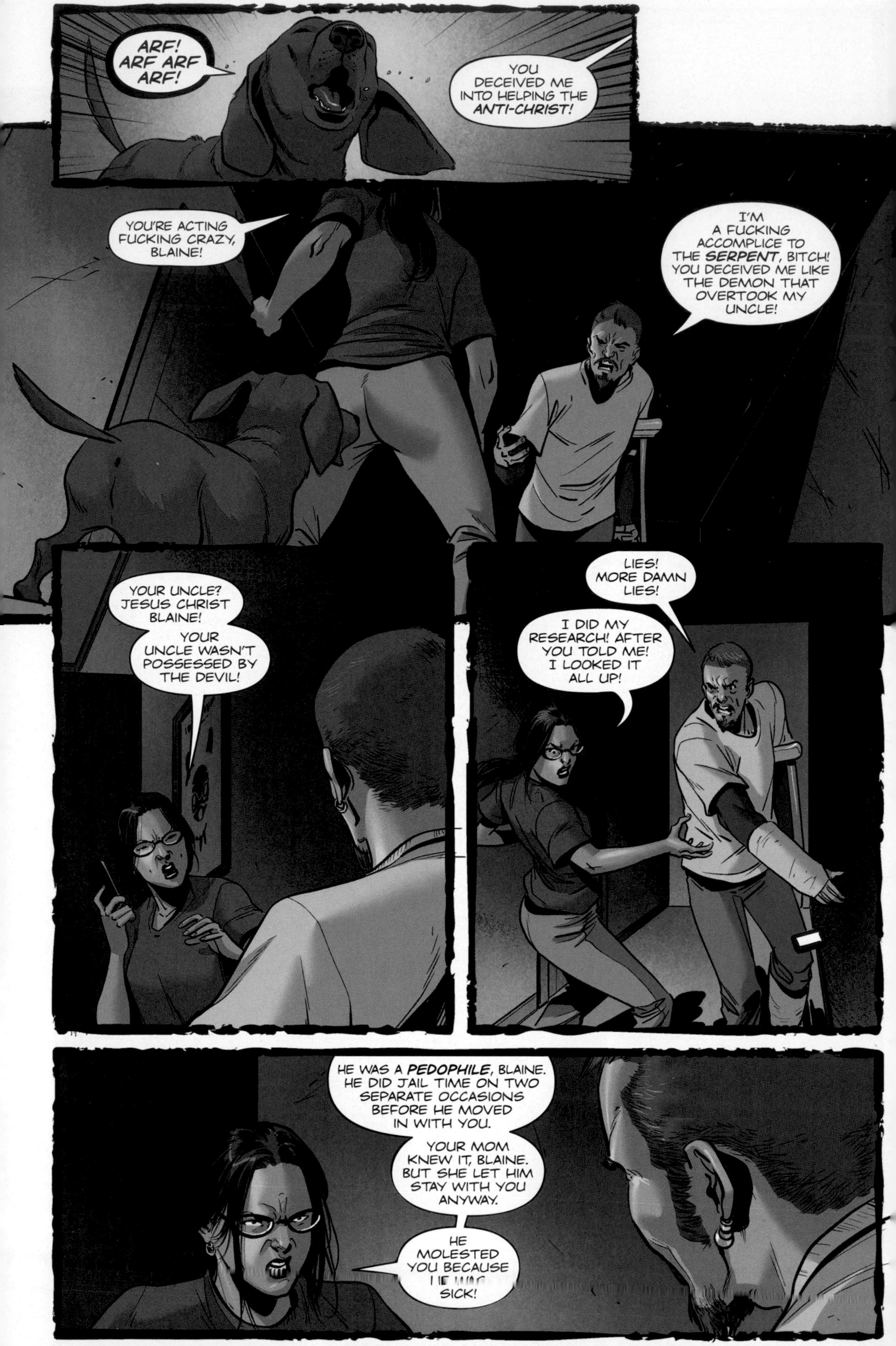
ARF! ARF ARF ARF!
YOU DECEIVED ME INTO HELPING THE ANTI-CHRIST!
YOU'RE ACTING FUCKING CRAZY, BLAINE!
I'M A FUCKING ACCOMPLICE TO THE SERPENT, BITCH! YOU DECEIVED ME LIKE THE DEMON THAT OVERTOOK MY UNCLE!
YOUR UNCLE? JESUS CHRIST BLAINE!
YOUR UNCLE WASN'T POSSESSED BY THE DEVIL!
LIES! MORE DAMN LIES!
I DID MY RESEARCH! AFTER YOU TOLD ME! I LOOKED IT ALL UP!
HE WAS A PEDOPHILE, BLAINE. HE DID JAIL TIME ON TWO SEPARATE OCCASIONS BEFORE HE MOVED IN WITH YOU.
YOUR MOM KNEW IT, BLAINE. BUT SHE LET HIM STAY WITH YOU ANYWAY.
HE MOLESTED YOU BECAUSE
SICK!

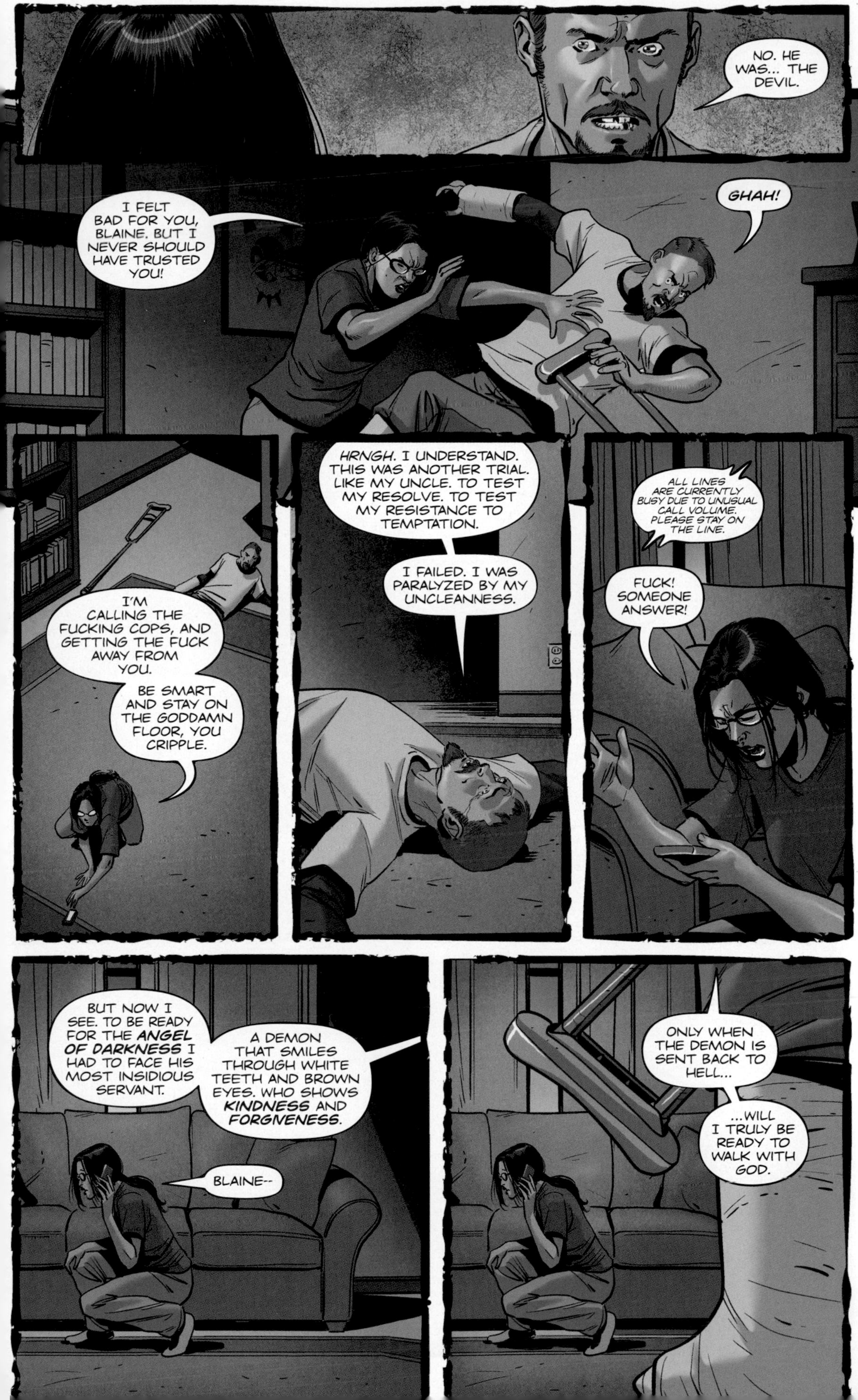
NO. HE WAS... THE DEVIL.
I FELT BAD FOR YOU, BLAINE. BUT I NEVER SHOULD HAVE TRUSTED YOU!
GHAH!
I'M CALLING THE FUCKING COPS, AND GETTING THE FUCK AWAY FROM YOU.
BE SMART AND STAY ON THE GODDAMN FLOOR, YOU CRIPPLE.
HRNGH. I UNDERSTAND. THIS WAS ANOTHER TRIAL. LIKE MY UNCLE. TO TEST MY RESOLVE. TO TEST MY RESISTANCE TO TEMPTATION.
I FAILED. I WAS PARALYZED BY MY UNCLEANNESS.
ALL LINES ARE CURRENTLY BUSY DUE TO UNUSUAL CALL VOLUME. PLEASE STAY ON THE LINE.
FUCK! SOMEONE ANSWER!
BUT NOW I SEE. TO BE READY FOR THE ANGEL OF DARKNESS I HAD TO FACE HIS MOST INSIDIOUS SERVANT.
A DEMON THAT SMILES THROUGH WHITE TEETH AND BROWN EYES. WHO SHOWS KINDNESS AND FORGIVENESS.
BLAINE--
ONLY WHEN THE DEMON IS SENT BACK TO HELL...
...WILL I TRULY BE READY TO WALK WITH GOD.

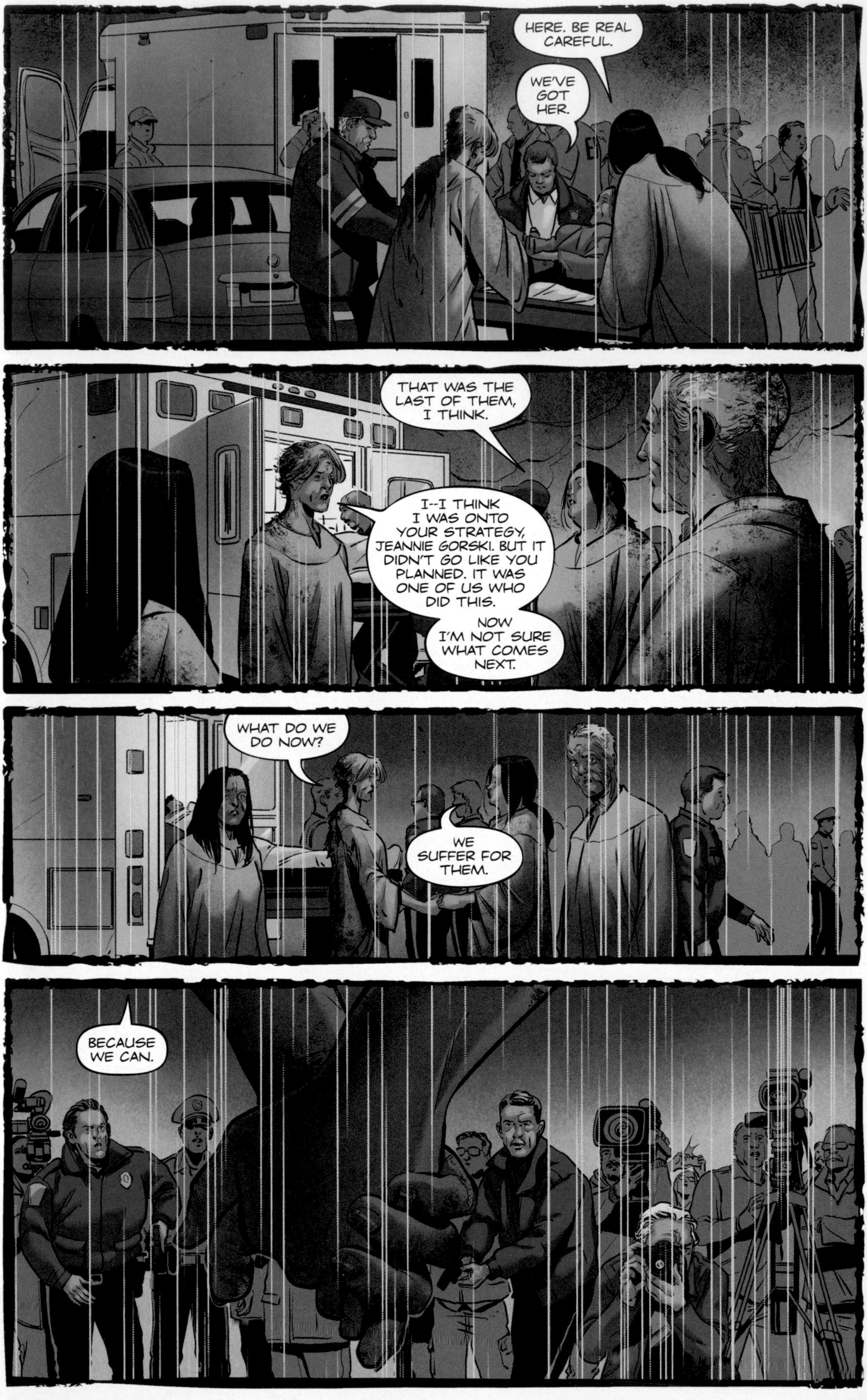
HERE. BE REAL CAREFUL.
WE'VE GOT HER.
THAT WAS THE LAST OF THEM, I THINK.
I--I THINK I WAS ONTO YOUR STRATEGY, JEANNIE GORSKI. BUT IT DIDN'T GO LIKE YOU PLANNED. IT WAS ONE OF US WHO DID THIS.
NOW I'M NOT SURE WHAT COMES NEXT.
WHAT DO WE DO NOW?
WE SUFFER FOR THEM.
BECAUSE WE CAN.

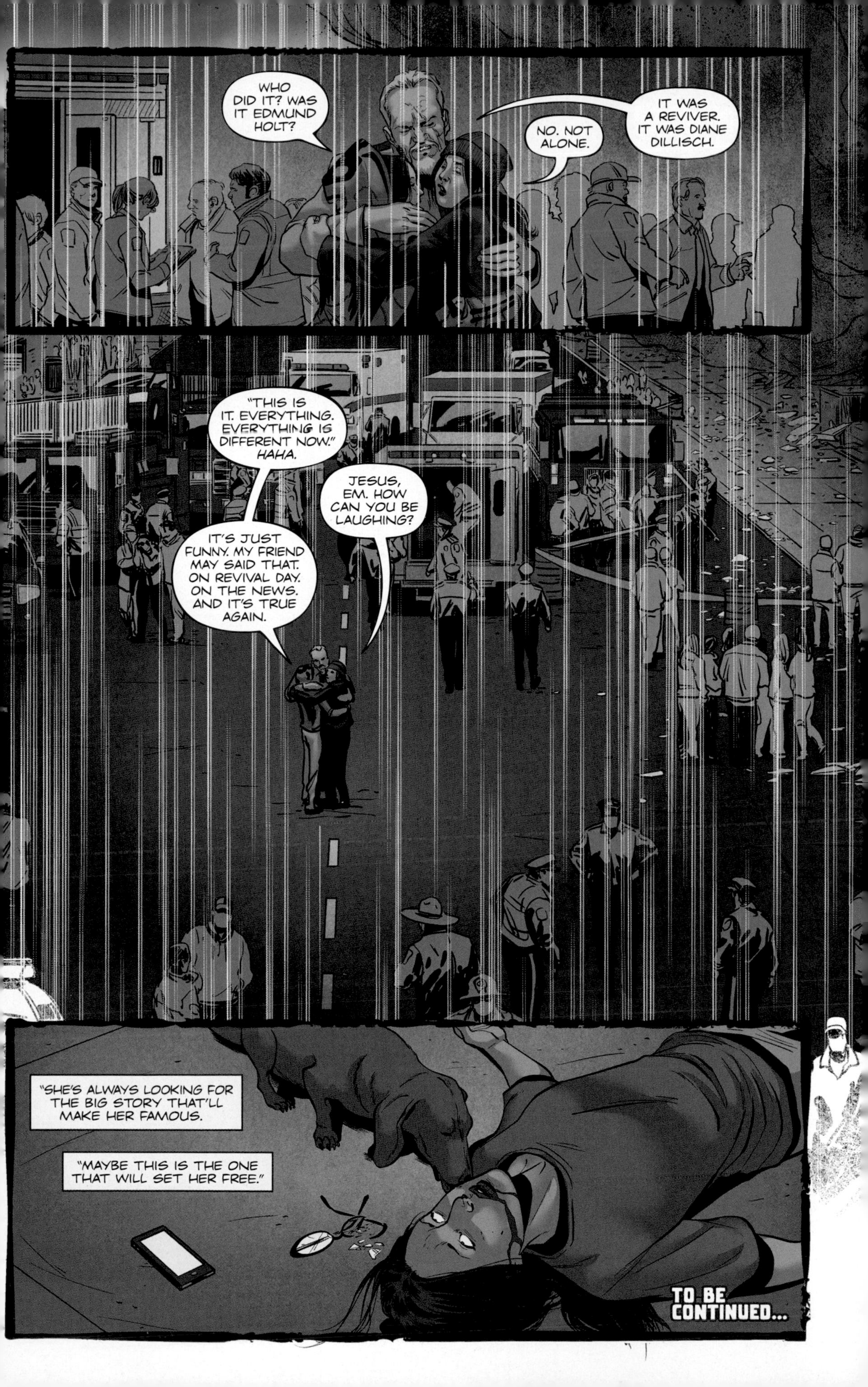
WHO DID IT? WAS IT EDMUND HOLT?
NO. NOT ALONE.
IT WAS A REVIVER. IT WAS DIANE DILLISCH.
"THIS IS IT. EVERYTHING. EVERYTHING IS DIFFERENT NOW." HAHA.
JESUS, EM. HOW CAN YOU BE LAUGHING?
IT'S JUST FUNNY. MY FRIEND MAY SAID THAT. ON REVIVAL DAY. ON THE NEWS. AND IT'S TRUE AGAIN.
"SHE'S ALWAYS LOOKING FOR THE BIG STORY THAT'LL MAKE HER FAMOUS.
"MAYBE THIS IS THE ONE THAT WILL SET HER FREE."
TO BE CONTINUED...

WORKS BY TIM SEELEY

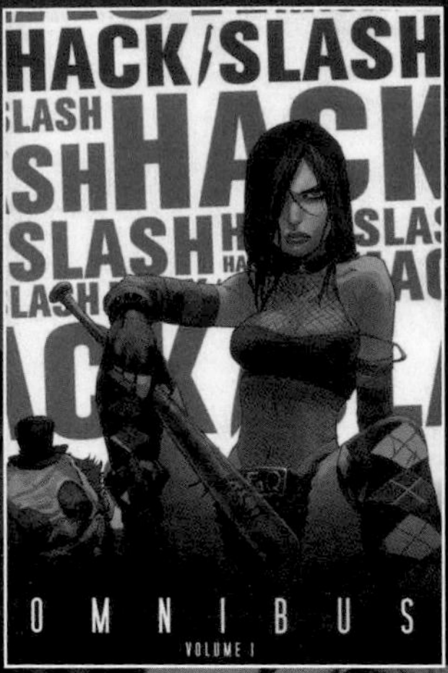
HACK/SLASH
OMNIBUS
VOLUME I

HACK SLASH

At the end of every horror movie, one girl always survives... in this case, Cassie Hack not only survives, she turns the tables by hunting and destroying the horrible slashers that would do harm to the innocent! Alongside the gentle giant known as Vlad, the two cut a bloody path through those who deserve to be put down... hard!

Omnibus TP Vol 1
ISBN: 978-1-60706-273-8
$29.99

Omnibus TP Vol 2
ISBN: 978-1-60706-274-5
$29.99

Omnibus TP Vol 3
ISBN: 978-1-60706-275-2
$34.99

Omnibus TP Vol 4
ISBN: 978-1-60706-526-5
$34.99

My First Maniac TP Vol 1
ISBN: 978-1-60706-338-4
$9.99

Hack Slash TP Vol 1 First Cut
ISBN: 978-1-60706-605-7
$12.99

Hack Slash TP Vol 2 Death by Sequel
ISBN: 978-1-60706-606-4
$14.99

Hack Slash TP Vol 3 Friday the 31st
ISBN: 978-1-60706-286-8
$18.99

Hack Slash TP Vol 8 Super Sidekick Sleepover Slaughter
ISBN: 978-1-60706-291-2
$18.99

Hack Slash TP Vol 9 Torture Prone
ISBN: 978-1-60706-409-1
$16.99

Hack Slash TP Vol 10 Dead Celebriti
ISBN: 978-1-60706-508-1
$16.99

Hack Slash TP Vol 11 Marry F*ck Ki
ISBN: 978-1-60706-273-8
$16.99

Hack Slash TP Vol 12
ISBN: 978-1-60706-731-3
$18.99

Hack Slash TP Vol 13 Final
ISBN: 978-1-60706-747-4
$18.99

Son of Samhain TP Vol 1
ISBN: 978-1-63215-244-2
$12.99

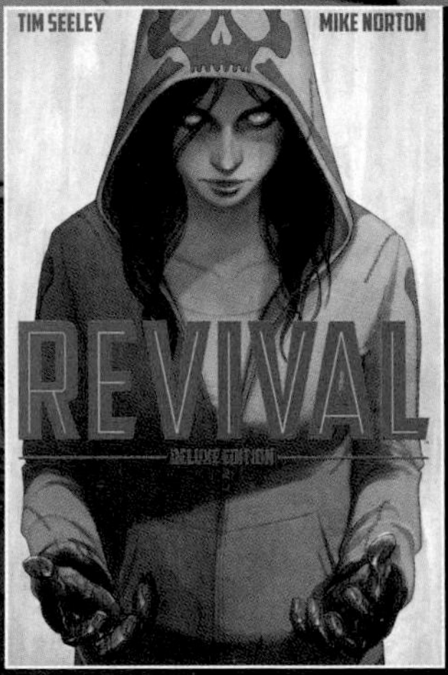
TIM SEELEY
MIKE NORTON
REVIVAL

REVIVAL

For one day in rural central Wisconsin, the dead came back to life. Now it's up to Officer Dana Cypress to deal with the media scrutiny, religious zealots, and government quarantine that has come with them. In a town where the living have to learn to deal with those who are supposed to be dead, Officer Cypress must solve a brutal murder, and everyone, alive or undead, is a suspect.

Revival TP Vol 1 You're Among Friends
ISBN: 978-1-60706-659-0
$12.99

Revival TP Vol 2 Live Like You Mean It
ISBN: 978-1-60706-754-2
$14.99

Revival TP Vol 3 A Faraway Place (MR)
ISBN: 978-1-60706-860-0
$14.99

Revival TP Vol 4 Escape to Wisconsin
ISBN: 978-1-63215-012-7
$16.99

Revival TP Vol 5 Gathering of Waters
ISBN: 978-1-63215-379-1
$14.99

Revival DLX Collection Hardcover Vol 1
ISBN: 978-1-60706-814-3
$34.99

Revival DLX Collection Hardcover Vol 2
ISBN: 978-1-63215-102-5
$34.99

MORE WORKS

Bloodstrike TP Vol 1 Reborn Under a Bad Sign
ISBN: 978-1-60706-625-5
$14.99

Loaded Bible TP Vol 1
ISBN: 978-158240-957-3
$16.99

Lovebunny & Mr. Hell TP Vol 1
ISBN: 978-1-60706-353-7
$14.99

Witchblade Rebirth TP Vol 1
ISBN: 978-1-60706-532-6
$9.99

Witchblade Rebirth TP Vol 2
ISBN: 978-1-60706-637-8
$16.99

Witchblade Rebirth TP Vol 3
ISBN: 978-1-60706-681-1
$16.99

Witchblade Rebirth TP Vol 4
ISBN: 978-1-60706-800-6
$16.99